MAGI͟C̶ ͟T̶O̶U̶C̶H̶

"Come away with me, lass." He moved to the rock where she stood, and held out his arms.

She could fight it no longer. She went to him, into his arms, and he scooped her up, holding her against the solid, silky warmth of his chest, as he started back into the sea.

"Are you ready, lass?" he whispered, his mouth hovering near hers.

"I'm ready," she said. "But I cannot swim."

"I'll show you." And he dived beneath the water, taking her with him.

He kissed her then, breathing into her mouth, and she felt as if she would burst with pleasure as she drifted through the shimmering sea, at one with her selkie lover. This was what she had dreamed about, this was what she had longed for. Nothing else mattered but his mouth, wet and open against hers, taking her, down and down and down, into the murky, velvet depths of the Scottish sea . . .

—From "Under an Enchantment"
by Anne Stuart

ROMANCE COLLECTIONS FROM
THE BERKLEY PUBLISHING GROUP

Love Stories for Every Season . . .

SECRET LOVES: Passionate tales of crushes, secret admirers, and other wonders of love, by Constance O'Day Flannery, Wendy Haley, Cheryl Lanham, and Catherine Palmer.

HIGHLAND FLING: The romance of Scottish hearts, captured by Anne Stuart, Caitlin McBride, Jill Barnett, and Linda Shertzer.

HARVEST HEARTS: Heartwarming stories of love's rich bounty, by Kristin Hannah, Rebecca Paisley, Jo Anne Cassity, and Sharon Harlow.

SUMMER MAGIC: Splendid summertime love stories featuring Pamela Morsi, Jean Anne Caldwell, Ann Carberry, and Karen Lockwood.

SWEET HEARTS: Celebrate Cupid's magical matchmaking with Jill Marie Landis, Jodi Thomas, Colleen Quinn, and Kathleen Kane.

A CHRISTMAS TREASURE: Festive tales for a true Regency holiday, by Elizabeth Mansfield, Holly Newman, Sheila Rabe, and Ellen Rawlings.

SUMMERTIME SPLENDOR: A golden celebration of romance, featuring today's most popular Regency authors . . . Marion Chesney, Cynthia Bailey-Pratt, Sarah Eagle, and Melinda Pryce.

LOVING HEARTS: Valentine stories that warm the heart, by Jill Marie Landis, Jodi Thomas, Colleen Quinn, and Maureen Child.

A REGENCY HOLIDAY: Delightful treasures of Christmastime romance, by Elizabeth Mansfield, Monette Cummings, Martha Powers, Judith Nelson, and Sarah Eagle.

Highland Fling

by

Anne Stuart

Caitlin McBride

Jill Barnett

Linda Shertzer

JOVE BOOKS, NEW YORK

HIGHLAND FLING

A Jove Book / published by arrangement with
the authors

PRINTING HISTORY
Jove edition / December 1993

ISBN: 0-515-11271-2

A JOVE BOOK®
Jove Books are published by The Berkley Publishing Group,
200 Madison Avenue, New York, New York 10016.
JOVE and the "J" design are trademarks belonging to
Jove Publications, Inc.

PRINTED IN THE UNITED STATES OF AMERICA

10 9 8 7 6 5 4 3 2 1

CONTENTS

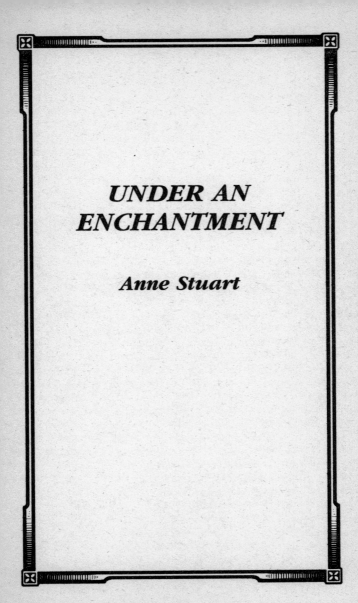

UNDER AN ENCHANTMENT

Anne Stuart

Dear Reader:

With a name like Anne Stuart, I would obviously have an affinity for Scotland and all things Scottish. When I was a girl I used to fantasize that I was the lost queen of Scotland, and when the time came I would kick Queen Elizabeth out of my spot and rule my highland kingdom. Back then I imagined border lords and fierce lairds and all manner of dark, dour passion, and while I now accept (regretfully) that I'll never be queen of Scotland, I still believe in all the romance of that country.

I've always loved selkies. The idea of a graceful seal coming to land and taking the shape of a man, with the sole purpose of begetting a child, is the sort of thing that stirs my blood, and at heart I'm just as gullible as my heroine. I'd believe, simply because I wanted to and because reality is far too cold and lonely.

Fortunately when you write stories you can shape reality to suit you. This little island exists only in my imagination, and the characters come from my heart. But the lovely thing about books is that, once released into words, they'll live forever.

I hope you enjoy reading this as much as I enjoyed writing it.

> Best always,
> Anne Stuart (who is much better looking and nicer than the Anne Stuart who *was* queen of Scotland.)

CHAPTER
1

Malcolm James Kendrick MacLaren walked out of the sea one fine autumn day. The villagers of St. Columba stopped in the midst of their labors, staring, as he strode from the surf with a purposeful grace.

He was a tall man, though perhaps not as tall as some. The clothes that clung to his wet body were plain, dark, and he was leanly built, well muscled, wiry. His black hair hung down his back, overlong, and his face was narrow, secretive, with dark eyes, strongly marked brows, a fierce blade of a nose, and a thin-lipped mouth that was surprisingly erotic.

In all, he didn't look the slightest bit like a seal.

That didn't stop Collis from staring, his gnarled hands motionless on the thick net. The man kept walking, straight and true, and his dark gaze met Collis's. He came toward him, ignoring the others who stood and watched, stopping in front of him.

The seawater clung to his sun-darkened skin, and up close those dark eyes were neither black nor brown. They were the deep, dark green of an angry ocean.

"Can I help you, lad?" Collis's voice came out strained, and he cursed his sudden weakness. This wasn't a lad, this was a man. One who was eerily familiar.

The man from the sea didn't seem to take offense. "Collis MacDewar?"

His voice was deep, rich, and Collis turned pale, wondering if it was the voice of his nightmares, coming to haunt him. "Do I know ye?" he asked.

"You know my people."

Collis shivered. He'd never hunted seals—like most of the people of St. Columba, he viewed them as friendly spirits. Only the few more hard-hearted of the fisherfolk, such as Domnhall, hunted the gentle creatures for their rich pelts.

"Have you come for me, then?" he asked. He was an old man, nearly seventy, and had seen many things. If his time had come, then he'd go willingly. Though he never thought death would come to him in the form of seal-man.

It was so faint he almost thought he'd imagined it. The slight upturning of that narrow mouth, the glint of light that reflected in his eyes. "I've come from Catriona," he said.

Collis shut his eyes for a brief moment. Catriona had been lost some thirty years ago—the sea had taken her and her body had never been found. "I'll go with you," he said resolutely.

There was no missing the smile this time. "No," he said. "I'll go with you."

Collis didn't hesitate. He dropped his nets, turned, and started toward the road leading into the hills. The man from the sea came behind him, following closely, and the townspeople watched, silent, respectful, as they made their way through the village, away from the shore. All their lives they had heard stories of the selkie, the seal people who took the form of humans when they walked upon the land. This was the first time they'd been blessed enough to see one.

Collis lived alone in a tiny croft halfway up the small hill in the midst of the island. He'd never married, never found any reason to. He worked hard, as all the people of St. Columba did, hewing out a living from his rocky soil and the merciless sea. It had been a long life, a decent life, and his only regret would be to leave behind his border collie, Tammas.

The dog rushed out of the croft, scenting their approach, his ears back with sudden wariness as he approached the stranger. The man held out one elegant hand, and the dog sniffed it, testing. And then his ears came up, he barked a greeting, and moved past to fling himself on his master, all lolling tongue and besotted doggy gaze.

Collis paused in the doorway of his cottage, staring at the man who'd followed him up the hill in silence. "I'd've thought she'd be afraid of you."

The man smiled again, and there was something bewitching about that smile as he leaned down and scratched behind Tammas's ears. "Why?"

"Dogs don't like the supernatural."

"Is that what I am?"

"You walked out of the sea, didn't you? Without so much as a boat in sight. We've heard stories of the selkie all our lives, here in the islands. You'd be the first one we've seen in the flesh."

"A selkie," Malcolm said, considering it. "It's as good an explanation as any. Have you got a fire going, Collis?"

"Of course," he said, affronted. "I'm not daft enough to let the coals die out. You'll want to come in and warm yourself. You're soaked to the bone."

"You're right." Malcolm ducked his head to step inside the small, tidy cottage. He seemed to dwarf the place, not so much by his sheer size, but by the force of his presence. He moved to the banked fire, holding out his hands to warm them over the coals.

They were long, elegant, the hands of a lord and yet not. They were tanned, well made, yet obviously used to hard work. The man looked at him over his shoulder with a slashing, mocking smile, and there was something uncannily familiar about his eyes.

Collis stared at him, fighting the superstitious fear that filled him. "Who are you?" he demanded in a hoarse voice.

"I told you. I've come from Catriona."

"She drowned."

The man shook his head, and his long black hair hung damply against his shoulders. "She talked about you, old man. The only friend she trusted. You would have saved her if you could."

"Saved her from what?"

"From the brutality of men. But you were too late. She was beaten and thrown into the sea, and it was only by the grace of God that she survived. The grace of God, and my father."

"Who did this?" Collis demanded hoarsely, knowing the answer anyway.

"I don't know whose hand struck the blow. But I know the men who planned her death. Sir Duncan Spens. His cousin Torquil. And Sir Finlay Wallace."

Collis shut his eyes in sorrow. "Aye," he said heavily. "I'd always suspected as much."

"You were too late to save her, old man. But you aren't too late to avenge her."

"She's dead, then?"

Not a flicker of expression passed over the younger man's face, and yet Collis could feel the depth of his grief and fury. "This past Christmastide."

Collis stared into the coals of the banked fire, unseeing. "I thought she'd been dead these past thirty years. Why should it grieve me so?"

"You can avenge her, Collis. You can avenge a sweet lass whose only crime was to run afoul of a group of murderous rich men. You can help me."

"Aye," he said slowly. "I can help you." His gaze narrowed as he looked at the stranger in his tiny croft. "And who are you?" he asked again.

"Malcolm."

Collis digested the name, with its history of kings and murder. "And what of your father, lad? You said Catriona was saved by the grace of God and your father. Who's your father?"

Malcolm smiled, the dark, sardonic smile. "The king of the seals, Collis. Who else would he be?"

Ailie had forgotten her shoes again. Nay, that wasn't strictly the truth. She'd remembered, once she'd set her bare feet on the thick grass outside the dower house, but she hadn't wanted to go back and fetch them. She didn't like them, enclosing her narrow feet, cramping her toes. She liked the feel of the grass, the sand, the gravel beneath her soles. Whenever she could she dispensed with her shoes, and her maid, Margery, had given up chasing after her. Now that Sir Duncan was dead, there was no one to try to force her into standard modes of behavior. Until Torquil decided to marry her.

No, he'd already decided, Ailie knew it in the depths of her heart. He was already making the financial arrangements with her brothers, and she was to have no say in the matter. It mattered not that she walked in to tea with her feet unshod, her thick reddish-blond hair a tangle down her back, her dress unfastened, her mind on faraway dreams. It wasn't her mind or her clothing that seemed to interest Torquil.

She knew lust when she saw it in a man's eyes. She'd seen it in her husband's eyes, recognized it when she was a young lass of seventeen and been given in marriage to a randy old man in his late sixties. The lust Duncan had felt for her traveled no farther than his eyes, and when he'd died four years after their wedding day, Ailie was still a virgin.

Torquil was a good ten years younger, still in his fifties, and the desire he felt for her would move beyond his eyes; she knew it with a sinking feeling. He'd been watching her for the past few years as his older cousin grew more and more feeble, and he'd even touched her, his thick-fingered hands skimming her breasts when he thought she was too feather-headed and dreaming to notice.

She didn't like his hands. They were the hands of a pig, with short, thick fingers and stubby palms, and she didn't want him touching her, taking her. He wasn't a bad man, a cruel man, but she wanted no man at all, not as much as she wanted her freedom.

However, it wasn't going to be up to her. She'd heard her brothers talking, their loud voices carrying through the cozy dower house where she'd taken up residence once Sir Duncan had died. They assumed she was witless, and she

encouraged that belief quite shamelessly. They might as
well have assumed she was deaf, so loudly did they plan
her upcoming nuptials. As soon as they ascertained that she
wasn't carrying Duncan's child.

Scant chance of that, she thought, moving through the
thick woods toward the town. Even if Duncan had been
able, she was hardly likely to conceive after four supposedly
barren years. But her brothers were careful men, as was
Torquil. They wanted no questions to stain the marriage of
Torquil Spens to his cousin's half-mad widow.

She was humming under her breath, an old tune about
Bonnie Prince Charlie, just the sort of song bound to drive
her protective family mad. Such songs had been outlawed
a century ago, and to sing them still courted trouble.

But sing them she did, as well as songs about faeries
and nymphs and broonies. There were times when she
wondered whether she might be a changeling. Perhaps some
enterprising troll had stolen the real Ailie Wallace from
her cradle, stolen her from a father who had no interest
in daughters and a mother who'd turned her face to the
wall and died as she'd lived, quietly, once she'd brought
forth a sixth offspring, her only daughter. Perhaps the real
Ailie lived with the wee folk, leaving the changeling Ailie
behind. It would explain her oddness, her affinity for things
that most people insisted weren't quite real.

She should be living in the woods on fairy dust and moon
milk. Instead she'd grown up surrounded by five bullying
brothers, dreaming her dreams, singing her songs, growing
steadily more peculiar until her family was ready to send
her away and have done with her. Someplace where they
wouldn't have to be shamed by her odd behavior and
dreaming ways.

Had it not been for Sir Duncan Spens, that future would
have been hers. It was sheer bad luck that she'd wandered
into the dining room one night when both her father and
his old friend had drunk far too much whiskey, sheer bad
luck that in his drunken state Sir Duncan had seen her
height and her red-gold hair and fancied himself ready for
a second wife.

She'd tried to escape the trap fate had provided for her. She smeared dirt on her face, let her hair hang in tangles down her back, and done her best imitation of poor mad Ophelia. She'd sung "Wae Is Me for Charlie" and the like, but to no avail. Sir Duncan declared himself pleased with a half-witted bride—she'd provide no distressing intellectual conversation. She'd be content to spend her married life on her back, where he wanted her to be.

She'd tried to run away, but her brother Angus had come after her, and being a brute and a bully, he'd beaten her unmercifully. And so she'd married, and lain on her back in Sir Duncan's huge bed.

But Sir Duncan's desire outstripped his capabilities. And as the weeks turned into months, and then into years, he no longer attempted to claim his child bride. He was content simply to watch her.

Torquil would never be satisfied with so little. And while she hadn't yet given up the notion of running, St. Columba was a small island, and she was well-known. Escape would be well nigh impossible. Since Torquil as well as her brothers would come after her.

She had time enough. Her brothers were very conventional Scots, true followers of the kirk and the laws of God and man. They wouldn't marry her off to Torquil until the customary year of mourning was up. She was safe and snug in the dower house, while Torquil had moved into his cousin's manor house, the huge drafty building he'd always coveted, as he'd coveted his cousin's wife. Sir Duncan had fathered no children—Torquil and Ailie were his only heirs—and Torquil's desire to unify the inheritance was a good part of his lust for her.

Duncan had been dead six weeks. She had a little over ten months of freedom left, and she intended to enjoy them to their fullest.

"Good day to you, Lady Spens," Jane Morrow, the baker's wife, greeted her. They looked after her, the people of St. Columba did, watching over her with anxious affection that was only faintly stifling.

Ailie flung back her hair and smiled at the woman. "Good

day to you, Jane. It's a lovely day, is it not? A good day for the faeries."

Jane gave her that kindly smile. "Indeed it is, mistress. Have ye heard about the selkie?"

Ailie stopped in her tracks, her toes chilled on the cobbled roadway. "A selkie?" she said. "Have you heard a new story?"

"Nay, lass," Jane said comfortably. "We've seen one."

For a moment Ailie didn't move. "Seen one?" she echoed. "Are you certain?"

"And wouldn't I be knowing, me being bred of stock that mated with the seal people in centuries past?" Jane demanded. "As were half the inhabitants of this village, and well you know it. He walked out of the ocean, miss, straight up to Collis MacDewar, and took him up to the hill."

"Did he look like a seal?"

"Faith, no!" Jane laughed. "He took the form of a man, of course. They always do. And what a man! Handsome as sin. Of course, he'd have to be."

"Why?" Ailie asked.

"He's come for a bairn."

"He's going to steal children?" Ailie asked, horror breaking through her usually airy demeanor.

"Nay, lass. He's going to find a young girl and get her with child. Then he'll go back to the sea. That's what they do, you know. That's why most of us on this island are descended from the seal people. Except for that bastard Domnhall." She spat as she said the name of the seal hunter.

"He's handsome, you say?"

"As the devil. With eyes that could look right through you," Jane said vigorously.

Ailie smiled. The sun was bright overhead, and at least for now, no one had any power over her. "I'm going to see him," she said. "I've never seen an enchanted creature before. Not up close."

"Ye mustn't!" Jane said, suddenly sober. "Haven't I warned you? He's looking for an innocent young lass to seduce."

"I'm a widow, Jane. Hardly an innocent."

"Lass, you're one of God's creatures, innocent as a babe, and I imagine you always will be. I wouldn't want you hurt."

"He won't hurt me," Ailie said serenely. "Old Morag will see that I'm kept safe."

Jane shook her head, but Ailie had already moved onward, through the town, heading up the narrow track that led to Collis's croft. The people of St. Columba called out to her as she passed, but she didn't hesitate. They would worry about her, when there was no need. No selkie from the great dark green sea would hurt her. She wanted to see a faerie up close, look into those dark wondrous eyes Jane had talked about, and learn if she could see her future.

She could just imagine her brothers' reaction when they heard of Collis's visitor. Fortunately most of them were in Edinburgh, only Angus remaining behind to watch over their half-mad little sister. If he caught wind of an enchanted creature come to St. Columba, he'd probably send word to Domnhall the seal hunter to dispatch him.

She couldn't let that happen. Collis would warn him, no doubt, but he might not listen. She'd never met a selkie before, she had no idea how practical they might be. Having lived their lives at the bottom of the sea, they might not know of the treachery of man.

It was a warm day for September. She climbed steadily, up the narrow path, rolling up her loose sleeves as she went, baring her strong forearms to the bright sun, shaking her thick hair out behind her. This time next year she'd be trapped once more. Torquil might own her in bed, but he couldn't force her to behave. He would have to stand by as she forgot her bonnet, her hairpins, her shoes. With any luck, if he insisted on marrying her, he might at least grow tired of her witlessness. Leaving her free to live her life of dreams.

She wandered the hills often, knowing where each croft lay, knowing the names and temperaments of the animals, the children, the inhabitants. Collis was a crusty old bachelor, one who suffered from the ague and the long nights. She liked him, and he liked her. He'd often tell her stories of piskies and broonies and the like, and never once did he suggest that he didn't believe just as devoutly as she did. Though she suspected he was far more practical than he let on with her.

She hadn't brought anything for him, a failing that sorrowed her. She should have brought some fresh fish from the harbor. A seal-man would eat fish, wouldn't he? Would he eat it raw, like a sea gull?

The croft lay nestled in a tiny pocket by the hill, a thin plume of smoke coming out of the chimney. Tammas stood in the doorway, watching her approach with unabashed pleasure, his tail wagging wildly as he rushed out to greet her.

She knelt down, her skirts trailing in the dirt, and let him lick her face, crooning to him as she did so. He smelled sweet and doggy, like the sea and the hills and the gorse, and she leaned her forehead against his shaggy coat.

He was watching her. She could feel his eyes upon her, watching her, touching her, and she lifted her head, like a doe sensing a predator.

He was standing in the doorway of the old croft, filling it, yet he wasn't that broad or tall. He was very still, and his eyes danced over her, skimming across her skin like a physical touch.

It was disturbing, but not unpleasant. Invading, but not encroaching. She sat back on her heels, her mussed skirts around her, and looked at him.

"Are you the selkie?" she asked, her voice cool and calm.

"So they say." His voice unnerving, deep and sure like his steady gaze. A voice that could reach out and touch her. Was this what enchantment was?

"And what do you say?" She allowed her curiosity free rein.

"My name is Malcolm."

She smiled at him. Surely no one named Malcolm could be that great a danger, enchanted or no. "I'm Ailie," she said.

"Ailie. A pretty name. Were you looking for Collis?"

"I was looking for you."

He looked startled by her artless speech. "For what reason?"

"I've never seen a faerie creature before."

"And you have now?"

She smiled, a shy, secret smile, staring at him, wondering what his skin would feel like. It was a golden brown, the color of a man who spent long hours in the sun. "Are you a golden-brown seal?" she asked, not answering his question. "Or is your pelt the color of your hair?"

His hair had dried on his shoulders, and he picked up a strand, staring at it as if he'd never seen it before. As indeed, thought Ailie, he might not have. "I'm black, like my hair," he said. "Like my heart."

"No," she said, slowly shaking her head. "Selkies aren't evil. They mean humans no harm."

"I'm an exception," he said. "I've come to cause harm to three humans. If I can find them."

She stared at him, nonplussed. Then she rose, crossing the dirt-packed front yard to the door of the croft. "But you won't harm me," she said. "You have no need."

He didn't move. "Mistress, have you any idea how dangerous this might be?"

"Why?"

"Collis is nowhere around. I'm a stranger who walked out of the sea, and there's no knowing who and what I might be. I could do you grave harm."

She shook her head. "You won't," she said. "I know these things." He had the faintest growth of beard on his face, as if he hadn't shaved in several days. She wondered how his skin would feel against her hand. Without hesitation she reached up and touched him.

He was so startled he jerked away as if burned, catching her wrist in his strong hand. "What are you doing?"

"I wanted to see if you were warm or cold."

He shook his head in amazement. "Hot, mistress," he said flatly. "Looking at you."

She took a step backward, but he didn't release her. "Jane

said you were here to father a bairn," she said, wishing his skin wasn't so warm, so tantalizingly rough on her wrist. The men who had touched her, her husband, Torquil, all had soft, useless skin.

"She did, did she? Are you offering?" The question was low-voiced, dangerous, but Ailie didn't flinch.

She shook her head, and her hair flowed round her shoulders, catching his eye. "Not I," she said. "You wouldn't want to get a babe on a woman who was daft, would you?"

"Are you?"

She smiled up at him, her own, secret smile. "So they say." She repeated his own words.

He echoed hers right back. "And what do you say?"

She looked down at the hand that covered her wrist. The dark, suntanned skin, the long fingers. "I dance to my own waltz, Malcolm," she said. "Beware of Domnhall."

"Domnhall?"

"The seal hunter. He would kill you the moment you changed back. He might not even wait that long. Collis will tell you." She tugged her hand away, and he released her. Her wrist felt cold without his flesh touching hers. She backed away from him, her gaze not leaving his dark green eyes. She could see the future there, and the past. She could see the dark roiling sea that was his home.

"Are you afraid of me?"

She considered the notion, still moving. "I'm not certain yet."

"Are you running from me?"

She paused in the midst of her retreat, and a smile spread over her face. "Yes," she said simply. And she turned and scampered back down the hillside, her skirts and her long hair flying out behind her.

"Ye'll not harm her," Collis said, appearing in the door behind him.

Malcolm stood very still, watching as the overgrown sprite raced down the hill with nary a glance backward. "Why should I?"

"She's an innocent. We all watch out for her on the island, since she's scarce capable of watching out for herself. She's a simple creature, one who means no harm, and it would go ill with you were you to hurt her."

"A simple creature," Malcolm murmured. "I'm not sure if I agree with that. I think she's far more complex than she appears."

"She believes in faeries and elves and broonies."

"And you believe in selkies," Malcolm pointed out.

"That's different. Most folk on this island are descended from the seals. It's a matter of history."

Malcolm didn't bother to look at him. "I won't hurt the lass," he said. "I don't know why you think I should."

"Because she's Ailie Wallace Spens. Daughter of your enemy. Widow of your enemy. Affianced bride of your enemy."

Every muscle in Malcolm's body tightened. He was more than adept at hiding his reactions, and he kept his face like granite.

"She's been busy in her short life," he replied in a casual tone to the man who'd been his mother's servant and friend a lifetime ago.

"Ye're not to harm her."

Malcolm turned to look at the little old man whose help he needed. "Of course not," he said simply.

Collis stared at him sharply, and then he nodded. Believing Malcolm's lie.

Because Malcolm James Kendrick MacLaren had every intention of harming Ailie Wallace Spens, if need be. He wasn't about to let sentiment stop him. She might be the only way he could get to his last surviving enemy. The only way he could strike beyond the grave of her father and husband.

And if he had to hurt an innocent, half-mazed creature to do so, then he wouldn't hesitate. He'd traveled too far to weaken.

CHAPTER
2

"Torquil's been looking for you."

Ailie paused at the gate of the dower house, fighting the frisson of uneasiness that stretched up her backbone. She wasn't afraid of man or beast, enchanted creature or wild animal, but Domnhall the seal hunter came close to making her cower. Not that she was about to let him see it.

She turned, smiling up at him with a particularly witless look, meant to disarm. "He knows where to find me, Domnhall," she said in a tranquil voice. "When did you start taking his messages?"

"I don't mind doing him a favor or two," Domnhall said, his small, dark eyes sweeping over her in a look that could only be called predatory. "Knowing he'll be paying his debts, sooner or later."

"He has debts to you?"

Domnhall looked displeased at her quick question. He was a huge man, broad, just beginning to go to fat as he reached into middle age, with mean eyes, rough hands, and a cruel nature that had been whispered of on St. Columba for years. He took delight in killing innocent things: the seals who came too close to his fishing nets, the birds that flocked near the hovel he called home. It was rumored he'd even killed the young woman he'd married and buried in record time, but there'd been no proof. People steered clear of him, eyeing him warily. All, that is, except for Torquil Spens, who wasn't averse to using any tool that came to hand, no matter how tainted.

"You're smart enough when you're paying attention," he said. "Not quite as mazed as you'd have one think, are ye?"

She smiled sweetly. "Not mazed at all, Domnhall."

"Where were ye just now?"

She could have told him it was none of his business. If she were the sort of woman her family wished her to be, she would have done just that, with cool dignity. But she wasn't the woman they wished her to be, and never would be. "I was off to see the selkie."

His reaction was instantaneous, and she cursed her flapping tongue. "He's either a seal or a man," he said in a low, evil voice. "And I kill seals." He looked down at his brutish hands, and Ailie could see the dried blood beneath his dirty fingernails. "I wonder what color his pelt will be."

"You'll leave him alone, Domnhall MacAlpin," she said fiercely.

He looked at her from his great height, unmoved by her fury. "And who would make me?"

She fought the panic that swept over her at the thought of brutish Domnhall going after the man at Collis's croft. He was swift and brutal with a knife—she'd watched him skin a seal once, and been heartily sick afterward. The slender, wiry strength of the selkie would be no match for him.

"There are powers, Domnhall," she said. "Creatures of the night, who could haunt you and chase you. The spirits of the ones you've murdered, following after you, driving you mad. There'll be no escape for you, none at all, until you run screaming into the sea." Her voice sounded like an ancient curse, called down upon his head, and he turned pale.

"I don't believe in such things," he said, backing away from her.

Ailie smiled at him serenely. "You'd be wise to do so. You never know when your deeds will come back to haunt you." And turning her back on him, she continued down the narrow path to the dower house. She could feel him watching her, and the skin at the back of her neck prickled. He meant her harm. She knew it, with instincts ancient and sure. She just wasn't certain what form that harm might take.

The dower house was small, cozy and snug, even in its current state of disrepair. She and Margery had left the manor house, taking up residence in the abandoned cottage as soon as Duncan was safely in the ground, and despite the cobwebs, the rotting wood, and drafty corners, she felt more at home than she'd ever felt in the grander residences of her father or her husband. Margery did her best, gradually making inroads on the ruined house, and Ailie was content with the ramshackle existence.

There was a fire burning in the grate in the small drawing room, and the smell of roast chicken filled the house. Ailie sank down in the shabby chair, holding out her bare toes to the warming fire.

"There you are, mistress," Margery said, appearing in the doorway, her broad, kindly face creased with worry. "People have been looking for you." Ailie had steadfastly refused to answer when addressed as Lady Spens, and Margery had given in with weary grace, settling for the more general term when she couldn't be prevailed upon to call her Ailie.

"So I gather. Torquil for one," she said, trying to keep the unhappiness out of her voice.

"Your brother for another. And me without a clue as to where you'd gone. You're not wearing black either. It's not decent, mistress. Your husband isn't even cold in the ground, and you're wearing colors. It shows a lack of respect."

"I forget," Ailie murmured, though she hadn't forgotten a thing.

"And your shoes, mistress!" Margery clucked. "You'll catch your death, wandering around like a bairn in the summer. Dinna ye realize that we're living here by your family's permission? If your brothers think I can't watch over you, they'll make you come back to Angus's house, and you wouldn't like that one bit. His wife's a spoiled young shrew, particularly now that she's carrying a bairn, and Angus has never shown ye much kindness."

Ailie simply shook her head, feeling her long hair fan out around her. "They can't make me," she said.

"Yes, mistress, they can. Try to behave yourself, my lady. It wouldn't take so much. Let me braid your hair, put away your colors, find your shoes. Walk quietly, with your head tucked down. You don't want any more whispers."

Ailie glanced at her maid curiously. Margery had been with her since she turned fourteen and confounded her family with her airy ways, and while she'd never understood her fey mistress, she had a stubborn, well-placed loyalty to Ailie's welfare. She simply didn't always recognize what was best for Ailie.

"And what would the whispers say, Margery?" she asked calmly enough, tucking her legs underneath her, settling her skirt around her. The hem was caked with mud from Collis's front yard, and absently she remembered the feel of the selkie's hand on her wrist. She could still feel the warmth of his flesh against hers. She would have thought a seal-man would be cold to the touch.

"They'd say you were mad, mistress. They could put you away, in a place where no one could see you, no one could help you."

"It might be better than marrying Torquil."

"Have a care, mistress. Torquil Spens is a decent enough man, and he wants ye. He's your best hope of any kind of happy life."

Ailie thought of Torquil, of the bland blue eyes and plump mouth, the silvering hair and sturdy jowls. He was a much kinder man than Domnhall MacAlpin, for all that he used the seal hunter for his dirty work. He'd take good care of her, Ailie knew. Keep her safe. Protected. Imprisoned. With no chance of escape or freedom ever again.

Ailie leaned back in the chair, smiling wearily. "I've accepted it, haven't I? Sooner or later he'll wed me, whether I say him aye or nay. At least I'll have a chance to dance with the faeries beforehand."

Margery shook her head in affectionate worry. "You and your faeries, mistress. They'll be the death of you."

Ailie thought back to the selkie. Malcolm, with the sea-green eyes that reached out and touched her. He was mysterious, enchanted, a far cry from the ordinary men and tedious everydayness of life. It was no wonder she was drawn to him like a moth to a flame.

"The faeries won't hurt me, Margery," she said softly. "Nor the selkies. Man is the only creature I have to fear."

Margery looked at her with perplexed tolerance. "The sooner you're wed," she said heavily, "the better for you. At least Torquil will protect you from your family." She started out the drawing-room door, her tread heavy on the worn floorboards.

"Aye," whispered Ailie to herself. "But who will protect me from Torquil?"

And unbidden, the memory of the selkie rose before her, like a faerie vision. And in the overwarm drawing room, Ailie shivered.

His mother had been a strong woman. A sturdy, gentle creature, with a fearless sense of right and wrong, one she'd done her best to instill in her wild young son, Catriona MacLaren had a saint's heart and a poet's soul, and Malcolm had loved her with all his reckless being.

He'd been a sore trial to her, growing up. He'd been rebellious, reckless, and the guilt still plagued him. Catriona had known he'd been devoted to her, just as she'd known how much he cared about his younger sisters and the man he knew as his father. She'd understood his uncertain temper, his rashness, his fierce need for justice and revenge. She'd always been able to reason with him, make him see both sides of the issue. But she was gone now, died of a fever last Christmas, holding the hand of her husband and her son, the two men she'd loved dearly and had never been able to see.

It was James MacLaren who'd told him the story, the man he loved and respected, the man he thought was his father. James MacLaren, who let his grief drive him too deep into the whisky bottle and loosen his tongue, who told his son the truth, and then regretted it ever since.

"I found her, lad," he'd said, staring into the fire, the unfamiliar power of the whiskey clouding his gaze. "She'd managed to cling to an old piece of jetsam, and she was bobbing up and down in the angry sea, her black hair spread out around her, matted with blood. It was a chance in a thousand that she'd survived so far, a chance in a thousand that I was out that day in the dory, more for sport than for duty, and happened to see her in the distance. By the time I reached her, she'd slipped beneath the waves, and I dived down after her.

"I was afraid I'd lost her," James continued, pouring himself another dram from the now half-empty dark bottle. "I couldn't see her anywhere in the murky depths of the sea. And then a dark shape swam by, sleek and graceful, and I knew it was a seal. I followed it, until I thought my lungs would burst, and he led me to your mother as she drifted down through the water, her hair flowing out around her.

"Even as I brought her into the boat I was afraid it was too late. She was scarce breathing, and her skin was dead white. I tried to force air into her, and she began to choke and cough. And she opened her eyes to me, her beautiful green eyes, and she was blind." His voice broke.

Malcolm held himself very still. He'd heard this story, he and his sisters, throughout their lives. The wondrous, romantic story of how their parents met and fell in love, when his father saved Catriona from the sea.

But this time it was different. There were ominous undertones to the tale, and it was his father's deep, angry voice that told it, not his mother's soft, sentimental one.

"They'd done it to her, lad. She told me the truth, and she made me swear I wouldn't take vengeance for it. It was my cross to bear, along with hers, and I thought I'd made my peace with it. But now . . . now . . ."

Malcolm took a step closer. His mother would never talk about her childhood or the years before she married James. Now, finally, the empty spaces would be filled. "Tell me," he said.

James looked up at his son, with love and affection in his blue eyes. "She lived on the island of St. Columba. She was the only daughter of a good family who'd fallen on hard times. She was a bonnie lass, one who made the dire mistake of thinking she was in love with the wrong man."

He'd known what was coming. He almost stopped his father, afraid to hear. But Malcolm MacLaren had never admitted fear in his entire life.

"Your mother knew right from wrong. She had no intention of giving herself without the blessing of the kirk. But yon Lordship had other ideas. He took her, by force, and she was too ashamed to tell anyone. In truth, there was no one she could tell. Her parents were old, bowed down with worry, and there was naught they could do against the power of a man like His Lordship."

"What happened?" He barely recognized the sound of his own voice. He sounded like a hungry wolf, raw and angry.

James looked away, into the fire. "She found she was carrying a bairn. And when she went to the man, to make him take responsibility, he drove her from his manor house with threats. But he knew he couldn't get away with his behavior. It wasn't as if Catriona was a simple village lass, made to be despoiled by the gentry. She was from an old family, a good family, and he'd be made to pay the price.

"So he and his friends got together. His best friend and his cousin and the man hired someone to kill her, to get rid of her with no questions asked. She never told me who'd done it, who'd taken her into a boat, out into the sea. The one thing she told me was that she'd fought, and he'd hit her in the head, knocking the sense from her, and thrown her into the sea. And she'd never seen again."

"How did she survive?"

James shook his head. "Heaven only knows. The seals saved her, perhaps. Or the grace of God. Somehow she found herself clinging to a piece of wood, her vision gone, clinging until I found her. I brought her back to Glen Corrie and nursed her myself. I wouldn't let any of the servants come near her. Even my own mother wasn't allowed to touch her. She almost died then, caught in a fever and a terror so deep I feared for her mind as well as her body. And then one day the fever left her, as fast as it came upon her. And as soon as the banns could be read, we were married." He leaned back against the wooden settle, looking older than his son had ever seen him.

Malcolm didn't want to ask the question. He loved his father. James MacLaren was a fair, good man who'd brought up his son to fear God and love nature, and a better father he couldn't have asked for. But he had to know the truth.

He leaned forward, took the bottle of fine Scotch whisky and brought it to his mouth, tipping the fiery stuff down his throat in a deep swallow. "When was I born?"

There was no mistaking the sorrow and regret in James's eyes. "You were a tough, fierce little laddie from the very beginning," he said.

"When?"

James closed his eyes. "Five months after we were married." He rose on unsteady feet. "Lad, you're my son. My heir, my firstborn child. It matters not to me that some other man fathered you. I was the one who was there when you came from your mother's body, red-faced and squalling. I was the one who taught you to ride and to hunt, who comforted you when you were sorrowed and laughed when you were joyful."

"Who was he?" Malcolm demanded in a harsh voice. "Who was the man who ordered my mother killed, along with her bastard?"

"Malcolm, he's the bastard, not you."

"Who was he? And who were the other men?"

If James hadn't been drunk, if he hadn't been desperate with grief, he never would have told him. "Sir Duncan Spens," James said finally. "His cousin Torquil. And his friend Wallace."

Malcolm drained the bottle of whisky, but the strong liquor only fanned the flames of his despair and fury. "You didn't kill them," he said flatly.

"I promised your mother."

Malcolm looked the man he'd known as his father in the

eye. "I made no such promise. They'll pay for it."

"Do you think that's what your mother would have wanted? She was gentle-hearted, forgiving. Do you think she'd want a blood vengeance?"

Malcolm started for the door, the cold winter wind swirling around the large manor house that had housed him all his life. "It's what I want," he said, his voice flat and deadly. And he'd slammed the door behind him as he walked out into the bitter night air.

And now he was here, on St. Columba, ready for the revenge that had eaten into his heart in the nine months since his mother had died. His father had watched him, with grief and regret, but none of his gentle words could turn him from his self-appointed task. He would make them pay for what they'd done to his mother. Stealing her sight, leaving her to live out her life in darkness. Had it been up to them, her life would have been forfeit. His as well.

Things were moving at a steady pace. He'd found Collis MacDewar easily enough. The old man had once been the only servant Catriona's parents could afford, and he'd been loyal and fond of the young mistress. His name had been one of the few his mother had mentioned when pressed to speak of her youth, and she'd done so with fondness in her voice. He would help him, Malcolm knew it full well, and instinct had taken him to the right man when he'd walked out of the sea after ditching his boat beyond the headland.

And then he'd suffered his first crushing blow. Six weeks too late. The bastard who'd raped his mother and tried to send her to her death had died peacefully in his bed, his sins unrepented. There was no way he would ever look into his son's eyes and see his nemesis.

His friend was dead as well, long gone of apoplexy. But the third of that group, Torquil Spens, lived on. And one woman was at the center. Ailie Wallace Spens. Barren wife of his father. Daughter of his father's friend. Beloved of the only remaining villain.

He would use her, he would hurt her, if that was the only way to hurt the three who'd transgressed so grievously against his gentle mother. He would strike at Finlay

Wallace from beyond the grave, despoiling his daughter.
He would cuckold his dead father, and if he managed to
give the old man's wife the child he'd never had, so much
the better. Catriona MacDugald's blood would inherit Sir
Duncan Spens's fortune. And he would take from Torquil
Spens the woman he lusted after.

And then perhaps the dark hole of pain and rage in his
heart would be filled.

The Wallaces were among the wealthiest on the
prosperous island of St. Columba. According to Collis,
they'd come from the lowlands several generations back,
their pockets filled with English gold. They'd built a
sprawling house, one that owed more to ostentation than
grace, and the family was large and greedy. The current
generation boasted five sons, all hearty bullies, and the
half-mad Ailie, Lady Spens.

She hadn't seemed half-mad, or half-witted to him, despite
what Collis told him, despite what her family seemed to
believe. There'd been intelligence and humor in her wide
blue eyes, as if she knew exactly what she was doing when
she talked of faeries and selkies and the like.

He would have liked to see how deep those fancies
went. In another life he could have, but now his need
for vengeance overcame any gentler feelings. If she was
half-mad, or fully mad, then perhaps that madness would
protect her from the results of his quest. Perhaps not. He
couldn't afford to worry about her.

His father, for so he couldn't stop thinking of James
MacLaren despite the truth, was prosperous and generous.
Malcolm was his heir, fair or not, and he had already been
given a large farm and four hundred acres of decent soil.
He'd left his inheritance behind in the capable hands of
his steward and come to St. Columba in search of his
destiny.

That destiny started with the Wallaces. With the five
brothers and the sister. He'd move on to Torquil Spens
in his own good time.

The Wallace house loomed before him, and he eyed it
with calm interest that was only partly feigned. It wasn't

as large as his father's manor house, or as pretty. Its lack of grace suited him well.

The household was in disarray. He could hear the loud voices raised in argument as he waited in the overdecorated anteroom that looked more as if it belonged in an Edinburgh brothel than a highland manor house. The servant who'd told him to wait had scurried away, and doubtless had forgotten about him in the uproar. He could make out a woman's shrill, complaining tone, and the sound of a deep male voice, bullying and blustering. There was another voice, quieter, and he wondered who among them were his enemies. All of them, if their name was Wallace.

The door to the room was flung open and a very pretty woman with the face of an angel, the expression of a shrew, and the belly of a woman eight months into pregnancy stormed into the room. "She's being impossible, Angus. I told her she wasn't to come down—someone will take her back to that wretched little hovel and keep her there. She's an embarrassment—she ought to be put away."

The man who followed her into the room was largish, inclined to fat, with the small eyes and thick lips of a bully. "She'll come down for tea if I have to beat her," he announced. "She does it on purpose, Fiona, playing her little tricks. She's smart enough when she tries—she can behave herself if she wants to. And by God I'll make her want to."

Neither of them noticed Malcolm standing in the shadows, utterly still, watching them with no little interest. He knew perfectly well who they had to be discussing. The daft Ailie Wallace Spens.

"She has no sympathy for my situation," Fiona continued in a voice that was halfway between a screech and a whine. "Just because she's barren . . ."

"We don't know that for certain," Angus said. "Though it seems likely enough by now. Bring her down, Fiona. Torquil's waiting to see her, and he might as well see her at her worst. It won't come as any surprise—he's seen her often enough when she was married to his cousin. If he's going to cry off, he might as well do it now. Then we can see about putting her away someplace."

"Very well," Fiona said, sulking, turning toward the door. At that moment her eyes caught sight of Malcolm, and they widened. "Who are you?"

Angus followed her gaze, taking a belligerent step forward. "Aye, who are you, to be listening in on a family conversation?"

Malcolm calmly considered how far he'd get if he shoved his fist against Angus Wallace's mouth. It might provide some immediate satisfaction, but he was after something more complex, more complete.

"I didn't mean to intrude," he said politely enough. "I'm Malcolm MacLaren, newly arrived on St. Columba. I was informed that you were the owner of a certain house I'm interested in leasing."

Angus's eyes narrowed, but the light of greed shone forth. "What house is that?"

"It's a tumbledown place out by the seal rocks. It doesn't look as if anyone's been living there for a while, but it would suit me."

"The old MacDugald place? It's been empty for almost thirty years. The old couple who lived there died out, soon after their only child drowned. Why would you be wanting that particular spot?"

Malcolm managed a charming, diffident smile when he wanted to rip the man's throat out. "I haven't much money. It looked to be within my funds."

Angus's smile was just as false as he promptly named a sum far too high for such a tumbledown place. That smile broadened when Malcolm agreed without argument, and his good humor was such that he invited him to tea. An invitation Malcolm accepted.

The withdrawing room was decorated in puce silk, a color obviously designed to complement Lady Fiona's complexion. It did no justice to Sir Angus's high color, and it made the dark-clothed man who awaited them look sallow. Malcolm shuttered his expression as he looked at the other man, heard his greeting in that soft voice.

"Torquil Spens," Sir Angus introduced him. "MacLaren

is a newcomer to the isle. He's leasing the old MacDugald house from me."

"I didn't hear of any newcomers," Torquil said smoothly, not bothering to rise from his chair. "I usually make it my business to hear of any new arrivals."

"I'm here, am I not?" Malcolm said politely enough.

"So you are. I wonder why?"

"It's a lovely island," he said in a noncommittal voice.

"But I wonder—"

"Here she is," Fiona announced in an aggrieved voice.

Malcolm watched Torquil's expression carefully as he rose to greet his intended, and he felt the exultation rush through him. He'd been right. Torquil was staring at the doorway with such avidity that it could only be called obsession, a lust of the body that would be his downfall.

"For God's sake, Ailie, are ye daft?" Angus thundered. "Why didn't ye warn me, Fiona?"

"I tried," Lady Fiona said, flouncing past into the room, pausing long enough to give Malcolm an arch, assessing look before she sank onto a puce-colored settee. He was right; it had been chosen specifically for her coloring.

He turned to follow the other men's gaze, and he had to swallow a sudden burst of laughter. Ailie Spens stood there, Lady Spens, to be more accurate. She was barefoot, as she had been the day before, wearing a bright blue dress that was much too small for her long, strapping body. The hemline came midcalf, the bodice was pulled tight across her chest, accentuating her very pleasing curves. The sleeves had ripped when she'd pulled the outfit on, and her thick hair hung down to her waist, golden, lit with sunlight, so that a foolish man might want to sift his hands through its rich length.

She was humming, something tuneless, swaying back and forth with eerie grace, unaware of him as he stood behind her bulky, glowering brother. The words were familiar, and he recognized them with a shock of misplaced amusement. She was singing one of Ophelia's mad songs from *Hamlet*.

He was more than conversant with Shakespeare. What his mother missed most, after not being able to look into the faces of her bairns, was the joy of reading. He gave that to her, reading anything she wished, from Shakespeare and Byron and Bobbie Burns to racy French novels that made her blush and laugh with pleasure. He knew *Hamlet* very well.

And then her eyes met his, across the room, and her voice faltered in shock. "You wear your rue with a difference, lady," he murmured.

And then the shock disappeared. "The selkie!" she cried, an enchanting smile wreathing her face as she started toward him. "You've come to take me to the sea."

CHAPTER
3

"You're daft, woman," Angus said angrily. "There's no such thing as a selkie."

"So that's who you are," Torquil murmured at the same time, eyeing Malcolm with an arrested expression. "I'd forgotten about our so-called supernatural visitor. Remiss of me. Ailie, love, aren't you going to greet your cousin?"

Ailie didn't even glance his way, skirting the bullish figure of her brother to come up to Malcolm. He could see deliberate wildness in her blue, blue eyes, and found himself thinking irrelevantly of bluebonnets on a hillside, waving free and careless in the breeze. "You aren't my cousin, Torquil," she said, looking into Malcolm's eyes.

He wanted to reach out and touch her, but he didn't dare, not with her brother and her fiancé standing by. "Lady Spens," he said, greeting her.

The tension in the room increased threefold. "How do you know my sister?" Sir Angus demanded in a belligerent voice.

"Don't be absurd, Angus," Ailie answered for him. "Of course he knows my name. He's come for me. To take me to the sea."

It was unnervingly close to the truth. Malcolm shook his head. "No, my lady," he said politely enough. "I've just come for a bit of quiet."

She didn't pout. He doubted she had such an artificial feminine expression in her makeup. Instead she shook her head. "If it's quiet you want, you won't find it here. Go back to the sea, selkie, before the seal hunters come after you."

"Ailie, you are without a doubt the most tiresome creature," Fiona said loudly. "Don't bother Mr. MacLaren—he has better things to do than listen to your half-witted ravings."

The smile Ailie gave her pregnant sister-in-law was full of cheerful good humor, and Malcolm wondered whether he imagined the trace of mischief in her eyes as she turned back to him. "Have you been well fed, Malcolm?" she asked. "Collis is an indifferent fisherman."

"I can take care of my own needs, my lady."

He was included in her mischief, he knew it. "I was wondering," she said, putting a strong hand on his arm. "I know you eat only fish. But do you smash them against a rock and then bite their heads off, or do you swallow them while they're still alive and wiggling?"

"Oh, God," Fiona mumbled in a strangled voice, and rushed from the room, her face pale.

"You did that on purpose," Angus said furiously, going after her.

"Did what?" Ailie asked, patently mystified.

Torquil came up beside her, taking her hand from Malcolm's arm. Malcolm felt her sudden clinging in surprise, and then she released him, so quickly that he wondered whether he might have imagined it. "You mustn't disturb Mr. MacLaren, dear Ailie," Torquil said in an avuncular voice. "He's a visitor, and he doesn't understand how very special you are."

"You don't think I'm simple, do you, Torquil?" she asked in a plaintive voice that sounded madder than anything Malcolm had heard from her before.

Torquil looked very pleased. "Of course not, my love."

"Because you wouldn't want to marry a woman who was half-mad, would you?" she continued. "Even for the sake of my inheritance you wouldn't want to be saddled with a barren idiot."

"Ailie!" he protested, his good humor vanished.

"Though we don't know for sure I'm barren, do we?" she continued in that light, singsong voice. "That's what you and Angus are waiting for. To see whether I'm breeding or not. It certainly would complicate matters if I were. Though I suppose I could ask old Morag the witch to take care of it for me."

She'd managed to shock even the phlegmatic Torquil into silence, and she took advantage of that fact, pulling away from him with gentle force. "I'm going back to the dower house," she said. "It doesn't appear as if we're going to be getting any tea today."

Malcolm wanted to go with her. He told himself it was out of his need for revenge, but he knew he lied. He wanted to see what else she might say, what outrageous things might come from that artless mouth. He wanted to touch her hair, to see if it felt as soft and silky as it looked.

"I'll accompany you," Torquil said hurriedly.

She spared one brief, sly glance at Malcolm. "No," she said to Torquil. "You won't." And with a whirl of her skirts and her rich golden hair she was gone.

"Damn," Torquil said, watching her run. He turned and shrugged his shoulders, giving Malcolm a smile that was no doubt meant to be man-to-man. "She's a rare handful. She's safe enough here on the island—if any man were to offer her insult, half the villagers would gut him."

"Is that a warning?" Malcolm murmured.

"Of course not, dear fellow. You can see as well as I that she's not quite right in the head. Never has been, for that matter, though no one has ever been sure of the reason. Why, she thinks you're a selkie! Of all the absurd fancies. I know I can count on you not to pay too much attention to the things she says. She's a complete innocent, unaware of how her words might sound."

Malcolm doubted that. Mistress Ailie seemed fully aware of the havoc she was wreaking. He simply smiled, a wintry, noncommittal smile. He'd always been adept at patience, at hunting for his prey. His prey stood before him, fat and sleek and ready for the slaughter. Malcolm was going to enjoy himself immensely.

But not yet. There'd be time to savor his revenge. To get it right. "I'd best be getting home," he murmured to the man he'd sworn to destroy.

"I'll convey your regrets to Sir Angus and Lady Wallace," Torquil murmured, making no effort to stop him.

The air was cool, crisp when he left the Wallace manor house, and Malcolm took a deep, cleansing breath. He'd met his enemy, face-to-face. The last remaining villain who'd engineered his mother's near murder. Odd to think that the fat, smug old man was some sort of blood kin to him. A few hours on St. Columba and the truth of James MacLaren's words came home to him. James was his father, the only one worth having. His kin lay back in Glen Corrie, not on this beautiful rocky island.

He started up the pathway to the northern coast of the small isle, wanting to investigate the house where his mother had been born, to see if any trace of the once carefree lass remained. Not that she'd been careworn during his childhood. She'd taken her blindness in stride, doing more than most sighted women could have accomplished, and doing it with calm good humor, ordering her servants, raising her brood of children, loving her husband.

Collis would meet him when he finished with the day's catch. Like most highland crofters, he counted on a number of things to scratch a living out of the unfriendly soil—the sparse crops he could grow, the sheep he tended, and the fish he could draw from the sea.

He found himself grinning, remembering Ailie Spens's deliberately artless question. He almost wished he had the strength of purpose to swallow a live fish, just to see the reactions of the good people of St. Columba.

The sky was fading into the dim halflight that would linger well toward midnight. He walked swiftly, trying to still the restlessness that danced in his veins. He needed to be patient. His revenge must be delicately taken for it to provide a mortal sting. He couldn't rush into anything.

His grandparents' house was a small, sturdy stone cottage

by the edge of the sea. Part of the roof had fallen in, some of the windows were broken, and the garden was a riot of overgrowth and color. Collis had taken him there this morning, and he'd immediately felt an affinity for the place. It was all he had left of his mother's family—a deserted old farmhouse. It both soothed him and strengthened his determination.

The shadows were lengthening when he opened the front door, listening to it creak noisily. He wouldn't oil it—it would prove a warning if Torquil began to suspect he had other reasons for being here. He stepped inside, staring around him at the dust-shrouded hallway.

His mother had grown up here. He could imagine her, a bonnie lass, racing down the steep front stairs. He could almost sense her presence, hear her breathing, smell the faint trace of flowers.

It wasn't his imagination, or wishful thinking. He wasn't alone in the old house. Someone was there with him. And he had a fair idea who it might be.

He walked into the empty drawing room. Ailie was standing by a window, staring out at the sea, her long hair hanging down her back. She'd heard him, of course, but she paid him no notice, intent on the rough water that lay beyond the rocks.

"Do you love the sea?" she asked in a vague, faraway voice.

"You shouldn't be here."

She turned then, to smile at him. "A daft question," she said, ignoring his comment. "Of course you love the sea. It's your home."

"Does your cousin know you're here?" She looked like a ghost, standing there in the shadowed room, and while he ought to thank the fates for putting her in his hands so rapidly, he wasn't ready for her. He wasn't going to take her in his mother's house, against her will. This house had known too much joy, too much sorrow, as it was. His grandparents had died shortly after Catriona had gone into the sea, never to know that their daughter lived and prospered, blind but loved.

And he wasn't going to take her at all if she was anywhere near as mad as she pretended to be. He was a bastard in deed as well as name, but even he had limits. There would have to be another way to get to Torquil Spens. Another way to avenge his mother.

"No one knows where I am," she said simply. "I like it that way. They'll tie me down soon enough. For now I simply disappear when I want to, go where I want to. I wanted to come here."

"Why?"

"I've never been here," she said, wandering past him, looking around her with a curious eye. "They say it's haunted. The old couple died long before I was born, and their daughter was lost at sea." She turned to glance at him. "I don't suppose you knew her? Her name was Catriona MacDugald."

It took an effort to control the shock her eerie words had given him. "How should I have known her?" he demanded hoarsely.

"In the sea, Malcolm," Ailie replied patiently, as if he were the one who was mad. "Maybe she didn't drown at all. Maybe a selkie came and stole her away, and she's living there still, with a dozen seal pups to watch over. I wonder if she'd miss her family."

"I doubt it," he said wryly.

"Well, I wouldn't if I were her," Ailie said, whirling around, the skirts dancing about her long, shapely calves. "Family is a mixed blessing, and mine has proved more of a curse. If you're here to take me to the sea, I won't argue. I imagine living beneath the waves is very grand."

Heaven preserve him, he thought wearily. He reached out and stopped her in the midst of her turning, holding her steadily. "You have too much of an affinity for Ophelia, mistress," he said. "She ended badly."

He'd hoped to startle her. She simply smiled at him, her face almost at a level with his, and he wondered what it would be like to hold such a tall woman in his arms. How would she fit against him? Beneath him? "That's a matter of opinion," she said. "She went where no one could reach her. I consider that to be a triumph."

"Suicide, Ailie? Isn't that a wee bit drastic?"

She stood there, staring at him, suddenly serious. "No, Malcolm. I might go into the sea with you if you asked me, but otherwise I'm promised to this life. I wonder . . ." And her voice trailed off.

"You wonder what?"

Once more the mischief lit her blue eyes, and she raised her hand to his face. Her fingers brushed his mouth, lightly, and it took all his self-control to keep still beneath her touch. "Whether your lips are cold as the sea. Or warm."

"And what have you discovered?"

"They're warm," she said, her fingertips tracing the outline of his lips. They were soft, gentle, and then to his shock she reached up and brushed her mouth against his as well, a feather-light caress. Before he could react, could pull her into his arms, she pulled away, moving across the room toward the door.

He watched her go, relief and regret and the slow burning coals of desire at war within his body. "Are you leaving?"

"They want to lock me away," she said, seemingly a non sequitur. "If I won't marry Torquil and sleep in his bed, then they'll lock me away. I wouldn't mind, but I should miss the sea, and the hills, and the creatures of the forest. So I'd best behave myself, for now. You'd best behave yourself as well, my selkie."

He didn't correct her address. "Why should I?"

"Because they don't trust you. Neither my brother nor Torquil, and while they smile and say all the right things, they are capable of great evil. Smiling, damnable villains," she said.

"You read too much Shakespeare."

"I know," she said. "It was ever a failing of mine." And she disappeared, humming beneath her breath. An old Jacobite song that had been outlawed years ago. "Over the Water to Charlie."

*   *   *

"Making war on women is a shameful business."

Malcolm didn't turn. He'd heard Collis's approach, and while he'd wondered just how much he'd observed, the old man's caustic observation gave him the answer. "I won't hurt her," he said.

"You already have. Were you to go into the sea this night and never return, she'd mourn ye."

"That's not my problem."

Collis shook his head in a disapproval. "I'll help ye," he said. "For the sake of Catriona. But I don't hold with hurting helpless craitures. If you wound Ailie, you'll have me to answer to."

Malcolm looked down at the sturdy, bandy-legged old man and told himself he should be amused. Unfortunately there was little to lighten his dark mood. "You and half the island," he said. "She won't suffer for anything I've done."

Collis just looked at him, uncertain whether to believe him or not. And then he nodded. "Ye're a man of your word," he said. "I've brought fish for your dinner."

Malcolm almost asked him if they were still alive and wiggling, but he controlled his dark humor. Collis wasn't quite sure what he thought of Malcolm. He'd asked him very little—they'd come to an agreement without much talking. He knew Malcolm came from Catriona, but he didn't know he was her son. For all Malcolm knew, Collis might truly think he was a selkie.

It didn't matter. People could believe what they wished. It would prove nothing but useful to have people think he was a seal creature, an enchanted being. The less people knew, the better.

He wouldn't hurt Ailie. Seduce her, yes, so that Torquil was painfully aware of it. Get her with a babe, as his father had failed to do. A fitting revenge on the man who'd sired him and then tried to have him killed.

And then he'd disappear, leaving the daughter of Finlay Wallace pregnant. There'd be gossip, of course. From what little he'd seen of Ailie, she'd probably scarcely notice her disgrace.

Perhaps Collis was right—it was a shameful thing to hurt

an innocent like Ailie. But his dark revenge would be far
sweeter than a dirk in the belly of Torquil Spens. She'd
spent her life being prey to the whim of her menfolk.
His use of her would be nothing new. And he had every
intention of giving her pleasure as well as a bairn.

He glanced around him, surprised to notice he was now
alone. Collis was moving around in some other part of the
deserted cottage, and Malcolm could smell grilling fish. At
least tonight he wouldn't be expected to bite the head off
a trout.

He could still feel the touch of her fingertips on his lips
and her lips. He wanted more than the brush of her mouth
against his. He wanted her body wrapped around him, her
hair a plaid for them both. He never thought revenge would
be near so sweet.

Deep in the forest that fanned out behind the village,
covering half the tiny isle of St. Columba, lay a clearing.
In that clearing stood a circle of stones, ancient, beyond
time, towering above the ground. The villagers kept away
from the spot, known as the Seal's Dance. It was haunted,
they said, a place for faeries and broonies and the like. It
was Ailie's favorite place in the world.

The old witch Morag was rumored to live there, though
no one had ever actually admitted to seeing her but Ailie,
and everyone knew the lass was mazed. The old woman
was powerful nonetheless, and she was known to cast a
spell on souls, a spell that rendered their fishing nets
empty and their sheep dead. She'd put such a spell on
Domnhall MacAlpin when he'd murdered Ailie's cat, but
the villagers didn't consider it one of her happier acts.
Domnhall had turned to seal hunting, and the good folk
of St. Columba were waiting for the selkies to take
their revenge.

It was the time for faeries, that endless twilight of the
northern isles, and Ailie's bare feet were light on the
pathway. Even if they suspected where she was, no one
would come after her. They were afraid of the Seal's Dance,
all of them, even Margery. They would wait till she came to

them, secure in the knowledge that the spirit of old Morag would protect her.

They were the simple ones, Ailie thought with gentle derision. So busy looking just beyond the end of their noses that they could see no farther. They trusted only what they could see, smell, and touch. They were missing a world of glory.

"There you are, lassie." Morag's voice came to her on the soft breeze, and she turned, gracefully, to see the bent-over old lady sitting on the ground by one of the stones. "I knew ye'd come to me this night."

Ailie didn't bother to ask how she knew. In her experience Morag was as wise and as old as time. She crossed the thick mossy grass and knelt beside the old woman. "Who is he?" she asked, knowing she need explain no further.

"He comes from the sea," Morag said. "Dinna ye ken his eyes? He comes from the seal people."

"So do half the people of St. Columba."

"Aye," she said, as if that answered everything.

"What does he want?"

Morag turned to look at her. Her eyes were milky, practically sightless, and yet she could see into Ailie's heart more truly than any soul with perfect vision. "He means ye harm, mistress. He'll change yer life, turn it upside down, and there's no telling how it will end."

"Why would he wish to harm me?"

"Not for your sake. For others'. It's a blood vengeance, and you stand right in the midst of it. Keep away from him, mistress. I don't want to lose ye."

"You won't lose me," Ailie said in a fierce, quiet voice that none of her kin would even recognize. "Haven't you been more than a mother to me? I'll keep away from the man."

"Ye don't want to. I can hear it in your voice. He fascinates you."

Ailie didn't bother to deny it. "I've never known an enchanted creature before," she said. "It's little wonder I'm drawn to him. He's bonnie enough to make even a lackwit take notice."

"And ye're no lackwit, for all the pretense ye make of it," Morag said.

"I'm lackwit enough to come here tonight with no food for you," she said wryly. "I'll bring you a basket tomorrow."

"And ye'll keep away from yon fine craiture?"

Ailie thought back to him. To the eyes the color of the sea, the tall, strong body, thin but powerful, the strong nose, and firm mouth. And she remembered the warmth of his mouth beneath her fingertips. Beneath her lips. Morag had never asked anything of her—she'd been a lap to weep into, a voice of wisdom, the keeper of the stories, and a source of magic. Ailie would do as she asked, without regret.

"I'll keep away from him," she said firmly, meaning every word of it. But she hadn't accounted for her dreams.

She slept soundly that night, in the high, soft bed in the dower house, at peace, knowing no one would come to her side, no one would insist on watching as she disrobed, his eyes bleary and hungry, his body aged and sick. She had no one to bother her, no one to question her, for at least the next few months. She could snuggle down in the feathery softness and know she would be blessedly, peacefully alone. Until she was forced to marry Torquil.

She was standing alone on a rocky stretch of beach, her bare feet on a boulder as the water swirled around her. There was a cool breeze, tossing her long skirts against her legs, spilling her hair around her face, but she stood there, shivering in the chill air, motionless, as she watched him emerge from the angry green depths of the sea.

His long black hair clung to his bare shoulders, beads of water glistened on his narrow, enigmatic face, his bronzed torso. He stood thigh-deep in the surf, and the icy sea swelled around his black pants.

He stared at her, silent, demanding. And then he held out a hand to her and beckoned her.

She shook her head. The water was too icy, she was too frightened, she who'd never been frightened of a man in her life. But then, he wasn't a man beckoning to her, calling to her. He was an enchanted creature, one who would take her down, down into the frigid depths of the water to live among the seal folk.

He moved closer, so that the water only reached his strong calves, and beckoned to her again. Once more she shook her head, denying him, denying the yearning that surged in her heart. He would hurt her, Morag had warned her, and Morag was always right. If she stayed on the rock and didn't touch the water, she'd be safe.

Finally he spoke, and his voice was low, musical. "Come away with me, lass." And he moved to the rock where she stood, and held out his arms.

She could fight it no longer. She went to him, into his arms, and he scooped her up, holding her against the solid, silky warmth of his chest, as he started back into the sea.

She braced herself for the cold, but as the water lapped around her skirts it was warm, balmy, like a Sunday bath. He paused when the water reached his chest, covering most of her body, and looked at her.

"Are you ready, lass?" he whispered, his mouth hovering near hers.

She no longer hesitated. If he meant her harm, then she wanted that harm, more than she wanted the stifling safety of her life, where everyone tried to order her and everyone failed. This would be her final triumph.

"I'm ready," she said. "But I cannot swim."

"I'll show you." And he dived beneath the warm water, taking her with him.

She held her breath at first, closed her eyes, as he loosed her, holding her hand as he pulled her through the sea. When it seemed as if her lungs would burst, she took a breath, certain she would drown. But life filled her lungs, rich warm life, surging through her, and she opened her eyes in surprise, looking around her as she glided through the depths of the North Sea.

The selkie was beside her. Malcolm, his long black hair trailing behind him, his limbs strong and graceful as he moved through the water. Surrounding them were a dozen seals, of varying colors, dark and golden, honey-colored and white, but the two of them still held their human shape. He came up to her, drawing her against his body, and she flowed against him, graceful, inevitable, wrapping her arms around him, her hair a cloud in the warm water, floating around them.

He kissed her then, breathing into her mouth, and she felt as if she would burst with pleasure as she drifted through the shimmering sea, at one with her selkie lover. This was what she had dreamed about, this was what she had longed for. Nothing else mattered but his mouth, wet and open against hers, taking her, down and down and down, into the murky, velvet depths of the Scottish sea.

Rough hands reached out, trying to pull her back, away from him, but she fought, struggling to hold on to him. His skin was smooth, slippery beneath her fingers, and she felt herself torn away, hauled toward the surface, and suddenly she could no longer breathe, the weight of the water pressing down around her, and it was icy, numbing. She opened her mouth to call to him, a cry of longing and despair, but the sea filled her mouth and throat, choking her, and she was drawn to the blinding glare of the surface without being able to make a sound of protest.

"Mistress," Margery said urgently, shaking her.

Ailie opened her eyes, reluctant, angry, and released the pent-up breath she'd been holding in her lungs. She was lying in her bed, warm, dry, and bereft. Her arms felt empty. "I was dreaming," she said.

"It's late morning, mistress. I've never known you to sleep so late. I was afeart you might be sickening."

"No," Ailie said. The dream was gone, there'd be no calling it back. The sunlight was bright outside the casement window, glistening through the changing color of the trees, and she knew she had to get up.

"Your family's here," Margery said. "You brother and sister-in-law, and Mr. Spens."

Ailie flopped back down in the bed and pulled the covers around her. "Tell them to go away."

Margery pulled the covers back. "Ye'd best come down, mistress. I ken they won't be leaving at all."

Sudden alarm filled Ailie. "What do you mean?"

"They came with baggage, and Lady Fiona's maidservant, and the cook, and a case of French wine. They've come to stay, mistress."

"I won't have them here."

"Didn't I warn you? If you kept walking out with your clothes and hair all which way, people were bound to talk. That brother of yours has been looking for an excuse to put you under lock and key, and his wife hates you. They know they can't take you back to their house without you screaming your head off, and the people of St. Columba wouldn't let you be harmed. So they're going to move in on you and watch over you here."

"Tell them to leave," Ailie said furiously.

"It won't do any good. They're here to stay. Best behave yourself and it'll be easier for the both of us. To be truthful, I'd like a bit of company, and you're a rare handful for me to watch over."

"I don't need watching over, Margery. I can take care of myself."

"By going off to see the selkie at all hours of the night? They heard of it, mistress, and that decided them. This is all for the best. You'll realize that, sooner or later."

"You told them to come." Ailie scrambled from the bed, her long white nightrail trailing behind her as she headed for the door.

"You can't go downstairs like that!" Margery protested, scandalized.

"Watch me."

Angus and Fiona were ensconced in the tiny parlor, having made themselves at home. Fiona was sitting by the fire that was unneeded on a warm day, her hands clasped over her pregnant belly, a petulant expression on her perfect face.

"I want you to leave," Ailie said without preamble.

Her brother was already drinking wine, and he choked on his mouthful, spitting it on the floor as he glared at her. "Have you no sense of decency at all, missie?" he demanded.

"This is my house. I'm a widow, with an inheritance and a jointure. I don't want you here."

"Now, lass," Angus said with a poor attempt at placating her. "You know you need the wise council of your family during your time of mourning. All this time alone hasn't been good for you. Not when your mind is far from clear in the best of times. We're here to watch over you, Fiona and I. You need rest and quiet."

"I need my freedom!" she cried.

She could have saved her breath. "You haven't been able to look after yourself, and while Margery does her best, she's not up to the rigors of watching over you. We'll do that for you, lass. Keep you safe here in the house where you won't be bothered by strangers during your time of mourning. There'll be no visitors, saving for family."

She fought the panic that surged up inside her. "You're my only family on the island," she said carefully.

"And Torquil, of course. He's your cousin by marriage, and hopes to be much more. But now isn't the time to be discussing such things. Rest and quiet, Ailie. For the next few months."

"And if I don't agree?"

"Why shouldn't you, lass? A sweet, cloth-headed girl like yourself? We're just doing what's best for you. It would grieve my heart to have to send you away."

"Send me away where?"

"There's a hospital in Edinburgh where they keep people like you. With bars on the windows and locked doors," Fiona piped up, and her voice had a cruel edge to it.

"Is that so much worse than being locked up here?"

"We'll be more than happy to give you a chance to find out," her brother said smoothly.

Don't, Ailie told herself. Don't scream, or fight, or say a word. It won't save you. "Welcome to the dower house," she murmured.

She plastered a bright, sunny smile on her face, made her eyes lose their focus, and picked up the trailing hem of her white nightrail. And then she wandered away, forcing her movements to be light and airy, as she hummed beneath her breath.

"She's mad," Fiona snapped at Angus.

"Perhaps," Ailie heard her brother reply. "Perhaps."

CHAPTER
4

"Dinna ye plan to go to the kirk?" Collis's accusing voice broke through Malcolm's reverie.

He roused himself to glance up at the old man. "Sunday, is it?" he replied lazily, knowing full well what day it was. Four days since he'd walked ashore on the island of St. Columba. Two days since he'd last caught sight of Ailie Wallace Spens.

"It would do ye no harm to observe the sabbath," Collis said sourly.

Malcolm shook his head. "I can't do that, old man."

"And why not?"

He smiled with a sweetness that left the old man stonily unmoved. "Because the kirk is no place for faerie craitures," he said. "Yon minister would doubtless cast me out if I tried to enter."

"Yon minister might surprise you," Collis said. "He's a fine preacher, never bedeviling a man about too much whisky and minor sins such as that. The entire island goes to service every Sunday."

There was no missing Collis's message. "Everyone?"

"Even those half-mazed," Collis said. "Torquil usually takes her."

Malcolm rose from his perch by the rocky shore. He'd taken to staring at the dark water, so angry and different from the sea near the MacLaren lands in Glen Corrie. "Then it would probably behoove me to go as well," he said. "I haven't seen Lady Spens since Thursday. I would have thought she'd be around." He made his voice sound careless, noncommittal, and he wondered whether he fooled Collis.

"I doubt she's had any choice in the matter. It's that family of hers. They moved in on her, and word has it they're keeping her under lock and key."

"Why would they do that?"

"To keep her away from you."

Malcolm looked at him in surprise. "Why would they think I would mean her harm?" They didn't strike him as clever enough to see beneath the surface.

"It's not you they don't trust, laddie. It's the girl. She's mazed, you know."

"So they say."

"And they're afraid for her. Afraid she'll come to harm. That someone might misunderstand her simple friendliness for something more sinful."

"They're afraid I'll seduce her?"

"Aye."

"A wicked thing to do, Collis. To seduce an innocent lass and then abandon her," Malcolm said dryly. "Anyone who's party to such an act should be punished. Don't you agree?"

Collis stared at him strangely. "If ye say so. Is that what happened to Catriona? Did she find herself with an unwanted bairn and then walk into the sea to escape her shame?"

"No!" Malcolm snapped. He glared at the old man. "You knew her, back then. Was she the sort of lass who'd give in to a man's lies? Who'd kill herself and her bairn rather than face the consequences? Was she a coward and a whore, Collis?" His voice was low, deceptively dangerous, as if he were waiting for an excuse to vent his fury.

But Collis shook his head slowly. "She was a sweet lass. One who might have made the mistake of giving herself in love to the wrong man."

"She didn't," Malcolm said flatly.

"But she would never have killed herself."

Malcolm felt some of the tension drain from him. In the far distance they could hear the tolling of the church bell, calling the people of St. Columba to worship. "Let's go to the kirk, old man," he said heavily. "I have sins to confess."

They sat near the back, he and Collis, and he almost didn't recognize her when she walked by. It was the sight of Torquil's smug bulk that alerted him, and his first glance slid over the demure creature by his side, then returned for a second shocked look.

It was the faerie-mad Ailie. Her thick golden hair was plaited in tight braids, wrapped and pinned close to her head. Her clothes were the dull black of mourning, high-necked, long-sleeved, reaching to the floor. There were no bare toes today, just sensible black shoes. Her face was pale beneath the weight of her coiled hair, and her eyes were dull and lifeless.

For a moment he wanted to leap out of his seat and haul her away from Torquil. "What have you done with her?" he wanted to shout, but he held still, mesmerized, knowing Collis watched him, knowing others did as well. It was too small an island for the people not to know that Ailie had been drawn to the stranger who'd walked from the sea, and he was damned if he'd give them food for gossip.

He plastered a bland, solemn expression on his face as the service started, hoping he looked suitably reverent. In truth, he paid no attention to the dominie who presided over the kirk. He was too caught up in staring at the back of Ailie's neck. How could a woman so tall, so strapping, suddenly look fragile?

Torquil's meaty hand was clamped around her arm, drawing her up, pushing her down, keeping a possessive grip on her as they moved through the endless service. Under cover of the offering Malcolm leaned over and muttered underneath his breath, "Distract Torquil after kirk."

"Easier said than done," Collis replied with a snort.

"Do it." If Collis failed him, there was no telling when

he'd have a chance to get close to Ailie. She looked ill, cramped and laced and strangled by her proper clothes and her proper behavior. He wanted to see her running barefoot and free, her long hair flowing behind her. He wanted to see her running to him.

In the end, Collis proved surprisingly creative. Torquil paused long enough to greet the dominie, and Ailie stood beside him, head bowed, eyes downcast.

Look at me, Malcolm demanded silently from his place in the kirkyard. Lift your head, lass, and see me.

He didn't know how she knew. But suddenly she'd turned, her blue eyes found his with a sureness that almost made him believe in faeries, and her pale face lit up with something that almost frightened him.

Torquil's hand clamped down on her arm once more, pulling her along as they headed for his carriage, when Collis moved down on them. He'd managed to retrieve a basket of fish, heaven only knew where, and in the bright sunlight the smell could carry all the way to Malcolm.

"Begging your pardon, Mr. Spens," Collis said, knocking into him, keeping an unsteady hand on the basket. "But I've need of a word with you on a matter of important business."

Torquil wasn't so easily moved. "The Sabbath is no day for conducting business, Collis." He waved him away. "Come see me tomorrow."

"But, sir," Collis protested, stumbling forward.

The basket, of course, upended. Silvery fish skittered over Torquil Spens's fine Sunday clothes, and his shriek of fury was almost lost in the sound of laughter from the assembled churchgoers. He released his grip on Ailie and turned in fury to Collis, shouting his outrage at the top of his lungs.

She disappeared. If Malcolm hadn't been watching her so closely, he would have thought it magic. Instead she chose the moment's confusion to vanish into the woods in back of the kirk, and much as Malcolm would have liked to have seen the outcome between Torquil's outraged sensibility and Collis's impersonation of an addled old man, he had more important things to do. He backed away from the amused crowd, skirting behind the old stone church and following Ailie into the woods.

She was already gone, out of sight, moving light and free despite her regimented clothes. He headed after her, relying on instinct, an instinct that was rewarded when he came across a discarded pair of shiny black shoes.

Her black stockings were a few yards onward. His feet crunched on the hairpins scattered in the path, and he found himself hoping there'd be further pieces of clothing leading the way.

Deeper and deeper into the woods he went, following the path, and the trees grew tall and dark over him, and the scent of pine and gorse was strong in the air.

The path ended abruptly, and he halted at the edge of the forest, unmoving, caught by the sight that met his eyes.

She was standing in a clearing on top of a small knoll. Surrounding her was a stone circle, looming over her, making her look suddenly dainty. She'd freed her hair, and it hung down her back like a rich curtain of silk. She'd tucked her long black skirts up in her waistband, exposing her slim calves beneath a froth of petticoats, and the high neck of the plain dress had been unbuttoned down to her generous breasts. She seemed completely unaware of him as she drifted over the grassy mound, humming beneath her breath, her movements airy and graceful. The bright sun overhead surrounded her, almost giving her a nimbus, and he leaned against a tree, watching her, momentarily entranced.

"Go away, selkie," she said suddenly in a stern voice, halting in her dancelike movements to meet his eye.

"I thought you liked enchanted creatures," he said, moving into the stone circle, slowly, stalking, ready should she suddenly take flight.

She didn't move, staring at him, and her blue eyes were wide and wary. "I've been warned," she said.

"I wouldn't have thought you'd listen to your family. Anyone who'd lock you away and dress you in such drear clothes doesn't have your best interests at heart."

Her sudden smile was mocking. "And you do, selkie? Somehow I doubt that. But you're right—I wouldn't think of listening to my family, or to Torquil either."

"Then who warned you? The faeries? The wind?"

"Don't be ridiculous," she said, suddenly dignified. "It was a witch."

She was so tall, so graceful. He'd always thought he liked his women small and plump. Perhaps he did. Perhaps the feeling that drove him with Ailie Spens had nothing to do with his occasional affairs. It was stronger, deeper, and he was finding it had very little to do with revenge.

"And what did the witch tell you? Beware of strange men who walk from the sea?" he said, keeping his voice light and mocking, controlling his sudden overwhelming desire to reach out and catch her shoulders in his hands, to draw her strong, graceful body up against his.

"She said you mean me harm. For the sake of a blood vengeance."

He stifled the uneasy feeling that only intensified his desire for her. "I've never been on St. Columba in my life," he said. "Four days is too short for a blood vengeance."

"Four minutes is long enough, in certain cases." There was a trace of asperity in her voice, one that sounded far too matter-of-fact for a half-mad creature. She seemed to realize it, for she immediately gave him an enchanting smile. "You'll turn my life upside down, Morag says."

"And you don't want that?"

That stopped her. She cocked her head to one side, considering it. "Perhaps," she said sweetly. "But not from a man who cares more for vengeance than for me. I've spent my life being a pawn for the men around me. I have no need to add another man to my life, to push me around and use me for their own gain. I don't need you, selkie. I can dance alone." She started away from him, but he caught her arm, turning her back to him with inexorable pressure so that she was close to him, so close he could smell the lavender in her hair, so close her bunched up skirts brushed against his thighs.

"I'm to let you go?" he murmured. "Just like that?"

There was no fear in her eyes. Alone in a deserted part of the woods, held by a man far stronger than she, Ailie Wallace Spens simply looked up at him expectantly. "Just like that," she said, giving her arm a faint tug.

He didn't release her. "No," he said simply.

Still no fear. They widened, those deliberately vague blue eyes, and her lips parted as if she would argue with him.

He didn't want an argument. He wanted her mouth, and he took it, pulling her up against him as he kissed her.

She tasted of sunshine and the meadows, of the sea breeze and lavender, she tasted of warmth and innocence and destiny, and her mouth opened beneath the pressure of his, as her strong hands reached up and caught his shoulders, not to push him away, but to steady herself.

He kissed her fully, as a man kisses a woman, using his mouth, his teeth, his tongue, holding her against him as he took her. She trembled slightly, a shudder passing over her body, and then her arms slid around his neck and she kissed him back, an endearing, inexpert kiss that hinted of the passion hidden beneath her airy demeanor.

He had to force himself to stop. He couldn't push her down on the hillock and take her in broad daylight, much as his body and soul cried out for it. For one thing, Torquil would be hot after them, and while nothing would please Malcolm more than to be caught debauching Torquil's beloved, he doubted he'd have enough time to do the deed before Torquil showed up. And if he were caught, there'd be no second chance.

He still held her in his arms, pressed up tight against his aroused body, staring down at her. Her mouth was soft, red from his kisses, and her eyes were, for the first time, genuinely confused. "Is that the way selkies kiss?" she whispered.

"It's the way I kiss. What's wrong with the lads of St. Columba that no one ever kissed you like that?"

She shook her head. "I like it," she said ingenuously. "Why don't you do it again?" And she offered her mouth to him, closing her eyes.

He could no more resist her than he could will his heart

to stop beating. He kissed her harder this time, slanting his mouth across hers, and he felt the fire burning through his veins, the wanting that threatened to consume him.

He groaned, not for the first time regretting the course he'd taken, and he reluctantly released her. "No more, lass."

Her eyes flew open again, and there was a definite disgruntled expression in them. "Why not?" she said. "Don't you like to kiss me?"

"I like it fine. But your fiancé is about to show up here, and he might take exception to me showing you how to kiss."

She considered that for a moment, stepping back from him. "I'd forgotten," she said.

"Forgotten about Torquil?"

"No. Forgotten you mean me harm. Don't you?"

He wanted to deny it. If he had any sense at all, he'd tell her bland, pretty lies, and if she were even twice as sharp as most women, she'd believe him. Women wanted to believe such things, and he knew the right words.

But he didn't want to use those words with her. So he said nothing at all, simply stood watching her, as he heard Torquil's graceless approach through the woods.

"There you are!" he said breathlessly, standing on the edge of the stone circle. "And MacLaren. I appreciate your looking out for her. I don't know how she could have run off so swiftly, but she's a dear, feckless creature."

Ailie's mouth curved up in a secret smile. "Am I, Torquil?" she murmured.

"Come on out of there," Torquil said. "You know how superstitious people are about the Dance."

"You're the only one here, Torquil," she said serenely. "Are you superstitious?"

"Not at all," he said stoutly, eyeing the stone circle warily. "Come with me, Ailie. You need to get back to the dower house." He was holding her shoes and stockings in his plump hands. Malcolm wanted to cross the stretch of grass and tear them away from him. He kept himself very still, wondering why Ailie didn't go to him, wondering why Torquil didn't move to claim her.

"Back under lock and key?" Malcolm said lightly.

Torquil's expression might have daunted another man. "You'd best keep your nose out of other people's business, MacLaren. You're a stranger here, you don't understand about Ailie. I have a responsibility to her. She's not safe on her own. You saw how she ran off the moment my back was turned."

"Perhaps she had a reason to run."

Torquil took a belligerent step forward, to the edge of the stone circle. "It's none of your concern. Go back to where you came from, and leave us alone."

The tension rose between then, hot and acrid, open warfare, and Malcolm knew a sudden elation. He was going to have his revenge, and he was going to take it with his own hands, wring it out of Torquil's sturdy body.

But Ailie was already moving past Malcolm. "He's not ready to go back to the sea," she said in a gentle voice. "And when he goes, I go with him. I'm to be a selkie as well, Torquil. Won't that be splendid? I always wanted to be under an enchantment."

"Don't be daft, Ailie!" Torquil snapped, still glaring into Malcolm's equally hostile eyes.

"Ah, but I am," she said sweetly, taking Torquil's arm and turning him away from the incipient confrontation that would have slaked Malcolm's blood lust. "Why should that have changed?"

"You're not to go near him again," he said, his body stiff with rage. "I don't trust him. He means you harm."

Ailie simply moved toward the path. "You're the second person to tell me that. I suppose I should pay heed." She glanced over her shoulder at Malcolm, and the clarity in her blue eyes unsettled him almost as much as the taste of her mouth had. She smiled then, a brief, distant smile, before she moved away with Torquil.

Malcolm said nothing, watching her as she disappeared down the pathway, Torquil's sturdy figure by her side. They would lock her away once more. If it were up to her family, he wouldn't see her again.

Overhead the sun was bright, the thick fleecy clouds

scudded by, and it took all Malcolm's enormous self-control not to go after them.

Her family would have nothing to say in the matter. She would come to him again, he knew it. He would call to her, and she would come, and damn all to the warnings of witches and family and whatever common sense she possessed. He would call, and she would come to him.

But whose downfall would it be? Faerie-mad Lady Spens, with her dreams and her dancing, her Jacobite songs and her soft, kissable mouth? She was a widow, he would take nothing she hadn't given before.

Ah, but in his case it would be different. He'd bedded a number of willing women, to their mutual pleasure. But he'd never given more than the moment and his skill as a lover.

Were he to lie with Ailie Spens, she would take more than his seed. She was the enchanted creature, not he. She would steal his heart and soul, with her gentle eyes and wicked smile, and she would haunt him until the day he died.

Surely there must be another way to punish Torquil. One that didn't put his own soul in jeopardy.

He would give himself one more day. One more day to claim his vengeance, one more day in the dangerous vicinity of Ailie Wallace Spens. And then he'd be gone, and she'd be released from her prison, to marry the fat old man who'd take her money and her body but let her dream her dreams.

Twenty-four hours. And then he'd leave St. Columba to go back to where he belonged. Back to his real father, his family. Vengeance wouldn't return his mother to him, or give her back her youth and her vision. Too much time had passed, and he'd been a grief-mad fool to think he could change things.

He would leave. And do his best never to think of a half-mad lass named Ailie, who danced with the faeries and stirred his blood to fire.

The night was warm and laden with mist. Ailie sat in the darkness, the pillows piled high behind her back, and considered her options.

The door was locked. Fiona had seen to it, making certain Ailie was fully aware of the turn of the key. But they hadn't seen fit to bar her windows.

Even now she could hear them in the drawing room below. It always astonished her that they considered her deaf as well as witless, so loud did they discuss their plans for her. Torquil Spens would settle ten thousand pounds upon Angus in return for his help in securing her hand in marriage as soon as a decent period had passed. Not that Torquil would miss it. Once he wed Ailie, he would have control of her substantial inheritance. As well as control of her body.

She rose from her bed, moving silently to the open window. The warmth of the day combined with the coolness of the land created a faerie mist that eddied and swirled around the dower house. It was past ten at night, and Ailie had no interest in sleeping. She wanted to find the selkie.

He was calling to her, she knew it. She could feel it in her blood, her bones, all the dreams and fancies she'd nurtured were coming to fruition. She'd believed so long and so hard in that unseen world that she was being rewarded. Illusion made flesh, made glorious, enticing male flesh, and she was going to go to him.

She knew what would happen, and she wasn't afraid. He would take her, a demon lover and his earthly bride, he would take her body and give her a bairn, and in doing so he would turn her into a seal creature, as he was. There had been a reason that Sir Duncan could never claim his husbandly rights. She'd been kept, safe, untouched, for Malcolm MacLaren to walk from the sea and take her.

It wasn't the first time she'd climbed down the thick vines that covered the dower house. Granted, before it had been in broad daylight, and there'd been no cause for stealth. If Margery had caught her at it, she would have screeched at her, but there was little to risk but a bruised backside.

Angus was drinking heavily, arguing with Fiona about

how they'd spend the ten thousand pounds. Angus was all for paying off a portion of the gaming debts he'd run up in Edinburgh, Fiona wanted to finance a trip to London and a season of gaiety as soon as she produced the bairn who'd swollen her body and roiled her indigestion. They didn't hear a thing as Ailie scrambled down the vines as thick as her wrist, her bare feet clinging precariously, her flowing white nightrail billowing around her. If they were to glance outside, they might think it was a ghost come to haunt them.

She rather liked that idea. The ghost of Sir Duncan's first wife, the immensely wealthy Lady Barbara, who'd failed to produce an offspring despite Sir Duncan's best efforts. It was her money that had ensured the prosperity of the Spens family. Her money that her brother and sister-in-law were wrangling over.

Or perhaps they might think it was the ghost of Sir Duncan himself. She could do a fair imitation of his harrumphing voice, enough to terrorize the superstitious Fiona into running screaming up to her room.

Tempting as the thought might be, she didn't dare risk it. Angus was more hardheaded than his shrewish wife, and he'd be more likely to check out the apparition. He'd stop her from going to the selkie, and she didn't think she could bear that.

He was leaving. She knew that as well, knew in her blood and bones. He was leaving, and if she didn't go to him, he'd leave her behind.

It was time, past time, for her final reckless act. She dropped the last few feet to the ground, leaning for a moment against the thick stone of the dower house. She had loved St. Columba, the hills, the oceans, old Morag, and the mystery of the Seal Dance. She had even loved her family, and had a sneaking fondness for Torquil.

But she wanted to dance with the faeries. Swim with the seals. To live a life she'd never lived before. And she was ready to take any risk to claim it.

She knew where she'd find him. In the midst of the enchanted faerie circle, where she'd last seen him. He'd come back there, through the mist-shrouded moonlight; he would come to her, wait for her, through the long night. And if she failed him, he would walk into the ocean without her, leaving her to harsh mortal hands.

She wanted immortality. She wanted freedom and beauty and glory and dreams.

But most of all, she wanted Malcolm.

There was no sign of Morag's spirit when she reached the enchanted knoll. No sign of Malcolm as well. The moss-covered hillock within the circle of stones was deserted, silent, bewitched. She sank down on the softness, her white nightrail flowing around her, feeling the damp of the mist settle on her skin. She would look like a ghost. Perhaps she already was one. Perhaps she'd followed him into the sea and drowned there, as poor Catriona MacDugald had more than thirty years ago, and she was doomed to wander the hills of St. Columba, looking for the demon lover who lured her to her doom.

She considered the notion, well pleased with the high-flown romance of it. She considered summoning forth a few tragic tears, then thought better of it. She wasn't cold, but the dampness reached into her bones, and she shivered. Wanting a shawl to wrap around her, wanting a blanket to lie on. Wanting a demon lover to come to her.

She heard him in the forest, moving closer. She knew his footsteps, sure enough on land, even though he must be unused to walking on solid ground. He was coming to her, though he wouldn't know she was waiting.

She saw him on the edge of the clearing, wreathed in mist. His long black hair flowed loose around his shoulders, his eyes were dark and intent, but when he saw her in the midst of the stones, he stopped, coming no farther.

"You're not afraid of the stones, are you, selkie?" she asked, her voice light and carrying on the mist. "You should recognize them. They were seal people, frozen into stone in the midst of a dance. They mean us no harm."

Still he didn't move, and she had the sudden fear that he would turn and leave her. She could feel the warring in his soul, the fight that she didn't want him to win. She rose to her knees, wraithlike in the swirling fog, and held out her hands to him.

"Come to me, selkie," she whispered, so softly he wouldn't be able to hear.

But he moved, slowly forward, as if impelled by a force outside himself. He moved through the circle of stones, moved to stand in front of her, and he was immensely tall and dark, a danger to her heart and soul.

"Go home, Ailie," he said in a rough voice. "You shouldn't be here."

"You came for me," she said. "You called me. Why else would we both be here?"

"Go home, Ailie," he said again. "You were right, I mean you harm. For blood vengeance, for no fault of yours. Run away from me, *m'eudail*."

"*M'eudail,*" she breathed. "You love me." She took his hands in hers. "Make me a selkie, beloved. Enchant me." And she pressed his hand against her breast, feeling his start of shock. His hand cupped her, he sank down to his knees in front of her, and the faerie mist settled down around them like a fleecy blanket, a bridal veil, a benediction.

And Ailie knew that she would finally know true magic this night. And madness as well.

CHAPTER
5

She looked like a ghost. A wraith, in her white nightrail with the mist surrounding her, kneeling in the center of the stone ring. Her breast was soft beneath his hand, but the tip hardened against his palm, and her blue eyes clouded in wonder and a longing that he'd have to be mad to deny.

Perhaps he was mad, as mad as she was, to be kneeling in the soft grass in the midst of a faerie ring, ready to take a lass who ought to be left in peace. He couldn't tell himself it was revenge, or anger, or anything but a longing for her, stronger than the rage and grief that had filled him, stronger than his failed mission.

He wasn't going to avenge his mother. He wasn't going to punish Torquil Spens and his cohorts. He was going to make love to the girl kneeling in front of him, and he was going to remember her every day of his life.

If he had any decency at all, he'd let her be. But right then he was a stranger to decency, to honor. He lifted his hands and threaded them through her thick fall of golden hair, pushing it away from her face, telling himself he'd kiss her, just kiss her, and then he'd send her away. But her mouth was so sweet beneath his, as her body swayed against him, and he could feel the softness of her breasts against his open shirt, and he wanted to feel the warmth of her flesh against his, skin to skin, heat to heat.

Her lips were soft. It didn't take much pressure to make her open her mouth, and he used his tongue, shocking her. He didn't want to think about who had kissed her before. Who had been the first to take her body. All he could think about was how much he wanted her, needed her. Needed to lie with her in the grass with the sweet scent of crushed heather beneath them.

He took her hand in his, drawing it down his body, placing it on him, half hoping he'd shock her into running away. Instead she touched him with delicacy and wonder, her fingertips tracing his swollen length until he had to bite back a groan of need that threatened to shake him apart. He forced himself to endure the pleasure of it, until he could stand no more, pulling her hand away.

"Don't," he said in a harsh voice.

"You started it," she said simply, looking up at him. "Ach, you make me crazy, selkie. Do you want me or no? I thought you'd come to the island to father a bairn. You're not going about it very effectively."

God, he wanted to smile at her. "I thought you were already crazy, Ailie. To be kneeling in the moonlight with a man you think is half seal isn't the wisest act."

She smiled then, and he was the one who was bewitched. "There's a difference between wisdom and sanity. I believe what I wish to believe, I'm just as daft as I care to be. Until you came along. You upset me, selkie. Confuse me. I don't know what I want from you."

"Don't you?"

She shook back her hair. "Yes, I do," she said suddenly. "I want to run away with you. Live in the clouds, live in the sea, I don't care where. I want to lie with you and give you bairns, I want to walk barefoot with you and sing songs and dance. I want a man who's as mad as I am, who'll never make me be what he expects but only what I am."

"And you think I'm that man?"

She shook her head, and her expression was wry. "I think you're here for cruel reasons, selkie. And I think I'm not wise enough to care. All I know is I want you to put your hands on me, and let the devil take the consequences."

He stared at her, telling himself he was a bastard in deed as well as name if he took her. Knowing that there was no longer any question of "if."

He rose to his feet then, with one fluid movement, and he took her with him. Without a word he pulled her, away from the stone circle, into the scrubby forest, back the way he'd come. She followed behind him, her hand secured in his, barefoot, silent, and graceful, along the woodland path that led to the north end of the island.

His grandparents' house was dark, deserted, as he pushed open the creaking door and drew her inside. He moved with unerring instinct, up the narrow, dusty stairs, and she followed after him, foolishly trusting him.

The mist had lifted by the sea, and a full moon shone down, in the window of the little bedroom under the eaves, turning the narrow iron bed silver in the moonlight, creating a halo around Ailie Spens's rich mane of hair. She looked up at him, guileless, believing in him, and he told himself he'd give her one more chance to save herself.

He took her hand and placed it against his chest, against the thudding certainty of his heart. "I can't promise you anything. Not true love, nor tenderness, nor even tomorrow. You think I'm a selkie, come from the sea to claim you."

She smiled at him, a tall woman, looking almost directly into his eyes, and the room was filled with the scent of the sea, the ancient wood, the pine and the heather and the crushed grass that clung to her white nightdress. "You've come from the sea to claim me," she said in a hushed voice. "As to whether you're a selkie or not, I don't really give a damn. All I know is that I want you. Put your hands on me, Malcolm. Please."

There was no way he could resist her, looking at him with such beguiling sweetness, asking for what he needed to give her. The past, the future slid away, so that there was only the two of them, standing by the bed in the moonlight, she in her nightdress, he in breeches and an old shirt that would be all too easily discarded.

"Run away, Ailie," he forced himself to say. "This is your last chance."

Sudden confusion crossed her face, and she began to pull her hand away from him. "Don't you want me?" she whispered.

It finished him. "Lass, I'd have to be mad not to want you. And you're supposed to be the daft one around here." He pulled her up against him, her strong, slender body fitting against his, perfectly, and he groaned, a harsh sound of longing and regret in the back of his throat.

Ailie told herself she ought to be frightened. Frightened of the tall, dark man in the bedroom with her, his hands at the neck of her nightgown, unfastening the buttons with an unnerving dexterity, his eyes intent. He'd done this before, she thought. Many many times. It would mean nothing to him, and it would mean the world to her.

She wanted him to leave her with a bairn. Because leave he would, she knew it. He'd walk back into the sea and disappear, leaving her to grieve and mourn, and she wanted something of his to cherish.

Crazy she might be, but she loved him. She knew that what lay between them had nothing to do with common sense or practicality, with sanity and wisdom. It was basic, elemental, and magic, and if it was one-sided, so be it. She would take what he was willing to give her, claim him as he claimed her.

The night air was cool on her shoulders as he slipped the gown away from her, and it pooled at her feet, leaving her naked in the moonlight.

She had no false modesty as he looked down at her, his sea-green eyes hooded, unreadable. She was as she was, and he could either accept her or not.

"Get on the bed," he said.

"In a moment," she replied in a deceptively tranquil voice, and reached up to unfasten his loose white shirt.

She wanted him to think she was calm, used to this sort of thing, when in truth she'd never seen an undressed man in her life. Sir Duncan's few attempts had been made under the cover of darkness, and while Fiona had given her detailed explanations of what went on between the two sexes, it was still all a matter of theory. She wanted to see what he looked like. She wanted to learn all of him. And she didn't want him to know she was nervous.

He tried so hard to be cool and wicked, but beneath that mocking exterior was the soul of a selkie, gentle and pure. If he knew she was untouched, if he knew she loved him, he would leave her be, and that would be the cruelest blow of all. Better he thought her experienced and bold. She could only hope that he didn't notice her hands were trembling as she pulled the shirttails from his tight black breeches.

But Malcolm was a man who noticed everything. He caught her hands in his, stilling them. "You're cold," he said.

Cold from fear, but she wouldn't tell him that. Not when she was blazingly hot as well. His hands slid up her wrists, to her elbows, and she swayed against him, looking up, hoping he wouldn't notice the faint shadow of worry that haunted her. If he'd simply kiss her again, she wouldn't notice the cold. If he lay with her on the bed, his big strong body covering hers, she wouldn't notice the cold.

His mouth was hot and wet against hers, and she felt that familiar/unfamiliar coil of desire in the pit of her stomach. He released her hands, and she slid them around his waist, against his bare, taut skin that was burningly hot, and she wanted his warmth, wanted his heat.

The bed was small and sagging beneath her, but she scarcely noticed as he followed her down, covering her, still half-clothed, his body pressed against her, between her legs, as he cupped her face in his hands and began to kiss her. His lips against her eyelids, her cheekbones, the corner of her mouth, were tempting, arousing, and she tried to turn her head, to catch his mouth with hers and kiss him back, but he was having none of it. His hands covered her breasts and she shivered with the wonder of it, arching against him.

His hands were rough, callused, the hands of a man who wasn't afraid of working for a living. The moonlight was like a benediction, blanketing their bodies, and she closed her eyes, giving in to the wonder of it, as his mouth moved down the line of her throat, to taste her hammering pulse, and then to capture her breast, like a wee babe suckling.

But this was no maternal feeling pounding through her. This was no gentle faerie coupling such as she'd long imagined. This was desire, hot, heavy in her blood, something that was a far cry from her daydreams of lying down in the heather with a selkie.

His hand moved between her legs, touching her there, and she knew a sudden fear. His fingers slid deep, into her heated dampness, and she moaned, a sound of entreaty and protest. He was a deft man, able to kiss her as his hand kept up its inexorable stroking, and she wanted to stop him, to change her mind. This was rapidly spiraling out of her control, and it frightened her, she who was frightened of nothing. The pleasure was too sharp, too overwhelming, and she wanted nothing more than to run away and hide.

She tried to pull away, but he was having none of it. His mouth left hers, to trail a path of damp, erotic kisses across her cheekbone to her ear. He caught the lobe between his teeth, biting gently, and she jerked against the wondrous encroachment of his hand, as new warmth suffused her body.

"Easy, *m'eudail*," he whispered in her ear. "I won't hurt you. You've given yourself to me. Are you wanting to change your mind?"

Her eyes met his in the moon-gilded darkness. He would leave her if she asked. If she told him the truth. And that was the worst fear, the worst devastation of all.

She ran her hands up the smooth, heated length of his body. "No," she whispered, brushing her lips against his. Wishing she'd paid just a wee bit more attention when Morag had told her of the things that went on between men and women. At the time she hadn't been interested, faced only with the prospect of Torquil.

Now she wished she had more solid knowledge to allay her fears. She could feel him through his tight black breeches, and he was very large indeed. She didn't think it was going to work.

She told him so, not wishing to discourage him. He

kissed her then, silencing most of her doubts, and then he rose, shucking his breeches and tossing them over the side of the narrow bed.

Lord, he was a bonnie man in the moonlight! It was no wonder that no sensible woman could ever resist a selkie. Ailie's sense had been banished long ago, and she stared up at him, lean and strong, with gilded skin and long black hair.

He knelt between her legs, and she could feel him, hard and hot against her. She closed her eyes, bracing for the first stroke, bracing for the pain, and she clamped her teeth down on her lip to stifle any errant cry.

He didn't move. "Open your eyes, Ailie," he said in a soft voice that brooked no denial.

She did so, unwillingly. She could see the rigid cord of the muscles in his arms as he braced himself over her, see the faint sheen of sweat that covered his beautiful body.

"That's right," he murmured approvingly. "You look as if you're expecting the worst. It's not going to hurt, love." He took her hands and placed them on his shoulders. "I know fine how to do this without making a botch of it. Trust me, Ailie."

Oh, but she did, in ways he couldn't begin to know. She smiled up at him, a wary smile, but a smile nonetheless, hoping he wouldn't see the fear in her eyes.

He smiled back at her, and the pressure increased as he pushed his hips forward. "You should remember it only hurt the first time you did this."

She said nothing, closing her eyes again, the better to savor his relentless invasion. His breathing was harsh, labored, as he struggled to control himself, and she was afraid of that control. Afraid that he still might leave her.

She slid her arms past his shoulders, around his neck, under the long black hair. She raised her hips to meet his steady advance, she put her mouth against his, and her tongue met his, mimicking what he'd taught her and what she'd learned to like so well.

His groan was muffled by her kiss, and his control

shattered as he sank into her, breaking past the unwelcome barrier of her virginity to claim her.

He held very still in her arms, rigid, and she could feel the tension ripple through his body, and she knew he wanted to pull away, to leave her.

Despite the discomfort she couldn't let him. She clung to him, fiercely, reveling in the feel of his strong, sleek body, on top of her, around her, within her. It was painful, smothering, and quite glorious. She wanted it to last forever, she wanted something more that she didn't comprehend.

He said something low under his breath, a curse, a benediction, and then the words "too late." He started to pull away from her, and she clung to him in panic, only to have him move back, sliding, smoothly, deeply, the discomfort fading as he rocked against her. His hands cupped her hips, pulling her legs around him, as he taught her the ancient rhythm of advance and retreat, and she felt herself begin to drift, awash in a sensual dance of wonder and delight, sweet and dreaming, content to move beneath him in the moonlit darkness, until it changed, the first harsh tendrils spiraling up from her belly, and suddenly, sharply, there was no peace but a clawing kind of wonder. She clutched at him, her heart pounding, her breath strangled in her throat, reaching for something lost and mysterious, and she felt the waters of the sea close around her as her selkie pulled her deeper, deeper into the inky darkness, and she struggled, fighting him, until suddenly it erupted into a shower of stars, drifting through the darkness.

She felt him shudder in her arms, the warmth and wetness of him flooding her, claiming her, giving her a child. Not a lad, but a wee girl. And her name would be Catriona.

It seemed forever before the madness left her, the madness that was unlike anything she'd ever feigned. She didn't want to move, didn't want to loose her hold of him. He was wet and slippery with sweat, like a seal, and it would be far too easy for him to vanish.

"Ailie." His voice was harsh, labored, but she wouldn't respond, afraid to give him an excuse to leave her. "Lass, why didn't you tell me?"

She hid her face against his shoulder, unwilling to talk. She wanted to stay wrapped in his arms forever, she wanted to fall asleep and wake in the ocean, swimming beside him. Failing that, she wanted to fall asleep beneath him and never wake again.

But Malcolm was having none of it. He moved away from her, ignoring her clinging arms, to sit beside her on the bed. He caught her chin in his hand and shook her. "Answer me, Ailie," he said sternly. "Why were you still a maid? And why didn't you tell me when you knew I'd have you?"

She opened her eyes then, cold and forlorn, the warm, loving glow of her body fading in the suddenly chill night air. "You wouldn't have," she said.

"Wouldn't have what?"

"Wouldn't have touched me. I know you, Malcolm MacLaren. You're no demon spirit, for all you'd like to be. You wouldn't take a lass and harm her if you'd a reason not to. As long as I was a widow, already pledged to another man, I was fair game. If you thought I was untouched, you wouldn't have come near me."

He shook his head, and beneath his dark, austere face was wry self-reproach. "I wish I could be as sure as you that I possess some shred of honor," he said.

"You wanted to hurt my family. I know that well—I may be half-mazed, but there's nothing wrong with my reasoning when I care to use it. It doesn't take any special powers to know that you've been wronged. By my family, by my husband, by Torquil. And I'm the instrument of your revenge." She said it quite calmly, wondering that it failed to hurt her.

He looked shocked. "What makes you say such a daft thing?"

"I thought we agreed, I am daft," she replied, her voice as cool as her blood ran hot. "Morag told me. You'll harm me for the sake of those you hate."

"Then why did you let me?"

She lay on her back in the moonlight, the marks of his possession still full on her body. He looked beautiful in the moonlight, a magical creature, and she would have given anything to be able truly to believe he was a selkie.

She reached up her hand to touch his face, wondering if he'd jerk away. He held still for her caress, his sea-green eyes distant as he watched her. "Because you're my fate, selkie. My destiny. You've come from the sea to claim me, and claim me you have. When you leave tomorrow, I'll be carrying your bairn to remember you."

"You're a madwoman, Ailie Spens," he said, taking her hand in his and moving it to his mouth. "And you make me mad as well." He placed a kiss against her palm, his mouth open, using his tongue, and his eyes met hers. "Send me away from you, before I break your heart."

"It's already too late to stop it. Lie down with me again, selkie," she whispered. "No one ever died of a broken heart."

He stared at her for a long moment, and she could almost believe he came from some dark otherworld. A world where she belonged. And then he leaned over and blocked out the moonlight once more, and there was no more room for talk.

He lay sleeping in the narrow bed. She'd marked him, Ailie thought, though not as thoroughly or as deeply as he'd marked her. She could see the scratches on his back, where'd she'd clung to him, sobbing. She could see where she'd bitten him on the shoulder, hard, when he'd carried her past any kind of sense or reason.

She stood at the side of the bed, the white nightrail once more around her, an old shawl wrapped around her as well, and wished she could throw them off once more and climb back in the bed with him.

It would be a mistake. As it was, she could barely walk. Her knees were weak, and parts of her body that she'd heretofore paid no attention to were sore and aching. She needed a hot bath, and hours of sleep. She wanted those hours with Malcolm, but the sun would rise soon enough, and the enchanted night would be over. She needed to be back in her own bed before they found her gone.

She didn't trust her family. Not Torquil or Angus or Fiona. As for the people of St. Columba, they loved her in their way, but if they were convinced the selkie had harmed her, it would go ill with him, and she couldn't bear for even an unwanted drop of rain to fall on his silky black hair.

She was mazed for sure. Foolishly in love, bewitched by the selkie who was most likely nothing but a man after all, but a man like none she'd ever known.

He'd leave, and he wouldn't take her with him. And she couldn't bear to see him go.

She'd make her way through the mist-shrouded dawn, back to the dower house, and from that moment on she'd be *douce* and mild, the meekest of young ladies, and in her belly she'd carry his bairn to love and cherish. Torquil would have nothing to do with a whore, and her brother and sister would wash their hands of her. It would be a quiet life, raising her daughter in the dower house, never leaving the island, but a happy life.

She couldn't bear to watch him any longer. To watch him was to long to touch him, and if she touched him, he'd awaken once more, and make love to her, and then she probably wouldn't be able to stand up, much less make it across the small island to her house.

But she gave in to temptation, leaning over to brush a feather-light kiss against his mouth. Her hair drifted against him, and his hand closed around a strand of it, reflexively, caressing it in his sleep.

With a tug she pulled free. And then she ran from the house, silent, swift, before she could weaken in her resolve.

She could scarcely see in the heavy mist that shrouded the village. It filled her eyes, poured down her face, blinding her, and she paused on the edge of the woods, using the back of her hand to brush away the moisture. It tasted of seawater. No, it didn't, she realized. It tasted of salt tears. She was crying, something she hadn't done since she was a wee lass of fourteen summers. She was crying over the selkie and lost love.

The moment she realized it, the dam broke. She sank to the wet ground, leaning against a tree, and began to cry full

force, weeping with unabashed noisiness, bewailing what
she could not have. There was a sour kind of pleasure in
it, to curse fate and her own twisted nobility, to howl her
misery to the morning star, and the noise of it filled the
forest around her, so that she couldn't hear the approaching
footsteps, couldn't know that danger lurked close at hand.

He loomed up out of the mist, huge and horrifying.
Domnhall the seal hunter, and there was a body slung
over his shoulder, gutted, bloody, a dead seal. The sight
of him was so shocking her tears strangled into silence, and
she stared at the corpse as he dumped it at her feet.

It was a plain brown seal, staring at her out of lifeless
black eyes. Malcolm's eyes were the green of the sea, and
his pelt would be black and shiny. He was safe.

"Ye're a noisy one this morrow, Lady Spens," Domnhall
said, and his semblance of a smile showed dark and broken
teeth. "Greeting for your seal lover?"

Panic overtook wisdom. "You're not to touch him!"

Domnhall reached down and caught her arm, hauling her
to her feet. The bloody imprint of his hand stained the
sleeve of the white nightgown, and Ailie shut her eyes in
sudden horror. "I'll skin him, lass. I doubt I'll wait till he
changes back to a seal. Have you ever seen a man skinned?
It would take a steady hand to do the job, but I don't doubt
I have the knack. You can watch, lass."

"You'll leave him alone. Torquil—"

"Torquil will thank me for punishing him. You as well.
He won't like it that you've betrayed him, lifting your skirts
for that trash. You've been with him, I can tell fine that you
have. You've the look and the smell of it. It'll make Torquil
mad with rage, it will. I've done the dirty work for him and
his family, and yours as well, before. I can do it again. I'll
kill the selkie, whatever he may be. And forebye I'll have
a taste of what he's going to die for."

She tried to back away from the ravening look in
Domnhall's dark, evil eyes, but his grip was unbreakable.
"I'll have you know what a real man is," he continued.
"Before you end up with yon Torquil. Not that he'll marry
you now. But he's too daft about you to let you alone.

He'll keep you locked away, and you'll never wander free again, barefoot through the grass like a madwoman. Your own kind of prison, mistress."

"I'd rather die," she said in a hoarse voice.

"Aye, you would. But you won't have that choice," Domnhall said. He started down the pathway, hauling her after him, leaving the gutted corpse of the seal in the middle of the forest.

She tried to call out, to scream for help, but Domnhall's bloody hand clamped down over her mouth. He was a huge man, endlessly strong, and her struggles availed her nothing. She tried to bite him, but he simply skelped her across the face, knocking her backward against a tree. Through the gathering mist she stared up at him, and she thought she saw Morag nearby, watching. But no one ever saw Morag but Ailie, and she would be no help.

There was no help for her at all. He hit her again, harder this time, and she sank to the damp earth as the blackness closed around her. And her last thought was of Malcolm. Pray God he walked into the sea once more, before Domnhall could hurt him.

CHAPTER
6

Malcolm let her go. He felt her hair brush his face, and he couldn't keep himself from catching hold of it, clinging to it for a moment, before letting it slip through his fingers. It was for the best. He'd taken her maidenhead, something the man who sired him had obviously never managed to do, and he'd taken more than that. He'd taken her love and trust, and what did he have to offer her in return?

He wasn't sure. The anger still burned deep inside him, but the longing for her burned brighter still, and even a night of passion couldn't dull it. He was hard for her again, and if she hadn't moved away, the taste of her lips lingering against his, he would have pulled her down once more, and to the devil with vows and the like.

She knew far too much. She was a *spaewife*, a seer, and indeed, she knew far too much of things she should have no inkling about. Unless Collis had chosen to talk, and a more dour, closemouthed creature Malcolm had yet to meet.

She would get back to her house safely enough, he had no doubt of that. Everyone had made it more than clear that the entire population of the island looked out for her—no one would dare harm her, not even her friends the faerie folk. The only danger to her on this island was himself, and he'd already done his worst.

He rolled over in the bed, staring out the open window.

The moon had set long ago, the dawn was just beginning to lighten the sky, and the mist had increased, swirling around the house. She would make it back safely enough, with no one the wiser as to her traveling during the night. Indeed, it was like one of her damned stories—the princess who slipped out at night to dance with the faeries. It had been a dance he'd led her on last night, one he wasn't ready to end.

He had no choice but to tell her. She was right, he was leaving this day. Going back to Glen Corrie, back to his father and sisters, back to the prosperous farm and the good, decent life he'd learned to love. Back without vengeance.

But would he go back with a bride?

How daft was she? Her dreaming, feckless ways, her mad Jacobite songs, her bare feet and unbound hair belonged to a creature unused to civilized ways. His mother would have sorted her out soon enough, with stern affection and common sense and love. He doubted anyone had ever shown her those things, and her response had been to slip deeper and deeper into a twilight world. Could she step out of it, into the light, if she wanted to? Would she for him?

He could only ask. When the sun rose, he would rise as well, dress, and make his way to the dower house. If they refused to let him see her, he'd find a way to get to her. He'd tell her the truth. He was no bewitched creature, come to claim her to a faerie world. He was nemesis, and she'd gotten in his way.

It was his duty, he told himself. His responsibility, to take her back with him, to wed her, in case, as she insisted, there was a bairn from this night's work. But despite what he told himself, it felt like no duty he'd ever performed in his life. It felt like his heart's desire.

He closed his eyes, drifting into sleep, when he heard the voice. It was a true *spaewife*, keening, eerie, soft on the morning dampness, insinuating itself into his sleeping mind. "Mind yon lassie," the voice moaned. "The seal hunter has her."

A nightmare, he told himself, opening one eye to glance around the deserted bedroom. There was no one there, but the voice came at him from the corners of the room. "Domnhall's ta'en her," the voice said. "And only you can save her."

He sat up, throwing back the covers as panic speared through him. "Who's there?"

No answer from the empty house. Just the keening of the rising wind, the rush of the surf against the shore, and the sense of dread that seeped into his bones. He knew. This was no nightmare. Ailie was in danger from the seal hunter.

He threw on his clothes as he ran, still fastening his shirt on the stairs as he barreled into Collis. The dawn had scarcely risen, and the house was dark with shadows, yet there was no missing the expression on the old man's face.

"Something's wrong," Collis said abruptly. "I was pulled from a good night's sleep and sent to ye, and I dinna like it one bit. Where's the mistress? Did ye harm her?"

A brief vision flashed through Malcolm's mind—Ailie in his arms, crying out in pleasure and sorrow. "No," he said, wondering if he lied. "I think the seal hunter's taken her."

"Are ye daft yourself, man? Why in God's name would Domnhall dare touch her? Torquil would have his heart for it."

Malcolm shook his head. "I don't know. I heard a voice as I was sleeping. I think I saw a face. An old woman, with streaky white-and-black hair and eyes like coals, and she told me only I could rescue Ailie."

"Christ!" Collis looked properly shocked. "You've seen Morag then. She never shows herself to most folk. Mayhap you're a selkie after all."

"Don't waste my time, old man. Where would Domnhall have taken her?"

Collis shook his head. "He knows this island better than almost anyone. Except for Ailie. He has a croft not far from mine, though I doubt he'd take her there. There's a storehouse by the water where he keeps his sealskins. No one goes there—the smell is dreadful, and people say it's cursed. He might have taken her there."

"I'll check the storehouse—you go to the croft."

"He's a dangerous man, selkie. Bigger than you, forebye, with a dirty way of fighting. Mind you don't find yourself gutted and skinned."

"A fine end for a selkie. I have to save Ailie first." Malcolm moved past him, heading for the door, when Collis's voice followed him.

"And what was the mistress doing out at this hour of the day, that Domnhall could have ta'en her?"

Malcolm paused by the door, turning to look up at the dour old man. "Giving herself to the selkie, old man. And I'm not about to lose her now."

His grandparents' cottage was at the far end of the island, away from the tiny harbor town. He started through the woods, going by instinct alone, half-blind in the shadows and mist, until he sprawled across something that had once been living flesh.

It wasn't Ailie's lifeless body. That knowledge made him shake, with relief and fury, as he stared at the corpse of the gentle seal. The man who had done this had taken his love, putting his filthy, murderous hands on her, and every moment she was with him would be torment for her airy, gentle soul.

He ran through the mist and the gradually lightening day, past sleeping houses and silent fields, the smell of the sea in the air. He knew where to find her, not with his mind but with his heart and soul. With the help of the *spaewife* echoing in his ears.

The storehouse was at the far end of the village, set off from the other buildings, sagging into the ground, a dark, dour place. Not even grass grew nearby, and Malcolm could see why the people of St. Columba would consider it haunted. The thought of his gentle lass trapped inside there at the bloody hands of a murderer sent his own murderous rage sweeping over him.

The voice came to him again, on the mist, on the wind, a keening, warning voice. "Mind the front door, MacLaren. He's waiting for you."

He didn't stop to question that voice, or the warning; he

simply heeded it, moving to skirt the edge of the building. There were no windows, and the stench of death and sea was strong and gagging in his nostrils. The smell of dead seals. MacLaren, the voice had called him. The voice knew who he was, better than he knew himself. He was a MacLaren, if not by blood, by heart and soul. By all that mattered.

He put his ear against the damp, rotting wood of the old shack, listening, but only silence issued forth. If Domnhall had touched her, he'd kill him, but he'd cut his balls off first and feed them to the gentle seals while the seal hunter watched.

And then he heard her voice, calm, steady, and he knew she was still safe. "He won't come, Domnhall. He's a selkie, he knows when he's in danger. He's not going to walk into your trap."

"You misjudge your charms, mistress. If he's a selkie, then he came to St. Columba for you, and he willna leave you in my hands without a fight."

"If he's not a selkie, why would you want to harm him?" She sounded a far cry from his deliberately daft lady, Malcolm thought. He could almost smile at the practical note in her voice, if he weren't so terrified of the danger she ran.

"Because he's had you, mistress. And yon Torquil won't like that one wee bit. He'll be best pleased if I rid him of the competition, and give him a taste of revenge in the bargain. Torquil's a shy man when it comes to blood and violence, but he's more than happy to have me take care of things for him."

"He won't be happy to hear you've touched me."

"Torquil can't have everything. I hate this island, and the people here. They think you're their sweet, daft lass. They all love you. How will they feel when they find you're a whore? That you rutted with the selkie, and then gave yourself to me hours later."

"I'd never give myself to you," she said flatly.

"Nay, mistress. But they'll not believe you, will they? Your family will lock you away, Torquil and Angus will split your inheritance, and I'll be well paid. And you, poor lady, will spend your days locked away, mourning your dead selkie."

"I'd rather die myself." Malcolm could hear the first trembling traces of emotion in her voice.

"Mayhap I'll oblige you. After I finish with the selkie." There was an ominous silence. "In the meantime, lay back and lift yer skirts, Yer Ladyship. I'd like to see if you're equipped any differently than the trulls in Inverness."

There was a backdoor to the shanty, half in the cold gray water of the sea. Malcolm slammed through it, using his shoulder, rolling to the ground as he went. He had no knife, no weapon at all, and he could wait no longer.

He had the element of surprise, and that was all, and he used it, coming in low and knocking the huge form of the seal hunter onto the ground as well. The stench of the place, of the man, was awful. The sealskins were piled high all around in the murky darkness, and he could sense Ailie in the corner, shocked, immobile, but still unharmed.

He slammed his fist against the man's face, again and again, feeling the skin of his knuckles split as Domnhall groaned. And then Domnhall surged up, taking Malcolm with him, knocking him against the wall, and Malcolm could feel the cold steel of the knife at the base of his belly.

He went very still, waiting for his chance.

"Shall I spill your guts for yon lass?" Domnhall said in a thick, panting voice. "Do you have the heart of a seal, or a man? I'd like well to know." The knife pressed hard against him, and it wouldn't take much for the seal hunter to split him, stem to stern.

Oddly enough Malcolm felt no fear. Merely an odd, disembodied regret, that Ailie should have to see it. It would turn her truly mad.

"Selkie." Her voice was cool and eerie, halting Domnhall's stroke. "You need your pelt. Domnhall must have taken it, or you would have been back in the sea already. Which is his pelt, Domnhall? Ye must give it back to him, or his soul will haunt you."

"Get away from me," Domnhall snarled. "I'm not afraid

of ghosts. He's a man, no more no less. . . ."

"It's black, you told me," Ailie said in that dreamy voice, and Malcolm heard her move closer. "Like your hair, black and silky and very soft. I like your hair, did I tell you that, selkie? I don't want him to kill you."

"Get away from me," Domnhall snarled, momentarily distracted as he turned to kick her away.

It was all the advantage Malcolm needed. In a flash he came up under Domnhall's burly arm, taking it and twisting it back, so that the knife fell with a thud on the dirt-packed floor, and the two of them were locked together in a deathly embrace, rolling onto the ground, over onto the pile of soft skins, rolling back to thud against the side of the small building, until the rotting wood splintered and they crashed out into the gathering daylight.

Domnhall had him pinned on the ground, and he grinned at him in evil triumph. "I don't believe in selkies, or ghosts. I'll kill you while the lassie watches, and that'll be the end to it."

Malcolm stared up at him, panting, filled with an icy calm. "Will it? Look at my face, seal hunter. Have you seen it before?"

Domnhall's thick, cruel countenance grew still as his eyes narrowed. "You're a stranger," he said, but he sounded suddenly uneasy.

"Am I? Or do I look like another lass you killed, years ago, and threw into the sea? She didn't die, Domnhall. She joined the seals, and sent me here to claim her vengeance."

Domnhall released him, staggering to his feet as superstitious horror swept over his face. "Catriona," he gasped. "You've the look of her."

"She sent me after you, Domnhall," Malcolm said, coming to his feet, moving after him. "I'm just one of many. We'll all come for you, we'll haunt your days and nights, until you give yourself to us. We'll eat your flesh, seal hunter, as you ate ours, and your soul will rot in hell."

He'd pushed him too far. Domnhall let out a low, keening sound, more mazed than Ailie could ever fabricate, and he turned and scooped up the knife that had fallen. "You have her eyes," he said hoarsely. "I'll cut them out. . . ." He lurched back toward him, murder in his face, as Ailie screamed in terror.

The pile of sealskins, still bloody, couldn't have moved, Malcolm told himself afterward. Domnhall was too blinded with murderous rage, and as he lunged for Malcolm, knife held at the ready, he stumbled, sprawling across the pile of skins, and lay still, as blood pooled underneath him.

"Ailie!" It wasn't his voice calling to her, it was Torquil Spens's rich, panicked tones as he rounded the corner, winded, his moon face crimson from exertion. Collis was close behind him, and Malcolm flashed him a bitter, reproachful look.

Ailie stood in the middle of the shanty, her face in darkness, and Domnhall's motionless body lay between them. She looked at Malcolm, and her voice was soft, and very sane. "Catriona?" she said.

And then Torquil reached her, pulling her into his arms, hiding her face against his burly shoulders as if to shield her from the sight of Domnhall's body, the blood flowing from underneath him, soaking the sealskins. He glared at Malcolm, and it took all Malcolm's self-control not to leap over the body of his fallen nemesis and rip Ailie from his arms. "Who the hell are you, MacLaren?"

"Catriona MacDugald's son."

Torquil's ruddy face turned pale. "I didn't believe Collis when he came for me. You're here for vengeance, lad, but you're too late. Your father's dead these last six weeks."

Ailie lifted her head to look at him, and in the gathering daylight he could see the mark of Domnhall's fists on her pale face. There was no daftness in her face now as full understanding of who and what he was hit her. Just a dark, impossible sorrow.

It didn't matter, Malcolm told himself, ignoring the searing pain in his heart. He'd come for one reason, and one reason alone, and he meant to have the answer. "Who gave the order?" he demanded. "Who paid the seal hunter to take my mother and cast her into the sea?"

Torquil shook his head. "Ye'll not believe it, lad, but

Duncan paid him good money to take her to the mainland and see her safely settled. None of us meant her ill."

"You can't prove it."

"No," said Torquil, releasing Ailie to face him bravely. "And I'm supposing you'll want your vengeance on me as well. Or did taking a poor daft maid prove vengeance enough?"

She was so pale. He wanted to go to her, to kiss the bloom back into her cheeks, he wanted to hear her singing her mad songs about Bonnie Prince Charlie. He'd taken her innocence, not in the taking of her maidenhead, but the betraying of her trust. She was better off with the old man who'd love and care for her.

"Vengeance enough," he said. And he turned and walked away.

Ailie Wallace Spens said not a word as Torquil led her back to the dower house. She barely paid heed to his soothing words, the promise of a swift wedding should there be an early bairn, the promise of devotion and forgiveness and cherishing and love. He'd watch over her, would Torquil, hold her so close she couldn't breathe. She was a lucky woman, she told herself, and a fool to greet for a man who'd lied and betrayed her.

Margery took her to her room, fussing and crooning over her. The bath was warm and soothing, but Ailie refused to get in it until she was left alone. She wanted no curious eyes assessing the changes in her body. She sank into the scented warmth, closing her eyes and letting the memories come.

Torquil, Angus, and Fiona were busy arranging a swift marriage. The dominie would oblige, given the circumstances, and if there was talk on the island, well, after all, it was only mad Ailie.

Margery had laid the clothes out on her bed. Black, sober garb, with heavy black stockings and shoes. Even the corset had black trim, a corset to tie her up and lace her in and keep her prisoner.

He'd loved her. Selkie or no, out for vengeance or justice, he'd loved her, she knew it deep in her soul. She could stay here in safety and comfort, and slowly strangle to death. Or she could run to him and risk everything.

She rose steaming from the tub, looking down at her woman's body. It was different now. It was no longer her own, it was his as well. And it would never, never be Torquil's.

She locked the door, then shoved a chair under it. She moved to her cupboard, but all her colorful clothes were gone. It was the sight of those black clothes that decided her, drab and dour and lifeless. Torquil loved her, but he'd end up destroying her. Better to destroy herself in her last chance at happiness.

She dressed in her drab clothes, for the last time, then went out the window. It was getting on toward midday, and she hadn't time to waste. He might be gone already, but something, old Morag perhaps, told her there was still time. She scrambled down the vines and was off, the black shoes pinching her feet, heading for the tumbledown house that had belonged to her lad's family.

It was empty. The sheets lay tumbled on the bed, stained with the blood of her innocence, and she found she could smile. She wanted to rip them from the bed and hang them from the window to announce her triumph, but she hadn't the time to waste. She ran back from the house, singing as she went.

Collis sat outside his croft, his mangy dog at his feet. "He's gone, lass," he said when she raced up to him.

"Where?"

"You dinna want a lad like that one. He came to hurt ye. He came for vengeance. Not that I blame him—his mother was a sweet one, who didn't deserve what happened to her. But he shouldna touched you. I told him that. I told him making war on women was a shameful business, and I thought he listened."

"Where is he, Collis?"

"Down by yon cove. That's where he left his boat when he first came here. He's no a selkie, lass. He didna come from the sea for ye."

"He did, Collis. Fine I know it, and I'm away with him.

Tell Torquil he needs a meek and *douce* lass, who'll give him bairns and never shame him."

Collis rose, worry creasing his ancient face. "You'd never shame a man, mistress."

"I'd never shame Malcolm, Collis. He came for me, whether he knows it or not. Wish me luck."

He shook his head, but there was the faint trace of a reluctant grin on his face. "You're daft, lass."

"Haven't they always said so?" And she took off down the winding path to the small cove as fast as her tightly shod feet could take her.

He was already out into the surf when she reached the sand. It was a small, trim boat, and he was more than adept at it, handling it in the waves with an expert touch.

"Selkie," she called, but the wind took her voice and hurled it away. His back was toward her, and he was looking out to the sea, to his home.

She threw herself down on the sand and began to rip her shoes off, throwing them away. She'd half a mind to tear off her clothes as well, but he was moving farther and farther away, and she couldn't take the time.

"Malcolm!" she shrieked, and ran into the surf.

This time he heard her. The wind whipped his long black hair and hurled it in his face, and his expression was both shocked and unreadable.

"Go back!" he shouted to her.

"I can't."

"I'm no good for you," he said desperately. "I'm wild and selfish. Go back to Torquil. He loves you."

"So do you, Malcolm. I belong with you. By land or by sea, selkie, I'm coming with you." The water was cold, lapping up around her thighs, the surf slapping against her, dragging her down with the heavy skirts, but still she came on.

"Are you mad, Ailie?" he shouted furiously. "You'll drown!"

"Mad for you, selkie. You will not let me drown." As if to mock her certainty, a wave came up and knocked her over, and she was down under the chilly brine.

She let herself drift for a moment, willing for what fate had in store for her. It would be easy enough to be pulled down, out to sea by the tide and the current and her heavy black clothes that were too much like a shroud. If Malcolm didn't want her, she'd let the sea take her, and she might end up a selkie after all.

The hands were hard, hurting, as he hauled her to the surface, and his expression was glittering with rage. He said not a word, wrapping his strong arm around her shoulders and hauling her through the rough water. Hauling her toward his drifting boat, not toward the shore.

He pushed her up and over the side, so that she landed in a frozen, sodden pile in the middle of the small boat, and then he came up after her, surging over the side with the grace of a seal, to collapse beside her, panting, furious, pulling her into his arms to rest against his hard, warm, wet body.

"If you ever do such a mad thing again," he said in a tight, furious voice, "I'll beat you."

She smiled against his chest. "Nay," she said. "You wouldna beat your poor daft wife, Malcolm."

"Who says I'm marrying you?" He pushed the wet hair away from her face and kissed her eyelids. "I should throw you back into the sea."

"You came for me, selkie. You'll wed me, and you'd best not take your time with it. We'll have a bairn in nine months' time, and people will gossip enough. Fetching a wife from the sea is unco'strange."

He cupped her face and looked down at her, and the smile on his face was like nothing she'd ever seen. Full of love and peace, and future. "Not in my family," he murmured, brushing his lips against her. "It's a tradition. Let's away, love. Before we both freeze to death."

He released her, reluctantly, and wrapped her in a thick wool blanket that lay stowed beneath the bench before he took hold of the sail and set them on their course once more.

Ailie watched him, his graceful, efficient movements. "I'll wear shoes for you," she said suddenly, overwhelmed with love. "I'll bind my hair and lower my eyes and sing no more Jacobite songs."

He glanced at her, and his sea-green eyes were full of love and longing. "I thought you loved me, lass. That's not the way to prove it. You wear what you want, sing what you want, give me bairns, and make me laugh. We'll tell the people of Glen Corrie that you're the selkie. I fetched you from the sea, and if you're a bit strange, it's no concern of theirs."

"Malcolm," she said, rising to her knees, the happiness spilling out of her. "I do love you."

"And I love you, lass, though it makes no sense. You'll make me a glorious wife if you don't drive me mad first." He leaned down and kissed her, full on the mouth, and he tasted of icy seawater and a wondrous future. He pulled her against him tightly, his arm holding the rough blanket around her, and as he looked down at her his dark, haunted face was light and joyful.

She flung her arms around him and kissed him back, and the sound of their laughter echoed over the sea as he steered the boat into the sunset, into the bright, blazing future.

THE SPRING BEGINS

Caitlin McBride

Dear Reader:

It was a thrill to be asked to write a novella for *Highland Fling*. Researching my latest novel, *Journey of the Heart,* which takes place in Edinburgh, I fell in love with Scotland. What a grand and sweeping landscape! What fascinating history and stoic patriotism! What a setting for a romance! So it was an immense pleasure conjuring up a story about the widower, Adam McAllister, his two bonny bairns, Mary and Kyle, and their feisty governess, Letitia Webster.

Ever since reading *Jane Eyre,* I have wanted to do a governess story. In the nineteenth century it was impossible for a respectable, educated female to live in the same house with an unattached male without kissing her good name good-bye, unless, of course, she was a governess. Getting my hero and heroine under the same roof opened up all sorts of possibilities for relationship-building, and for plain and simple fun.

Beyond the romance, "The Spring Begins" is a story of redemption. Adam McAllister is a man who needs to put aside the past in order to embrace the future. He has been grieving over his dead wife for two years, emotionally isolating himself from his children, and generally shrouding himself in the gloom of perpetual winter. As implied by the title, for Adam the spring begins when Letitia enters his life. And Letitia has found a love that transcends social boundaries and helps heal some wounds of her own.

I hope you enjoy your visit to Leys Castle in the Highlands of Scotland and learn to love the McAllister family as much as I loved creating them!

Catlin McBride

"And time remembered is grief forgotten,
And frosts are slain and flowers begotten,
And in green underwood and cover,
Blossom by blossom the spring begins."
—*Swinburne, "A Vision of Spring"*

May 1814
Near Inverness, Scotland

Adam McAllister, Viscount Blair, was late, and he hated
not being punctual above just about any other imperfection
he might be plagued with on any given day. There simply
was no excuse for it, barring, of course, the occasional
blizzard or hail storm that might understandably impede
his progress. But today . . .

Adam lowered the edifying instructional pamphlet
he'd bought at Woolsy's Book Emporium entitled *The
Guardian's Guide to the Scheduling of Children's Activities*
and looked about him for the first time since his barouche
had left Inverness at half past noon. His coachman had
folded the hood back on the vehicle, and Adam had
an unobstructed view of the surrounding countryside.

Spring had indeed sprung, as the saying went. The
air was as soft as eiderdown and sweet-scented by the

96 Caitlin McBride

the woodsy knots of rowan and birch trees, interspersed
with ruddy-barked Scots pine, that were nestled against the
cool green foothills. The cloudless sky was a deep cerulean,
dotted with startled grouse taking wing at the sound of
Adam's carriage trundling by. Brown hare gamboled in
the heather. The scene was idyllic. So Scottish. So full
of life. So alien to someone, like himself, who was dead
inside, and had been for the two years since he'd lost his
Maggie.

Maggie had been the sort of wife a man would sell his
soul for. And mayhap he had made such a bargain with
the devil on the eve of his wedding, because now that
Maggie was dead he felt no soaring of spiritual awareness,
no affection for Mother Nature when he was confronted by
beauty such as this. Euphoric feelings were functions of the
soul, matters of the heart, after all. And he felt nothing.

"Spring 'em, Will," he ordered his coachman.

Will turned in his seat and frowned at his master. "Tsk-tsk,
me lord! On such a bonny day as this ye want me t' be
drivin' harem-scarem and missin' all the beauty what's t'
be seen?"

Neighboring gentry would be surprised to hear Adam's
coachman speak to him so familiarly, but Will had been
in the former Lord Blair's employ long before Adam was
even a twinkle in his father's eye; therefore he allowed Will
privileges that weren't extended to the other servants.

"I've an appointment to keep, as well you know."

"And ye dinna think that a wee scrap of a female can be
left waitin', do ye?" Will had a habit of turning most of
his conversation into questions. It was an idiosyncrasy that
could be either endearing or irritating, depending on one's
mood. Despite his impatience to be home and comfortably
settled in the library at Leys Castle to greet his new employee
officially, thereby setting a formal tone from the very first
meeting, Adam couldn't help but be a little amused by Will's
affectionate grousing. He decided to reply to Will's questions
with more of the same.

"How do you know she's a wee scrap? The last one wasn't.

And don't you think a female deserves the same courtesy as someone of the male gender, Will? Do you object to her being English? I should hope not, since I, myself, am half-Sassenach. Or do you deem her unimportant because she's a governess?"

Will made a scoffing noise with his tongue and talked over his shoulder. "And do ye think I'm such a bounder as that, me lord? As a servant meself, do ye think I'd look down on me own lot? B'sides, a fine-speakin', well-learned governess is more than a servant, she's a lady—dinna ye ken? And aren't ladies supposed t' be forgivin'?"

"If she's the lenient and forgiving sort, Will, do you think she's the kind of governess I'm wanting for Kyle and Mary?"

Will squirmed on his high wooden seat till Adam feared he'd catch splinters. The man was overcome, no doubt, with exasperation. "And did that old battle-ax, Miss McCall, the one what ye just gave the heave-ho to, do any good by the wee ones? I dinna think she did! Or wasn't she mean enough to scare the very starch out of Miss Grundy's apron? That'd be quite a piece of work, since the apron could stand up and walk by itself it's so full of the stuff—hmmm?"

Adam chuckled despite himself, imagining his fastidious housekeeper's apron marching about the kitchen disembodied. Then he sobered, considering himself bound by duty to instruct Will on the principles of correct child rearing. " 'Tis important for a governess to be quite firm, Will. Kyle and Mary are high-spirited and require a governess who will hold them in tight rein. Those two little scapegraces would run roughshod over a tenderhearted creature, such as Miss Kimble was."

Will snorted. "Miss Kimble was a snivelin' peahen! If ye be wantin' my opinion, me lord, there's got t' be some sort of governess between Miss McCall and Miss Kimble what the bairns could take to. The poor wee mites! Ever since me lady—"

"That will be enough, Will," Adam interrupted sternly, his good humor thoroughly doused by Will's implication that the children had suffered since Maggie's death. Will immediately turned to sit fully forward in his seat and urged the horses to a spanking pace. He probably recognized that he'd blundered by mentioning Maggie at all, much less the children's behavior. Adam knew that Will, and probably all of the servants, thought he was too strict with the children. Certainly Maggie had been much more loving and spontaneous in her relationship with them. Adam's mouth stretched into a thin line. Her spontaneity had killed her.

Even on such a bright day as this, his dark memories could still intrude. But Adam was saved from too deep an immersion in the past by a sudden jarring of the carriage, followed by violent wobbling. "What the devil . . . ?"

While Will managed the horses, endeavoring to slow the vehicle, Adam raised up to look over the side of the carriage. Surely they'd run over a rock and damaged one of the wheels. While he balanced in this precarious position—his point of gravity being far above the seat where it belonged—the right forward wheel separated from the carriage and bounced off the road into a field of heather. The carriage came to an abrupt halt, and Adam somersaulted over the side, landing on his aforementioned point of gravity in a large rut filled to the brim with mud.

Adam was so taken by surprise at this untoward event that he didn't move immediately. Cold, slimy mud covered him in large splotches from head to toe. His hat had spun off in another direction while he'd been catapulted through the air, and he could feel mud creeping along his scalp.

By now Will had calmed the horses and tied them to a nearby tree. He scurried over as fast as his spindly aging legs would allow and stood looking down at his master with an oddly controlled expression that Adam suspected was three parts amusement.

"Ye dinna hurt yerself?"

"No."

"But ye're a mite mucked up . . . would ye say so, me lord?"

"I'd say so," Adam growled.

"Aye. Yer yellow locks are takin' on a decided shade of

brown. Mayhap you'll be needin' a bath afore ye meet the new governess, eh?"

Adam lifted one grimy hand and flicked a glob of mud at Will, hitting the coachman square on the nose. Surprised, Will grunted in protest, then performed a series of facial acrobatics that would make the great actor Edmund Keene green with envy.

"Go ahead and laugh," Adam advised him with grim good humor. "I can see you're holding it back with all your might. You won't be any use to me till you've let loose, I suspect."

Thus given permission, Will doubled over and laughed out loud. His hoots and guffaws lasted a moderate amount of time, allowing Adam sufficient opportunity to stand up and encourage the mud to slide off his person by the shaking of each arm and leg in turn. Finally Will composed himself, wiped his eyes with his sleeve, and inquired, "What will we do, me lord?"

"I don't know," was Adam's succinct reply. "I don't wish to go into town looking like this. Yet I don't wish to sit here waiting for you to return, either. I say, Will, how roomy are those breeks you're wearing?"

"Not big enough fer the likes of you, me lord, I'm happy . . . er . . . *sorry* t' say! But saints be thanked, here's a fellow what ought to be glad t' sell ye the shirt off'n his back."

Adam looked up and saw a yeoman leading his mule down the road toward Inverness. His clothes, although rough and simple, appeared to be relatively clean, a fact that recommended itself highly to Adam, especially in the present circumstances. The man was also very close to being Adam's size, which was unusual. Adam was all of six-foot-three, broad-shouldered and lean-flanked. After a short dickering session, he bought the man's clothes.

The two men retired to separate clumps of crowberry bushes near a sparkling, quick-flowing beck, disrobed, and handed their clothes to Will, who then exchanged them. Adam briefly bathed in the gurgling water and flapped his arms in the air to dry more speedily, feeling for all the world like a duck preening his feathers.

As for the yeoman, it was to be assumed that he would wash Adam's fashionable toggery in the beck, hang them up to dry in the bright midday sunshine, then put them on as dusk approached. He would then be in possession of the most expensive and fashionable pair of pantaloons, shirt, waistcoat, and jacket as he had ever hoped to own, quite impressing his family when he arrived home for supper. And he'd been paid as well.

On the other hand, Adam would be dry and less embarrassed to approach the wheelwright in the small village of Culcabock than to have regaled the locals with the muddy sight of him in his ruined finery. The wheelwright knew Adam, as did just about everyone thereabouts, but if he kept his hat pulled low over his brow, perhaps his clothing would allow him to go about his business unrecognized by most. He knew the wheelwright would obey his directions immediately to take his tools out to Will and the carriage to make the necessary reparations.

"Ye'll be goin', then?" Will had sat down in the shade of a tree and was chewing on a blade of grass.

Adam placed the floppy dun-colored hat atop his head, yanked the sleeves of his shirt to cover his wrists, and wished that his trousers at least met the top of his ankles. "Yes, I'll be going. Never fear, Will. The wheelwright will come to rescue you shortly. I'll try to catch the mail coach at Culcabock. The driver will quite handily deposit me at Balloan, which, as you know, is but a stone's throw from home, easily walkable in fifteen minutes or less."

"Aye, for legs such as yours, me lord," agreed Will, grinning and staring pointedly at Adam's bare ankles. "But won't the governess be takin' the mail coach? Mayhap ye'll be meetin' her afore ye've tidied yerself, me lord, and I dinna ken she'll be impressed seein' ye dressed thus!"

"She said she was hiring private transportation from Inverness. I haven't the slightest expectation of seeing her before the agreed-upon time. And possibly, *just possibly,*

I'll still be able to keep that three o'clock appointment with Miss Letitia Webster."

"Miss Letitia, eh?" Will rolled his tongue around the inside of his mouth and scowled. "Hope she's as stiff-rumped as ye're wishin', me lord. But judgin' by the name . . . I knew a Letitia once't. I called her Letty. Sweet as a cherry comfit, she was. Soft as the feathers of a dove. Such a name dinna belong to no dragon."

"The Lord knows I hope you're wrong, Will," Adam grumbled, stuffing into his deep jacket pocket the pamphlet he'd bought at Woolsy's. Then he turned and strode quickly down the road toward Culcabock.

"I do wish you'd confine yourself to your side of the coach, madam," drawled Mr. Rumey, a solicitor from Inverness who'd just begun a long journey on the mail coach to the lowlands, only to be made most uncomfortable by a huge butcher's wife in possession of a basket of yowling kittens sitting just opposite him. "You've a whole seat to yourself. Miss Webster and I have politely kept our appendages, clothes, and sundry articles of luggage entirely on our side of the coach."

"I dinna ken why ye're such a complainer, Mr. Rumey," wailed the woman, clutching her basket and eyeing the solicitor reprovingly. "I canna help it if the kittens are missin' their mother. I wouldna ha' brung them at all from me sister's in Inverness, 'cept me new-married daughter was so needful of a few toms t' fend off the mice at the farm. Seems to me it wouldna hurt ye a bit t' be more accommodatin'. I'm only goin' so far as Culcabock, and it's only a wee mile or so down the road."

"Here, Mrs. Dodd," said Letitia, reaching forth her arms. "Give me the basket. Then you won't have to . . . er . . . *sprawl* so, and Mr. Rumey will be made more comfortable."

Mr. Rumey immediately withdrew a large handkerchief from his waistcoat pocket and covered his face with it. "Animals make my eyes tear and my nose itch most unbearably. I can't think having those cats right next to me would be the most desirable alternative."

Letitia sighed and smiled. "Well, I was only trying to help, Mr. Rumey. Heavens! I hope the two children I'm going to be teaching won't be as difficult as the two of you!"

Mrs. Dodd patted Letitia on the knee. "Och, how I feel for ye, Miss Webster. A fair, sweet thing like you, with such bonny blue eyes and chestnut hair, having t' fend fer herself in the wild world. And on top of it all, ye had the bad luck to hobble yerself to the likes of Lord Blair."

As soon as she'd said it, Mrs. Dodd appeared to wish back her comment. Her mouth gaped open in surprise at her own lack of judgment, and she took a sudden interest in the landscape as it skimmed past the carriage window. Mr. Rumey put his handkerchief back in his pocket, shook his head, and tsk-tsked in a melancholy manner.

"Mrs. Dodd, what do you mean?" Letitia asked her, alarmed. "You said nothing about Lord Blair when I first mentioned that I'd be governess at Leys Castle. I know he is a widower, but please don't tell me he's a libertine! If he is, I'll simply have to catch the next coach back to Inverness!" Letitia had had her share of fending off amorous employers, and sometimes even the elder brothers of her small charges, and she was in no mind to repeat the ordeal, no matter how empty her purse was.

"Naw, lass, he ain't *that*!" Mrs. Dodd assured her, shifting the basket of kittens to one side and leaning close. Casting Mr. Rumey a sideways glance as if to indicate that he wasn't supposed to be privy to their conversation, and being rewarded with Mr. Rumey's upturned nose and "hmmph" of disdain, she whispered, "If'n he were beddin' th' servants, I'd have heard tale of it. It's not *that* what makes 'im a hard man. 'Tis his cold heart, lass. Ever since his wife died, he's run Leys Castle like a prison. And he expects the governess to be the warden over those dear bairns of his. Strict, hard, demandin', and downright mean, he is, lass." Mrs. Dodd leaned back and nodded sagely.

Letitia frowned and chewed on her bottom lip. "That's very discouraging because *I'm* not strict at all. I've found that it's much easier to teach the children if they are

comfortable with me and aren't always thinking up some
way to discompose me, such as with a frog in my bed or
some such thing, you know. Naturally I require a certain
amount of respect and decorum during lessons, but I must
admit that I've been known to romp with the children during
their play periods."

"Play periods?" Mrs. Dodd gave a cackle of disbelief. "I
dinna ken he'll allow ye t' have play periods, lass."

"But children must be allowed to play," Letitia insisted
worriedly.

"Well, dinna fret," Mrs. Dodd advised her kindly, ready
to soothe Letitia now that she'd set her to worrying. "I'm
sure ye'll manage somehow! At least he'll not reject ye fer
yer English ways. Lord Blair's father died when the lad was
just a wee bairn, and his mother—born and raised as she
was in Kent—hired an English governess, then later sent
him to English schools. He's as much a Sassenach as he is
a Highlander. Ah, here's Culcabock."

Mr. Rumey cheered up considerably when the outskirts
of town came into view, for he would soon be rid of Mrs.
Dodd and her mewling kittens. Truth to tell, Letitia would
be glad of a little less noise so that she could think about Mrs.
Dodd's description of Lord Blair's character. The woman
at the registry office in Edinburgh who'd interviewed her
for the position of governess had mentioned that Letitia
had been preceded by three governesses already, none of
whom had lasted more than six months. Letitia had not
dared to question why their employment at Leys Castle had
been terminated so soon, because she herself had had four
governess jobs in the past eighteen months and was thankful
simply to be granted another opportunity to work.

Not that it had been her fault that the previous jobs hadn't
lasted. Indeed, could she help it if the young men of the
households took a fancy to her and set their aristocratic
mamas to worrying that their darling sons would shackle
themselves to a mere governess? Even more often the
husbands turned speculative eyes in her direction and
cornered her in dark corridors to "chat."

Letitia felt tears spring to her eyes, and she resolutely

fought them back. The great ladies of the households where she'd served as governess needn't have worried that their sons would propose marriage to her or that their husbands would demand a divorce. The proposals she'd received from the gentlemen—if they could be called that!—had never been anything so binding, or so respectable, as marriage. Drat these good looks she'd been "blessed" with. They'd not served her well in the past two years.

Letitia had been raised as a gentlewoman. In fact, her father was a baron. But when her mother deserted the family to marry Letitia's dancing instructor five years ago, Letitia's papa developed a weakness for gambling, which finally left their family destitute. Sir Arnold Webster responded to these dire circumstances by drinking himself into a stupor one night and falling out of his bedchamber window, breaking his neck on the gravel drive below.

These were grave and trying times for Letitia and her two younger brothers, but she ignored, as best she could, the murmurs of scandalized neighbors and "friends" who suggested that their family was tainted with bad blood. After all, wasn't their father a drunk and a wastrel, and worse still, wasn't their mother a doxy? Doxy or not, Letitia had sorely missed her mother after she went away. And the odd part of it was that Mrs. Webster had never shown signs of such weakness of character before she met Letitia's dancing instructor. This fact made Letitia rather nervous. Was it possible that beneath her own proper exterior she had the makings of a fallen woman, too? So far in her brief life she'd felt no urge to embark upon a life of sin, but she had moments of doubt and worry.

Letitia arranged for her brothers to live with distant cousins, but at the age of one and twenty she considered herself old enough to fend for herself in the "wild world," as Mrs. Dodd so aptly put it. Letitia was glad her brothers had a safe place to live for now, but she'd every intention of discovering some way to earn enough blunt to set up a humble cottage for the three of them. How she would accomplish such a feat remained a mystery. She couldn't even keep a governess position for very long, and all the money she did manage to save was spent on food and lodgings while she looked for yet another position.

Her first position had been in a household in Yorkshire, far away from her old neighborhood in Nottinghamshire. But as opportunity and desperation dictated, she'd gradually ended up in Inverness, the center of the Scottish highlands. From the registry office there she'd learned about Lord Blair's need of a governess. She had planned to hire private transportation from Inverness, but lack of funds prohibited such a luxury. She had inquired about Leys Castle and had discovered that it was in walkable distance from Balloon. Though she would arrive at the Castle windblown and hot, she felt she had no choice.

Letitia smoothed her hands down her best blue kerseymere dress as the carriage slowed to a halt in front of a small black-and-white inn. Mrs. Dodd, in a knocking, elbow-poking, grunting flurry of activity, gathered her belongings in preparation to alight. Pressed against the squabs of the carriage to avoid most of Mrs. Dodd's clumsy movements, Mr. Rumey watched with undisguised irritation.

A jostled bandbox or satchel hit Letitia in the knee more than once, but she stoically bit back any exclamation of pain she was tempted to utter. After all, Mrs. Dodd was a good-natured lady who meant no harm. Though, thought Letitia, grimacing from another blow to her knee, she certainly inflicted enough harm unintentionally. Not the least of Mrs. Dodd's blows was the one to Letitia's hope of happiness in her new home. Those stories about Lord Blair had filled her with foreboding.

Finally Mrs. Dodd squeezed out of the carriage, and Mr. Rumey heaved a giant sigh of relief. This was not to be a stop during which travelers would be allowed a moment to stretch their legs. The coach would stay only long enough to deposit departing passengers or pick up new ones. But Mrs. Dodd's absence gave Mr. Rumey and Letitia considerable stretching space.

Mrs. Dodd's round, rosy face appeared at the window. "As I said, Miss Webster, dinna you worry none about Lord

Blair. Mayhap I misheard how mean he is."

Letitia smiled weakly. "Perhaps so. I hope the kittens prove to be excellent mousers. Good-bye."

Her conscience apparently soothed by Letitia's composed farewell, Mrs. Dodd stepped back and waved her hand, causing several boxes that hung from her beefy arm to clap together noisily.

During this process, a man stepped from behind her and reached for the door handle of the coach. "Excuse me, madam," he said in a low tone, his face turned toward Mrs. Dodd as he tugged on his hat rim politely. "If I dinna board the coach now, the driver says he'll be leavin' me in the dust."

The door opened wide, and a very tall man dressed in simple farmer's attire entirely eclipsed Letitia's view of Mrs. Dodd standing on the walkway. But when she was able to see Mrs. Dodd again, Letitia was puzzled by the shocked, slack-jawed expression on the lady's face and the frozen manner in which she still held her arm in the air.

"What is it, Mrs. Dodd?" Letitia inquired, sticking her head out the window and looking about for the source of Mrs. Dodd's discomposure.

"He . . . he . . ." she uttered faintly, her eyes bulging.

But it appeared that Letitia would never understand Mrs. Dodd's sudden startled look because the carriage rolled forward and jerked into a fast departure. In her last glimpse of Mrs. Dodd, the lady was pointing a fat finger at the coach as it drove off.

"Well, that was odd," Letitia remarked, settling back into her seat. "Mr. Rumey, why do you think Mrs. Dodd acted so . . ."

But Letitia's words died in her throat. Sitting across from her was a man in possession of a pair of the most arresting green eyes she'd ever seen. *Emerald* green. And they were boring into her with eerie intensity, creating the same sort of unease one might feel when being observed by a wild beast at the London Tower menagerie. As she stared back he turned his gaze toward the window.

Most improperly Letitia continued to stare at the man. There was an unsettling incongruity about him. Judging from his attire and a stiff, muddy lock of blond hair sticking out from beneath his hat brim, she had to conclude that he was a common farmer. But his features were so . . . noble. And his skin . . . Though it was not lily-white like the skin of so many dandified men she'd seen, it was also not weather-roughened as she'd expect from a person who labored in the sun.

She glanced down at the man's hands. Like his face, they were a light, golden brown. His fingers were long and tapered, the nails neatly trimmed. Why, she wondered, would a man pay such attention to the trimming of his nails, yet not wash his hair?

Intrigued, Letitia allowed her gaze to travel slowly up his broad chest to his face. She was dismayed to observe him returning her stare again, and she felt embarrassment, like a living thing, creep up her neck to warm her cheeks.

"You were saying, Miss Webster?"

Letitia turned to Mr. Rumey, who looked the very model of tried patience. "I was only commenting on Mrs. Dodd. It was nothing," Letitia replied with a vague waving of one hand. "I'm sure you'd rather rest till our next stop, sir, so I won't bother you with idle conversation."

"Well, I do rather wish to catch a little snooze. I advise you to do the same, Miss Webster, now that we're no more to be plagued by that *woman*. I can't imagine why she thought herself duty bound to repeat common gossip about Lord Blair. You should try to forget everything she said. Very likely she was misquoting someone."

"I hope so," Letitia returned earnestly, her worry over her employer's temperament and child-rearing philosophies compounded by the agitation she felt in the company of the new passenger. His legs were so long that his knees were but a fraction of an inch from touching hers. While his narrow hips covered a mere third of the space Mrs. Dodd's derriere and copious skirts had occupied, Letitia was much more aware than before of being crowded. In fact, she could hardly breathe. She had no notion where to look, either, so she gazed steadfastly at her hands, which were clenched together in her lap.

"Ye're goin' to Leys Castle, lass?"

Letitia felt a thrill at the sound of the man's voice. Goodness, he was talking to her! Since she had felt no qualms in holding a conversation with any other of her traveling companions, she did not feel it fair to poker up and snub the fellow, even though Mr. Rumey's rebuking glare at the poor farmer would seem to indicate that he thought the man entirely too coming. Letitia ignored Mr. Rumey's disapproval and shyly looked up at the farmer.

"Yes. Do you know Lord Blair?"

The farmer's mouth quirked into a small smile. He had a beautiful mouth, she noticed. "Aye. Everyone hereabouts knows His Lordship."

"Recognition by the masses is an unfortunate disadvantage to belonging to the peerage," Mr. Rumey opined dampeningly.

Disregarding Mr. Rumey's remark, Letitia leaned forward. "I mean, sir, do you know Lord Blair's reputation? Have you an opinion of his character?"

"Ye're goin' to the castle, yet ye dinna ken the man's character?" queried the farmer.

"I'm to be governess to his children. I've . . . I've heard he's very strict and demanding. I'm afraid he may find me lacking."

The farmer's hat rim lifted slightly, as if he'd raised a brow. "Lackin' in what way, lass?"

Letitia had no idea why she was confiding in this total stranger, and apparently neither did Mr. Rumey. The solicitor had pursed his lips in an expression of injured propriety. "Well, I like to enjoy the children, and I want the children to enjoy me. I believe a governess needs to have fun with her charges if she's to be effective as an instructress."

"I've heard tell that the bairns are a rambunctious pair, needful of a firm hand," he told her. "Mayhap ye'll be wise not t' indulge 'em. And mayhap ye hadna better cross His Lordship, either. Mayhap he kens what's best for the bairns. 'Tis better t' be paid than not, eh, lass?"

"Well, as to that," began Letitia, bristling at the notion that money was the deciding factor when principles were at stake, "if I disagree with Lord Blair, I shall tell him so, whether my salary is in jeopardy or not! Sometimes one is so close to a problem that one cannot see it clearly, you know. Possibly His Lordship has unreasonable expectations for his children. Did you know, sir, that he's had three governesses before me, and all in eighteen months' time?"

The farmer's smile vanished for an instant, an unreadable emotion flashing in his green eyes. "I've heard as much." There was a pause, during which his smile returned. "And how many positions have ye held, lass, in the same space of time?"

Letitia felt herself blushing to her roots. "Four," she admitted, shrugging her shoulders. "But none of the dismissals were my fault," she hurriedly added. "You see . . ." Letitia's explanation trailed off. It would be awkward to tell him how she'd been compelled to leave each position because she was too comely. And would such a man, who appeared to have no vanity himself, believe such a tale?

Adam was highly diverted, much more so than in a very long time. When he'd been about to board the mail coach and heard his own name on the lips of the notorious tattle-tongue Mrs. Dodd, the butcher's wife, he could not resist a little amusement for himself. First of all, he'd made quite sure that Mrs. Dodd had seen his face as he'd stepped into the coach. Her look of astonished chagrin had more than repaid him for the inconvenience of plunging into a mud puddle.

Then, since he was traveling incognito and was presented with such a tempting opportunity to familiarize himself with his children's new governess without the encumbrance of her employer's real identity, he impetuously decided to playact as a farmer. He was dressed thus, wasn't he? And what harm would his little ruse do? The worst that might happen would be that Miss Webster would reveal herself to be not at all the type of governess he wanted for the children. If that were the case, they'd both be saved a great deal of time and trouble. He'd put her back on the mail coach on the morrow.

Miss Webster was silent now, overcome by miserable embarrassment. She'd been about to explain why she'd been turned away by four previous employers. He thought he knew why. She was too pretty. Nay, she was beautiful. Even though she was sitting, he summed up her height at about five-foot-seven. Tall, but not too thin, as was so often the case with "Long Megs" like this one. In fact, she appeared quite shapely. Her hair was a rich chestnut brown, and her eyes were as blue as the spring sky outside the carriage window. Will had been right. This Letitia was very like the Letitia he'd spoken of. Too sweet, too soft for a governess.

To add to her considerable physical impediments, she was opinionated into the bargain. Obviously her approach to child rearing was at odds with his own. Near hedonistic, he'd wager. Far too lenient, far too . . . spontaneous. A niggling voice of self-truth suggested that he, too, was being too spontaneous in playacting as a farmer, but he pushed the thought aside.

"You don't think he'll approve me, do you?"

Adam felt a twinge of sympathy, a singular sensation for someone so used to being numb. "Perhaps it would be better if he didn't."

When Miss Webster's eyes widened, he realized that he'd abandoned his brogue and had spoken in his usual Oxford-educated tones. To try to undo the confusion this had inspired, he hurriedly added, "Mayhap ye dinna want t' be the governess His Lordship be needin'."

Miss Webster did not reply, her look one of aroused suspicion. The farce was over, apparently. She knew he wasn't a farmer. But did she guess . . . ?

Letitia was angry. Who was this person masquerading as a farmer? His little slip of the tongue—that giving way to correct English—had stamped the man as decidedly upper-class. Had Lord Blair sent someone to spy on her? What a dreadful thought, but such a trick was certainly in keeping with the unpleasant picture her mind was painting of Lord Blair. There was nothing Letitia despised more than deliberate deceit.

If her suspicions proved to be correct, and if she were determined to act upon principle, she should board the mail coach tomorrow morning. But where would she go? Her funds were nearly depleted. Principles were wonderful things, but they couldn't buy one's supper.

"What be ye thinkin', lass?" The farmer's soft inquiry insinuated itself into her tumbled and angry thoughts. Her eyes leveled with his, and her heart skipped a beat despite herself. Lord Blair had erred in sending such a devastatingly attractive man to do his spying. Spies were supposed to be inconspicuous. This man could never be that.

"I'm thinking that I'll take a nap, just as Mr. Rumey advised me at the outset," said Letitia, leaning her head against the back of the seat and closing her eyes, shutting them against the onslaught of emerald green.

Leys Castle stood on the crest of a grassy hill, the highest point in what Letitia thought must be acres and acres of beautiful parklike grounds. The castle itself wasn't terribly large, which pleased her, since she'd expected to be awed by a cold palatial stronghold. Instead the castle was no larger than a comfortably sized manor home. It had a main tower, dating probably from the fourteenth century, complete with turrets and battlements, but additional buildings added within the last century gave the castle a more modern look.

The stone of the building was a mottled gray. Flowers bordered the walkway from the main gate, which Letitia was surprised to discover unlocked and unguarded. If Lord Blair managed his household like a prison, as Mrs. Dodd had suggested, he wasn't very diligent about locking things up. This fact gave her a modicum of hope. She really wanted to believe that this castle could be her home for a while. Letitia loved the rugged grandeur of the highlands. She actually felt more at home in Scotland than she ever had in England. If only her brothers could be with her.

Letitia enjoyed the flowers as she strode up the walkway toward the main door, trying to forget her trepidation about meeting Lord Blair, whom she had magnified in her imagination to be an ogrelike creature. She tried to forget that sham farmer from the coach, too, who was probably a despicable spy, but that was an even harder task. He was by far the most electrifying man she'd ever met, even in his ill-fitting toggery. Her strong attraction to the stranger confused and troubled her. She hoped she wasn't showing signs of that bad blood her neighbors had talked about.

The day was exquisite, the mild temperature a keen complement to the bright wash of spring colors all about her. Too soon Letitia was nose to nose with the door knocker—a fierce-looking lion's head. She lifted the brass ring hanging from the lion's mouth and thumped it twice against the huge wooden door. Then she waited.

Instead of a dignified majordomo, a tall, thin, middle-aged woman answered the door. Judging by her attire and the heavy cluster of keys hanging from her apron string, she was the housekeeper—a flushed, harried-looking housekeeper. Before Letitia could open her mouth, the housekeeper drew her inside.

"Och, lass, 'tis glad I am at the sight of ye! Th' master's just come home, and the bairns are up t' their usual rigs and rows! Lambs they were, all day, mind ye! Precious lambs! But soon as ever their father steps over the threshold, the very devil takes hold of 'em! And me with the scullery maids t' watch over whilst they kill the fowls fer dinner!"

Letitia set down her portmanteau, taken aback by the housekeeper's apparent expectation that she'd immediately assume her responsibilities as governess without first being shown to her chamber or given the opportunity to freshen up. "Where are the children, madam?"

Letitia's question was answered when the housekeeper's eyes widened with dismay as she looked past Letitia's shoulder. Turning about, Letitia observed a most interesting scene. At the top of a flight of stairs two children sat astride the wide wooden railing, prepared to slide down at any moment. Their faces were aglow with naughty expectation of forbidden fun. A footman was cautiously ascending the

stairs with his hands posed in front of him, obviously
hoping to snatch them off the rail before their wild ride
began. At the bottom of the stairs stood the majordomo,
a short, portly, balding fellow with a large nose.

"Master Kyle," he stated in a deep, ministerial voice, "if
you insist upon riding the banister again—the very thing
your father has expressly forbid you to do—you know I will
have to take you to his library for yet another reprimand.
Involving your little sister in this mischief will only make
matters worse."

Master Kyle did not seem the least discomposed by the
butler's threats. His cherubic face, framed with blond curls,
lit with glee. His sister, who sat behind him with her chubby
arms clasped about his waist, giggled. Letitia knew from the
information given her at the registry office that Kyle was six
and Mary was four. She could feel a smile curving her lips.
They were impishly adorable . . . just her sort of charges.
How could their father have the heart to be so stern with
them?

"Master Kyle," intoned the butler ominously. "These are
not idle threats!"

"Oh, pooh, Belnap," lisped the little girl, peering around
her brother's shoulder. "I don't care a fig if Dada's mad.
Dada's al'ays mad about somethin'!"

Then, apparently having timed their departure to coincide
with the frustrated footman coming within inches of grabbing
them, Kyle gave a little push and off they sailed down the
railing. Blond curls bounced behind them as they slid easily
and quickly down the glossy, beeswax-polished cherrywood,
their faces beaming with enjoyment that was half pleasure,
half fright. Mary shrieked her way down, but Kyle forbore
to vocalize his excitement in such a childish display.

Belnap caught them at the bottom and stood them on their
feet, pinching Kyle's ear between thumb and forefinger and
taking hold of Mary's hand. "Just as I told you, Master
Kyle, it's off you go to His Lordship's library." Letitia
noticed that rather than looking unhappy about his fate,
Kyle looked pleased.

"Dear me, no, ye mustn't take 'em there just yet, Belnap,"

the housekeeper told him, glancing at the cabinet clock that stood in the spacious hall.

"And why is that, Miss Grundy?" inquired the butler, giving the housekeeper his full attention.

"Because 'tis five minutes afore the hour, and the governess here is supposed t' meet His Lordship sharp at three. The bairns will have to wait their turn!" Miss Grundy, apparently ever-diligent, rubbed the end of her apron over the dulled shine of an arm attached to a suit of armor standing sentry in the hall.

Awakened to the fact that they were in the presence of their new governess, Kyle and Mary turned their wide green eyes toward Letitia. Their smiles vanished. She felt her heart wrench at their forlorn looks and she wished she could somehow reassure them. But once the spy had made his report to Lord Blair, it was very unlikely that she would be staying past breakfast on the morrow, so there was really no point in trying to make friends with them.

As soon as the registry office coughed up another unfortunate female, the poor things would be subjected to another governess whose philosophy was more in keeping with Lord Blair's notions of strictness. Kyle even looked as though he resented Letitia taking his place in the library, though very likely Lord Blair meant to chastise her as certainly as if she'd slid down the banisters along with the children.

"Show her to the library, Miss Grundy, won't you?" suggested Belnap. "I don't dare give over these ruffians to you!" he explained, nodding his head meaningfully at the children, who had begun to squirm. "They'd tie you in a knot!"

"Yes, give them to Nurse," said Miss Grundy with a grateful nod at the butler, who responded by looking pleased and turning the color of a ripe pomegranate. "She's had a long enough spell away from 'em! And *she* dinna have dinner to get on the table sharp at seven!"

"I had hoped to freshen up a bit before meeting His Lordship," Letitia asserted, lifting her chin a little. "Surely Lord Blair would understand that I've just arrived and am wishful of washing my hands and face." It seemed barbaric, this rushing about just to keep to Lord Blair's time schedule.

Miss Grundy looked askance. "Naw, lass, I dinna ken he'd understand *any* reason t' be late. His Lordship's *never* late for anything!" With these final words, Miss Grundy quickly ushered Letitia down the hall to a double-paneled door near the back. "Knock, lass, then wait," the housekeeper advised her. "I'd stay t' introduce ye, but I'm needed in the kitchen." Then she was gone, her stiff apron making a scratching noise against her skirts as she bustled away.

Letitia wiped her hand over her upper lip. She was perspiring from the heat of her walk from the village and from nervousness. She felt sticky strands of hair lying flat against the back of her neck and an uncomfortable wetness between her breasts. Clearly she was in no proper state to meet Lord Blair. It rankled her to be treated so inconsiderately. But she desperately needed this position. Taking a fortifying deep breath, she knocked on the door.

"Come." The voice was low and cultured, not a beastlike growl such as one might expect from an ogre. She entered the room and closed the door softly behind her. The room was dim and cool and smelled of leather and sweet smoking tobacco. A man stood with his back toward her, looking out a wide, many-paned window. He was very tall, and blond.

She walked a few steps forward and stood in the middle of the room near a heavy antique-looking desk, her hands clasped tightly together. She supposed that he would interview her from the massive wing chair behind the desk. There was a narrow hard-bottomed chair positioned in front of the desk. The difference between the two pieces of furniture clearly implied the superiority of the interrogator who would sit in the wing chair, and the inferiority and guilt of the child, servant, or governess who was obliged to sit opposite him in the rump-numbing wooden seat. Letitia winced. She could almost feel the hard wood digging into her tender bottom.

"Miss Webster?"

Letitia's attention returned to the man standing across

the room. He had swiveled around and now faced her.
He approached, his hands behind his back, causing his
well-fitted forest-green jacket to pull slightly across his
broad chest. His legs were long and incredibly well shaped—
very lean and muscular. He was extremely handsome. His
features were noble and his eyes were . . . emerald green.

"You!"

"So, you do know me, despite my change of clothing."
He stretched his arms wide and made a slow circle, like a
modiste's model pirouetting for inspection. His brows were
raised in a mocking inquiry.

"Only a simpleton would fail to recognize you, my lord,"
Letitia retorted, "and Mrs. Dodd did recognize you, I gather,
even in your farmer's costume. But she had the advantage
of me. She has seen you before!"

Lord Blair had the grace to look slightly ashamed of
himself. " 'Twas a sad trick, I admit, but I did not plan it.
You see, I had an unfortunate encounter with a mud puddle
when my carriage lost a wheel, and I was forced to trade
clothes with a passing farmer. When I found myself on the
same mail coach as you, I could not resist the temptation
to discuss myself with a stranger."

"By so doing, you've put me in a very awkward position!
I need this job, my lord, and you've already decided that I
shan't do!"

Lord Blair's brows lifted again. "Your impudent manner
of speaking makes me suppose that you are not terribly
anxious to secure my good opinion, Miss Webster. Actually
I thought *you* had decided against taking the position, since
I'm rumored to be such an ogre."

Letitia winced, all too aware that that was exactly what
she'd thought of him. He might look like a Michelangelo
angel—and be the father of two little wingless cherubs—
but he could still have an ogre's heart. But as she looked
at him now, the corners of his mouth upturned in a rueful
smile, he did not look very menacing.

The rueful smile disappeared, and Lord Blair turned to
pace three steps to the side and back, very slowly, very . . .
distractingly. His legs were incredible. Was it proper to

admire a man's legs so much? "If you're not dead set against leaving, however, I've decided to keep you on," he said. "Once you are more familiar with my rules regarding the children's schooling and discipline, perhaps our differences of opinion can be reconciled."

Letitia's heart flip-flopped. He wanted her to stay? But what of her own misgivings? What of her *principles*? Well, at least he hadn't actually sent someone to spy on her, as she'd suspected. Still, his deceit was unforgivable. How could she work for such a man? But what registry office would dare send her out again with so many failures on her record?

"You are wrestling with your conscience, Miss Webster," Lord Blair suggested, walking to the wing chair behind his desk and resting his hand on the curved velvet back. "Honor and pride versus expediency." He motioned to the hard-bottomed chair opposite him. "Won't you sit down?"

Letitia cast a disparaging glance at the chair, resting there in all its punitive simplicity, and said, "I'd rather stand, my lord."

Lord Blair's lips pursed. "If you don't sit, I'm obliged to stand as well. 'Twould not be gentlemanly to do otherwise. It would very much *please* me, Miss Webster, if you would sit down!"

Letitia's eyes flashed. "Certainly it would please you, because by placing me in that chair, you immediately put me at a decided disadvantage."

Lord Blair blinked, confusion clearly written on his face. "I must confess myself totally at a loss, Miss Webster. Please explain." He eased one trim, muscular thigh over the corner of the desk and leaned. It was a compromise. He wasn't sitting, but he wasn't standing, either. Did that mean she was something between a lady and a servant? Goodness, he had wonderful legs! But where was her mind wandering?

She pulled her gaze away from that manly thigh and stuttered, "I—I am a student of behavior, my lord. Sometimes the things we *unintentionally* do or say send a more potent message than anything we might *intentionally* do or say. By placing me in that punishingly uncomfortable chair, you are already conveying your disapproval and meting out discipline. Or, at the very least, you are making me humble and more receptive to instruction."

Adam was stunned, and impressed. Lord, how did a provincial governess come up with such an insightful hypothesis? She was probably right, too. He'd never thought about it before, but he most likely *had* subconsciously chosen such an uncomfortable chair for the humbling effect it had on the people who sat in it; his solicitor, the vicar, the servants, the children . . . He always sat near the fire with his friends, offering them deep "cushy" chairs and a place to put their feet up. Equally comfortable, equally . . . equal.

She was an original, all right. And extremely bright. Maybe that's why he had decided to keep her on, if she was willing.

Maybe.

Adam stood up and leaned on his hands against the glossy surface of the desk. "Have you observed anything else about me, Miss Webster, or about anyone in my household, which gives you a better understanding of their behavior?"

To his surprise, Miss Webster's brows knitted in serious thought. The question was not meant to be taken literally. He had spoken sarcastically. "Well, since you mention it, I've noticed something about Kyle."

Adam straightened up abruptly, crossed his arms, and scowled. "Kyle? But you haven't even met the children. How could you . . . ?"

"Ah, but I have," Miss Webster replied with a smile. "Utterly charming little scapegraces. I liked them immediately. I used to enjoy sliding down the banisters when I was a child, too."

Adam's scowl deepened. "At it again, is he?"

"Mary, too," Miss Webster confessed, still smiling. "I'm not tattling on them. They were quite blatant in their misbehavior. Belnap intends to bring them to you as soon as you're . . . er . . . through with me."

Adam shook his head. "Drat, I don't know what else to do to keep them from breaking their necks in such a dangerous game. They think they're immortal, much like their mother did when she used to—but never mind that! I've given them lengthy talking-tos and deprived them of their favorite tea cakes. I've sent them to bed without supper a few times as well, but nothing seems to work."

"Their misbehavior attracts your instant and lengthy attention, I gather?" said Miss Webster.

"Shouldn't it?" he challenged.

"I'm merely suggesting that the children have hit upon the very thing to catch their father's attention and to find themselves frequently in his company. How often would you see them if they didn't need to be lectured and punished?"

Adam was annoyed. A small, intuitive voice inside him told him she was right, but he spurned such simple logic. He suppressed the small voice and listened instead to his manly pride. He drew himself up to tower over her, glowering. "It is presumptuous of you to sum up a man's relationship with his children ten minutes after meeting them."

"Miss Grundy mentioned that they'd been lambs all day till you came home. She implied that this is frequently the case."

He paused, trying to control his temper. His next words were deceptively calm. "I thought you said you *wanted* this job, Miss Webster."

She didn't flinch. "Not if we can't talk honestly about the children."

Adam did not reply. He felt cornered. Lord, why did he want her, anyway? She surprised him by vocalizing his very thoughts.

"Why do you want me, anyway?" she asked him.

Why? Damnation, he didn't know why! His eyes raked over her person in a quick but thorough perusal. She was comely, but he'd no intention of complicating his life and hers by trying to woo and bed the chit. Despite this resolve, an unbidden, most unwelcome image of her lying naked in the center of his bed with her arms lifted in a beckoning pose flashed through his mind. For the first time in two years, Adam felt a yearning to hold and be held. He gritted his teeth and dispelled the tantalizing image. He reminded himself that wanting something . . . someone . . . made one vulnerable to a great deal of pain.

"Because I'm desperate," he said finally. "Because the registry office is less prompt in responding each time I request another governess. None of my friends and acquaintances will recommend anyone for the position, either. I'm hard to please, they say."

Miss Webster was trying to suppress a knowing smile. Drat the baggage! Why did he find such impudence so beguiling? He rubbed the back of his neck and paced the floor. "Mayhap since you are desperate for money and not likely to be well received at the registry office, and I, too, am needful of immediate supervision for my . . . er . . . energetic children, we should give it a go."

He shifted a look at Miss Webster and was not encouraged by her skeptical frown. Before she could say anything, he rushed on, "I will allow you to speak your mind about the children—talk honestly, as it were—if you agree to allow *me* the final word."

Letitia could hardly believe her ears. Lord Blair was proposing a compromise. He'd even used the phrase "if you agree to allow me," implying that Letitia had equal power in their control of the children. A singular idea, that, and not at all what one would expect from a tyrant. She began to be hopeful that a position that seemed so unpromising at the outset could well be the most satisfying of all her jobs. Now, if only she could trust that he wouldn't make advances toward her . . . He was a young man—she supposed he wasn't a day over thirty—and he'd been without a wife for two years.

"To help you decide, Miss Webster"—Lord Blair interrupted her troubled thoughts—"I will speak frankly." She saw his chest rise and fall in a deep breath. Every movement he made was intriguing to her, even his breathing. "You need not fear that I will make . . . er . . . improper advances. I assume that you've been made the object of unwanted and highly reprehensible attention from previous employers. . . ."

Letitia felt her stomach tighten. "How did you know? I never said anything to the woman at the registry office."

His eyes grew suddenly piercing, his jaw tense as he flicked a searing look over her person. "I deduced as much."

She felt that telltale warmth creep up her neck again. He had complimented her, in a way. She had continually cursed her good looks these past two years, yet it somehow pleased her to think that he considered her attractive.

"I give you my word, Miss Webster," he said in a low voice. "I will not press unwanted attentions on you."

"Then I will stay," she said.

And so it was settled, thought Adam, nodding his approval. But why had he used such ambiguous phraseology in making his promise to her? He should have simply said, "I won't touch you." But he had qualified his statement by promising only to refrain from pressing "unwanted" attentions on her. Adam mentally shook himself. Lord, why was he being so analytical? Certainly he meant to stay well away from Miss Webster and her charms. She was the children's governess and nothing more to him than that.

There was a scratching at the door, followed by Belnap and the children. Letitia was thankful for the interruption. Although he was not an ogre, Lord Blair's presence was a little intimidating. She would be glad of additional people in the room. Perhaps then she wouldn't feel so crowded. She knew her logic wasn't sound, but it made perfect sense to her. She'd felt crowded sharing a carriage with this man, too.

"I'm sorry, my lord. I thought I had allowed enough time for your interview with Miss Webster," Belnap apologized. Letitia was glad to see that Belnap no longer kept Kyle to his side by pinching his ear. He held both children's hands. Mary and Kyle's eyes were fixed on their father, paying no attention to Letitia.

Lord Blair moved to the front of the desk, next to Letitia. A faint scent of sandalwood soap teased her nose. She glanced up at him and saw that the ends of his hair were still damp from a hasty bath. She liked the shiny color of it much better without the dulling layer of mud. "It's quite all right, Belnap," he said. "This will be a good time for the children to be introduced to their new governess."

Lord Blair's tone was very formal, almost stiff. Letitia supposed that he had assumed such a demeanor because he was about to reprimand the children for misbehaving. But it was heart-wrenching to watch the children's tentative smiles waver and then completely disappear.

"Kyle, Mary, this is Miss Webster, your new governess."

Two pairs of green eyes obediently turned to her. Kyle bowed, and Mary curtsied with sober dignity. They had been well taught in minding their manners, at least while their father was watching. The proprieties met, they immediately returned their gaze to their father. Clearly they adored him. And, just as clearly, he seemed determined to keep them at a distance.

"Now, Belnap, you may leave the children with me and show Miss Webster to her chamber. Send Nurse for the children in exactly ten minutes."

"Yes, my lord," Belnap murmured, holding the door for Letitia.

Letitia moved toward the open door, but was forestalled when Lord Blair called out, "Oh, I almost forgot, Miss Webster, I've something for you."

Letitia turned about and watched and waited while Lord Blair picked up a pamphlet and a sheet of parchment paper from the desk and handed them to her. The title of the book was *The Guardian's Guide to the Scheduling of Children's Activities*. On the paper was a schedule, written in a strong, elegant hand, detailing the children's activities for the coming week.

"Study the book, Miss Webster," he ordered her. "The schedule I've outlined for the children closely follows the advice put forth by the scholarly gentleman who penned this remarkable volume. I am very much impressed with his wisdom."

Letitia skimmed the grueling agenda, noting that no play periods were included. "Indeed, I make no doubt that the gentleman who wrote this book is scholarly, my lord," she murmured. "I'm equally convinced he hasn't the least understanding of children."

Belnap made a little coughing noise, and Lord Blair drew

himself up in a rigid pose of indignation. "You said I might be honest," she reminded him as she quickly exited the room.

Letitia's first two weeks at Leys Castle went by amazingly fast. The better part of each day was spent with the children in lessons or in meals. Letitia did not insist on a play period for the children—though she fully intended to, eventually—but she made the lessons fun, which somewhat made up for the lack of romping. But not quite. Spring beckoned constantly, its tantalizing rays of soft sunshine casting prisms of light on the schoolroom floor, the smell of blooming flowers and sweet new grass wafting on the breezes that blew through the open windows.

Lord Blair's schedule allowed for a fifteen-minute walk in the formal gardens, but the trek through clipped shrubs and organized flower beds was meant to combine decorous exercise with instruction on local flora and fauna, and His Lordship duly quizzed the children each evening before they went to bed. Therefore Letitia was obliged to forgo the romping or risk being called to the carpet for neglecting the children's botanical education.

Letitia was biding her time. After acquainting herself with the routines and personalities of Leys Castle, and getting to know her charges as best she could in a few days' time, she meant to launch a full-fledged attack on Lord Blair's too rigid notions of child rearing. Her resolve to make the children's lives more bearable grew as she came to be very fond of Kyle and Mary. In truth, they were starved for affection.

Sometimes during lessons Lord Blair would appear at the door of the schoolroom and bend his penetrating gaze on the three of them, as earnestly watching her as he watched the children. She would invite him to come in, but he always refused politely and withdrew, bidding the children to be good and to learn their lessons well. A momentary pall would fall on the group whenever Lord Blair made these unexpected and frustratingly distant appearances. Kyle's hungry eyes would linger on the empty doorway long after

his father went away. Letitia always tried that much harder
to amuse them when this happened, and she delighted in
their responding smiles and laughter.

Miss Grundy and Belnap warmed toward her as well,
their seeming inhospitality on the day she arrived apparently
a result of their being at wit's end, and having met too many
governesses over too few months. "There's no use, lass, in
gettin' attached to someone who's bound t' be gone in three
shakes of a lamb's tail," Miss Grundy told her, then smiled
broadly. "But Belnap and meself, we're hopeful that ye'll
be the one who stays!"

Letitia hoped so, too. She was becoming very fond of the
inhabitants of Leys Castle and took a lively interest in all
their concerns. She had discovered almost immediately that
Miss Grundy and Belnap fancied each other, but they seemed
determined to pretend that they didn't. Letitia supposed that
they might have scruples about indulging in a romance while
both of them were employed at the castle, thinking it not
seemly. Or perhaps they were just shy.

Lord Blair had asked Letitia to meet him in the library
after dinner—sharply at nine o'clock—to review the past
two weeks, and she was very nervous. They had spoken
little since the initial interview in that same chamber. He
was frequently out in the evening, dining with gentry and
no doubt enjoying the company of drawing rooms full of
interesting people.

Letitia wondered how many of the local beauties found
Lord Blair as attractive as she did. And did *he* find one
of *them* attractive? From what Miss Grundy had told her,
Lord Blair had been immune to female charms since his
wife died. The portrait of Lady Blair, which hung in the
drawing room, revealed Margaret McAllister to have been
blond, with a gamine face and speaking eyes. She was very
pretty, but her real charm seemed to lie in the liveliness of
her expression, so well caught by the artist. No wonder
the children were full of life and mischief! They were
miniatures of their mother, except for their green eyes,
which they obviously inherited from their father.

It was a pity Lord Blair had so little to do with Kyle

and Mary beyond discipline and education. Perhaps if he'd turned to them for comfort and affection after his wife died, he'd not have suffered her loss as much.

Miss Grundy had told her that the most painful source of Lord Blair's suffering, however, had to do with the way his wife died. It was a senseless accident that could have been easily avoided. She had ridden an untrained horse and impetuously taken a jump that would have been dangerous even with a mount that was accustomed to jumping. The resulting fall had killed her instantly.

Letitia pitied him. But she also blamed him for alienating himself from the children and making them bear the brunt of his sorrow. The result was that they'd not only lost their mother, but their father, too. Letitia wanted very much to remedy this situation. Her mission at Leys Castle expanded. Now, instead of simply wanting to improve the children's schooling, she wanted to mend a family.

That evening, as Letitia prepared to meet Lord Blair in the library, she found herself fretfully peering into the mirror above her dressing table. She wore a simple sarcenet gown with a high prim neckline, the only adornment of the gown being the goffered lace of her collar. The sleeves were tight and so long they hid the fine bones of her wrist. The high-waisted, slim-skirted gown was a deep russet, a color she deemed properly subdued for a governess to wear.

When a young man from her last place of employment had declared that the color was the very same as the highlights in her hair, she dismissed his words as claptrap spouted by a silly moonling. But tonight, as the candlelight picked out shimmering strands in her smoothly combed chignon, she wondered if the fellow had been telling the truth. And if he had, she wondered if Lord Blair would notice, too.

Letitia's wayward thoughts were brought abruptly back to reality by a loud clap of thunder and a flicker of lightning. A storm had been brewing all afternoon, and in the past hour she'd heard the distant rumbles growing ever closer. Rain pattered against the windows. She walked to one window that had been left partially open, breathed in the fresh, vitalizing smell of rain, then pulled shut the sash.

There was another flash of lightning, followed by an even louder roar of thunder directly overhead. Letitia loved a good storm. Somehow the movements of the churning clouds and the restless wind made her feel more alive . . . more excited about being alive.

It was five minutes before the hour of nine, and Letitia knew she dare not be late for her appointment with Lord Blair. She left her chamber and proceeded down the hall to the stairs. Just as she was about to descend, the children's nurse, whom everyone simply called Nurse, came rushing down from the direction of the nursery clad in her nightrail, her gray hair falling in a long braid down her slightly humped back. Nurse had taken care of Lord Blair as a child, too, and her age probably encumbered her a little in caring for the children, because they easily wore her out. But she obviously loved them and they loved her. Letitia knew this counted for very much, especially in this particular case.

"Miss Webster, can ye come t' th' nursery wi' me? It's Mary callin' fer ye, lass. Scared of the storm, she is. I can usually calm 'er down, but she dinna want me. She be wantin' her Miss Tish, she says!" Nurse's mouth turned up in a smile, the multitude of tiny lines that creased her lips smoothing out and giving her a younger look. "That's a sweet name the wee thing's given ye, eh, lass?"

Letitia was grateful that Nurse didn't begrudge her a share of the children's affection. In truth, the elderly woman was probably grateful to have someone who could help them. "I've an appointment with Lord Blair, but I—"

"Och, I understand, lass," Nurse said, nodding. "Ye'd better be goin', then."

"But he can wait," Letitia finished decisively. "After all, I'm residing in this house for the benefit of the children. I should think that their welfare would be my first priority."

"His Lordship might argue that it be *my* place t' soothe the bairns back t' sleep, lass. I dinna want t' put ye in the way of trouble," Nurse cautioned.

"Nonsense," Letitia said cheerfully, turning and walking down the hall toward the nursery. Another rumble of thunder shook the windowpanes, and she heard Mary scream. Letitia lifted her skirts and hurried into the nursery. Mary had pulled her knees up under her chin and buried her face in her hands. Her outcry had awakened Kyle, and he sat by her on the bed, one arm thrown around her shoulders.

In white nightdresses to their ankles and their fair heads bent close together, they reminded Letitia of a couple of angels. Heaven knew, however, they weren't that. At the moment they were just two frightened children. Yes, Kyle was frightened, too, though he'd never admit it. Letitia's heart went out to both of them.

"There, there, you two!" she called gaily as she entered the room. "With all the commotion outside, it appears that mighty Thor has misplaced his hammer again!"

Mary lifted her face from her hands and held out her arms. "Miss Tish!" Kyle's troubled face brightened, too, as Letitia sat down beside them and pulled them into a comfortable cuddle, arranging the coverlet snugly about them. Nurse watched from the end of the bed, smiling.

"Miss Tish," said Kyle, gazing up at her, his eyes as wide as saucers. "Who's Thor?"

Before Letitia could answer, another clap of thunder rumbled through the room. Mary grabbed Letitia about the neck and squeezed while Kyle stiffened to the rigidity of a broomstick. Letitia waited till the children relaxed a little before continuing with her story.

"I don't suppose your dada would object if I told you an amusing tale to help you back to sleep. You see, according to Norse legend, Thor the Thunderer is the protector of Asgard, or Cloud Land, whichever you choose to call it."

"I like Cloud Land," Mary said.

Letitia smiled. "Then Cloud Land it is. Well, one morning Thor woke up, and his hammer was missing. . . ."

Adam paced restlessly in front of the fire, the nubby fabric of his kilt swishing against the back of his knees. It was five minutes after the hour. Miss Webster was late. He supposed her tardiness might have something to do with the storm, since women were frequently made nervous by thunder and lightning—although Maggie had always been energized by the electricity in the air during one of Mother Nature's kickups.

Adam walked to the wide window, which gave an expansive view of the grounds behind the castle. He, too, loved a good storm. Spidery forks of lightning split the darkness and, for a brief, dramatic instant, imbued the landscape with an otherworldly glow. A crash of thunder followed, the sound and vibration stirring up a rush of vague but disturbing yearnings. God, how he wanted . . . wanted . . . What did he want?

Adam moved away from the window and back to the fire. He held his palms to the warmth and tried to pretend that the gesture was comforting. Yes, maybe he was cold. He gave this up in less than a minute and walked over to the round cloth-covered table next to the sofa.

Though he seldom ate after dinner, Miss Grundy had brought him a tray that held a dish of shortbread and a steaming pot of chocolate. She set the tray on the table, explaining—with an odd little smile—that "Mayhap you and Miss Webster will be wantin' a wee bit of refreshment whilst ye talk about th' bairns." Then she had backed out, her faded blue eyes twinkling with some sort of secret amusement. Adam didn't know what to make of her, but he attributed her uncharacteristic coyness to the cyclical whims women were prone to, and resumed his pacing of the carpet.

Now Adam was glad for the shortbread, because he was hungry. He bit into the buttery biscuit, and though he appreciated the flavor, he knew immediately that he wasn't really hungry after all. He tossed the half-eaten biscuit into the fire and returned to his former position at the window. Another flash of lightning revealed the fragile limbs of a young birch tree near the building to be writhing and swirling in the wind, like the loose tresses of a woman's hair. *A woman's hair.* He could almost feel his fingers threading through the silky mass of chestnut. . . .

Adam jerked into motion, marching toward the door. "Damnation, where is that governess, anyway? I haven't all night to sit about the house waiting for her!"

He knew he should probably send a servant to fetch Miss Webster, but he craved movement. Like the leaves of the trees outside, he wanted to be part of something exciting, something bigger than himself. Tonight, more than any other night since Maggie's death, he felt the constraints of his self-inflicted isolation. Sure, he dined with the neighbors, he danced and conversed—but he still kept his soul to himself. Lately his soul struggled for recognition, for expression. It was a damned frustrating and unwelcome sensation, this *wanting*.

Action, any sort of action, was just the ticket, he decided. Inactivity only allowed him to think and feel more than he wished to. And if giving that impudent little governess a blistering set-down for being late made him feel better, so be it!

Adam ascended the stairs to the upper story and turned down the hall toward Miss Webster's room, just a few doors from the nursery. There was no answer to his firm knocking, so he retraced his steps down the hall, past the stairs to the nursery. The door was open. He peered into the dim chamber, where a single candle lit the comfortable scene before him. Miss Webster was curled up on Mary's bed, her arms around both children. Something bittersweet twisted inside Adam at the sight of the three of them so cozily occupied and so happy in one another's company. Miss Webster spoke in a whisper, and Kyle and Mary appeared to be hanging on every word. Arrested by the homey scene, he strained to hear.

"Not once after that was there mention in Cloud Land of the time when Thor dressed as a girl and won his hammer back from Thrym the giant. No one dared laugh at Thor's expense, you see. Now whenever you hear the thunder, you might imagine that someone has stolen Thor's hammer and is playing a rather noisy game with it."

Adam stepped forward. "It has also been said that whenever Thor drives his chariot, pulled by his golden-hooved twin goats, the clouds roll and the thunder booms."

Letitia started at the sound of Lord Blair's deep voice.

The worst of the storm had passed, and the thunder was now just a distant rumble. Raindrops rolled lazily down the window glass in an unpredictable, meandering fashion. Nurse had gone back to bed and was fast asleep by now in her small chamber adjacent to the nursery. The children had been nodding with returning sleepiness, but they, too, were wide-eyed at the sight of their father at this late hour.

And what a sight he was. Dressed in a kilt, he was more handsome than ever. Letitia's stomach tightened at the sight of his beautiful legs below the pleated hem of the green plaid kilt; golden-furred, lean, and shapely. She pulled her fascinated stare away from those gorgeous shanks of his and met his gaze straight on. Had he seen her admiring his legs? she wondered. Heavens, she hoped not!

"Lord Blair, I'm sorry to be late for our appointment," she began briskly, trying to hide her flustered feelings. "But the children were having a little trouble sleeping, what with the storm and all. We were just—"

Lord Blair forestalled any further explanation with a dismissive wave of his hand. "The storm is passed now. Tuck them in, Miss Webster, and we shall have our meeting."

Always prompt to do his father's bidding, Kyle jumped up and scrambled into his bed. As Letitia bent to pull Mary's covers up she was struck with a sudden inspiration. "Perhaps you'd like to tuck Kyle in, my lord, while I do Mary?" she suggested offhandedly. She did not look at Lord Blair to see how he responded to the hint, but she saw Kyle's face light up hopefully.

Letitia was relieved and grateful when, after a short pause, Lord Blair moved to Kyle's bed and began straightening the child's covers.

"You know about Thor, too, Dada?" Kyle looked shyly at his father.

Lord Blair had pulled Kyle's blanket up to just under the child's chin. His hand rested on Kyle's chest. "Yes, a little. My father used to tell me stories of the Norse gods when I was a boy."

"Dada, tomorrow night will you tell us a story?"

Again Lord Blair paused, this time a longer and more

painful pause to Letitia. Had she set the children up to be disappointed?

"We'll see, Kyle," said Lord Blair in a restrained voice. "I'm invited to the McFarrs for the evening, but I haven't decided whether or not I'm going."

Kyle nodded, satisfied with this small morsel of hope. Lord Blair patted his son's head then, rather awkwardly, as if he hadn't done it for a long time. He moved to Mary's bed and smiled down at the child, tracing a forefinger along the soft curve of her plump cheek. Mary smiled back.

It was a tender moment, apparently too tender for Lord Blair to stand for any length of time, because he suddenly straightened up and moved to the door. There he turned around, saying in a stern voice, "I'll be waiting in the library, Miss Webster. Snuff the candle and do not tarry, if you please."

Letitia sighed as she listened to his slippers' soft thud against the hall carpet as Lord Blair marched away to the library. His determined resistance to Kyle and Mary's need for their father's affection saddened her very much. She kissed the children good night, then descended to the library. What waited for her on the other side of the thick-paneled door, she hardly dared to wonder. She only hoped His Lordship would grant her more time with the children and not dismiss her willy-nilly because of the laughter so frequently heard coming from the schoolroom. She opened the door and entered the library.

As he did the last time they'd met in this chamber, Lord Blair stood by the window. But this time he was swathed in darkness, his silhouette barely discernible against the ghostly gray of the rain-drenched night. She moved to the fireplace and turned her back to it, waiting.

He walked slowly toward her, his hands, as before, clasped loosely behind him. As he moved into the light of the fireplace and the candelabra set on the table by the sofa, she cursed the attraction she felt for this man. She could speak her mind more easily if her serious thoughts weren't jostled aside to make room for such shocking notions as how delightful it would feel to be held in his arms. Was it natural to feel that way, or was she becoming all too much her mother's daughter? He faced her, not quite twelve inches away. If she backed up, she'd catch her skirt afire. If she sidled away, she'd appear the coward. She stood her ground.

His black velvet jacket looked so touchable, so well fitted to the muscular contours of the chest beneath it. Did soft blond curls cover his chest, as they covered his legs? she wondered. Oh, those legs . . .

"So, Miss Webster, two weeks have passed."

She lifted her downcast eyes to clash with his deep green ones and felt a shiver of pleasure. "Yes, my lord, they have." What an inane reply. Why didn't she just announce herself a simpleton and be done with it?

"And how do you reckon the value of this past fortnight, Miss Webster? Have you fared well with the children? Have they learned anything?"

She rallied her senses. "I feel very good about this fortnight's work, my lord. The children seem to have accepted me—"

"That's obvious."

"I believe it is important to gain the children's trust and affection."

"I know. I have conceded that you've accomplished as much." He flicked his hand impatiently. "But let us move on to educational matters. Have they learned anything?"

"You quiz them nightly. I should think you'd have formed an opinion about that already."

He surprised her with a quick smile and stepped back, motioning to a well-padded wing chair by the table, adjacent to the sofa. "Won't you sit down, Miss Webster? Miss Grundy has so kindly supplied us with shortbread and chocolate. Notice I haven't requested that you sit in the punishment chair by the desk. I don't want you to feel intimidated in any way. We're going to talk honestly about the children."

Letitia registered the slightly sarcastic tone of his voice and lamented that he routinely hid behind mockery. She suspected how much he felt for the children beneath that hard exterior, and she wanted, ever so much, to break through that shell of protection. She sat down in the chair, smoothing her skirts over her knees. She was a trifle discomposed when she looked up and saw that he'd been watching her modest preenings.

Lord, why was she so fetching? Adam sat down on the sofa and negligently crossed his legs at the ankle. Perhaps if he feigned a relaxed attitude, he would eventually begin to feel relaxed.

"Would you pour the chocolate, Miss Webster?"

"If you'd care for some, my lord. I couldn't swallow a drop myself."

He leaned forward, surprised. "You're nervous? Do I make you nervous, Miss Webster?"

"My immediate future lies in your hands. Why wouldn't I be nervous?" She threw him a challenging look.

Still restless, he stood and paced the floor in front of her. "You're an excellent governess. I haven't a bone to pick with you about the children's education. They've learned a great deal these past few days and seem to enjoy it. A singular talent, that, making children enjoy the process of education. Will you concede that my schedule has helped you succeed in this endeavor?" He stopped pacing and stood before her.

She looked him square in the eye, her voice wavering only slightly as she replied, "I cannot, in good conscience, concede such a thing, my lord, though you may very well sack me for saying so. I have succeeded with the children *despite* your restrictive schedule."

His jaw hardened. "Is that so?"

"Quite so. I implore you to allow the children a play period each day after nuncheon," she rushed on, seeming to gather resolve. " 'Tis unnatural to be inside all day when spring beckons us outside." She paused, her manner suddenly irresolute, her voice wistful. "Don't you feel it, my lord?"

"Feel what, Miss Webster?" He knew he sounded caustic, cynical.

"Spring, my lord. Don't you feel spring? The air, the scent, the softness of it?"

"No, I do *not.*"

He saw the pained expression in her eyes. "Then I pity you."

Adam could stand impertinence. He could tolerate scorn, or even fear. But he could not bear to be pitied. Leaning forward, he grasped the arms of the chair Miss Webster sat in and pushed his face close to hers. "Save your pity, my dear, for yourself," he hissed. "If you don't quit meddling in matters that are not your concern, you'll be sacked soon enough, despite your teaching abilities."

Letitia was stunned by the intensity of Lord Blair's reaction to her words, and just as equally amazed by her own urge to gather him close to her and soothe away the bitterness—her gaze dropped to his lips—or to tenderly kiss away the grim set of his mouth.

Letitia got her wish, but when Lord Blair grasped her by her upper arms and pulled her to a standing position, then kissed her, there was nothing tender about it. He held her flush against his chest, their bodies intimately touching from head to toe. His legs, those long, beautiful legs, were pressed against hers. His mouth was warm and urgent, his hands here firm and sure as they circled her waist and pulled her closer still.

Letitia had been kissed before, but never had she had the urge to kiss back. Caught up in such a novel and thrilling sensation, Letitia forgot propriety, caution, wisdom—all those pesky principles—and kissed him back. Her hands moved up the fluid musculature of his back and around to the sinewy cords of his neck. Her fingers felt the soft texture of his hair where it waved above his collar. She was in tactile paradise.

Adam was in a state of dementia, he was sure of it. Why else would he be doing the very thing he'd promised Miss Webster he wouldn't do? But she felt so right in his arms, so pliant, so responsive. He couldn't get enough of her mouth. He wanted . . . He wanted . . .

So this was what he wanted. Miss Letitia Webster. The children's governess, for Christ's sake. He released her.

Letitia eased down into the chair. Her lips still throbbed

from Lord Blair's demanding kisses. Her heart beat erratically; her breath came shallow and fast. She had completely lost control of herself as soon as this man took it into his head to kiss her. He had broken his promise. Or had he? He told her he'd not force unwanted attentions on her. Judging from her response to his kisses, on a very basic level she'd apparently wanted them very much. But she shouldn't want them. She was a moral young woman. She was nothing like her mother . . . was she?

"I'm sorry, Miss Webster."

Letitia looked up into Lord Blair's troubled expression. He had backed away and had folded his arms across his chest, perhaps to indicate that he'd behave and keep his hands to himself.

"My conduct was unforgivable. I don't know what came over me." He walked to the fireplace and supported himself against the mantel with one elbow flexed, staring into the flames. "I expect I'm just like your other employers." He laughed uneasily. "Indeed, Miss Webster, you're too comely by half to be safe in the world."

Letitia knew that Lord Blair was nothing like the other men who'd forced kisses on her. She'd felt no attraction to them, nor did she feel heart stirrings for her former employers as she did for Lord Blair. "None of them ever apologized, my lord. At least you have done that."

"It doesn't change my guilt, however. I expect you'll be leaving, then?"

Letitia looked at her hands. Leave Kyle and Mary, Miss Grundy and Belnap? Leave Leys Castle and . . . Lord Blair? "I don't want to leave."

"I don't want you to leave, either."

Letitia's eyes darted up. What did he mean? Did she dare hope . . . ?

Lord Blair began pacing again. He appeared to be weighing his words before he uttered them. He stopped in front of her and blew a long breath between his teeth. "You're an excellent governess, and the children like you very much. They've been behaving much better, Belnap tells me. No more banister rides."

He smiled wanly. She responded with an equally unconvincing smile. She was foolish to hope that he might have an interest in her beyond a physical attraction. She was a mere governess, daughter to a disgraced baron who had died ignominiously and with pockets to let. Her best hope of sharing something like love with such a man as Lord Blair would be to live with him as his mistress. She could never do that. For two reasons she prayed God he'd never ask her: first, it would lower him in her estimation, and second, she might be tempted to say yes.

"Besides, Miss Webster, what would you do? I think it is requisite that you stay in one place for at least a year to establish your credibility. Don't you?"

He was right. But how could she bear being near this man for a whole year? What if he kissed her again? Would she have the moral strength to resist him?

"As God is my witness, Miss Webster, I will not touch you again. Do you believe me?"

Letitia looked into Lord Blair's green eyes and saw the sincerity, the resolve. She believed him. It made her unaccountably sad.

"I believe you, my lord, and I will stay under one condition."

"Which is?"

"That you will allow me to establish my own schedule for the children, which will include play periods."

"You drive a hard bargain," he said dryly. "But I begin to think you know what you're about when it comes to teaching children, so I shan't dispute you. We will have another interview in a month. Next time, however, I will arrange a chaperon to be present for your safety."

"But I trust you. After all, you promised."

"If I must use outside help in keeping that promise, it is still kept, I suppose." He paused, leveling a piercing gaze at her. "I do not trust myself."

Letitia felt a thrill, knowing he desired her so powerfully that he needed a chaperon to help him resist her—even if it was just a physical attraction. She stood up and moved to the door. She turned to face him. "You said before that you didn't know what came over you. I think *I* know what came over you tonight."

"You do?"

"Spring, my lord."

"Ah . . . *spring*." He smiled genuinely this time, almost tenderly. Letitia was reminded of another Norse tale of the golden-haired god, Balder the Beautiful, whose smile was the harbinger of spring.

"Good night, my lord," she whispered, and left the chamber.

Letitia watched from her bedchamber window as Lord Blair's coach left the front courtyard early the next morning. Since he usually rode his horse or took a small curricle to nearby social engagements, she knew he must be taking an extended leave of Leys Castle. Watching the coach get smaller and smaller, she felt her heart grow heavier and heavier. She would miss seeing him about the castle, even if it were only a glimpse of his coattail as he rounded a corner.

She finally admitted to herself that she was more than physically attracted to Lord Blair. She had developed a *tendre* for the man, however hopeless and unrequited it may be.

Later, Letitia casually "bumped into" Miss Grundy in the breakfast room in hopes of discovering the viscount's whereabouts, and just as casually mentioned that she'd seen His Lordship departing the premises. She learned that Lord Blair had gone to Edinburgh to stay with friends for a few weeks.

" 'Tis the Season, lass," Miss Grundy explained as she busily checked the silver for spots. "He dinna stay fer the whole thing, but he deems it proper t' make an appearance each year. Gets the matchmakers' hopes up every time he shows his handsome face in Edinburgh, I'll wager, but the silly lasses who bat their lashes at 'im might as well give up, I say. I ken he fancies a more mature sort. Like you, lass."

Letitia was startled by Miss Grundy's words and the sly look she slid in her direction. Letitia's hand fluttered to her throat. "Like me?"

"Aye, lass, like you," Miss Grundy confirmed with a shake of her head. "He left in a great hurry, dinna he?" she added, the dangling observation seemingly unrelated to her previous comment. It did make Letitia think, however, that their encounter last night might have discomposed him so much that he felt it necessary to leave quickly. His kisses certainly had had a powerful impact on *her*. She'd even dreamed about him.

Letitia's brow furrowed as she remembered Kyle's request to his father last night to tell him a story. "He didn't say good-bye to the children, I suppose."

"He went to their beds afore he left and kissed their wee sleeping faces. And he said t' tell Kyle that he'd bring a storybook back with 'im t' read, just as he promised."

Letitia felt an eddy of warmth curl around her heart. He'd remembered.

Miss Grundy had found a spot on a large serving spoon and was vigorously applying the hem of her apron to it. "He'd never have done such a thing afore you came, lass." Miss Grundy shifted her keen eyes to look at Letitia again. "Belnap and meself have seen how he's changed these past few days."

"Oh, Miss Grundy, you mustn't think that I've wrought any change in Lord Blair," Letitia sputtered, feeling her face warm with a mix of embarrassment and hope. "I've simply done my best to teach the children."

"Ye brought a breath of fresh air with ye, lass. A spirit of hope, I'd say. Just like spring on the moors." Miss Grundy replaced the silver spoon in the velvet-lined chest and turned to face Letitia with a big smile. "Belnap and meself—Nurse, too—we're grateful to ye."

Letitia's gaze dropped to the carpet. "Thank you. I only hope he lets me stay. We don't always agree about things."

"He'd be a fool t' let the likes of ye slip through his fingers!" Miss Grundy said with feeling. "Now off ye go, Miss Webster. I hear the bairns' breakfast bell ringin', and ye dinna dare miss a meal, what with that wee figure of yern t' keep from wastin' away t' nothin'."

And so Letitia was dispatched to the nursery to breakfast with the children, her mind reeling with the things Miss Grundy said, and the things she didn't say but seemingly implied. Did she dare to hope that the servants thought her worthy of such a man? But perhaps it was only wishful thinking on their part. They probably missed having a mistress about the castle, and also liked her management of the children.

The real issue, of course, was what His Lordship thought of her. In Edinburgh, thought Letitia, surrounded by all the fresh new faces of the females regularly carted off to the city by their parents to make marriage alliances, he'd no doubt forget all about his impudent governess back home. The best course to take would be to put the viscount right out of her head and devote herself to the children.

Easier said than done. Devoting herself to the children was no problem at all, but she found herself continually thinking how wonderful it would be to share the children's time with their father. How pleased he would be by Kyle's progress in mathematics. How charmed he would be by Mary's stitchery. How much fun it would be if he joined them in their rambles across the moor, knee-high in heather and bluebells.

He was always on her mind, his image forcefully brought to her attention by the similar way Kyle's chin thrust out when he was being obstinate. Or the crinkle of Mary's eyes when she smiled . . . just like her father's. No, putting the viscount out of her mind and heart would be a difficult, if not an impossible, task.

By a small sheltered inlet of the Firth of Forth, Adam joined a group of genteel Scottish society for a boating excursion and an al fresco luncheon. Just an hour's journey from Edinburgh; the ladies and gentlemen had traveled the distance easily and comfortably. The day was incredibly temperate. The breezes that blew off the firth, which could often be biting even in the summer, were mild. The sun's

persistent rays were neither too strong nor too hot, but
were gently warming. Everyone felt the friendly influence
of such congenial weather, and the prevailing mood was
one of genuine pleasure and cheerfulness.

Adam stepped out of the carriage he shared with Geddes
Wolfe, a professor at the University in Edinburgh, his wife,
Katherine, and their daughter, Jane. He turned to lend a
hand to the ladies as they alighted from the carriage in a
whisper of muslin skirts. Even at the advanced age of forty,
Mrs. Wolfe was still a trim woman. Her pelisse—dyed a
rich capucine—fit her figure well and complemented her
dark blond hair. But it was the sight of Jane that caused
everyone's eyes to turn in their direction, her dainty foot,
shod in soft kid, pointing a toe at the step in front of her,
her face framed by a straw poke bonnet, her mouth upturned
in a sweet smile.

"Oh, this is delightful," she said softly, pausing in the
door of the carriage to look about. Adam followed her
gaze. Indeed, he supposed there was much to be pleased
with if one had an eye for the beauty of nature. The
water was a sun-silvered blue, reflecting back the clouds
that swirled like tufts of pulled cotton against the bright
midmorning sky. The long, L-shaped dock was lined with
punts, dinghies, and sloops—floating, waiting. Ladies in
pastel muslins and ribbons, each carrying a matching parasol,
promenaded along the shore in the company of gentlemen
equally bedecked in springlike hues—white cravats, fawn
breeches, and richly dyed jackets. Here and there he noticed
a kilt, the tartan plaids lending a dash of piquancy to the
otherwise mellow color scheme.

Adam usually reserved his kilts for evening wear and
special occasions. Today he fit in perfectly with the
other gentlemen in his bottle-green jacket, champagne
pantaloons, pearl brocade waistcoat, and white cravat. He
had unintentionally worn clothes that complemented Jane's
ensemble, but which coincidence made them look all the
more like a couple. Jane was in sea-foam green, from the
ribbons that tied below her chin to the laces in her half
boots. Beneath her green pelisse, she wore a white gown

dotted with ivy sprigs. She was as blond as Adam, and her eyes were a light, translucent hazel. Jane was, simply said, beautiful. Her looks reminded Adam of Maggie's.

Professor Wolfe wet a finger with his tongue and lifted it high in the air. "Not much of a wind for sailing. I think I'll take Mrs. Wolfe out in a dinghy, Adam." His bushy brows waggled as he darted a meaningful look at his daughter.

Dutifully taking his cue and choosing a course that would ensure sufficient chaperonage for Jane, Adam said, "And so will Miss Wolfe and I. We can row out together to the middle of the lake, Professor, then drift till lunch. Is such a plan acceptable to you ladies?" He smiled, deferring to Mrs. Wolfe. He knew Jane would agree to anything he proposed. In the three weeks, since his arrival in Edinburgh, she had been consistently agreeable. Too agreeable. Today he hoped to get Jane alone, relatively speaking, and to pry out of her a few original opinions. So far everything she'd claimed to admire or enjoy were blatant parrotings of his own expressed preferences. He knew there must be substance behind the beauty and he was determined to unearth it. Surely there was one woman in Edinburgh who could take his mind off Miss Letitia Webster!

Stopping to chat with people as they went by, Adam and the Wolfes slowly worked their way to the dock and boarded two dinghies. Adam controlled his rowing so that the professor's boat stayed within a few yards of his, keeping a proper distance to preserve propriety yet drifting far enough apart that their conversations would be private.

Finally, floating in the middle of the lake, Adam pulled in the oars. Watching, Professor Wolfe did the same, throwing Adam a friendly salute. Adam felt a prick of conscience. Geddes and Katherine, acquaintances of his for over a decade, were hoping that Adam would ask for Jane's hand in marriage. He'd encouraged their hopes over the past weeks by spending more time with her than with any other young woman.

Adam had been careful, however, not to be too particular in his attentions or to treat Jane with exclusivity. The Wolfes would be disappointed if he didn't come up to scratch, but they wouldn't blame him or claim foul play. Besides, he knew there were other suitors waiting in the wings, several of whom the Wolfes would, in time, find equally acceptable as potential sons-in-law.

Adam had never implied any commitment. He was trying to discover for himself if commitment was something he really wanted to pursue. Ever since he'd kissed Miss Webster in the library at Leys Castle, he'd known that it was time he had a woman in his life . . . but not just any woman. That would be a heresy to Maggie's memory. The trouble was, no one in Edinburgh had triggered the urge to, well, *mate,* like Miss Webster had so aptly done that stormy night in May.

"Miss Wolfe," he began, "what think you of governesses?"

Taken aback by such an odd question, Jane blinked and said, "I hardly think of them at all. I had several as I grew up. I don't even remember all their names. What think you of governesses, my lord?"

He smiled. "I think they are necessary to the proper education of children."

She smiled back—a dazzling show of neat, white teeth—ready to go along with the conversation to please him, however pedestrian the topic. "Certainly, my lord."

"But there are many different approaches to teaching, Miss Wolfe. Governesses may be strict, they may be confiding, they may be aloof, they may like to play with the children, or they may not. What sort of governess would you prefer for your own children?"

Apparently awakened to the fact that Lord Blair could be quizzing her in matters that might determine her marriageability, Jane gave the question some thought. It was disappointing to Adam when she predictably inquired, "What type of governess do you prefer, my lord?"

Adam suppressed his exasperation. "There must have been one or two of your governesses you liked above the others, or one, at least, that you remember the most."

Again Jane paused, her nose wrinkling prettily, her lips pursed in thought. She had luscious lips—kissable lips. So why didn't he want to kiss them? Suddenly she giggled. "Well, there was one we liked rather well. She was so odd. I confess we laughed at her expense quite often, the poor, timid creature. She disliked worms, you see. . . ."

Adam assumed a look of smiling interest and let his thoughts wander. Her beauty notwithstanding, conversing with Jane was about as stimulating as watching the clock tick. Insipid, predictable, plodding. He could never say the same about Miss Letitia Webster. He played a game of word association, comparing Jane and Letitia to sundry everyday things. For example: Jane, vanilla. Letitia, cinnamon.

Jane, oatmeal. Letitia, Indian curry.

Jane, a daisy. Letitia, a wild, full-blown rose.

Jane, pale green—like her eyes, her dress, her conversation.

Letitia, red—like the highlights in her hair, like her spirit, her passion, her zest for life.

So why was he sitting in a rowboat with Jane while Letitia romped with his children on the highland moors? Why, indeed! But he supposed he'd needed this trip away from Leys Castle to understand the mixed and turbulent feelings Letitia Webster had caused in his life. He wanted to make sure he wasn't just desiring her because she was comely and because she was available. Newly reawakened to an awareness of the female sex, he wanted to make sure there was no one else who engendered in him that same urge to settle down. To hold and to be held. To entrust his heart into another human being's keeping. Yes, he was finally willing to take the chance of wanting something— someone—so badly that he was vulnerable to pain again. Ah, Letitia. Quick-witted, courageous, wise, loving, and impudent. Could he make her love him?

Letitia shook the grass, tiny flower petals, and stems from the linen and folded it neatly. Dark-bellied clouds had collected over the moor, and she and the children would need to hurry back to the castle to avoid a soaking. Kyle and Mary had been revivified by the tasty food Nurse packed for nuncheon, and now they chased each other, laughing, through the reddish-brown heather.

Letitia waved a summons. "Time to go!" Neither child seemed to hear her or to notice her upheld arm.

"Kyle! Mary! We're going to be rained on if we don't leave right away. Come along!"

The children stopped running, but their attention had been caught by something besides Letitia. They were faced away from her, staring in a southerly direction. She turned to see what they were looking at. It was a man on a horse. It was . . . Lord Blair! Like the children, Letitia could only stare. He had left in a coach, but he was returning on a horse, and much sooner than she had anticipated. It had only been a month ago when she'd watched sadly from her bedchamber window as the carriage disappeared down the Edinburgh road.

As complex feelings ran through her she watched him approach now. Excitement, fear, dread, toe-curling admiration . . . love. He had slowed his roan mount to a brisk walk. He was hatless, his hair tousled by the wind of the approaching storm. He wore a blue jacket, buckskin breeches, and top boots. He looked comfortable and agile on the horse, easily controlling the animal with the subtle movements of his fingers as they lightly held the reigns. His wonderfully long legs pressed just as subtly against the horse's flanks, reminding Letitia of the strength she'd felt in them as they'd pressed against her own legs that stormy night last month.

As he slowed to a halt next to the children, his eyes held hers for a moment before they lowered and focused on Kyle and Mary. In that instant, as their eyes met, she'd felt an electrifying connection. He hadn't smiled. He hadn't shown by any gesture that he was glad to see her. But there had been an intensity in that look that was at once gratifying and terrifying.

"Hello, children. Haven't you a word of welcome for your father?" His voice was cajoling, his smile broad and genuine.

"Hello, Dada," they chorused together, no doubt delighted by his unexpectedly warm greeting.

"Did you bring my book, Dada?" Kyle was emboldened to ask.

"Yes, but it's in the carriage, several miles behind me. I'll fetch it out of my portmanteau tonight, Kyle, and read to you and Mary, just as I promised."

"Why didn't you come in the carriage, Dada?" asked Mary. She pointed toward the darkened sky. "It's going to rain, and you'll get wet."

"It seems to me we're all going to get wet in a moment. Miss Webster, what are you doing exposing the children to a possible soaking?"

The words were disapproving, but Lord Blair's tone of voice was gently teasing. Letitia felt confusion overcome her. Apparently his softened attitude toward the children extended to her as well. There was no deciphering his feelings, however. His green eyes were unflinchingly direct, but unreadable.

Letitia avoided that unnerving steadfast gaze of his and answered, "The storm came up suddenly. We were just about to return to the castle when the children caught sight of you."

"I'm sure it was a surprise to see me so soon. I'm usually gone two months to Edinburgh."

"Oh." Another intelligent reply, Letitia derided herself, suddenly remembering that she was wearing her oldest dress, an ill-fitting faded blue sprigged muslin. Her hair, so neatly bundled into a chignon that morning, now fell loose down her neck, the wind blowing tendrils about her face. She made a fruitless effort to push back her hair with one hand, and with the other hand she smoothed her gown over her hip. She shivered when she noticed him watching her movements with interest.

"Oh, look at that bird, Dada!" Kyle was pointing at a large osprey flying in unusual circles and swoops above them. Lord Blair's keen gaze shifted away from Letitia, allowing her to breathe freely again.

"It's showin' off," said Mary disgustedly, her hands on her hips, her head bent back to watch the bird.

"But it is rather amazing, Mary," said Letitia, shading

her eyes as she, too, followed the bird's spiraling antics. Despite the unnerving presence of Lord Blair, Letitia was fascinated by the bird's acrobatic flying. She'd never seen anything like it before. "What does it have in its mouth? A twig?"

"A sprig of heather," said Lord Blair. Suddenly another bigger bird appeared and began flying with the first one. "She'll drop it soon."

"What's the heather for, Dada?" asked Kyle.

"It's a female osprey, Kyle. By carrying the heather in her beak, she's letting it be known that she wants a mate . . . a male osprey, you know. If she approves of this braw fellow who's trying so hard to impress her, she'll drop the heather, and they'll fly off to build a nest together."

"Oh!" said Mary, finally impressed. "Then there'll be baby birds!"

"Yes, Mary," said Lord Blair, a laugh in his voice.

"I had no idea birds were so . . . resourceful," said Letitia, still watching the birds.

"Rather I would call them romantic, Miss Webster."

Letitia's gaze clashed with Lord Blair's, then both pairs of eyes skittered away. The birds' behavior was easily comparable with that of human beings; for example, the way a lady used her fan to flirt and send messages of availability to the male sex. Even with her eyes a woman could quite ably convey an interest in a desirable gentleman of her acquaintance. And if the man chose to "fly" with her, they'd build a nest.

"Dada, Miss Tish says the moors are full of ed-u-ca-tion-al ma-ter-i-als," said Kyle self-importantly, proud to have said two long words in the same sentence.

"Indeed? Well, as usual, Miss Tish is quite right."

Thrilled to be conversing on such equal footing with his father, Kyle further informed him, "Miss Tish says curiosity didn't kill the cat, like other people say. It just made 'im smarter! She says we should be curious about everything around us so we'll learn."

Lord Blair shifted Letitia another swift enigmatic glance.

"Yes," he murmured, "there are merits to curiosity."

Letitia nervously bit her bottom lip. Why was he being so agreeable?

Finally the osprey did drop the heather, and soon the birds had become small brown dots against the gray clouds.

"They'd better hurry and build their nest or they'll get wet," said Mary.

"We'll all be wet in a minute," said Kyle, mimicking his father. "You were right to hurry ahead of the carriage, Dada."

"I timed my return very well, didn't I?" said Lord Blair.

"Why *did* you come back from Edinburgh so soon?" Letitia was stunned by her own audacity. It was certainly none of her concern why Lord Blair had concluded his business, or pleasure, in Edinburgh. Mayhap he'd found a bride and had come back to prepare for the wedding. Letitia prayed that wasn't true. If it *was* his reason for returning early, she'd have to leave Leys Castle for sure. She couldn't bear to see him with another woman. *Oh, Letitia, how foolish you are!* she scolded herself.

"I had an appointment to keep, Miss Webster," Lord Blair answered. "Don't you remember? I said we would meet in a month's time to discuss the children again."

"I hardly thought you would feel it necessary to curtail your trip to keep an appointment with me, Lord Blair," she whispered, dropping her gaze to the carpet of heather at her feet.

"I always keep my appointments." He paused, and she felt his scrutiny. "Tonight, at seven, you will dine with me."

Letitia's head jerked up. "Dine with you?"

"I promised you a chaperon, didn't I? What better way to ensure your safety during our interview than to have Belnap and his host of footmen hovering nearby, watching over the dinner courses and the governess at the same time? What think you of my plan, Miss Webster?"

If it had been Jane Wolfe he'd asked for an opinion, Adam knew exactly what response he'd get. But Miss Webster was not so eager to please at the expense of her own integrity. She'd been timid and humble—shy—so far. Showing up so unexpectedly, he'd taken her by surprise. And he'd been intentionally neutral in his treatment of her, trying to gauge her response to him and gradually introduce her to his own enlightened feelings. Though she had demonstrated a physical attraction to him the night of the storm, he didn't know how involved her emotions were. He must pace himself. Now he saw her old assertiveness returning. Her chin lifted fractionally. Her eyes sparkled.

"I do not care to be lumped in the same category as the pigeon pie, my Lord Blair, but Belnap's presence is welcome," she coolly pronounced. "I will dine with you if you deem it the most convenient way to dispatch your business with me."

Adam suppressed an almost overwhelming desire to laugh out loud. How he loved her feistiness! Poker-faced, he replied, "At seven, then." He pulled his gaze away from Miss Webster's delightfully flushed countenance and again regarded the children. They were staring at him, eager to be noticed. Why had he never realized how desperately they wanted his attention? Maggie's death, like the blight of winter, had deadened him to the influence of his children's love, to the very beauty of life around him—human and natural. He had to make up for his aloofness.

"Children, would you like a ride back to the castle?"

Kyle and Mary squealed and danced a jig, leaving no doubt that they were well pleased with such a plan. He reached down and pulled each one up, placing Mary in front of him and Kyle behind. They held on tightly, their faces alight with pleasure. Adam felt his own heart swell measurably. Allowing himself to love them felt quite satisfying. He looked down at Miss Webster. A tiny smile teased at her lips, though she seemed to be trying to suppress it.

"I'd offer you a ride, too, Miss Webster," he said soberly, "but there's no room, you see. I could come back for you."

The suggestion of a smile vanished. "That won't be necessary. I walk quickly."

Adam lifted a hand, palm up. "It begins to sprinkle."

"Nothing to signify. Children, we will recommence your lessons at one-thirty." She picked up the luncheon basket and cloth and, gripping her skirt in her spare hand, did truly begin to walk with admirable speed toward the castle. Adam watched her for a moment before urging his horse to a gentle canter. Lord, but she was a sassy lass! He could well imagine how spirited her lovemaking would be, if properly encouraged and nurtured by the right man. Would she consider him the right man? he wondered. Would she drop the heather sprig for him? Beginning with dinner, he'd soon find out.

Letitia was having considerable trouble swallowing. Course after course, her nervousness refused to desert her. Sitting with Lord Blair at the elegant dining table, Letitia felt as though she were in a particularly anxious dreamlike state.

Yes, she must be dreaming, because the scene before her couldn't be more perfect. The table was fashionably devoid of a cloth and softly lit by an ornate centerpiece candelabra. The gleaming china reflected in the mahogany finish of the well-polished table, and the crystal goblets and tumblers fairly shimmered. Imported from Denmark, she surmised, running her fingertip along the rim of her wineglass, and startling herself by the responding bell-like tone of authenticity that rang through the room.

Lord Blair looked up from carving his pheasant and raised a brow. Belnap eyed her, too, but he had an expression of compassion on his face. So far he'd been a stalwart chaperon, seeming to commiserate with her nervousness. But he did not appear to disapprove of her having dinner with Lord Blair. He should disapprove, she thought rather petulantly. It wasn't proper at all.

"Sorry. I didn't mean to make a noise," she said.

"I don't mind," Lord Blair returned amiably. "Little enough noise has come from that end of the table. You usually have so much to say, Miss Webster. Cat got your tongue, lass?"

He'd never called her "lass" before. Was it because she was wearing the russet dress again, the one she'd worn the night he kissed her? It had been a risky thing to do, but it was her best gown, and dining with an aristocrat did justify a little dressing up, didn't it? Or was it the wine that had loosened his Scottish brogue? She would prefer the latter explanation. Anything Scottish suited Letitia, especially the kilt Lord Blair wore tonight. She cleared her throat. "When it comes to the children, I suppose I can be quite vocal, yet you do not seem disposed to discuss them tonight. I thought that was the purpose of our dining together."

Lord Blair shrugged. She loved the way his shoulders looked in that green velvet jacket. "I spent some two hours with the children this afternoon. I could tell you've not wasted your time this past month." He paused and slid her a rueful smile. "Despite your play periods. I am impressed. Nothing further need be discussed. I wouldn't change a thing you're doing."

Letitia set down her fork and folded her hands in front of her, resting them on the table. Her fingers were intertwined tightly, all the better to keep them from shaking. He was being altogether too reasonable, too agreeable, too charming. "Then why are we dining together? 'Tis not the custom for a governess to sit at table with the lord and master of the household."

Lord Blair rested his elbows on the table, forming a steeple with his splayed fingers. Above this loosely constructed flesh-and-bones edifice, Lord Blair's eyes regarded her. "I thought you might be persuaded to tell me something about yourself. Not even the servants could tell me where you were born, or who your parents are."

Letitia stiffened. "How do my origins concern you, my lord?"

"I'm simply interested, that's all. I'd like to know more about you."

"Why?"

"Because you know a great deal about me. Miss Grundy told me about your strolls through the portrait gallery and all your many questions about my predecessors. I feel it only fair that you, in turn, answer my questions."

Letitia felt warmth flood her cheeks. "Living in a beautiful castle like this one, with so much history attached to it, you must be used to people's interest in the McAllister clan. My interest was inspired by curiosity. By comparison, the Webster family history is very dull. I would bore you to tears recounting it."

"I did not ask for a chronology of dates, events, and names." He smiled teasingly. "Aren't I entitled to indulge in a little curiosity, too? You deem it such a merit, you know. I was simply wondering about your immediate family. Do you have brothers and sisters?"

The last thing Letitia wanted to do was talk about her family; it was much too painful and embarrassing. She had loved her mother and father, but they'd each, in different but nonetheless definitive ways, deserted her and her two brothers. It was their fault that she was presently separated from her beloved younger brothers and must work for a living as a governess. It was her mother's fault, too, that she constantly doubted her own fortitude. She glanced at Lord Blair. Despite his teasing, friendly manner, he did not look as though he meant to retreat one iota. Resigned, she answered, "I've two younger brothers."

"At school?"

"No. They live with cousins in Nottinghamshire."

"And your parents?"

"Dead." Letitia's conscience jabbed her. "Well, at least my father's dead."

"Your brothers don't live with your mother?"

"No." Letitia reached for her knife and fork, pretending to be suddenly interested in the cooling food on her plate. "This salmon is delicious."

Adam knew he was being persistent to the point of impoliteness, but he wasn't simply trying to appease a vulgar, overactive curiosity. He was endeavoring to find out more about the woman he had fallen in love with. Miss Grundy seemed to enjoy a friendship with Letitia, yet even she could not tell him particulars about Letitia's family. Letitia had talked freely about her other positions as a governess, but her life before that she apparently considered a closed book.

Since it didn't seem likely that she would explain why her brothers did not live with their mother, Adam tried a different tack. "In looks, do you favor your mother or your father?"

Letitia's knife and fork clattered to the plate, and she abruptly stood up. Her eyes welled with tears. "I don't know why you persist in badgering me about my family, Lord Blair." Her voice held equal portions of dignity and despair. "But if you must know, my father was a drunk and a gambler, and my mother ran away with my dancing instructor! I hope I'm nothing like either of them! Perhaps now you'll understand why I choose not to discuss them."

Dropping her napkin on the table, she walked quickly out of the room. Adam followed her. He was appalled that he'd brought her to tears with his blundering questions! Her family's troubles did not lessen her in his eyes, however; rather, he instantly admired her all the more. How much she'd had to deal with and overcome, yet she still managed to be so uncynical, so courageous and unique!

She exited through the front door and moved hastily toward the gate to the formal garden, a maze of trees and flowers enclosed within an ancient stone wall. Long shadows stretched across the lawn. The misty pink gray of gloaming shrouded the land in an almost dreamlike beauty.

Despite the urgency he felt to catch up with Letitia and apologize for causing her pain, Adam truly recognized and appreciated the beauty around him for the first time since Maggie's death. He felt as if he'd been wearing blinders for two years. He felt the beauty, too, in the cool mist against his skin. He heard it in the song of the lark, serenading the tenacious sun that rode the horizon and held back the night. He inhaled the fragrance of lily of the valley, roses, and mock orange blossoms.

Adam's senses vibrated with awareness. He was alive to his surroundings again, thanks to Letitia. In fact, he'd never felt so attuned to nature as he did now. He wanted to pull this shining night close to him, embrace it all— from the opalescent twilight sky above his head to the dew-tipped grass beneath his feet. But most of all he wanted Letitia.

A narrow rock walkway winded through the picturesque chaos of the garden. Chamomile plants grew between the cracks and gave up their applelike scent as Adam trod over them. The cool, deep dark created by overhanging tree branches and crowding, flowering shrubs refreshed his spirit. He breathed in the crisp air and was filled with peace and hope. For Adam, spring had come at last.

Rounding a bend, he saw her. She was leaning against a tree, her face in profile as she gazed into the dense green waters of a moss-bottomed pond. She heard his approach, and her head jerked in his direction. Even from a distance, he could see the tear tracks on her cheeks. Embarrassed, she wrenched her whole body around, turning her back to him, surreptitiously wiping away the evidence of her distress.

Adam closed the distance between them with slow, cautious steps, approaching her as if she were a shy forest creature. At last he stood just behind her. She had finished wiping her tears and she held her head regally erect, though she still averted her face.

He gave a long sigh. "I've been intrusive and tactless."

No response. He lifted his hands, palms up. It was

a gesture of apology, of abject chagrin. "I'm a clumsy clodpole."

"Aye, my lord, that you are," she whispered.

Buoyed by the return of some sort of communication between them, he stepped closer. "Forgive me. I didn't mean to bring up a subject that is distressing to you."

He watched her head bow, the movement unwittingly revealing the beautiful, slender column of her neck. He wanted to slip his fingers around that smooth white flesh, then kiss her behind her shell-shaped ear.

She turned slightly, throwing him a self-conscious look over her shoulder. "You couldn't have known. It's embarrassing."

"All families have their closet skeletons, you know."

Letitia made a helpless gesture with one hand. "It's not just what they've done. It's hard to explain. I still love my parents and I think I actually feel guilty about blaming them for my misfortunes. Yet it *is* their fault that my brothers and I have had to suffer a great deal of unpleasantness in the past years, and I resent them for that." She turned fully around, her eyes pools of confusion. "My parents' weaknesses have made me afraid of my own fallibility."

Adam took one last step forward, bringing him within inches of Letitia. She did not retreat. He lifted his hands as if he were going to clasp her shoulders, left them poised in the air for half a moment, then dropped them again to his side. He'd promised her he wouldn't touch her. If he broke his promise, would she think he was implying that she was like her mother? Chances were, however, that her mother wasn't as bad as the gossips had undoubtedly painted her. She had probably been a casualty of a bad marriage, driven to make a choice between her children and the love of a man who was not her husband. A tough predicament, that.

"Life is never as black and white as we want it to be, Letitia," he said. "You have good reason to resent your parents, yet I think you know that they were probably dealing with their problems and needs the only way they knew how to at the time. You and your brothers unfortunately got caught in the middle."

Letitia's brow furrowed. "Most people don't see it the way you do. Most people want to categorize everyone as either good or bad. Even though they did some good things in their lives, my parents have been labeled as bad because of their mistakes. I've done the same thing. I've thought them very bad for the things they've done. But I still . . ."

"You still love them, which makes it all very confusing, doesn't it? Don't worry about it, Letitia. Realize that your parents were complex human beings with failings, as we all are. It's perfectly all right to love imperfect people. If that weren't true, none of us could ever possibly hope to be loved."

Her face lit up. "How wise you are! You have such a compassionate view of people and their foibles!"

"You'd never have said that to me six weeks ago," he reminded her, smiling and feeling sheepishly proud of himself.

"Nor six hours ago!" she retorted, smiling back.

They stood there, grinning at each other like two infatuated children. But the yearning Adam felt to pull Letitia into his arms and kiss her was very adult. His smile fell away as he studied her face, trying to read her thoughts, to gauge her emotions. She looked so beautiful . . . and so vulnerable.

"God, how I want to break my promise to you, Letitia. How I want to touch you."

Letitia's heart ached with wanting him. He was so wonderful in every way! She'd come to the castle expecting to be turned away by a tyrannical ogre. She'd been led to believe that he was a cold man, beyond the reach of his children's affection and no longer interested in the love of a woman since his wife's death. There were seeds of truth in this pat tale told by the gossip mongers, but the real, complex truth lay far afield.

Adam was a loving man who'd been caught off guard by his beloved wife's sudden death. He had grieved deeply for her and inwardly railed against the injustice of it. To gain back a semblance of sanity in his life, he'd forced everything and everyone around him into neat little schedules. Then he'd removed his emotions to a safe place where no one could hurt him again. But there was a price to pay for that sort of protective isolation. Had he realized that? Was that why he wanted to touch her? No matter what had brought on Adam's desire to touch her—to hold her—Letitia's own desire to return his embrace was just as strong.

"I want you to touch me, too, my lord, but I—"

"Call me Adam, Letitia."

She drew in a sharp breath. "I'm afraid."

"That I'll make you like your mother?"

"Worse than that. I'm afraid that if you touch me, I won't care who or what I am anymore! I lose all sense of propriety just *thinking* about you kissing me! I've thought about it a lot, you know," she confessed impetuously, darting him a quick, embarrassed look. "And . . . and if you kissed me very much, I'm afraid I'd be so drunk with love and pleasure that I'd gladly sell my soul to stay in your arms!" Letitia spoke with fervid sincerity, not weighing her words or considering Adam's response to them.

Adam knew she spoke from the heart, and his question concerning the state of her feelings for him was sufficiently answered. She'd said it! She'd said she loved him! That was all he needed to know.

Adam pulled her into his arms and kissed her, tenderly at first, then, against his own determination to go slowly, the kiss deepened and intensified. A fire of desire ignited inside him. She felt so right in his embrace, her slim, rounded curves molding so perfectly to the hard, straight planes of his chest. Her thighs pressed against his, the delicate fabric of her skirt brushing against the bare skin of his legs below the hem of his kilt.

God, how he wanted to make that early fantasy of

his come true; the image of her lying in his bed with her arms upheld in a beckoning pose!

He pulled away and cradled Letitia's face in his hands, his eyes exulting in the sight of her passion-flushed cheeks, her parted lips, her heavy-lidded eyes.

"I've a question to ask you, Letitia." He was surprised and humbled by the huskiness of his own voice. The lass had a devastating effect on his self-control.

She gave a little moan, her face turning in his hands to look away. "Oh, don't ask me. You know I can't refuse you when you hold me thus. Don't ask me to be your—"

"My wife, Letitia. Sweetheart, be my *wife*."

Letitia knew now that her earlier suspicion that she was dreaming this whole unbelievable episode must indeed be true. She stared at him, her body braced and still for the inevitable return of reality.

Adam chuckled. "You look as though I've asked you to swim the North Sea, *mo he'rt*. Is it such a horrible thing to contemplate being my wife?"

Hope soared inside Letitia. "But I'm your children's governess, my lord!"

"We'll get another."

"You know that's not what I mean! You're a viscount, and I'm just a—"

"A woman very much my equal in every way. I don't know any more about your parents than what you've told me, Tish. May I call you that, my love? I like the way it sounds when the children call you thus." Then, not waiting for an answer, he continued. "You are obviously gently bred, well educated, and of high moral fiber. Whether your father was an earl or a merchant makes no difference to me. I love you, Tish. I love your spirit, your compassion, your wisdom. I want you to be the children's mother. But more importantly, I want you to be my wife."

Emotion ached in the back of Letitia's throat, making speech difficult. But there was something more she had to know. "What about Maggie, Adam?"

"I'll always love Maggie. She'll always be a part of my life, but my *past* life. I want you to be my future, Tish. You've given me back the happiness I lost when Maggie died. I know Maggie would want something . . . someone . . . who's so very good for me and the children."

Joy filled Letitia, emboldening her to taunt playfully, "Even though I'm impudent and outspoken, unstructured and prone to romping?"

"Especially because you are all those things and more, lass. Now shut up and let me kiss you."

For once Letitia agreed without an argument.

A wedding in Scotland could be a simple or an elaborate undertaking. A spoken agreement to marry between the participating couple need only be confirmed by two witnesses to make a marriage union legal under Scots law. This easy manner of shackling oneself to another for life made hasty marriages a frequent occurrence in Scotland, especially among couples fleeing England and their disapproving parents to the border towns of Gretna Green and the like.

For Adam and Letitia a hasty marriage was desirable simply because they could hardly wait to be wed. Since Adam was determined not to bed his betrothed before they were legally married, by mutual agreement they decided on a simple ceremony in the castle chapel in a week's time. Although Letitia knew Adam loved her and respected her, and she herself had more than once been tempted to visit his bedchamber before their vows had been exchanged, he wanted to prove his respect for her by waiting till after the ceremony to make love to her. Letitia knew he was being sensitive to her confused feelings about her mother, and she was touched and pleased. At the same time, however, she was in a constant state of pleasant frustration.

Oh, how she loved him! They spent the week before the wedding in the blissful occupation of getting to know each other better. They passed long evenings sitting in the library in the "cushy" chairs by the fire, with sherry, chocolate, and shortbread to sustain their marathon conversations, and with a nodding maid as chaperon, sitting in a far corner. Childhood memories, politics, literature, and every other conceivable subject was exhausted, then renewed with vigor the following evening. They didn't always agree about certain topics, but their disagreements were stimulating and made each of them think hard about both sides of the issue.

Mornings they paid social calls, with Adam proudly introducing his betrothed to the local gentry as well as the tenant farmers. Some people raised their brows when Letitia revealed that she had come to the castle as the children's governess, but for the most part the obvious love between Lord Blair and his bride-to-be quieted any unkind speculation about the appropriateness of their match. After all, she was the daughter of a baron, and though not a Scot, as would be preferable, they decided that for a Sassenach lass she would do quite well. Besides, Letitia glowed with such happiness that her animation and gracious charm won over everyone within the first few moments after meeting her.

The children, of course, were ecstatic at the prospect of having Letitia for a stepmama. They saw that Dada was much more fun now, too. These facts, coupled with the cheerful servants bustling about the castle in preparation for the wedding, gave the castle such a festive air of excitement that Kyle and Mary were bursting with high spirits. Adam and Letitia spent each afternoon with the children, and they invariably spent the hours till dinnertime on the moors, running the children about till they settled down enough to eat a meal without bouncing off the walls.

Some patches of heather on the high moors were turning purple, and the days were long and warm, the twilights seemingly endless. It seemed that Mother Nature had conspired to make the week before Letitia's fairy-tale wedding a romantic idyll of all that was best about the Scottish highlands. With an atmosphere so conducive to romance, it was only with considerable force of will that Adam managed to refrain from making love to his delectable fiancée before the wedding night.

She was no help, he often thought with a tender, grudging look at his betrothed. She always looked so fetching, so aglow with sweet, seductive sensuality! And Letitia knew she was tormenting him, albeit without much conscious effort.

Letitia, on the other hand, claimed that Adam's misery were his just deserts for tempting her constantly with the sight of him in a kilt each and every day. She had confessed her fascination with his legs, and he had responded by wearing his kilt *all the time*! It really wasn't fair of him to flaunt those gorgeous shanks like that, she'd told him. Ever so badly she wanted to slide a curious hand beneath the kilt to clasp his knee. And those stories she'd heard about kilts . . . She was prodigiously curious. . . . Did he wear trews beneath his kilt, or was he an *authentic* Scotsman?

Thankfully, when Adam and Letitia's tenuous hold on their passion seemed about ready to break, an announcement from Miss Grundy and Belnap gave them something else to think about.

"Miss Grundy and I are getting married, my lord," Belnap soberly informed Adam as he shared breakfast with Letitia one morning.

Adam and Letitia responded in unison, but displayed a very different understanding of goings-on at the castle.

"How splendid!" chirped Letitia. "I was wondering when you'd get on with it, Belnap!"

"Good God, Belnap!" Adam exclaimed, clearly astonished. "I hadn't the slightest notion! How long has this been going on?"

"Didn't you know, Adam?" Letitia laughed.

"Tish! You knew about this?" countered Adam.

"Since the first day I set foot in the castle," she informed him cheerfully, then turned and smiled at Belnap. "You and Miss Grundy have loved each other a long time, haven't you? Why did you wait so long to marry?"

Belnap's eyes twinkled. "Right you are, miss, about Miss Grundy and myself. We've loved each other from the minute I started work here at Leys Castle three years ago. But it didn't seem right nor proper to carry on in a loverlike manner with His Lordship so unsettled. We were waiting for him to marry before we thought it appropriate to tie the nuptial knot ourselves. Naturally we were made quite hopeful when you showed up at the castle and caught His Lordship's fancy."

"Was it so obvious?" inquired Adam with a tender smile for Letitia.

"Quite so, my lord." Belnap grinned at Adam in a most unbutlerlike fashion. "And begging your pardon, my lord, but with the two of you smelling of April and May, and with the castle all abuzz with preparations for the wedding and the party afterward, Miss Grundy and I couldn't wait a minute longer. We don't mean to make things more muddled around here, but we hope you'll understand, my lord, and will grant us permission to call on the village vicar this very afternoon."

Adam's mouth curved with knowing, amused sympathy. The roles of master and servant dissolved in this shared dilemma of lovesick impatience. "I understand your eagerness completely, Belnap. By all means, marry today. I only hope you'll allow Miss Webster and me to attend the ceremony?"

And so it was settled. Miss Grundy, in a sunshine-yellow dress she'd sewn herself in the hope-filled hours of many long winter nights, stood before the altar with a dapper-dressed Belnap to exchange marriage vows. With a wreath of myrtle in her hair and a radiant smile on her wrinkled face, Miss Grundy looked almost young. Ah, thought Letitia, what love can do.

On the eve of her own wedding, with a mere few hours separating her from the pleasure of calling herself Letitia McAllister, Viscountess Blair, legally deserving of all the pleasures attached to such a title, Letitia was seriously considering a visit to His Lordship's bedchamber once lights were out. In her opinion, the title of Lady Blair was nothing compared with the title of wife to the man Adam McAllister, and she could hardly wait to share his bed.

During dinner, however, unexpected guests arrived— Letitia's brothers, James and Frederick. They were not unexpected by Adam, who wanted to give Letitia a surprise wedding present. The sight of her twelve- and thirteen-year-old brothers brought tears of grateful joy to her eyes. Adam watched, beaming.

Letitia had of course written to her brothers and announced her wedding plans, hinting of her hope that they'd be reunited in the near future. Adam had also sent the boys a missive and some money, along with Will, the coachman, who'd gladly accepted orders to carry the Webster lads back to Scotland in the viscount's traveling chaise in time for the wedding. The boys were instructed to bring all their belongings because Adam fully intended to keep them at Leys Castle till time for them to be sent away to a boarding school.

All Letitia's fondest hopes had been realized. She had a home, a family, and the man of her dreams. So, when she was wed on the following morning beneath a bower of bluebells and myrtle sprigs, her white dress decorated with a sash of McAllister tartan, and with a golden-haired god—her husband—smiling an eternal promise of spring, Letitia could not possibly believe that more happiness was possible. That night she learned differently.

The party ended. The guests had gone home or had bedded down in extra bedchambers for the night. Letitia sat in her own room in front of the dressing table while one of the maids brushed her hair. She wore a diaphanous white dressing gown that was gathered below her bosom and fell in soft folds to her feet. Loose sleeves flared at the elbows. The neckline was low and revealing, bringing a blush to Letitia's cheeks as she observed herself in the mirror. But choosing the white was quite a good idea, she decided. The shimmering paleness of her gown made her chestnut hair look that much darker and shinier. Free from the usual chignon, her wavy hair cascaded to the middle of her back.

Adam opened the door that joined his chamber with hers and stepped into the room. Letitia could see his reflection in the mirror. The maid immediately bowed herself out the other door that opened to the main hall and left them alone.

Alone. At last.

Letitia turned around. She thought she'd been imagining it when Adam's reflection in the mirror revealed him to be in full Scottish regalia, just like at the wedding. She thought he would have changed into something more . . . comfortable. Her eyes hadn't deceived her, however. He still wore his green plaid kilt, black velvet jacket, white shirt, a sealskin sporran, a handcrafted dirk tucked into his belt, and with the *sqian dhu* in place in his right stocking. Truth to tell, Letitia found this toggery more stirring to her senses than even the silkiest dressing gown Adam might have worn for his first visit to her bedchamber.

He pirouetted for her inspection, as he'd done that first afternoon in the library. "For you, Tish, I'm completely authentic."

Letitia swallowed. "*Completely* authentic, Adam?"

He smiled, his lips slowly upturning in a sensuous invitation. "Completely, *mo he'rt*." He removed the dirk and the *sgian dhu* and placed them on a nearby chest. "Come here, Tish."

Letitia moved readily into Adam's outstretched arms. As they held each other with no threat of interruption and no doubt of one another's love, the passion Letitia and Adam had been keeping in check for so long flowed in a torrent.

Adam's tongue slipped between her lips, and he kissed her deeply, exploring her mouth with urgent intensity. He caressed her, the flimsy material of her gown the only barrier between his warm hands and Letitia's sensitive skin. He found her nipple and tugged on it gently, persistently, rhythmically, till she thought she might pass out from the pleasure of it. She felt a thrill surge through her body, leaving her legs weak and languid. She wanted to lie down with him. But first . . .

"Come, love," he said, holding her at arm's length, his eyes trailing lovingly over the curvaceous front of her gown. "Let me undress you."

"No, Adam."

Adam raised a brow, a questioning, almost uncertain smile tilting his lips.

She put her hands on his upper arms and gently pushed

him toward the bed. He looked puzzled but pleased, ready to allow her to be assertive. When the backs of his knees hit the edge of the high bed, he abruptly sat down. She knelt in front of him and put her hands on his bared knees.

"What are you doing, Tish?" he asked her, wetting his bottom lip.

Her hands slid up his legs—those long, slim, beautiful legs—the kilt crumpling and rolling up her arms, the blond hairs on his legs curling around the tips of her fingers. She stopped midthigh. "Don't be shy, Adam," she said, smiling impishly. "I just want to see if you're truly authentic. My love, I'm curious. I just want to *see!*"

Adam's green eyes glittered dangerously. He laughed deep in his throat, causing a delicious shiver of yearning to rack Letitia's body. "Aye, Tish, you shall see. . . ." Then he pulled her onto the bed with him and satisfied his wife's prodigious curiosity once and for all—or at least until the next time he wore a kilt.

Ah . . . spring.

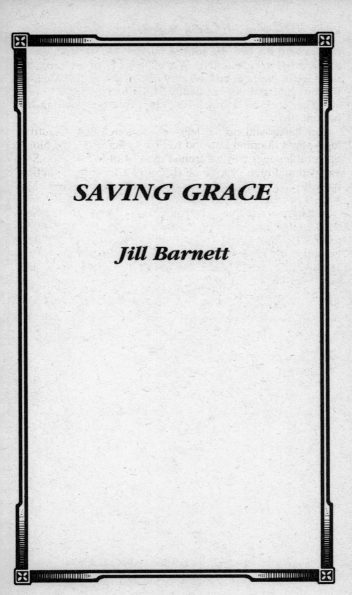

SAVING GRACE

Jill Barnett

Dear Reader:

I have a confession to make. These letters are harder to write than the stories. At first, I was going to tell you about my Scottish ancestors, but after a few sentences I began to doze off. Besides which the Scottish ancestors I knew something of were born in Texas. Next I made an attempt to write about Scottish thriftiness, but then my charge-card bill arrived.

So I moved on to things Scottish—oats, for instance, which immediately brought on a desperate craving for oatmeal cookies. This gives you some insight into how my mind works. Two hours and four handfuls of cookie dough later, I waddled back to my computer and tried something else Scottish: plaids—something I won't be able to wear because of that cookie dough.

Write to them about something you love, I told myself. *But I've already mentioned oatmeal-cookie dough!* Then I remembered some Scottish things I loved—characters, females in particular. Some of the best historical romance heroines I've ever read about were Scottish: Bronwyn, Cameron, Annie, Frances, Kayleigh—young women as bold and brash as the land in which they were born.

Naturally, when I think of Scotland, my mind's eye doesn't see mists and moors, kilts and claymores. I see women with a strong sense of pride, women who fight stubbornly for those they love . . . sometimes a wee tad too stubbornly.

This is how Grace McNish was born. There's an old Scots saying: give your tongue more holidays than your head. Good advice, right? Grace doesn't take advice well, and her tongue has never seen a holiday. She's a different character for me—a feisty Scot who's a bit of a shrew.

She needed taming, a job that called for a special kind of man. "Saving Grace" is the story of how she meets her match, someone stronger than she, yet someone with a great deal of patience, a man who falls in love with her because of her loyalty and fight, and who channels her fire in a different direction. He teaches her tongue to take a holiday.

Well, I believe it's time for my tongue to take a holiday, or another glob of cookie dough. Keep smiling.

Jill Barnett
P.O. Box 785
Pleasanton, CA 94566

The Devil is always good to beginners, and even God
Himself protects simple animals . . . and women.
                                    —*Auld Scottish proverb*

CHAPTER
1

The man was out cold. And Grace McNish had done it.
Awkwardly perched atop his brawny chest, she leaned
closer, an ancient dirk clutched tightly in one hand while
the other fanned away a brown-and-red cloud of settling
autumn leaves. Her green eyes were surprisingly clear and
calm for someone who had just slipped and fallen from her
prized hiding place in an old rowan tree, and had had the
blessed good fortune to land upon a dastardly McNab.

She searched his face for signs of deceit, for everyone
knew a McNab couldn't be trusted. His breath was slow
and shallow, and a red, egg-sized knot swelled on his
forehead just above his thick dark brows. His hair was
streaked blond, long—almost touching his shoulders—and
surprisingly, his face was strong, angled, his jaw square and
firm and shaven—an oddity for the McNabs who usually
wore beards, most likely to hide their weak chins.

With her dirk a scant inch from the man's brawny neck,
she scanned the wee glen for signs of others. There was
no one. The only change in the surroundings was a small
area of trampled bracken where his spooked horse had fled.
Leave it to a McNab to be too cattle-handed to control a
poor horse, she thought in disgust. She leaned a tad closer,
then touched his skin with the old dull blade, watching for
signs of consciousness.

A female head covered in bright red hair popped into her line of view, peering down at the man. "Is he dead?" Fiona asked in a loud whisper. She sat on her heels and looked at Grace through wide and frightened eyes. "Tell me ye've no killed the mon."

Satisfied he was truly out, Grace relaxed and slid the dirk into her belt. "He's hardly dead, only knocked senseless— a fine state for a McNab." She glanced up, careful to speak toward Fiona's left ear, the right one being nearly deaf. "And what are you doing over here? You're supposed to be hiding in the broom bush across the road."

"I was worried."

"Why are you worrying? Scotland would be a finer land with one less McNab." Grace tugged fiercely at her ragged and time-frayed plaid, which was caught beneath the man, and muttered, "Naught but the devil's spawn, they are."

" 'Twas ye what had me worrying. Ye screamed so loud I heard ye with my right ear."

"You needn't be worrying yourself about me," Grace said, her pride stung. "I am, after all, the laird's grand-daughter."

"Aye, that's what ye always say," Fiona paused, then said under her breath, "and laird's granddaughter or no, something always goes wrong."

Grace gave her black hair a toss, a gesture that showed she was not concerned about consequences, at least not when her newest plot was taking root. Her green eyes lit with wicked glee, then she grinned. "Not this time." She arched her shoulders back and pointed to the unconscious man. "I've nabbed a McNab."

One look at that gleam in Grace's eyes and Fiona turned her face heavenward and muttered a prayer with the words "trouble coming."

"The only trouble coming is called McNab," Grace shot back, then stared at her captive. "Look at him." She pointed toward his powerful arm. "All hearty and muscled." Her empty stomach picked that exact moment to growl, and she scowled at him. "Unlike we McNishes, the McNabs aren't wanting for food."

Fiona eyed him thoroughly. "From those brawny shoulders and legs I'd say ye were right."

"Probably been stuffing himself with McNish mutton." Grace stared at the man. Then her face became pensive, and a scant minute later brightened with the glimmer of an idea—a truly frightening thing to anyone who knew Grace McNish or had been privy to one of her frequently disastrous and woebegotten plots.

She grinned. "It'll be no puny ransom for this one. We'll not settle on a sum based upon their past thievery." She rubbed her hands together and smiled in anticipation. "We'll collect the ransom by his weight."

Slowly, assessingly, she looked him over, starting at his blond head, over the plaid-covered shoulders that were nearly as wide as her arm span, past his narrow waist and hips, down his thick muscular legs covered in trews that declared the importance of his rank within his clan, down to the man's costly leather shoes with the woven silk laces. "Should be enough to feed the clan for two winters at least."

"Grace . . ." Fiona's face was wary. "The auld laird might not see this in the same light as ye do. What with the Campbell himself, Lord of the Isles, coming in less than a fortnight. Ye ken all the clans be keeping to their own, not wanting to kindle the Campbell's bad side."

"Och! As if I care one wee bit for the almighty Campbell's good or bad side," Grace said with more braggartry than sense. "We've not seen any succor from himself, the great and powerful Campbell. Kindle the Campbell's bad side . . . I'd like to light a bonfire under it."

Her jaw took on a stubborn set and she railed on. "The McNishes wouldn't be starving and living on a wee barren isle in the middle of Loch Earn if the McNabs hadn't driven us from our lands and stolen everything we once had. And what has the almighty Campbell done? Naught!" She made a sound of disgust. "No doubt he's too busy belly-crawling to the Sassenach king or chasing after the wild MacGregors to have a care for the wee troubled clans." She fiddled with a hole in her plaid and said quietly, "The clan won't make it through another winter with no food, no cattle, naught but the thin, puny clothes on our backs."

She tugged at the worn plaid and freed it from beneath the fallen man. She stood proudly, as proudly as one who was four-foot-eleven could. What Grace McNish lacked in stature she made up for in unflailing tenaciousness, vivid imagination, and, as her grandfather had been prone to say, "more pigheaded obstinence than a Sassenach has lies."

She straightened the folds of her tartan so they hid the tattered holes and spots of unraveled cloth, then adjusted her old cracked belt with a sharp tug that was bound to soon sever the weak, worn leather. "My grandfather's first duty is to the clan. He will relish the prize of a McNab."

Fiona searched her face. "Do ye think a prize might make him forget about the fire?"

Grace nodded, then frowned slightly.

Fiona shook her head dismally. " 'Twas yer worst blunder yet." She shuddered. "I can still smell the smoke and see the auld laird's red face."

" 'Twas only a wee error in judgment."

"Even I wouldna give Seamus flaming arrows for his auld crossbow."

Grace placed her hands on her hips. "We have to protect the clan from the vile McNabs! My grandfather can do little with but one leg."

"He can still shout," Fiona said. "And shout he did. Even I heard him."

"The McNabs didn't cut out his tongue. But they took his leg, killed his sons and his pride. We're the only hope the clan has." Grace paused. "Besides I told Seamus to aim toward the loch."

"He was aiming for the loch."

"And the way to learn something is through practice. The flaming arrows . . ." She shrugged. "Seemed a fine idea at the time."

"Yer ideas usually do . . . at first. Somehow." Fiona sighed. "But that one ended like most."

No excuse readily popped into her head, so Grace changed the subject. "I cannot undo the damage, but we can feed the clan with the McNabs' Michaelmas provisions. 'Tis the chance we've been waiting for. I'll not let it pass."

"I dinna ken if that be such a fine idea." Fiona looked as if the sky were about to fall. On her.

Grace took a moment to stare at her captive, then she gauged Fiona's worried face to see how much justification she'd need to win her over. "Providence saw fit to have me fall at the exact moment he was riding past. Surely you . . ." She paused, placing a hand over her heart innocently as her face took on a fine look of blasphemous horror. "You wouldn't have me question the Lord's wise and perfect hand?"

Fiona didn't reply. She just looked heavenward as if she expected to see a sudden bolt of lightning. Eyes wide, she turned back to look at the fallen man and the broken tree branch, then turned toward Grace.

At that exact moment a clap of thunder echoed from the clouds around Ben Lawers. Grace grinned, thankful for her fine (if accidental) sense of timing.

Fiona shook her head vigorously.

"I thought not," Grace said, anxious to get on with her plan. She looked down at the unconscious man and felt Fiona take a step closer, too.

"Doesna look much like a McNab." Fiona scanned his features thoughtfully. "Look there! He has a chin!"

"Probably from some poor ancestor with strong blood who was forced to marry a McNab."

"Which one do ye think he be?"

Grace raised her own chin—a sign her pride was showing. "Old Donnell has twelve sons. How should I know which one he is?" She glared down at him. "They're all sniveling, murdering cowards who maim auld men and steal from women and children." Eyes glittering fiercely, she leaned closer to Fiona. "The *uruisg* was once a cruel McNab," she said grimly.

"The hairy wicked beast that hides under waterfalls?" Fiona asked, her voice uneasy.

"Aye." Grace stepped closer. "His deeds were so evil, himself so mean, a faerie of the moor mist changed him into the vile beast he should be." Her speech slowed for a tad of drama. " 'Tis said no bogey . . . no ogre . . . no evil warlock is as horrible as a McNab." She moved a step closer. "Every wee bairn in the Highlands knows of the gruesome McNabs, knows that hell has two McNabs astride wild, mad, frothing kelpies which guard the fiery gates, and that the devil himself looks exactly like the Laird McNab!"

Fiona's eyes grew wide as oatcakes. "The tales are true?"

Grace nodded, her face fierce and her chin jutting out. "They cut out their captives' livers and throw them to the wolves!" She waved her arm around, mimicking the dastardly deed she so vividly described.

Fiona paled.

Grace hunched her shoulders and her voice took on a sinister tone. "They skin their prisoners alive . . ."

Fiona stepped back as Grace really got into the thick of her story.

". . . *scalp* their heads bald." Grace wiggled her fingers near Fiona's red hair.

Fiona's eyes seemed to double in size and she covered her mouth with her hands.

"And the women," Grace went on, "ahhh the women . . ." She paused for the right amount of effect, then whispered dramatically into her friend's left ear, " 'Tis said they strip them naked and have their way with them."

"No!" Fiona gasped.

"Aye," Grace said with a smug nod. "They do."

There was a long pause before Fiona asked, "What does that mean?"

Caught in the thoughtful depths of creating her next grim detail, Grace looked up, her expression puzzled. "What do you mean, what does that mean?"

"Having their way with them."

Grace paused for a doubtful second then quickly caught herself and planted her hands on her hips. "Well, if you don't know, I'm surely not going to tell you."

"Do ye ken?"

"Of course I know," Grace said, chin in the air. "I am

the laird's granddaughter. I have to know these things."

"Then tell me."

"You're not the laird's granddaughter."

"I'm her friend."

Grace sighed. "And as your friend I'm going to spare you the gory and gruesome details. Now stop pestering me and help me tie this devil up."

"How do ye do that?" Fiona asked with a frown.

"Do what?"

"Manage to twist yer argument until ye make sense?"

" 'Tis a gift from God," Grace answered as she knelt beside the downed man and struggled to push him onto his side. He had to weigh close to fifteen stone. Must be that hard and heavy McNab head, she thought.

After a few hard shoves and grunts, she managed to wedge her knees beneath him and hold him a few inches off the damp ground. Gritting her teeth with Scots determination, she said, "Hand me the rope."

Fiona stood there for a moment, then turned this way and that, searching the area. "Where is the rope?"

Grace dropped the man's shoulder, scooting back so he thumped back flat to the ground. She eyed him quickly, looking for signs of consciousness. His breathing hadn't changed, so she whipped around, her face unbelieving. "What do you mean, where's the rope?"

"Don't ye have it?"

"No, I thought you had it."

Fiona shrugged. "I don't have it."

"I told you to get it."

"When?"

"Before we left. I distinctly remember telling you to take the rope from the stables."

Fiona winced and chewed her lip, then slowly, sheepishly, put her hand into the sporran that hung from her belt. A second later she opened her hand to show a brown waxy ball the size of a walnut.

"What is that?"

"The soap from the table."

Grace groaned. This happened occasionally. Sometimes

she would be in such a hurry to enact one of her plots that she would forget to speak to Fiona's good ear. She sighed the sigh of the long-suffering, then covered up her own mistake by taking charge as usual. "We'll have to make do. Stand over him, and if he so much as moves, clobber him on the head with that broken branch."

"Me?" Squeaked Fiona, eyeing the thick and knotted branch, the size of the man's head.

"Aye."

"What if I kill him?"

"He's a McNab. You probably couldn't hit him that hard."

Fiona balked, staring at the man as if he were the devil.

"Remember, the Lord in His infinite wisdom wouldn't have broken the branch if He didn't want us to use it," Grace justified.

"I thought *you* broke the branch."

"'Twas God's plan. I just happened to be part of it. Now," she said thoughtfully, tapping a finger against her pursed lips. "What can we use for a rope?"

Eyes wary, Fiona stood over the man, the branch in her shaking hands. Grace scanned her friend, then herself, speculatively eyeing their belts. Then she turned to the devil McNab. Now why should their plaids be left to billow in the icy highland air? Let the cruel McNab freeze.

Grace knelt beside him and eyed his belt. 'Twas fine wide leather, ornately tooled, and buckled with a huge piece of heavy sparkling silver. She could no longer stomach such extravagance. The past few years had changed her views on ornamental finery. What little was left them by the McNabs had been sold or bartered for food.

The haunting cries of hungry children were too real to her, too frequent a sound in the Clan McNish nowadays. The cost of that one precious buckle would feed those poor wee bairns for a year. She made a mental note to purloin the buckle as soon as she could find some rope to replace the belt.

A McNab. She looked at the man, knowing he represented everything cruel in her world, everything stolen from them.

She made quick work at the buckle, and a minute later, when her own stomach growled loudly, she scowled down at her enemy for a flicker of a second, then braced her knees, grasped the belt with two tight hands, and pulled the belt flap back just a tad too hard (with all her might).

The man grunted, loudly.

"Grace McNish!" Fiona screeched, the branch quivering in her hands "Have yer wits gone walking to Ross?" she whispered loudly. "Are ye trying to wake him?"

"I know, I know. I couldn't help myself," she muttered, doing her best to ignore her gnawing hunger. She spoke louder. "Now stand closer while I try to pull this belt out from under him. Remember, if he so much as opens an eye, clobber him."

CHAPTER
2

He'd like to clobber her.

Colin Campbell, Earl of Argyll, descendant of the King of the Scots, and as Lord of the Isles, the second most powerful man in all of Scotland, lay surprisingly still as the little shrew tried to belt his hands together. Eyes kept closed and breathing deceptively even—except for the moment she had near halved him when she wrenched his belt a good ten notches tighter—he played the captive, and waited.

Comfortable in the knowledge that time was on his side, he spent the minutes with his eyes closed imagining Grace McNish and her shrewish face—skin ruddy as an oakcake, a crooked hook of a nose, a wart or two, straggly brown hair, and small sneaky eyes, black to match her humor. Ugly.

"There," she said, and he heard her brush her hands together with a couple of claps before she stood and shouted, "Put the branch down, Fiona, and help me turn the oaf."

Colin's jaw tightened. *Uglier than sin*.

Two pairs of small hands gripped him; one pair lit tentatively onto his left shoulder and one pair with pinching little fingers on his left hip. He had no doubt who was who. He thought of those little fingers digging into his hip and pictured her all sharp-boned, pock-skinned, and dragon-tempered, yet a scrawny dragon since, when she was on his chest, he judged her weight to be no more than six stone. Six stone of vinegar.

With a few grunts and gasps, they rolled him onto his back, where he rocked slightly atop his belt-bound hands. He listened for their next move and contemplated when to make his.

"Grace!" came a shout from behind them. The sound of running feet thrashed from the nearby bracken. "Grace! Ohhhhh, no . . ."

There was a loud thud. The runner fell scant inches from Colin. Twigs, dirt, and damp leaves splattered the side of his face. He didn't flinch, even when the swearing lad scrambled to his feet in another shower of muck and gasped, "They're coming! The McNab supply wagons! They're almost here! And sure as St. Columba's faith, there's no guard!"

"I've captured their guard, Duncan," the shrew said arrogantly, placing a small bare foot atop his belly and pressing too hard.

Colin gritted his teeth and held his breath—something that wasn't easy with a jabbing little foot digging in one's gut. He could feel their stares, then the foot left him.

"Don't let's stand here and gawk at him. Where are the others?"

So there were more of them, Colin thought, waiting to see if they mentioned how many.

"Still in their hiding places," Duncan answered.

"Quickly, then! Drag this stupid oaf over in the bushes and hide him well. Then get back into your positions." She paused. "No, no, not those bushes. The really *big* bushes over there."

Covertly Colin tried to work his wrists free. He needed them free so he could wring her scrawny neck.

"What about his feet?" Duncan asked.

Colin froze. There was pensive silence.

"Tie his shoes together," the shrew ordered. "In knots."

Colin mentally swore, seeing his chance to run disappear. A moment later, with his cloak and beltless plaid dragging and bunching, they hauled him through the sharp bracken and into a bed of bushes. He imagined, savored, relished the vivid mental images of his revenge.

He lay there, hearing their muted voices, the shrew shushing the others and sounds of them shimmying up the nearby trees. Then there was naught but nature's silence. The same deceptive silence he'd blindly ridden into like a damned green fool. On a damned green and foolish horse, he thought, his pride stung.

His stallion had turned lame in the same fall that had ruined his own cloak and plaid and forced him to borrow these at the last inn. If he been astride Torquay, instead of some hired skittish nag, he wouldn't be lying in the thicket trussed up like a Michaelmas goose. Not that he was overly concerned. His men were but an hour's ride behind him, and the belt that bound his hands was beginning to give way.

'Twouldn't be long . . . He thought of the shrew. Soon she'd care much about his good and bad side. His smile held no humor.

The call of voices and the creak of wagons sounded from the road. He turned over, using their noise to camouflage any sound his motion might have made. He opened his eyes for the first time.

Three burgeoning provision wagons lumbered up the grade, their drivers appearing to be naught but servants, old men who tossed a wineskin between them, drinking and laughing and jesting as they drove right into a trap.

The lead wagon edged past. Colin glanced up at the nearest tree. Sunlight caught the glint of metal—a dirk pulled. A battle cry screamed out like the howl of a sick hellhound. The dirk moved. The branches shifted. A flash of wild black hair, brown plaid, and wiggling bare legs flew through the air.

Past the driver . . .

Past the wagon . . .

Past anything remotely near her target.

Mud splattering, she landed with all the grace of a tangled puppet. He choked back a bark of laughter. Covered in brown mud, she sprawled there no more than a blink, then scampered up, launching herself with better aim at the sotted driver.

"A McNish!" she cried, managing somehow to get her dirk poised near the stunned man's throat.

"A McNish!" came the answering battle cries of her band, then came a thud, a shout of pain, and a curse.

"Duncan?" she called out.

There was a grunt and the sound of a brief scuffle, then an out-of-breath "Aye?"

"Is all well?"

"Aye." He paused for a long telling moment. "I missed."

So did she, Colin thought, chuckling to himself.

Without warning a screechlike bellow rent the air. Head ringing, he turned toward the racket.

Standing in the road beside the first wagon was a red-haired lass, the reed of a bagpipe between her lips and her cheeks puffed and red as plump autumn apples. She blew the cursed thing again and the blare rang clear through his teeth. Atop the nearest wagon, the muddy shrew hunched her shoulders and shivered in reaction while the wagon driver, who looked more stunned than drunk, pounded the heel of his hand against an ear.

The lass readied to blow again, the horror of which prospect was enough to make Colin bolt from the bushes and forget his game of cat and mouse for the sake of his hearing.

Luckily the muddy shrew reached out with her free hand and grabbed a cord on the drone pipe, then shouted, "Fiona!"

The lass looked up.

"Enough pipes!"

"Could ye hear it?" the lass asked with a frown.

Colin shook his head. The Turks could have heard it.

"Aye," the shrew answered. "But next time sling the pipes from your left side, next to your good ear."

Good ear? A deaf piper, Colin thought with a sure nod. Now, why didn't that surprise him?

The shrew gave the next wagon a pointed look. His gaze followed hers. A brown-haired lad of about sixteen held a claymore on the driver. "I had thought those pipes were . . . lost," she commented too casually.

The lad blanched, then quickly turned away, promptly slipping on one of the goose cages, which in turn set the other geese to honking louder than the Battle of Bannockburn.

Duncan, he thought with a sense of surety, remembering the spray of mud as he watched the clumsy lad try to shush the geese.

" 'Twas fine luck." Fiona clung to the pipes. "Just this morn, when ye were still in bed, I found 'em in an auld arms chest with a big lock, beneath a blanket, under a pile of wood, behind an auld table, way o'er in a corner of the stable loft, in back of that huge haystack." Fiona paused for breath then added in a puzzled tone, "I dinna ken how they got there."

The shrew turned her head slightly and mumbled something that sounded like, "I don't ken how you found them." She turned back and watched the lass fiddle with her pipes. "Put the pipes down now and go guard the road," the shrew said, then called out, "Iain! Seamus! Is all well?"

"Aye!" came the reply.

Colin glanced toward the third wagon for the first time. Two lads of about twelve, one with an old pike and one with a rusty crossbow, aimed their weapons at the weaving driver. Colin judged the pike to be close to a century old and so bent with age it looked as if one good wallop would break the thing in two. He doubted the crossbow had even been shot in that same length of time, but it didn't matter since the lad had the arrow cocked backward.

He managed, at that precise moment, to slip his hands from the belt, stared at them for a moment, then shaking his head, he looked back to the scene on the road. Never had he seen a more inept band of reivers. Had the drivers been anything else but drunken old men, this band would be the captives—if they were very lucky and weren't dead instead.

As poor as their skills was their clothing. Every plaid was ragged, holed, or torn. The lads' shirt sleeves were too short, their seams frayed or split, and the rich saffron color dulled by time and wear. There wasn't a shoe among them.

He glanced back to the shrew, who still had her dirk on the servant. All he could discern was a muddy mask for a face and a waist-long tangle of equally muddied black hair.

"Hold still, you devil's lackey, or I'll cut out your drunken liver and feed it to the wolves!"

And that mouth, he thought. Anyone could recognize that mouth. He shifted position and began to untie the wad of knots on his shoes, but found his gaze kept returning to the absurd scene before him.

"You!" She pointed the dirk at the servant's neck. "Get down!"

The man wobbled drunkenly, then hiccuped before he climbed down. The other drivers joined him, prodded along by her ragtag thieves. The lad with the pike kept it near the throats of the men while the other lad fiddled with the crossbow and arrow, stopping every so often to scratch his head and frown in frustration. Two of the geese in the second wagon had Duncan's shirt sleeve gripped in their bills, and every time he'd tried to pull it loose, a third and fourth goose would stretch their long necks out and nip him.

"The Mc—hic—Nab isna—hic—going to like this," one of the servants warned.

The shrew laughed. "And I care what the McNab likes!" She slid down from the wagon seat, landing none too gracefully, but she spun around so fast, mud flew from her face and whipped from her hair.

Dirk still drawn, she stalked the servants. They stepped back, fumbling. She grinned, surprisingly straight white teeth showing through the crust of brown mud. "Tell him for me, auld man, that the Clan McNish sends their gratitude for the plump larder." She gestured toward the wagons. " 'Twill be a bonny fine Michaelmas on the Isle of Nish."

Her cohorts laughed. As if she were spurred on by the laughter, her shoulders went straight and her chin went up.

"But 'twill be a meager repayment for all that sniveling cur McNab has stolen from our poor wee bairns!"

She waved the dirk beneath their noses. "And be sure to give him this message. Tell him we have one of his oafish sons, the big one that doesn't have the sense needed to control a poor bridled horse."

Colin took a slow, long, deep breath.

"Tell him," she continued, "he'll see the cattle-handed lug in hell if a McNab sets one foot on what's left of McNish soil!"

The servant shook his head as if he were trying to comprehend, then he looked to the other two, who shrugged. "I dinna ken. No Mc—"

"Go!" Her chin jutted out and she fanned the dirk in their faces. "If you favor your liver, get your scrawny legs moving!"

"But—"

An arrow shot past her nose with a deadly whine.

She gasped.

Colin ducked.

The arrow thrummed into the tree next to him. He stared up at it for a stunned moment, then turned back toward the glen. The servants stood gaping at the arrow that had just passed inches from them. Their faces paled. A second later they were running down the road as if chased by the devil himself.

"Seamus . . ." The shrew turned slowly, very slowly.

The crossbow lay in the empty spot where the lad had been.

She glanced at the other lad. He turned quickly around, dropping the pike. She glared at him. "Iain, where's Seamus?"

He shrugged, a gesture of innocence, but his face reeked of guilt. She took a threatening step toward him. He hooked his thumbs into his belt and began to whistle, rocking on his bare heels and staring at the sky.

With a cool stare she stepped past him, scanning the area. "Seamus . . ."

A bush near the road quaked like an aspen.

She moved closer.

The bush stilled.

"Seamus!"

The bush rattled.

She took two more steps.

" 'Twas only a wee slip of trigger!" came a voice from the quivering bush.

"Come out, Seamus."

"I hit the tree."

"Come out, Seamus."

"Be ye vexed, Grace?" the bush asked.

"Aye." She spun around. "And Iain! Stop whistling!"

The whistling stopped abruptly.

She turned back toward the bush. "Now, Seamus."

The bush was silent and still.

"Seamus!" she shrieked.

His head popped up from the bush like a wide-eyed weasel.

"Grace! Grace!" Fiona came running up, something clutched in her hands. She skidded to a stop in front of the shrew and held out her hands. "Here."

Frowning, the shrew asked, "What's that?"

"The toad," Fiona answered proudly.

"What toad?"

"Ye ordered me to hoard the toad." She lifted it up. "This be it. Although why ye want to hoard toads I'll ne'er ken."

"I said . . . guard the road!"

"Huh?"

Grace leaned toward the girl's other ear and yelled, "I said guard the road!"

"Oh." Fiona stared at the toad for a long moment, then dropped it and wiped her hands on her plaid. She gave a relieved sigh. "I was afeared ye were turning to witchcraft."

Laughing to himself, Colin watched another one of their trout-brained conversations begin. While they argued, he again worked at the tight knots in his shoelaces. 'Twas the only thing they'd done well.

He glanced up again and saw the shrew had moved to a

water barrel, where she stood, toweling the mud from her face and hair. She tossed the cloth away and turned back around.

Colin stopped laughing. He stopped moving. He stopped breathing. For the mere glimpse of a face like that a man would bargain with the devil to stop living.

He'd been wrong. So wrong. Her skin wasn't pocked and ruddy. 'Twas the color of highland snow, the kind of skin that was soft enough to make a man crave its touch, crave its taste, the feel of it against his own.

Her features were proof of God's perfection—a heart-shaped face, fine high cheekbones with a barest hint of a blush, a full pink mouth that turned his thoughts carnal, and eyes that slanted slightly upward, misty, exotic, eyes that fired the lust in a man, because a sensual man knew that a woman's eyes turned slanted and misty when she had been loved long and well.

With that last thought he sat back, took a deep breath, and ceased working the knots. He just stared at her, unable for a while to will himself to look away. She was the most exquisitely perfect young woman he'd ever seen.

"Duncan! Go over to those bushes and check on the oaf!"

Except for her mouth.

Colin reached beneath his cloak and unfastened the Campbell brooch hidden beneath his borrowed plaid, then quickly retrieved the belt and slipped and twisted his hands so they appeared as if they were tightly bound, then he lay down as before—eyes closed, listening, the brooch clutched in his fist.

"He's still out!" Duncan shouted.

The sound of her footsteps rustled in the bracken. She stopped close by, but said nothing, so the silence dragged on. He waited.

"We'll lug him to the wagon," she said finally, and called the other lads.

Soon he felt four pairs of hands lift him; one set of fingers dug into his shoulder muscles with familiar fury. He let every muscle in his body relax. At six-foot-three and thirteen stone that was plenty of dead weight.

A grunt, a few groans, and a muttered she-curse on the black soul of the McNab who'd sired the heavy lummox, and they hauled him toward the wagon. They brushed past the bushes that lined the road and he covertly dropped his brooch, resisting the urge to smile with satisfaction when his captors continued on. They fumbled and staggered, trying to get him into the wagon. At this rate his men could be here before they had him loaded.

Short of rendering him deaf with a blast from those bagpipes, he knew he had little to fear from this group. Then his mind flashed with the image of the misshot arrow in the tree trunk. He amended that thought.

But before he could do much more thinking, the shrew had climbed into the wagon and conveniently settled his head in her lap, then tugged on his shoulders while the lads tried to heave him up. She smelled of lusty wet highland earth and female musk. The side of his face met the softness of a woman's full breast and he thought of that face, breathed that earthy scent. Perhaps he didn't want his men to come too soon.

"He's a brawny one, he is," one of the lads said when they finally managed to get him inside.

" 'Tis all that stolen mutton and beef," the shrew said, still cradling his head.

He moaned and turned so his mouth rested against the tip of that breast. Then he groaned loudly against it, trying not to laugh when she gasped and scooted away. 'Twas quiet for a long moment. He could feel her face just inches from his, searching. He could feel the warmth of her breath when she finally breathed. Then she moved away.

"Don't just stand around! Iain and Seamus, you take the last wagon. Fiona!" The shrew raised her voice. "You'll ride up here and guard the oaf." She paused, then asked, "Did you hear me?"

"Aye. Guard the loaf. Where is the bread?"

"The oaf!"

"Oh . . . him."

"Aye. But first go fetch that branch again. Duncan, you

take the second wagon." Grace paused, then whispered, "Is Fiona gone?"

"Aye," Duncan replied. "She's over by that tree."

"Good. First chance you have"—she took a quick look in Fiona's direction—"hide the pipes again."

Only a few minutes passed and the wagons lumbered down the road, wheels rattling, axles creaking, a band of ragged reivers bickering over their success; and in the back of the lead wagon, amid sacks of oat flour and barrels of ale, lay the Lord of the Isles, a wee ghost of a smile on his lips.

Colin Campbell hadn't laughed this much in years.

Not too long afterward a group of men entered the clearing. One knelt on the ground, carefully examining the footprints and the wheel ruts. Another walked the circumference, eyeing the broken bracken, tree branches, and bushes. The others stood silently. Little more than two minutes later they left the clearing in swift pursuit.

CHAPTER
3

Her stomach growled again. Grace looked down at her prized prisoner, a McNab, one of the very people who had caused those she loved so much pain. She took a deep breath and dumped a bucket of water on him.

He didn't sit up coughing as she'd hoped. He didn't even flinch. He just slowly opened his eyes, as if he had all day, as if he were dry as summer air instead of dripping icy water from a nearby burn. He stared straight at her through intense eyes that were not a cold blue as she expected, but an odd shade of yellow gold—the eyes of a highland wildcat, eyes that weren't blinded by the night, but sharper, keener eyes that seemed to know her . . . too well.

'Twas the most unsettling look she'd ever received. For a brief instant she forgot he was a McNab. She forgot to breathe. She forgot to move.

But she would never forget that look. Some weak part of her wanted to turn away, but she couldn't. He challenged her without a word, with only a look, a battle fought as surely as if their gazes were weapons, one trying to overpower the other. First.

They were enemies. Challengers. And the challenge held the boldness of a dare, and something else more primal. He was the captive, yet she felt hunted. For the first time in her eighteen years Grace McNish didn't feel the compulsion to go after something she faced, nipping at its heels with all the tenacity of an angry goose. Instead she wanted to turn on her own heels and run away. The feeling didn't set well with her, or with her pride.

Unconsciously her hands tightened into fists. Her lower teeth worried her upper lip for a brief second, then she stopped, realizing her nervousness was showing. Her chin came up, yet she didn't blink. She refused to. She couldn't guess his thoughts, but had the uncanny feeling that he knew hers better than she did.

"Grace! Come here!"

Startled, she blinked, then exhaled, reluctantly accepting that she'd been the first to break. She called out that she'd be there soon and looked back at him. He smiled mockingly—the victor, and they both knew it.

Her fingers tightened around the handle. She stared at the wooden bucket, then at his wooden head.

She was not a good loser. A fighter by instinct, she felt so strong an urge to battle this man that she almost gave in to it. But she was a survivor by necessity, something painfully taught her by the McNabs. His clan.

She tightened her jaw in an effort to hold her temper. He watched her as if he had read her every thought, then proved he had by glancing at the bucket she held with a look that said, Go ahead and do it. Immediately she tossed the bucket on the dank ground and realized too late that she'd played into his hands.

He smiled, slowly, arrogantly.

She drew her dirk and smiled slowly, arrogantly.

He didn't react. But she did. She could feel the sweat bead beneath her plaid. His lack of response taunted her and she felt the need to give back the same.

She moved the dirk toward him, waiting for his reaction. She got none. Yet her own traitorous heart began to pound in her ears.

Stubbornness made her move the dirk to hover above his neck. He never took his gaze from hers. A challenge met. Her smile faded.

Using all her willpower to keep her hand from shaking,

she moved the dirk down, pausing above his heart. His look was unchanged. She battled to keep her expression unreadable as she moved the dirk to his belly.

Still he watched, only her face. Her bluff wasn't working. She took a deep slow breath and moved the dirk lower, pausing above his male pride. She waited. And she waited, heart thrumming, her body stiff and the challenge between them piquing her until every hair on her body felt alive and her skin was naught but gooseflesh.

Time stopped. But the tension grew rapidly until the air was as taut and silent as a war ground before the battle charge.

"Grace!" came the impatient call again.

Damn his eyes for never flinching. She raised the dirk high.

Damn her for giving in. She sliced it downward and through the knotted shoelaces, then turned quickly away so she could take a badly needed breath.

After struggling to find her voice, she said, "Get down." She sheathed her dirk, placed a hand on the splintery gray rim of the wooden wagon bed, and leaped to the ground, anxious to flee that odd feeling over which she had no control.

She never saw the nail.

Two formidable steps and the sound of rending fabric ripped through the air. She turned. Her plaid had a hole the size of the oaf's grinning blond head. Glaring, she jerked the brown fabric from the nail, spun on a heel, and marched toward the others, her head high.

"McNish!"

She halted at the first sound of his deep voice. 'Twas the timbre of thunder in Cairngorms. It took a moment to realize that God was not calling her. She took a deep and settling breath, but did not turn around.

" 'Tis no bonnier and rosy a view in all of Scotland!"

She turned her head around to see what he was braying about. He stared at her back, grinning. She tried to follow his gaze, but couldn't see over her shoulder. With a sinking feeling of pure dread, she reached a hand around, over the

plaid . . . over her hip . . . over the tail of her shirt . . . and
lower.

She touched bare skin. The hole was right over her
rump. To her horror she felt the damning heat of a blush.
She jerked the folds of her plaid around to cover herself,
adjusting them in her belt. She stuck her chin high and
stormed off, calling vivid and vile curses down upon the
obnoxious and hardheaded McNab.

His head wasn't the only thing that was hard.

Colin's grin faded as he watched her stomp off. He
leaned against his bent knees that were still stiff from lying
prone for so long in the wagon. An interesting last few
minutes, he thought, still feeling the remnants of battle—not
a physical battle—but instead an intense mental challenge,
the kind of absorbing tactical war carried out in the world
of politics, the games he'd played with clan chieftains,
ambassadors, and kings, but never with a woman.

An armed woman. He took a deep breath. That armed
woman—a catapulting banshee whose uncontrolled fervor
for revenge could easily have gelded him, more than likely
by accident. He took a deep settling breath. He must be
daft.

Then he thought of her face and realized he was not daft,
just randy. He took a few minutes to get himself under
control, trying not to think about his reaction to the wee
shrew. He jumped down, then glanced over his shoulder at
her. She stood by the other wagons talking to Duncan while
Fiona burrowed through the supplies like a ferret scenting
a hare.

"Have ye seen my pipes?" Fiona shouted, rummaging
beneath a willow goose cage.

The shrew shook her head, gave Duncan a conspiratorial
smile, then, as if she'd felt Colin's stare, turned toward
him.

Her smile faded. For some reason he cared not to analyze,
that annoyed him. Her chin went up a notch, then her hand
slid to the handle of her dirk. Her eyes flared, challenging.

One for her.

He leaned casually against the side of the wagon, crossing his ankles in nonchalance before intentionally staring right at her butt.

One for him.

Quickly she shifted positions, slowly moving and nodding as the others talked until she now stood facing him.

One for her.

He slowly let his gaze roam up from her bare feet, stopping every so often to smile knowingly and linger on a certain intimate part of her anatomy before traveling on. By the time his gaze reached that incredible face, it was bright red. Glaring, she turned away.

One for him.

Colin laughed, using his loosely bound hands to shove away from the wagon. He twisted his wrist so the belt became tighter. 'Twouldn't do for his bonds to fall off in front of them. He shook his head for what must have been the tenth time. Should he have wanted to escape, he'd have been halfway to Crieff by now. He took a step.

"Don't move!" warned a wee and shaky voice.

He turned and froze.

Seamus stood nearby, pointing the quivering but perfectly loaded crossbow at him.

One for Seamus.

"Don't move!" the lad repeated with more bravado but no less shaking.

Colin didn't intend to move. He liked living. The sound of that misfired arrow was still potent enough a memory that he heartily hoped Seamus didn't move, hoped he didn't breathe, and in fact he wished the lad's finger was anywhere except on the damned crossbow trigger.

"Och!" cried Fiona. "Here they be!"

Screeching pipes bellowed through the small glen.

Colin hit the dirt.

An arrow whizzed overhead. It had long disappeared into the thick green forest before he expelled a relieved breath.

A pair of familiar little feminine feet stopped in front of him. He looked up, past her bare legs, past the ragged plaid, past the cracked belt where she rested her small fists, to that defiant face.

"You move quickly, McNab, for someone who cannot even control a poor wee horse."

"Not so quickly that I cannot see a nail." He paused. "Or feel a draft."

Her eyes narrowed and her face flushed a familiar rosy color that made him grin.

"I'll not banter with a sniveling devil who steals from poor women and wee bairns!"

Colin gave the wagons a pointed look. "And the Clan McNab has no women and bairns?"

"Don't spend your breath or tax your sly mind trying to make me feel guilty, McNab! Your clan's not starving!" Her eyes flared with a quick flame of anger. "You're no living on a rocky, barren isle in the middle of an icy loch, where there's little game and naught grows but hunger and the tears of your clan."

Her looked turned distant, and a little lost. She stared past him. "Where you watch a powerful, braw man become old because his sons were murdered, his body maimed, and his clan driven away in shame."

She was silent for a moment, then she took a deep breath and turned back, suddenly appearing very aware of him lying there, listening. She gave him a look so full of scorn that he almost forgot that he was not a "vile McNab." "Your clan's living off McNish mutton and beef, off vegetables grown on fertile land that once belonged to the McNish. Off plump geese, off priceless oranges and honeyed figs."

Whipping around, she grabbed a fat brown sack from the wagon, then bent over him, her face but a foot away, her jaw jutting out, and her body shaking in anger. "Starving people would crawl on their swollen bellies up the craggy granite face of Ben Lawers for the wee crumbs of a month-old bannock."

She dropped the bag in front of his face with a heavy plop. "Starving people don't dine on plump bags of honeyed figs!"

Silently he watched her walk away, her head high, her

shoulders and back as straight as a Scotch pine. She had sheer determination in every movement of her body, this shrew with a dagger-sharp tongue, Black Scots temper, and the face of an angel.

But for all the fascination sparked by that beauty, and the sure irritation of her blistery mouth, 'twas the passion of her ideals that had him thinking, and the vivid images brought to mind by her angry words that made him so pensive.

Grace McNish had a clear and true love of her clan, a loyalty that was fast fading among many Scots, what with England's slow pervasion of Scotland. The constant warring between the clans rendered them an easier land to conquer, subversively, with devious plots and power-hungry men's schemes to control the throne. Loyalty was something Colin understood, and respected.

He watched her for a moment longer, thoughtful, and a little confused himself. He sat up, thinking to end this deceptive game, but Iain approached him. The lad waved a heavy claymore near Colin's nose. "Ye're to move ov'r there." He nodded toward a large fir at the edge of the small clearing. "Where I can keep a better eye on ye."

Colin stood, towering over the lad whose wrists were too thin and frail to support even one strike of the heavy weapon. "Where's your pike?"

Iain glanced at the claymore with silent doubt, then looked at Colin and quietly nodded toward the last wagon. Duncan stood with Seamus, the crossbow slung on Duncan's arm while he appeared to explain to the younger lad how to hold and maneuver the long pike.

"Seamus had a wee bit of trouble with the crossbow," Iain said.

'Twas the most blatant example of understatement Colin had ever heard. His mind flashed with the sound of Duncan tripping, his losing battle with the pestering geese, and the image of his struggle to hold the claymore on the driver and at the same time stand on the wagon. He watched the bumbling lad play weapons tutor to Seamus, then he thought of Duncan with the crossbow and immediately came to a decision.

Colin would keep ducking.

This band of reivers was a sad lot, but as inept and inexperienced as they were, they had persistence, and they had heart. Smiling to himself, he glanced at Iain. The claymore was not easy for a brawny man to wield, much less a thin lad. Iain's face wore an expression of struggling pain.

Taking pity on him, Colin strolled over to the tree and could hear the lad trudging in his wake. He turned around to say something and Iain jumped back, startled, his fear showing and the claymore slipping to the ground with a dull thud.

The lad scrambled to pick up the weapon and Colin bit back a smile, pointed at the tree, and asked, "You want me here?"

Iain straightened and nodded, keeping his wary eyes on Colin, who sat on a pile of crisp fallen needles at the base of the pine. Then, apparently satisfied his prisoner wouldn't escape, Iain moved a distance away, slapped the claymore on one narrow shoulder with a grunt, and began to march back and forth.

He took his guard duty seriously. His frown showed his concentration and his lips moved as he silently counted, pivoting on the tenth step, then counting all over again. Again Colin found himself smiling. He relaxed, leaning his head against the tree trunk, and he watched the lad march.

The sudden taint of danger filled the air. A shower of green pine needles drifted to the base of a nearby tree. Colin stilled, feigning ignorance while he listened. He caught the barest hint of movement high in the thick branches. He rolled his shoulders and winced as if he were feeling stiff. The motion allowed him to change the direction of his gaze without arousing suspicion.

High in the tree was the familiar glint of polished steel—the blade of a drawn broadsword.

Slowly, with little movement, he edged his hands from the twisted belt. He leaned his head back against the rough trunk, feigning sleep, and he listened.

Behind the tree, within a near distance, came the soft sound of tentative steps. A warrior's tread—quiet, stealthy, and deadly.

CHAPTER
4

"You must be getting auld, Mungo. I could hear your tramping a good twenty feet away," Colin said quietly, keeping an eye on Iain. The lad marched about twenty feet away and was concentrating on counting his steps.

There was a grunt from behind the tree. "I'd like t' see how bloody quiet ye'd be after ye've had an arrow in yer foot," came a gruff reply.

Colin was silent while he tried to quell the urge to laugh at his friend. "Been here that long, have you?"

"Aye," Mungo whispered. "Been following ye for over three hours. Until the arrow, we figured ye had naught to fear. 'Cept mayhap for yer hearing."

"The pipes," Colin muttered with certainty.

"Thought the gates o' hell hae opened and the devil himself was comin'. An' speaking o' devils, who be the wee reivers?"

"McNishes."

"Who be the archer?"

"A lad called Seamus."

Mungo grunted something dire, then said, "Damned thing came out of nowhere."

"I take you're not maimed for life."

"Nay, just feeling meaner than usual. Shall I cut ye loose

so we can go after them together? I want this Seamus all to meself."

Colin didn't answer, just found himself looking at Grace McNish.

"We're ready whene'er ye say."

The silence continued and Mungo said, "Donnell McNab is expecting ye for Michaelmas. He's complaining that it's been too long since he petitioned for support against some wee and troublesome clan."

The McNishes, Colin thought, looking at the motley group in their bare feet and ragged plaids, a bit too thin— a fact that lent credence to McNish's claim that the clan was suffering. "Aye. McNab is right. It has been long, but I'll not be rushed into choosing sides."

Mungo grunted in agreement.

Colin watched Grace rummage through the food with the others. She picked up the bag of honeyed figs and opened it, looking inside with a look so covetous that he forgot what he was thinking. She took a deep breath, squared her shoulders, and drew the bag closed, placing it back on the wagon with a quick look of longing. He wondered why she didn't eat one when she obviously wanted to so badly, then remembered her fervent sense of nobility. No doubt she was saving them for the clan.

After another speculative look, Colin said, "I want you to ride ahead to the McNab. Tell him I've been delayed. And watch him, Mungo. See what you can find out about the feud."

"An' what about ye?"

"Leave me be," Colin said. "I want to see for myself if the McNish clan is as much of a problem as McNab claims."

"Aye," Mungo agreed, then added, "MacGregor's been seen about."

"Leave a few men behind, but tell them to stay out of sight."

There was a high whistle—the call of a lark—but Colin knew the sound well. Slowly and silently his men disappeared into the forest.

He watched Iain. In the past few minutes, under the

weight of the sword, Iain's pace had slowed to that of a slug. Like the slow swing of a clock's pendulum, his steady marching lulled Colin toward sleep, his head resting against the tree trunk and his eyes closed.

'Twas the sound of determined footsteps followed by the drifting scent of food that caused him to open his eyes. She stood watching him through suspicious green eyes, a bowl clutched tightly in a hand.

"Go an' get yourself something to eat, Iain," she told the lad, then drew her dirk and turned toward Colin with a sweet smile. "I'll guard the lummox."

He thought to tell her that her tongue could use the honey from those figs she found so contemptible yet wanted so badly, but he chose to keep silent. Instead he watched the lad eagerly lope over to the wagon, the sword dragging behind him, then he glanced back and caught her staring greedily at the bowl in her hand.

She looked up and quickly covered her hungry look with the belligerent one she usually wore when she looked at him. "Here's some food."

"You're not eating?"

"No, later," she answered curtly.

"After your earlier speech, I didn't think filling my stomach was of your concern."

"Unlike you McNabs, the McNishes are humane. We don't starve our enemies." Her chin shot up and she eyed him up and down. "Not that you look like you'd starve."

"Like what you see, do you?"

Her cheeks turned red and instinctively she swung the bowl high enough to heave it at him.

"Throw it," was all he said, then watched her expressive face bare every thought she had. She wanted to throw it. He watched her fight her instincts, knowing after what he'd just said that she wouldn't, contrary female that she was. Instead she would just stand there and glare at him, until she could find some way to get away from him with her pride still intact.

He pinned her with a hard stare, trying again to unsettle her. She didn't give in this time, but she wasn't unaffected

either, because after one deep breath, she lowered the bowl
and held it out as if she expected him to take it.

He said nothing.

"Do you want it or no?" She all but shoved it into his
face.

He gave her a lazy winner's smile. "My hands are
bound."

She didn't dare untie him. As if struck stupid she stood
there for a moment, then she glanced over her shoulder and
saw that the others had gathered around a circle between
the wagons and were busy eating. She knew they were as
famished as she, having had one meal in the last three days
and that only a few berries and an old bannock soaked in
water.

A brief prayer for patience and she looked at his mocking
face, took a deep breath, and knelt in front of him, determined
to remain calm, unaffected. One didn't give in to the devil,
especially not Grace McNish.

Kneeling in front of him only brought home the fact
that even when he was sitting, he was still taller. 'Twas
as unsettling as his stare, and made her feel as if she had
to be even more defiant, even harder-edged, to prove she
could hold her own against him.

He was her enemy, her means to avenge the wrong done
her clan, yet some weak part of her had soured to the taste
of revenge. And it seemed that this devil spawn could, with
one look, make her forget he was a McNab.

"Undo my hands," he suggested too lightly for her taste.

"I'll feed you."

He laughed again, as if this were only a game with him.
"I still think you'd prefer to let a McNab starve."

"A part of me would, but 'twouldn't do to let you starve."
She jabbed the spoon into the bowl, then looked up.

He arched an eyebrow inquisitively.

A small smile of satisfaction itched at her lips. "The
ransom will be paid in weight. You lose weight. We lose
gold." She paused then, and eyed him. "I'd say your head
alone is worth a small fortune."

He chuckled and shook his head. "Och, McNish. What does it take to close your shrewish mouth?"

She held up the spoon. "Och, McNab. What would it take to open your big one?"

"Are you referring to my mouth?"

It took her a moment to understand him, then her own mouth fell open in shock and she felt the sure heat of a blush that proved she'd understood his meaning too well. His laugh assured her he had her right where he wanted her.

Before she could react, he opened his big mouth and gave her a look of feigned innocence she knew well. She had used it often enough herself. She watched his grinning face, irritated, flustered, but bound and determined not to let it show.

From the sparkle in his eyes she could see he was enjoying this immensely. She wondered if he could tell how badly she wanted to retaliate. Taking a brief second, she relished the idea of her taking the loaded spoon and flicking it right at him. She smiled at the thought of oats dripping down that long nose, of his own surprised face turning red, of the wonderful sense of satisfaction she'd feel.

"Go ahead," he said, half dare, half command.

She blinked, then stilled. Twice now he'd maneuvered her to react as he'd wanted. She spent a moment trying to figure out how he wanted her to react this time so she could do the opposite.

She gave up and lifted the spoon toward his mouth, anxious to get the deed done. He watched her expectantly. For some reason her hand had slowed under his scrutiny, as if he could control her with only his eyes.

The spoon barely touched his mouth and his lips covered it. Slowly he pulled back, his lips swiping clean the bowl of the spoon. Not once did he look away. She resisted the urge to squirm and looked back down at the bowl, shoving the spoon in and scooping up the next bite. But she made the mistake of looking up and almost dropped the spoon.

His tongue traced his lips, cleaning them, wetting them. She inhaled sharply and her own lips parted. She watched him, not knowing she was gaping, fascinated for some reason she couldn't explain. She tried to lift the spoon toward his mouth and didn't realize that she moved with it, closer, her mouth still parted in awe as she stared at his.

He moved toward her simultaneously, his eyes locked on her mouth. His gaze did odd things to her belly. She could feel his warmth and smell the scent of leather and man. Unknowingly she raised to her knees, needing to come closer . . . and closer . . . and closer. . . .

Before she could think or move or stop, his tongue stroked the line of her parted lips. His mouth moved softly atop hers, a touch she'd never before known. Then suddenly his tongue filled her mouth with an urgent male possession that made her knees weaken, so her only thought was to lean into him, breast to chest, belly to belly, thigh to thigh.

His body moved slowly, brushing her as his mouth did the same. Instinctively she moved with him. He licked her lips, making her shiver, then his body twisted sharply. He shifted so his hard thighs were suddenly outside hers.

She knew his hands were bound, but she felt suddenly captive. He edged her back until they were shielded from the others by the tree.

Before she could react, his tongue filled her mouth, and he pinned her against the tree. His hard masculine body pressed into her softness and made her weaken to everything that wasn't absolute sensation. At that very moment the girl in her died a little, and the woman in her grew, because for the first time she experienced a taste of the reason man and woman existed.

This man whose lips drifted like snowflakes over her face had taught her life's lesson. Her eyes drifted open and met his look. 'Twas as misty as hers. He gently kissed her again, their lips melded as if demanded by fate to do so, and he watched her, his own look somewhat dazed.

There was no calculation in his expression, just surprise, and something more elemental—power, possession, and passion, an intensity that excited and frightened her at the same time. And there was a small bit of doubt, as if he didn't believe she was real.

She knew the feeling well.

He knew this feeling not at all.

'Twas a violent consuming need to possess the woman, here and now. A deep and passionate urge that felt as if it bordered on obsession. And such was foreign to him. He was a man known for his quiet control, his ability to think and not react, his powerful intelligence. He took supreme pride in that reputation. Colin Campbell was not a man to be guided by his own wants and needs.

As if his sanity and pride compelled him to, he broke the kiss, but not the eye contact. Sheer will was one thing, curiosity another. Their breath panted little clouds of ragged mist. He watched her close her eyes in an effort to deny what had passed between them. But it did no good. 'Twas undeniable.

Her face said the same when she opened her eyes. They were tinged with dampness, and her cheeks had begun to blotch. He watched her fight to control those tears. Watching her valiant struggle touched some kindred part in him, pride being something a Scot could understand.

"Go on, shed your tears," he said with grudging respect. " 'Tis not shameful, McNish."

She jerked her chin higher, and took a quivering breath. "I do not cry." But she didn't look at him. Instead she scrambled away. "Do not touch me again, McNab." Now standing—a power play if he'd ever seen one—she did look down at him. "I think you are the very devil himself."

She spun on a heel and walked away, her pride high, but he knew she was not as strong as she tried to be. She had to work too hard at it. In fact he'd never seen anyone who worked so hard to be what she wasn't.

She was no warrior. She did have an exuberance about her that he wasn't sure the most favorable of attributes, and she had an impulsive need to have the last word. Both of which had already kept him vastly entertained. She also had a quick mind. 'Twas just that her judgment was a tad daft, as shown by her choice of cohorts—also a tad daft.

He watched her, intrigued. One was not sure what she would next do. He'd been on the verge of telling her who he was. Yet now, as she strode away, he thought to wait a bit longer. Leaning back against the tree trunk, he adjusted his belted hands and closed his eyes.

He had no idea how long he'd dozed. He had no idea what woke him, except that Seamus was now on guard duty. He watched the lad walk twenty times the length Iain had. Pike resting atop a narrow shoulder, he would reach the edge of the glen and turn sharply, marching back past Colin and past the wagons to the other side. Seamus turned and the pike knocked the needles from an unfortunate pine, yet on he went, marching back and forth, pivoting when he reached some imaginary boundary.

"Ten hams!" Iain shouted down from one of the wagons.

Seamus marched past.

"Aye," Grace acknowledged, then turned toward the next wagon, where Fiona blasted the pipes again.

Colin gritted his teeth. *Christ!*

"Fiona!" Grace shouted.

The lass heaved a mighty sigh and looked down, a prideful and dreamy expression on her face. "Doesna the sound stir yer heart braw wi' the pride of the highlands?"

'Twould take more than a braw heart to suffer the horror of the lassie's piping, he thought. Was enough to send a loyal Scot fleeing to England.

"Fiona." Grace glared at Duncan, obviously for not hiding the pipes well enough. "Put the pipes down and tell us what's in the wagon."

The lass brightened. "Ye're right. I'll play for ye later," she said, oblivious to the winces and quiet groans of the others. She gave her bagpipes a pat that made them groan sickly and looked in at the wagon load beneath her. "A barrel of pickled herring, three barrels of ale, fifty partridges, and apples!"

Seamus pivoted and marched past.

"Fifteen . . . geese!" Duncan gritted in frustration while he tried to jerk his sleeve from the bill of one of the birds.

"Three barrels of oat flour!" Iain called out.

"Duck!"

"How many ducks?" Grace casually asked Duncan.

"Duck!" Duncan yelled again. He jumped in the air. The pike whipped past him and he shouted, "Seamus!"

"What?" The lad halted midpivot, the long pike still positioned atop his shoulder . . . scant inches from rapping Grace in the head. "Duncan? Where be ye?" Seamus called, searching.

Unfortunately he spun back toward Duncan.

There was a loud thud.

"Oh!" said Seamus. "There ye be. Duncan, what're ye doin' lyin' on the ground while we're doin' all the work?"

Duncan's face turned from red to purple.

"Look there," Seamus added, pointing at the shattered goose cage next to Duncan. "Ye let that goose get away." He moved toward the wagon. "Gie me the crossbow and I'll shoot it!"

"No!" everyone including Colin shouted in unison. There was a telling silence as the goose calmly waddled off into the forest.

"Seamus?" Grace asked with amazing patience. "See if you can lift the claymore."

CHAPTER
5

For over two hours the cumbersome wagons rattled and bumped over the rutted road. The higher they went, the thicker the forest and the mist. Duncan drove the lead wagon, Iain the second. Seamus drove the last, alongside Fiona, while Grace sat in the wagon bed and kept a watchful eye on the McNab.

Reaching up to the heavens like the bruised arms of some enormous god were the purple crags of Ben Lawers. Grace looked toward the mountains, using them as a reference, and judged they were only about six more hours from Loch Earn, and from the crumbling auld castle atop a barren rocky isle that was the only land left to the Clan McNish.

In the four bleak and desolate years since the Battle of Boltachan, her clan had suffered under the conquering sword of the McNabs. She'd been barely fourteen at the time, and had never known what had sparked so blazing a feud. But she'd seen the results of it, seen the cruelty of the rival clan, seen the toll taken on women and children and once proud men.

There was more food than her clan had seen in years inside these three lumbering wagons. They desperately needed this food—the geese, hams, and oat flour. She wanted to see the bairns' faces when they tasted the oranges and honeyed figs.

Children who had only known hunger would find their first taste of delight in those rare fruits.

She smiled at the image.

"What are you thinking, McNish?"

That deep voice killed her thoughts, and her smile. She took a breath and turned to see her captive reclining kinglike atop some bags of oat flour. When she'd last looked at him, he'd been asleep. She wished he still was. "You're awake."

"Aye."

"I wonder how a man who is responsible for almost destroying a whole clan can sleep so peacefully. Have you no conscience?"

"My conscience is clear, McNish."

She gave a huff of disbelief.

"And you didn't answer my question."

"I've forgotten it."

"I asked you what you were thinking."

"Why, McNab?"

He shrugged. "Humor me."

She stared past him. "I was thinking about the clan." She paused. "The bairns."

He was quiet, too quiet. She turned back, suddenly aware that he had tensed.

"Do you have bairns?" His eyes pinned her, searching for something. She could feel it.

Determined to hold her own with him, she looked him straight in those gold eyes. "If I said aye, would you look to steal them on your next raid?"

"I don't harm children."

"No, you just kill their fathers."

He watched her with no expression, then said, "Such bitterness from one so young, McNish. Did you lose a father?"

"My parents died when I was a child."

His voice changed, grew softer, yet she sensed there was no softness in his thoughts. "Did you lose a husband?"

"I am eighteen." She returned his look with a hard one of her own.

"Auld enough to have been wed for two years, perhaps three."

The silence stretched between them.

"I'm not wed."

He seemed to relax, but continued to watch her speculatively. It bothered her, though she tried to hide the fact.

"Tell me what it was about the bairns that made you smile so."

" 'Twasn't killing their fathers," she said, unable to stop herself.

He looked away for a minute, took a long, deep breath, then turned back to her. "Where did you get that mouth?"

"The same place you got your cowardice. I was born with it."

His eyes suddenly glittered with a fierce hardness and he seemed to be choosing his words carefully. "Men have died for calling another a coward," he said with a calm that she sensed was deadly. "I suggest you not use such again."

Her chin jutted out in defiance, but she couldn't quite look him in the eye. "I'll say whatever I like, McNab. You're the captive, not I."

Neither spoke. But she could feel the heat of his gaze. She fiddled with the ragged edge of her plaid for the tense minutes that followed.

Finally he broke the silence. "I wonder that you cannot find the courage to look me in the eye."

Her head shot up and she met his challenging look with a stubborn one of her own.

"Nor can you answer a civil question."

"What is this, McNab? Now that you're a captive you seek to suddenly become humane? Civil? Why should you suddenly care about the widows and children of the men you killed?"

He just looked at her until she finally glanced away and asked quietly, "Why should my thoughts concern you?"

Again he said naught.

Cursed man, she thought, opening her mouth to tell him what she thought of him, but her traitorous tongue went and answered him. "There are McNish bairns that have never tasted such fare as these wagons carry for one feast. Many of the wee ones have never had rosy cheeks and bairn-plump hands."

She stared at her hands for a moment, rubbing them together, looking at the ragged nails and the calluses from hoeing the granitelike ground that would grow naught but scrawny potatoes. "I want to see their eyes when they taste for the first time the tart sweetness of an orange, the juicy meat of plump roast goose, the pure pleasure of a honeyed fig."

She looked past him, in her memory seeing the gaiety that had always been so characteristic of her people. "I want to see them smile. I want their mothers to sing to them, their fathers to toss them high in the air. But most of them no longer have fathers, and their mothers have naught to sing about."

When he didn't say anything, she went on. "I want to see my grandfather laugh. I cannot give him back his leg, that I know, but I'm the only family he has left. Perhaps I can give him back his pride. I want life to be as it was before." She grew very quiet, remembering.

"How was it before?"

"Warm and safe and happy."

So his instincts about her had been correct. Her clan was her life, and her need to right the wrong done them, whatever that be, was what compelled her to do and say the things she did.

He knew of that kind of compulsion himself, righting the wrongs done by others. He'd spent a decade doing the same. It had taken him ten years to rebuild the Campbell name and the title of the Earl of Argyll. The title was his by inheritance. The respect was his by merit. His uncle, the last earl, had spent much time and effort inciting the clans, thereby ensuring his services to a king who preferred his kinsmen to be busy feuding with each other, rather than causing trouble to him and his precious throne.

It had taken Colin years to gain that respect and, more important, to regain trust, years to change the damage done by a man who cared naught for loyalty, heritage, respect, but only for the amount of gold paid him to divide his own homeland. 'Twas not an easy thing, living down a traitor.

He felt her gaze and glanced up. She scowled and turned away, digging beneath her and coming up with a dark red apple. She took out two more and handed one each to Seamus and Fiona, then pulled out her dirk and began to peel the remaining fruit.

'Twas like watching a child with a toy. Dirk in hand, she slowly drew the blade 'round and 'round so the peeling curled downward. She chewed her lip in deep concentration, and when the entire peel was naught but one long dark bouncing spiral, she grinned and cut it off, lifting the peel toward her open mouth.

Her gaze met his and she flushed as red as that apple. She stuck her chin up as if to deny what she'd been doing, then looked away, ferociously biting into the peeling in an apparent attempt to chew away her anger.

'Twas a shame. He found her game—he paused, then laughed to himself—charming, not a word he would have thought to associate with the muddy shrew from earlier that day. He watched her eat. She stubbornly refused to look at him.

He didn't care, for then he could observe her at his leisure. He had never felt such satisfaction from just looking at a woman. Perhaps it was the expressiveness of her features, the way every thought in that obstinate little mind flickered across her face as clear as spring water. She was in a fine temper. Yes, Grace McNish was lovely, in spite of her scowl, in spite of her zeal to chew the bloody apple peeling from here to kingdom come.

Interesting how his thoughts seemed to be focused on her mouth—the viperish words that came out of it and the ravenous way she was eating. In his mind he saw the other things that mouth could be doing. He smiled.

She looked at him out of the corner of her eye, and he winked, which just set her off again. Christ, but this was great fun, he thought, wondering what was next. He stared at the back of her head, and after some time she looked at the peeled apple in her hand, then muttered something.

"I cannot hear you, McNish, when you speak to the forest," he said, watching her cut off a chunk of the fruit.

Still she didn't look at him, but shouted, "I said . . . would you like some apple?"

"Sounds familiar, a woman offering a man an apple. . . ." He let the sentence hang.

She spun around as he'd expected she would, her eyes narrowed in understanding. "I see no man, McNab. Only the serpent."

"If only you knew how badly I want to say something right now."

"What?" she asked, her expression suspicious and curious. 'Twas an interesting combination to watch—stubbornness and innocence. He shook his head and tried not to smile.

"Say it."

"No. I don't think so."

"No courage, McNab."

"Just tact, McNish."

"Bah!" she said, and tossed the piece of apple at him.

With rapier speed, Colin sat up and caught the small chunk of apple in his open mouth. He heard her gasp of surprise and leaned back against the oat bags, grinning at her while he chewed. She stared openly, and for one brief second he thought she might smile, but she didn't.

He swallowed, looking at the apple, then gave her a dare he knew she wouldn't resist. "Is that one wee morsel all you're going to give me?"

Immediately she cut another chunk from the apple and paused, looking at it for a time, then with the inkling of a devilish smile, she tossed it high in the air, just as he'd expected. He watched the piece of apple fall, then smoothly moved to catch it the same way.

Once again, the challenge was on.

She flicked a second piece.

He caught it.

And another.

He caught it, too.

Faster and faster, chunks of apple flew through the air as

quickly as her dirk could slice. Cheeks bulging, he caught the last one, and she burst out laughing, the sound innocent and clear as the lilting skirl of the bagpipes.

Then he glanced at Fiona and her bagpipes. He blanched. There was no lilt to the lass's playing.

He chewed, unable to suppress a winner's smirk, and she sagged back against the wagon bed and looked at him, the first sincere smile he'd seen on her face. "Och, McNab, I was right, you do move quickly."

He swallowed and laughed to himself. She'd just conceded she had lost by telling him she was right. " 'Tis not speed that counts, McNish, but agility and patience." He grinned then, and added, "There are some things, some situations, when slow and easy is better."

Her face showed that she'd missed his meaning, but she covered her puzzlement well and swiftly, for her doubt only flickered for an instant, then she stuck up her chin, her expression suddenly filled with certainty. "Aye. Slow can be better." She paused, nodding. "Better for vengeance, for torture . . ."

Always the last word, he thought.

Fiona's bagpipes bellowed overhead, playing an auld Scottish victory song that sounded like the mating call of a sick goose. After one particularly spine-raking note, the poor geese in the second wagon honked loudly.

The road had narrowed, steepened, and become more pocked. The three wagons climbed the steep grade slowly, each driver having his hands full just to hold the bouncing wagons to the center of the bumpy road.

They neared the crest of the hill, and Grace slowly craned her neck over the side of the wagon to peer at the long, rocky drop below. From her angle, 'twas a sheer drop to a wee burn below. Her belly fluttered uneasily. Her clammy hands gripped the wagon rim tighter and she glanced back at McNab.

He appeared not the least bit concerned with the rough ride, which made her even more determined not to show that she was. In spite of her churning belly, she straightened

her shoulders, let go of the wagon rim, and calmly placed
her hands in her lap.

The wheel hit a chunk in the road. Fiona missed a note,
a painful experience to anyone nearby.

"Och! That wasna right, was it?" Fiona asked aloud,
pausing so that the only noise was that of the honking
geese. She played another wrong note, frowned, and shook
her head, then tried four or five more, until she gave up and
began the song all over again from the beginning, playing
so loud that she didn't hear the groans of the others.

McNab winced, then turned to Grace, who was taking in
deep breaths to calm her stomach. He shouted, "Have you
thought about hiding those pipes in a loch? A very deep
loch?"

Quickly she relaxed and once again released her death
grip on the wagon, not wanting him to see her fear. The
wagon hit a deep rut and bounced hard.

To the sick sound of off-key piping, Grace sailed over the
side. Her heart drummed in panic. Instinctively she grabbed
for the wagon rim. Splintery wood dug into her palms.

She hung on with everything she had. Her body dangled
helplessly over the crag and banged against the side of
the bouncing wagon. She screamed for help, but her voice
was drowned out by the skirling squeal of Fiona's bagpipes.

Suddenly McNab was there. His hands gripped her wrists.
His powerful arms pulled her upward. In less than a blink she
was back inside, kneeling atop the barrel and holding on to
him so tightly she could barely catch a breath.

She was safe. Her mind's eye pictured the long, steep
drop. She could still feel the sense of helpless fear. Shaking,
she buried her face in his neck, and at the feel of his
hands rubbing her back so soothingly, she finally allowed
herself to breathe. Still she clung to him, knee to knee,
his big arms around her, holding her, providing refuge, the
powerful hands that had saved her now calmly rubbing her
fears away.

His big hands . . . His big, free hands . . .

Free hands. Slowly her narrowed gaze traveled down
from one large arm to where his unbound hands were

still rubbing her back. She stiffened. "You devil's spawn! You're free!"

She jerked back, pulling him with her. The barrel beneath them wobbled just as Seamus drove the wagon into a hard rut.

"Dammit to hell!" McNab swore, falling into her.

They both went over the edge.

She felt nothing but cold misty air rushing past them. They would surely die. With an uncanny sense of acceptance, she waited.

Suddenly his warm arms clamped tightly around her. He twisted in midair, his body protecting her from the coming impact.

They slammed into the hillside so hard that both of them grunted, then they rolled together down and down. Sharp rocks scraped and gouged her and must have done the same to his arms, which were still wrapped protectively around her. Grace could feel him try to take the brunt of the battering, try to keep his body between her and the sharp, slick hillside. Shale splintered and scattered with them as they slid until they splashed to a stop in a shallow burn.

The water was like ice.

Head dripping, McNab came up coughing. "Dammit! Can you do nothing without throwing your whole body into it?"

She sat for only the time it took to blink, then pulled out her dirk and flew at him, water splattering with her. "No! I can't!" she shrieked. "Watch this!" And she hit him with her whole body.

He fell back with another splash, Grace astraddle his chest, her dirk on his neck. He opened his eyes and looked up at her, his gaze moving from her face to the dirk poised once again at his neck. She glared back. She'd won.

After a moment during which the idiot appeared to be fighting back a laugh, he said, "Och, McNish, we need to stop meeting like this."

She froze, her sense of victory quickly waning as her mind filled with the vivid image of the last time they had been in the same position. "You lying oaf! You were awake!"

In a wink he'd flipped her on her back. Stunned, she stared up at him, her body pinned between his splayed thighs, his hand gripping her wrists so tightly that the dirk plopped uselessly into the trickling water.

He grinned down at her. "Aye, McNish."

CHAPTER
6

"Nay, McNab! Not without a fight!" Her knees battered his lower back and she twisted upward, trying to unseat him.

He tightened his thighs, holding her more firmly, and his hands pinned her struggling wrists. She jerked her head from side to side, water spraying up with each motion. She fought wildly, until her breath came in exhausted pants and her chest heaved.

He could read the panic in her face and feel the rapid beat of her pulse in the wrists he held so tightly. Her desperate gaze left his face and turned toward the escarpment. She was searching for help.

In the distance, the weak wail of a bagpipe could be heard. Help was not forthcoming.

He watched the play of emotions upon her face and knew the second she'd resigned herself to fate.

"Go on." That chin went up. "Do it," she said in an emotional rasp, then she closed her eyes, sighed, and her body went surprisingly limp.

He knelt there, befuddled, watching her.

She held her breath for a long time, her eyes still closed. She turned her head away, then exhaled dramatically. "I'm ready." She took another deep breath and lay there very still.

It took a minute longer before her breathing returned to

normal. She cracked open one green eye, peering at him suspiciously. "What are you waiting for, McNab? Do it."

"Do what?"

"What you McNabs always do. Have your vile way with me!" She shut her eyes and flopped her head back in the most dramatic gesture of submission he'd ever witnessed.

He did a fine job of holding back his smile. "Ah, yes." He nodded. "I'd forgotten." He just let the silence drag on. "Now, how was I supposed to do that?" He knew the moment she had opened her eyes, and he frowned as if he couldn't for the life of him remember.

"You have to strip me naked first, you oaf!"

There was that mouth again. He nodded, then cocked his head thoughtfully. "There are alternatives. I could cut out your liver."

She eyed him, her face no longer so fierce.

He paused, then pointedly looked around. "But there are no wolves to throw it to."

She exhaled, loudly.

"Perhaps I should just strip you naked and have my way with you since I cannot seem to think of anything else. Although it seems to me there was something else we 'vile McNabs' do." He stopped, then muttered, "I cannot think of it."

Her eyes grew round and he could see her trying not to let her fear show. He decided she'd had enough teasing and released one wrist, then quickly snatched up the fallen dirk before she could beat him to it. Dirk in hand, he turned back toward her.

She screamed loud enough to crack heaven.

He sat on her to keep her from squirming away. "Hold still!"

"Oh, God . . . Please don't skin me alive, or scalp me! Please!" All her bravery gone, she fought and wiggled and battered his back again with her knees.

"Dammit, McNish! Hold still!" He gripped her flailing wrists just as a knee rapped his back hard. "I'm not going to hurt you!"

A second later she stilled, looking up at him with a

surprised expression. "You're not?"

He stood up and looked down at her, holding out a hand. "No, I'm not."

She eyed him warily. Stubborn to the last, she ignored his outstretched hand and scrambled to her feet on her own. She rammed her shoulders back and stuck her chin up high. "I was right. You are a coward," she said with complete stupidity.

He counted to ten, slowly, very slowly. Finally he looked up the hillside, searching for the best path back to the top. The sound of splashing water came from behind him. He waited a moment, then turned.

She stood there wringing out her sodden plaid. Her black hair hung damply down her back and her shirt and plaid clung to her wee body. The cloak and plaid he wore hung about him in a sodden mass, and his trews were wet from the thighs down.

He watched her twist the water from her clothing. She wrung out each section of fabric with the same zeal which he would have liked to use in wringing her stubborn neck. She didn't look up, didn't acknowledge him, yet he knew she was aware that he watched her. Finally he turned back and eyed the hillside.

"What are you going to do with me?"

She had purposely waited until he'd turned before speaking. He sought more patience—something that was running thin. He turned. "What do you think I should do with you?"

"I'm not a McNab. I couldn't think that cruelly."

He leaned back against the rock face and eyed her, deciding whether or not to tell her that he wasn't a McNab. "What would you say if I chose to remain your captive?"

She gaped at him, then quickly covered her surprise. "I'd say you were a coward and an idiot."

Her mouth made the decision for him. She didn't deserve the truth until she learned a few lessons, lessons he'd take great pleasure in teaching her.

With a narrow-eyed look of suspicion, she asked impatiently, "Why would you do that?"

"To prove to you that all McNabs aren't as you think."
He turned his back on her.

She snorted. "More than likely to spy on us."

He counted to fifty this time and surveyed the hillside.

After a few more too quiet minutes she said, "I don't
believe you."

He ignored her and stepped back so he could better see
the face of the cliff.

"What are you looking for?"

"A way back up to the road."

She followed his gaze to the steep hillside covered with
slick rock. The mist was slowly dropping and wisps of fog
hovered near the top of the cliffs. "They'll come back," she
said with a confidence he did not feel.

He grunted something noncommittal, then headed for a
small break in the rock. "Come this way."

"I think this way is better," she said, and moved in the
other direction.

He turned and grabbed her by the shoulder. He nodded
in his direction. "This way."

"But this is easier," she argued.

He ground his teeth together. It kept him from killing
her.

She tightened her jaw and lifted her chin in defiance.

He'd had enough. In one swift movement he picked
her up, ignoring her yelp of protest. He set her on the
ground directly in front of him, turned her around, and
said, "Walk."

She scowled at him over a shoulder, then foolishly opened
her mouth to argue.

"Now!" he barked, leaning over her and using his size
to try to intimidate her.

She glared at him, then muttered something about fools
that almost got her tossed back into the burn, and walked
toward the path he'd found. They traveled about ten yards
and hit a section of sheer rock.

She turned around and planted her fists on her hips. "So
now what, McNab?" Her tone said, I told you so.

Colin counted to a hundred this time, then scanned the

hillside for alternative routes. He didn't like her smug grin. He liked her casual humming even less. When she began to mutter about hardheaded McNabs, he mentally cursed the God that gave this woman the gift of speech.

If he hadn't wanted to observe the McNish condition for himself, uninfluenced by their knowledge of who he was, he would have told her that he wasn't a hardheaded McNab but a powerful Campbell and he'd teach her to care more than a whit for his good and bad side. But he hadn't achieved his position by giving in to his emotions. This wee shrew was, however, his hardest trial.

"Come here," he said.

"Why?"

"Because I told you to."

"I don't wish to." She crossed her arms and stood there.

"I *wish* you to. Now."

"No."

He saw red and took a long step toward her.

She wisely balked no more than a second longer and slowly took a few steps, then foolishly muttered, "I'm coming."

A long, patience-testing hour and many arguments later, during which she luckily escaped with her neck intact, they both sat staring down the narrow road waiting for some speck to appear on the horizon.

There was no sign of the returning wagons—no dust cloud above the road, no jangle of harnesses, no thud of horses' hooves, no creak of the wagon wheels, and most telling, no bellowing bagpipes. Nothing.

Colin had whistled twice, but there was no sign of the men Mungo was to have left behind.

"They'll be coming soon," she said for the tenth time.

The minutes moved like glaciers. She took to drawing circles in the dirt with a finger. He took to pacing. Neither worked to speed time nor to bring the wagons back.

"You'd have thought they'd have noticed we were gone when the song ended."

She looked away.

He looked down at her. "How long is that song?"

After a pause she said, "If Fiona can get through the entire thing with no mistakes, perhaps ten minutes."

"And if not?"

"She always starts over from the beginning."

He groaned, then sat down next to her on the hard ground.

She scooted over, scowling at him. He stretched his long legs out and rested his arms atop his knees. "It's going to be a long wait."

"You're wrong, McNab. They'll be back."

'Twas sunset when Colin finally stood. He dusted himself off and, without a word, started to walk down the road.

"Where are you going?" she called out.

He ignored her.

"McNab!"

He kept walking.

"You're my captive! Remember? You cannot just up and leave!"

It wasn't long before he heard the sound of her running feet. He grinned and lengthened his stride.

She scurried up to him, grumbling.

He looked down at her. "Learned your lesson, did you?"

Her mouth thinned and her eyes narrowed. She looked straight ahead and made a fierce attempt to match his pace. Her wee arms pumped and her feet scurried, but never once did she lower her determined chin. He caught her covert glance just before she said, "No McNab could ever teach a McNish anything."

"Och! I could teach you something, McNish."

"No doubt some inspiring tidbit, McNab." She paused, which put her a few steps behind him. He could hear her run to catch up. She rushed by him and stuck her chin up, still staring straight ahead. "Perhaps you can instruct me on how to command a horse."

"Perhaps I can teach you how to land where you aim."

She spun around, the ragged damp plaid floating about her. He caught her wee flying fist in one hand and looked down at her, his patience gone. She glared up at him, raised that chin a notch, and tried to punch him with the other fist.

He ducked under her fist and at the same time flung her over a shoulder, pinning her flailing legs with one arm.

"Perhaps, McNish," he shouted over her squeals of protest, "this will teach you when I've had enough."

And he kept on walking, one arm clamped across the backs of her thighs. He ignored her struggles, ignored her fists beating at his back, and did his best to ignore that mouth.

Grace stood back, quiet for the first time since McNab had decided she was a sack of oat flour and treated her as such. Unfortunately her subsequent screaming hadn't sparked a single response, other than that obnoxious whistling. The man thought he was a lark.

She turned back toward the small glen near the road. She watched the small covey of grouse and imagined them roasting on a fire. Her stomach growled, and she slapped a hand over it as if by doing so she could hush it. She was so very hungry, but she wouldn't admit it.

The McNab looked at her for a moment, then stepped toward the bushes that ringed the glen. He turned to her and raised a finger to his lips, pointing at the birds.

She glared at him. Did he think she didn't know enough to keep quiet?

He picked up a rock and threw it. They had one grouse. He picked up another stone and threw it. They had dinner.

He started to walk toward the fallen birds. Grace grabbed his arm and shook her head. Then she couldn't help herself; she raised a finger to her lips and frowned, like he had.

She picked up a rock that filled her palm. "My turn," she mouthed, and resisted the urge to throw it at him when he crossed his arms and appeared to be holding back a laugh.

Grace used her anger to best advantage and heaved a rock at another grouse.

"You hit it," McNab said in surprise.

She dusted her hands off and swaggered past a group of hazel bushes. "Of course. You needn't sound surprised."

"Nothing you do surprises me, McNish." He walked over to the birds and squatted down.

She stopped swaggering. He'd just called her boring. She planted her hands on her hips and gave him her best look of defiance. "I pretended it was your head."

He looked up at her and laughed as if he expected her to say exactly that.

"Mine's the biggest one," she added smugly, and pointed at the two smaller birds that he'd killed.

He didn't answer, but gathered the birds, then suddenly stilled.

"The puny ones are yours," she goaded.

Colin stood, then grabbed her and moved into the forest.

"Where are you going?" she shrieked, getting tired of his manhandling.

"This way. Hurry!"

"But that's the wrong—"

"Be quiet." He glanced back just as her eyes narrowed and her face became mulish.

"That road leads to Loch Earn! If you think I'm going this way, then you must think me a bigger idiot than you."

"Shut up, McNish."

She gasped and dug in her heels.

A horse whickered from the road, followed by laughter.

"They've come back!" She wrenched her hand from his and took off for the road, her words echoing in her wake, "I told the stupid oaf they'd come. But does he believe—"

His big hand closed over her mouth and he jerked her back against him, holding her still. She screamed in protest but it muffled against his hand. "Be quiet!"

She bit him. He grunted but held fast. She kicked him. He swore under his breath and tightened his grip before he turned around, pulling her with him into the thick brush. He leaned down and rasped into her ear, "Look, McNish!"

Her furious green gaze followed his. A small band of men moved onto the road from the dark forest opposite. They had the look of those who had sold their souls to the devil—men who reveled in murder and mayhem.

A big man with wild gray hair and a red beard stabbed

his pike into the road and turned. "Naught but an empty road, Tom."

"Aye," said a man wearing a red scarf about his head. "So where's this fine quarry ye were babbling about, Tom?"

A small, beady-eyed man with a collection of knives strapped to his belt turned to the big man. "They were coming this way, Sim." He turned to the big man. "I seen 'em meself, MacGregor."

"Dinna mind him, MacGregor," said Sim. "Auld Tom's been seeing kelpies and faeries ever since he polished off that jug earlier! What's a few wagons when yer pot-eyed?" All the men laughed except the beady-eyed Tom, who pulled a long dagger and leaped toward the other man, slashing.

They fell into the road and the others gathered around cheering and shouting and calling for a kill. MacGregor slowly walked into the fray, watched the men cut at each other, then planted his pike between them while he pinned Tom's wrist to the ground with his filthy boot. "Enough! We've wasted enough time."

The men grumbled slightly, but turned and disappeared like wraiths into the forest. Grace turned to McNab. "Were they looking for us?"

"Appears they were looking for the wagons. It's a good thing that band of yours didn't come back to find us."

Grace glanced back at the road and thought of her friends and what might have happened. She shivered slightly.

"Come along, McNish. We need to stay away from the road." He stood over her and held out a hand.

Still a little shaky, she placed her hand in his and let him pull her up. Just this once.

The night was black and moonless, but it wasn't silent. An owl hooted and insects chittered. However, Grace was silent, for the first time in hours. They'd traveled well into the depths of the forest and even farther way from her home. And she'd told McNab so, many times. He just pulled her along until he'd said he thought it was safe enough to make camp.

She glanced up at him, unable to help herself. He had his broad back to her as he reached for some more branches for the fire. She wondered about him. He didn't seem to have the McNabs' hot-blooded temper.

Oh, she'd tried everything she could to spark rage in this man, as his clan's action caused rage in her. But he'd ignored her. Her chin came up and she huddled deeper into her plaid. So she had decided not to say anything. Silence. That ought to get to him, she thought.

She glanced covertly at him, strangely drawn to do so repeatedly. She should have hated him, for she hated everything that was McNab. That hatred was a part of her, the one thing she'd clung to when it seemed as if there was no hope for the Clan McNish.

But she was having trouble hating this man. She couldn't look at him and see the pain of her clan. She looked at him and she saw—oh, God . . . she closed her eyes at the thought. She saw him as a man.

She refused to use the term "handsome." She remembered the strength of him, the strong lines of his profile, his mouth, the frustrating way he calmly reacted to almost everything she'd done to bait him.

She couldn't remember hunger or pain or vengeance. She remembered his kiss, his taste, remembered him acting so silly and catching those apple pieces. She remembered laughing for the first time in so very long.

And she remembered that he'd kept her from foolishly walking into a pack of thieves. She frowned, not liking the taste of guilt she was feeling, nor her reaction to McNab.

She couldn't let herself give in to this weakness. She couldn't. And she wouldn't cry, either, although part of her felt like doing so.

She sat there, weak with hunger, trying not to think about him, trying not to look at him, and concentrating on every past cruel act of his vile clan in the hope that she could dredge up some spark of fight.

In the distance a wolf howled and Grace pulled her plaid tighter around her. A woods owl called out. The fire crackled as he added the wood. Then finally it was quiet.

And her cursed stomach growled loudly.

He looked up at her while he turned the three grouse they had caught on a spit he'd made. "You were wrong, McNish. You are hungry."

"I wasn't wrong," she said, breaking her promise to keep silent. She crossed her arms over her plaid.

"I suppose that wasn't your empty stomach calling out just now?"

"Aye, it was. But I wasn't wrong," she added stubbornly. He looked at her until she admitted, "You just happened to be right for a change."

The Grace McNish rule: Never admit you were wrong.

He shook his head.

"Don't worry yourself about me, McNab. Hunger is a normal state for a McNish." She looked away from the meat, unable to watch it cook. She was so hungry she'd have almost eaten it raw. Her ribs hurt, too, from being carried like an oat sack on his big shoulder. The rich smell of the roasting birds finally got to her and she swallowed her pride and asked, "Aren't they cooked yet?"

He chuckled. "Almost."

"Remember the big one is mine."

There was long silence, then he asked, "I take it you're talking about the grouse?"

She should have seen that one coming. "You are a sick man, McNab."

He shrugged. "If you want the big one, you can have it. Just ask." He made a rotten attempt at hiding his smile.

She straightened and put her hands on her hips. "My stone hit the biggest grouse and we both saw it. I want it understood. The bird in the middle is mine."

"Are we having another challenge, McNish?"

"I don't know what you mean. I was just pointing out which bird belongs to whom. You McNabs have trouble keeping your hands off things that don't belong to you."

He waited a moment before calmly and arrogantly responding, "Who struck the first kill?"

"Why . . . you did," she said sweetly. "Don't the McNabs always kill first?"

His expression changed lightning quick. All sense of play was gone. He looked like he had murder on his mind. Hers. She resisted the urge to grin smugly—she did have some sense of prudence after all—and she changed the subject instead. "The birds are burning."

He looked down at the spit, where the birds on the outside, his birds, were aflame. He swore and jerked the spit from the fire.

'Twas her turn to control her smile. She did a lousy job of it. "May I have my bird, please?"

His narrowed gaze met hers. She pointed at the spit. "That nice plump one in the middle. The one that's not burned."

He used her dirk to pry off a charred bird. It crackled and the burned legs and wings crumbled to the ground. She almost felt sorry for him when she saw how he stared at it. Almost, but not quite. She smiled at him. "I'm waiting."

He stabbed the dirk into her bird and the meaty juices ran out, sputtering as they dropped into the hot ashes. He slid the bird from the spit and held it up for her.

She smiled sweetly and plucked it off the dirk before he could do anything rash, like steal it for himself. She ripped off a leg and just stared at it for a moment because it looked as good as it smelled.

She tasted it and closed her eyes. 'Twas heaven. She chewed slowly, savoring the rich gamy flavor. She licked her lips and sighed as she swallowed, not realizing the picture she made—eyes closed, lips moistened, pure pleasure radiating from her face.

She opened her eyes to find him staring at her with the look of a man starved. " 'Tis my bird, McNab," she warned, holding the bird close to her chest.

"What bird?" he asked distractedly, still watching her mouth.

"This bird!" She held it up in front of her face.

He seemed to find himself again and bit into one of the charred birds. His scowl changed to a look of someone who had just eaten a big lump of lowlands coal. He stopped chewing. His eyes teared slightly and his jaw twitched.

"Mmm." She took another plump mouthful and oohed and aahed over how perfect it was.

He crunched on the blackened meat, then paused, blanching slightly before he chewed again, very slowly.

"This is soooo good."

He swallowed, hard, then grunted something about his being only a little well done.

"Mine's perfect, McNab." She leaned over and looked at his bird. "I believe there's a piece of meat right there." She paused and pointed toward the breast of his bird. "A wee one that's not too well done." She looked up and grinned.

"It's fine," he growled, and bit off another charred bite before tossing the carcass over his shoulder.

"So's mine." She bit into the meat with great relish.

He frowned at the second bird, then tossed it and the spit over his shoulder, too.

"Mmm."

He pinned her with a look that said he knew exactly what she was doing and didn't like it one bit.

Just the kind of look that sparked her to say, "Delicious." She ducked her head to hide her grin. She munched some more and heard him stand. Och, she thought. Can't take it, McNab. She ignored the quiet sound of his footsteps and finished her delicious meal, then turned and tossed the bones into the fire.

She turned back around and looked up—her third mistake. Her second had been ignoring his footsteps. Her first had been pushing him too far.

He towered above her. "So torment is your game, McNish?"

"Aye, McNab," she said, returning his look. She wouldn't back down from this man. She would not.

Before she could contemplate her next move, he made his. He pulled her up with such speed her vision blurred. He held her fast against him. "You're about to learn a new game."

CHAPTER
7

Just as he'd guessed, she opened her mouth to speak. So he kissed her into silence. She struggled for a moment, a fight he'd expected.

His hand firmly holding the back of her head, he filled her mouth with his tongue. She stilled. Her fists, which she had raised to strike him, froze above his shoulders. He felt the fight in her die.

Her hands lowered and her warm palms slid around his neck. "Och, McNab. What are you doing to me?" she whispered against his mouth.

He pulled at her plaid. "Stripping you naked and having my vile way with you."

She shook her head. "Nay." Her lips moved over his softly. " 'Tis my battle." Her tongue darted past his, giving back just exactly what she had gotten.

His other hand roamed down her back, over the soft roundness of her buttocks. She arched her body against his, then her hand slid down his chest and around his waist, gripping him in the same way he held her.

No meek, submissive woman here. She responded with the same fierce fervor in his arms as she had in her revenge.

He moved his hips in answer. She caught the rhythm.

Once again the challenge was on.

Never leaving her mouth—that mouth that pushed his

patience to the limits now pushed his passion beyond
anything he'd known before. He bent and let her slide
lower, where her softness rubbed against the hard ache in
him. Her hands gripped him tighter and she matched him,
hip to hip, tongue to tongue, movement to movement.

He could feel her fight to hold her own sense of power
in this, as she did in everything. Yet Colin intended to win
this battle.

His hands moved lower, up under her plaid and shirt,
then skimmed the backs of her legs and moved to touch the
warm soft skin of her inner thighs. She gave a wee gasp at
his touch, a sound he wanted to hear again. Her skin was
silky, like touching a rose petal. He stroked downward until
he held the backs of her knees and pulled them up around
his circling hips. He molded her softness to his shaft.

She moaned something against his mouth, half plea, half
cry. Her hands tugged the back of his clothes up, then she
slid her palms inside his trews, trying to touch him as he
touched her. She muttered in protest against his tongue, then
struggled to reach lower.

Holding her tightly, he sank to his knees, then to the
ground, laying her down beneath him. He broke the kiss
for the first time and straddled her, running his fingers over
the soft skin of her eyelids, down her jaw. She opened her
misty eyes and he ran his finger over her damp lips.

He did not speak, because he couldn't find the words he
needed to say. He was lost in the look she gave him and
he wasn't sure he wanted to find his way out.

Just as he had done to her, she reached out and palmed
his jaw, then ran two fingers along his cheek to stroke
his eyelids, his brows, then touch his lips. He touched
her fingertips with his tongue, then drew her hand away,
holding it while his other opened her plaid and her shirt
and stroked the white skin of her neck downward to her
belly. She caught her breath at his touch, then her eyes
grew misty and she moistened her lips.

He parted her clothing more until her breasts were bared
and he teased them with a slow fingertip. She tried to sit up,
her hands moving to mimic his touch, but he slid his arm

under her back and pulled up so she arched toward him. He lowered his mouth to her bare waist, sucking until he had made his mark on her.

The whole time her hands were busy pulling at his clothing, baring his chest. She gave a cry when her hands scored through the hair on his chest and he wondered at the sound she would make when she came.

His lips closed over her breast, taking as much of it into his mouth as he could. 'Twas his turn to gasp when her lips and tongue kissed him until his blood grew hot.

"Such fire, McNish," he whispered into her ear. "Such hot fire. Burn for me." He cupped her womanhood and touched the nubbin of a woman's pleasure. She moaned.

He straightened and laid her back on the ground. Her nails scored over his flexed thighs. He touched her again and felt her body rise with the tide of passion his touch brought.

He slowed and she cried out and reached to give him the same touch. She gasped at the contact, then slowly her fingers stroked the length of him through the rough wool of his trews.

He moved out of her reach and slid his arms under her knees, lifting her to his mouth. He blew on her wetness, then kissed her. She gave a thin scream, then pulsed hard and fast. She had barely stopped throbbing and he did it again.

He lowered her legs to his hips and jerked down his trews, moving over her, the hard length of him lying against her sweet nether lips. He shifted slowly up and down, rubbing her with his shaft.

He kissed a path up her belly, ribs, and breasts, never once ceasing the motion of his hips. His mouth moved up her neck and he paused, the swollen tip of him settled barely inside her.

Her eyes grew wide and he slowly entered her, watching her face for fear or pain. She jerked his head down and filled his mouth with her tongue. He inched inside more, her tightness closing around him until he met her maidenhead.

He stilled, then slid his hand between them and fondled her

pleasure point. She found another quick release, tightening around him. He broke the kiss, closed his eyes, and threw his head back. With a swift thrust, he broke the barrier, filling her and possessing her where no man ever had.

She screamed, and punched him in the jaw.

His eyes shot open and he froze, then he shook his head and flinched slightly before looking down at her. "Damn . . . McNish. What the hell did you do that for?"

She glared up at him, accusation in her eyes. "You hurt me!"

"I had to."

"Why?"

Christ! He gritted his teeth together and took a deep breath. "It only hurts the first time."

"Oh." She paused, then looked up at him, her eyes narrowed in suspicion. "Are you in pain?"

"No," he answered without thinking.

"Then you've done this before?"

Oh, hell . . . The answer to that question would probably get him more than a swift punch in the jaw. He moved his hands to her head and kissed her slowly, then moved his mouth to her ear and whispered, "It doesn't hurt the man, McNish. Only the woman." He looked down at her, his lips almost touching hers. "Does it still hurt?"

She appeared to think about this for a moment, then wiggled her hips slightly.

He counted in Gaelic, searching for control, praying that he wouldn't have to stop.

"No."

Thank you, God. Watching her face for signs of pain, he pulled back to begin the timeless rhythm.

"Don't leave me," she said in a panicked rasp, her small hands holding onto his buttocks.

"I'm not leaving you, McNish. I'm becoming part of you." He slid forward. "Slow and easy." He slid back, beginning the motion.

Her eyes drifted closed.

"Feel me . . . as I feel you."

Her hands slid up his forearms and held them tight.

He ceased all motion and asked, "Am I hurting you?"

She opened her eyes, misty, slanted, green as the dark depths of a highland forest. She swallowed and shook her head, then, as if to prove it, she tightened her knees on his hips.

He loved her in long slow strokes that drew out the sensation, that taught them the feel and texture and pleasure of each other. Primitive need made him want to come, but he didn't want to leave such hot sweetness. He wanted to stay inside her forever, feel the tightness, hear her murmurs, revel in the depths of this rare woman until he died from the intensity of her.

"More," she softly chanted with each breath, impatiently prodding him with her body to move more swiftly.

He gritted his teeth and continued just as slowly. She opened those misty eyes and watched him, her expression half dare, half pleasure. She gripped his hips tightly and tried to quicken the pace. She pushed his patience to the limit, challenging him, whether 'twas arguing or loving.

Taking one deep breath, he locked his gaze with hers in a look meant to prove his power. Even if it killed him. And it almost did.

She drew a long breath that he felt to the very depths of her. "Quicker, McNab."

"Slower, McNish."

She flinched in reaction, then she watched him, biting her lip, her gaze never straying from his. He edged in and out so slowly, savoring each inch, the slow and easy friction that he knew would prolong their pleasure.

She tightened her knees on his hips impatiently and pushed up, hard and strong, and a slight smile touched her lips when suddenly he was inside her as deep as anyone could be. She closed her eyes, moaning in triumph, and moved against him. He matched the motion, but grasped her hips and slowed the movement as he bent to run his tongue over her shoulder and to tease down to a breast.

She arched up and he slid an arm under the small of her back, his hips beginning a slow deep grind that made her moan and reach to grip his forearms. He licked a path up her white belly and across each rib, then shifted his hold so his hands held her by the waist and he pulled her up against him as he knelt, until she could do little but cling to his shoulders.

Not once did either of them miss a motion, a beat. 'Twas another battle. Another challenge. Their hips circled together slowly at first, perfectly synchronized, then built like the passion that burned within them. He could feel every inch of her with each withdrawal, could feel the swollen woman's point that ran like a small tongue over his shaft.

Her release came hard and fast and on a scream that sent him so far over the edge that he filled her with warm life again and again and again, a sweet bliss that went on longer than any man could ever fathom.

When he came around, he was sure he was blind. No man could experience such fire and come out unscathed. He opened his eyes, expecting blackness, and he got it. Her black hair was wrapped around him, as were her warm legs and her nether lips. Had he been blinded, it would have been worth it.

He looked down at her. Her face held the flush of woman loved hard and long. If she were the only woman he could ever make love to, he'd die a happy man.

At that thought he took a long, slow breath. The air was filled with the musky scent of their loving and the clean pine smell of the woods in which they'd lain. He could still taste her essence on his lips.

He watched her eyes slowly change. She stared up at him and murmured, "My God . . ."

He realized with sharp clarity that he'd just lost the very battle he'd wanted to win.

To her.

She stared up at McNab's face. He looked like he'd been hit with a caber. She turned away, feeling exactly the same way.

She had liked it. How could she?

Traitor. Weakling. Coward. She could have stopped this.

She should have. But she didn't. She closed her eyes against the sharp pang of guilt that struck her. He was her enemy. A McNab. But the true horror was something she could no longer deny—she was in love with him.

"We need to talk," he said, his deep voice wrapping around her like chains. He reached out to brush the tangled hair from her face and she flinched. He paused, something unreadable flickered through his eyes, then he looked down at her. "I hurt you again."

She looked away and shook her head, then pushed at his shoulders. He moved off her and she jerked her clothing down, grasping the front of her plaid and shirt with one tight fist. She scrambled to her feet.

"McNish."

She couldn't face him. "You didn't hurt me. I hurt myself." And betrayed my clan, she thought, imagining her grandfather's face when he found out. *A McNab*.

"There's something I need to tell to you." He stepped toward her.

"Not now." She stiffened when his hand touched her shoulder. God . . . she was going to cry. She never cried.

"McNish."

"Not ever, McNab!" And she did something else she'd never done. She ran.

"Where the hell is she?" Colin muttered, stumbling through the black depths of the forest. No one could disappear that quickly. "Dammit, McNish!"

He walked farther, searching the bushes, the trees, every dark and dank nook and cranny.

A man's shout pierced the forest silence.

Colin froze and released a branch of a thick bush.

"You devil's spawn! Let go of me!"

He'd know that mouth anywhere. He edged closer to a thick copse of trees.

"Ouch, damn ye! Catch her, Sim! The wee bitch bit me!"

"I'll do more than bite you, you vermin! McNabbbb!" She kicked one of the thieves.

Colin drew his dirk and stepped into the clearing. "Let her go."

The two thieves turned, still struggling to hang on to her. He looked at her to see if she was all right.

"It's about time, McNab!" She glared at him.

There were times when she didn't have the sense to be afraid. This apparently was one of them.

She turned to the two thieves. "He's a McNab." Her face took on that stubborn look of challenge. "Surely you've heard about the McNabs. They'll cut out your liver and feed it to the wolves!"

Colin groaned. "McNish . . ."

"He'll skin you alive, you thieving cowards!" She jerked her arm away from one of the men and grabbed his hair in both fists, then yanked hard. "And scalp you bald!"

"Jesu! Get the viper off me! And get her hands out of me hair or I will be bloody bald!"

"You'd best let go of her," Colin ordered, although he wasn't quite sure who needed saving most.

"Aye, you sniveling—"

"McNish!"

Thankfully she clamped her mouth shut and released the man's hair. The men quickly let her go. With a sharp tug, she straightened her clothing, then stuck her chin up and strolled toward him. She stood next to him, then muttered, "Took you long enough."

"Sometime later I'll teach you what long is," he said, ignoring her snort. He pinned the men with a hard look. "Where's the rest of your band?"

The smaller man glanced slyly at the other, then responded meekly, "There be no others. Only we two poor souls."

McNish jammed her fists on her hips and shouted, "That's a lie! We saw the others! And the big one named MacGregor!"

"Goddammit, McNish!" Colin grabbed her with his free hand. "Shut up!"

Indignantly she turned to him. "Well, we did!"

"Thank you for telling them."

His sarcasm hit home. Her face flashed with guilt for an

instant, then she shrugged. "Too late now," she said. "And you don't have to be so sarcastic."

He ground his teeth together.

Something sharp poked him in the back.

"Dinna move! Neither of ye!" came a gruff voice from behind them.

"Well, McNab," she muttered. "I'd say that answers your question."

Always the last word . . .

CHAPTER
8

The thieves held the McNish reivers captive along with Grace's precious wagons. Fiona, Iain, Seamus, and Duncan all sat nearby, tied, but looking unharmed. Grace counted eight thieves, excluding the MacGregor, who couldn't be seen anywhere in camp.

She and McNab had been tied, too, and forced to walk to the camp at sword point. Grace was gagged.

The rest of the thieves huddled near a large fire and watched her through sly eyes. It made her skin crawl, but she'd not show it. She glared back at every one of them.

"What have ye there, Tom?" one of them asked. "A wee bit of skirt fer the men? This one's no child like the other." He nodded at Fiona.

Tom and Sim both looked at Grace and shuddered. "We don't want her, Lem!"

"Ye're fools, then. She's a beauty!" Lem walked toward her and she swung a foot back, planning to kick the fool when he got close enough.

Tom jerked the gag from her mouth. "See fer yerself, Lem."

Just the moment Grace was waiting for. "Stay away from me, you pocked rat!" She thought she heard Colin groan just before her band cheered.

"Ah," Lem said. "I like 'em with fight."

"Good!" She spat and kicked him hard.

"Get him, Grace!" Duncan shouted.

Scowling at her, Lem raised a fist.

McNab stepped in front of her.

Lem paused, then looked up at McNab. He was almost twice as big as Lem and threatening even with his hands bound.

"Don't," McNab said with deadly calm.

Grace grinned at his broad back.

"She's my wife."

"His wife?" Duncan squeaked in disbelief.

Her mouth fell open. *His wife?* Then it happened. . . .

Lem turned a suspicious gaze on Duncan, who flushed red, then Lem turned back to her and asked, "Yer friend there sounds surprised. Are ye his wife?"

'Twas worse than hitting her. If she said yes, it would be a public declaration, and by Scottish law they would be legally man and wife. She stepped beside Colin and looked up. There was something unreadable in his expression.

'Twould serve him right if I agreed, she thought. His face held a sudden challenge, as if he knew she'd say no. Her eyes narrowed. She looked Lem straight in the eye and said, "Aye! I'm his wife!"

Colin smiled. She'd done exactly as he had thought, and he could see in her colorless face that she'd just realized it.

Tom the thief stepped up to him, careful to stay out of McNish's range. He removed his battered hat and placed it over his chest. "Me heart goes out to ye, lad." Then, shaking his head, he and Sim shuffled away, muttering about hell on earth.

Lem looked at McNish first, then at Colin. He made a sound of disgust. "Get over there with yer friends! And keep yer wife quiet or I'll gag her again."

Grace stepped toward him. "You wouldn't—"

"Shut up, wife!"

The men all laughed, but she didn't. She waited until Lem had walked away then said, "You tricked me, McNab.

And you'll be sorry." With that dire threat she spun around, chin high, and walked over to her band.

Colin took in the camp as he walked over to join the captives. He stood over McNish. She scooted around until her back was to him. Her band stared up at him in awe, then Duncan foolishly said, "You just wed a McNab."

One blazing look from McNish and he cowered slightly and looked away.

Colin sat down next to her. She scooted away. He leaned to where Duncan huddled with Iain, Seamus, and Fiona. "Where are your weapons?"

"Over by the last wagon," Duncan answered, nodding toward the wagon that sat about twenty feet away. The pike, the claymore, and the crossbow were stacked by the wagon wheel. 'Twas about equal distance between the wagon and the campfire.

Colin leaned closer to McNish. She started to scoot away again, but he said quietly, "You'll hold still, wife, if you want to escape."

She turned to him, her face stubborn as an old ass.

He edged back until he was alongside her and partially blocked from view of the campfire. "Your dirk is inside my plaid. Don't look at it! Just move your hands back. Aye, that's right. And feel around for the handle."

She moved back a bit and reached inside.

"That's not it," he said, unable to keep the grin from his voice. She flushed and he added, "The dirk handle's smaller."

Her elbow jabbed into his stomach, and as he faked a cough to cover his grunt, she slid the dirk out.

He shifted and raised his bound hands slightly. "Cut the rope."

She paused, then he felt the dirk handle graze his hand. "Cut mine first."

"McNish," he warned through a clenched jaw. "Now is not the time for this."

She didn't move.

"You will obey me . . . wife."

" 'Tis not very smart to remind me of that mistake when

I have a dirk in my hand, McNab. 'Twould be easy enough to make myself a widow. Besides, there was no ceremony and I never promised to obey."

"Cut . . . the . . . damn . . . rope."

She waited just long enough to push his patience over the edge, then smiling, she did as he demanded, handed him the dirk, and raised her hands. "I'm ready."

Colin cut the laddies' ropes with a warning to keep their hands hidden, then tucked the dirk into his waist. "Not now."

"What do you mean, not now!" she whispered angrily.

He just smiled. "Be patient, wife."

"Damn you, McNab!" she spat.

He ignored her mumbled curses and scanned the camp. The men, who had been drinking heavily from an open ale barrel, had begun to sing.

"Sing with them," Colin said, and joined in.

They finished an auld Scottish ballad and Colin shouted, "We need some piping."

The thieves rumbled in agreement.

"Any of you play?" Colin asked casually.

They shook their heads.

"The wee red-haired lassie's a truly fine piper!" Colin called out to them, ignoring the gasps of the McNishes.

The thieves cheered and called out, "Gie her the pipes!"

Colin leaned toward a grinning Fiona and whispered into her left ear, "You can help us escape. Just play as loud as you can, then run and hide behind the wagon. Do you understand?" Her eyes widened and she nodded seriously.

Tom had risen and went to get the bagpipes that were sitting on a wagon seat. Colin leaned to the laddies. "When she plays that first note, run for the weapons. Duncan, take the pike. Iain, take the claymore. Seamus, you take the crossbow."

"Seamus and the crossbow?" they all asked in unison.

"Aye," Colin said in a tone that brooked no argument. "Be certain to keep your hands hidden when he brings the pipes here. Everyone understand?"

They nodded.

"What about me?" McNish asked.

"Quiet. He's coming," was all Colin said.

"Raise yer hands, lassie," Tom said to Fiona. He cut the rope, then handed her the pipes.

Colin had shifted earlier, so he was squatting, the dirk hidden in the folds of his cloak and plaid.

The thieves all looked at Fiona expectantly. She raised the reed to her lips and hit her loudest note. The thieves stood frozen in shock.

"Now!" Colin yelled, and ran toward the campfire. He grabbed Lem just as an armed Duncan turned from the wagon and ran toward them. He tripped, and Colin threw Lem to the ground. Duncan fell atop him, pinning him down with the pike.

One down.

Colin grabbed a thief in each hand and slammed their heads together. As they fell he glanced at Iain, who was struggling to raise the claymore. "Rest it on your shoulder, Iain!" Colin shouted. Iain took a deep breath and let the claymore fall on his shoulder, conking the thief that snuck up behind him on the head.

Four down.

A screeching flash of long black hair sped past him as he grabbed another one. McNish made a flying leap at Tom's back. She missed his back but managed to sling her bound hands about his neck as she went flying past him. Tom screamed, then choked, and Colin almost felt sorry for him. She and Tom landed on Sim, knocking both men out.

Six down.

Colin sidestepped a kick from the man he held and punched him just as Seamus loaded the crossbow backward.

"Shoot the arrow into the campfire, Seamus!" Colin yelled, and the lad turned and took aim. He pulled the trigger and the arrow shot out behind him, pinning the last thief to a thick pine tree.

All eight down.

Colin took a deep breath and glanced around the camp.

"McNaaaab!" came a muffled shriek.

He turned and saw two bare feet kicking from beneath

the unconscious bodies of Tom and Sim. He slowly walked over and watched her for a moment. Her head popped out from under Tom's arm and glared at him. "Well, don't just stand there, you grinning oaf! Get them off me and cut the ropes!"

Colin stood there a second longer than necessary, then bent down.

A dirk flew just over his bent head and stuck with deadly force into one of the wagons. Colin hit the ground next to McNish and quickly freed her hands.

"Behind ye!" Duncan warned.

"I've been waiting for this." MacGregor's deep voice sounded from the edge of the camp. He stood there casually tossing Colin's brooch in his left hand.

"Aye, MacGregor. So have I," Colin said, then lunged for MacGregor's knees. The huge man thudded to the ground. He grabbed Colin in a bear hold and squeezed. Colin kneed him and ducked a hammy fist.

"Get him, McNab! Punch him in the gullet!"

Colin turned toward McNish. She had burrowed out from under the men and sat atop them, punching the air with wicked fervor.

MacGregor connected, knocking Colin to the ground. He rolled and shot back up, seeing nothing but stars.

"Break his nose! Blacken his eyes! Strike him in the belly!"

Colin threw his hardest right and felt the satisfying crack of MacGregor's jaw. The man fell like a cut tree.

"Nice one, McNab!" McNish clapped her hands. "I knew you could do it."

Colin picked up a fallen dirk and held it over MacGregor, who shook his head and looked at McNish. "Who the hell is that?"

"My wife."

MacGregor scowled. "Who is McNab?"

McNish swaggered over to him and stopped, planting her hands on her hips and sticking her chin proudly in the air. "He is!"

MacGregor howled with laughter. "Might be a good idea,

Campbell, if ye told yer wife yer real name."

"Campbell?" McNish repeated. She eyed the brooch that lay on the ground next to MacGregor. She bent and picked it up, then turned a stunned face toward Colin. She stared at the brooch, then wobbled slightly.

"Aye," MacGregor said. "Colin Campbell himself. Lord of the Isles. Earl of Argyll."

There was a loud thud.

The Countess of Argyll was out cold.

EPILOGUE

'Twas Michaelmas, a very special time at Findon Castle, the home of the Earl and Countess of Argyll. The whole family had gathered for the celebration that had become tradition in the twelve years since Colin Campbell had brought home his feisty bride, Grace McNish Campbell.

She had not come peacefully. Colin's men had finally shown up, too late for the MacGregors, but in time to help him haul his angry wife home to his castle. Her pride was a little bruised. But her love for Colin was stronger than her bruised pride.

In the end, she had saved the starving McNish clan she so loved and had given her grandfather back a bit of his pride. Her husband had fined the McNabs and restored McNish lands, righting the wrongs done to them. He had also managed to tame her . . . a tad.

The last battle for the earl and countess had been to admit their mutual love. Colin had ducked five silver goblets, dodged three platters, and a brass ewer before he managed to get close enough to extract a confession from his sweet wife. Soon the castle that had played host to kings and queens, lairds and ladies, and many a foreign diplomat was filled with that love.

And on this day some twelve years later, while the earl and countess laughed and watched, the bells rang and called the Campbell children to the great hall for the cutting of the huge Dundee cake filled with currants, dried fruits, and—best of all—honeyed figs.

The two Campbell sons stood in the hall, waiting. Gavin, the eldest at eleven, and a handsome, tall young man who, like his ten-year-old brother, Lucas, held the promise of their father's stature and temperament. They were patient lads, and they needed to be with four younger sisters who were exactly like their mother.

Six-year-old Bridget came barreling into the hall with her twin sister, Isabel, in her wake. Bridget skidded to a halt, elbowed in front of her brothers, and gave her sister a smug grin before announcing that she was first. Isabel stuck her chin out like a mule, accused Bridget of cheating, and said she was worse than a vile McNab.

Annabella, who was eight, swaggered into the hall with the confidence of a conqueror and glanced at her siblings before laying claim to the very biggest piece of cake. But two-year-old Marta ignored them all and made a dive for the huge cake, landing in its center face first. She came up licking her lips, then blessed everyone with a wide, cake-crumbed grin and said, "Mine!"

Yes, the children argued and struggled and worked to be individuals, fought for their beliefs, but one thing remained constant—they loved each other. And that love and loyalty taught to them by their parents remained with them and their children, and their children's children, and so on, until this very day.

THE THISTLE
IN BLOOM

Linda Shertzer

Dear Reader:

Superstitious actors always refer to it as the "Scottish Play." No one will come right out and say *Macbeth,* for fear of bringing down some major catastrophe upon the theater, the acting company, or worse yet himself! I don't know where or when this superstition originated, or why the "Scottish Play" by any other name should hold such a curse. I don't really want to know, but I think I've been touched by it, anyway, just a little.

"The Thistle in Bloom" was almost completed, with a file on my disk and several notated hard copies lying about my office. Then a plot complication necessitated a great deal of rewriting. With a week and a half to go to my deadline, my substantial rewrite was more than half-completed. I felt good, but I was tired and thought I'd wait until the next morning to print it out.

Then the curse struck! For some reason best known only to my computer and Macbeth, the next day my file would not read. None of my hard copies contained the new material. I was lost!

I placed a frantic phone call to my husband, who has a master's in computer science. Like a knight in shining armor, bearing his Norton Utilities Program like a sword and shield, he came home from work immediately (a forty-five-minute drive) and spent the entire afternoon retrieving my lost file, enabling you to read "The Thistle in Bloom" today.

I set my story in the Highlands in 1817. Since I also write Regencies for Berkley as Melinda Pryce, it was a time period I could feel comfortable in. But the Highlands were not a happy place during this period. My hero and heroine must contend with poverty and crop failures and the lingering effects of the English taking over their ancestral lands. Had it not been for their deep and true love for each other and their sense of humor, they would never have overcome their problems.

While my little computer problem is hardly on a par with famine and war, I still don't know what I would have done without the unfailing help of my loving husband, and his unfailing faith in me. It's this type of love that makes a great romance even after twenty-one years of marriage, five children, and a huge house that we'll never finish remodeling.

I hope you enjoy my tale for *Highland Fling*, and that the "Scottish Play" brings better fortune to you.

I'd love to hear from you.

Linda Shertzer
P.O. Box 293
Pasadena, MD 21122

THE HIGHLANDS, 1817

"Seamus is home!" the Auld Laird announced excitedly as he hobbled across the murky laich toward the front door of Castle Dunkennet. His knobby cane thumped loudly on the bare flagstone floor.

Katherine MacKerlich hurried after him, her own softly slippered feet making no sound. "Do have a care or you'll fall," she warned.

"Now stop yer fussin' at me, lass." The Auld Laird's mouth was set in a determined grin. "I'm not some invalid auntie wha cannot find her own shoes at the end of her feet."

Katherine shook her head and sighed with affectionate exasperation as she continued to follow him closely. Her own father had served the Auld Laird well as his steward. When her parents had died when she was still very young, the Auld Laird had taken her to raise with his own children. The man might be aging and walk with a limp, but he was still a match for anyone half his age. Now that his only son had returned, nothing would stand in his way.

And Katherine had no intention of lagging behind.

She loved Seamus MacKenzie—had loved him for

many years. How wonderful to discover that he loved her, and wanted to marry her, too! If only there were enough money . . . If only this trip to London to make his fortune and restore their impoverished estates had been successful.

At last their seemingly interminable separation was over. She and Seamus would be together again!

The small black dog, his pointed ears twitching, ran ahead of both Katherine and the Auld Laird. His tiny claws tapped against the cold, stone floor. Reaching the door before them, he jumped up and down, barking sharply.

"Hush, Dughall," Katherine scolded. More sympathetically she added, "I know you've missed him, too, boy."

Whining instead, Dughall pranced back and forth on his short, bandy legs. He stopped occasionally to dig furiously, as if he could burrow under the door through solid stone just to reach his master.

Before Katherine could pull the door completely open, Dughall squeezed through the tiny space and sped, yapping, outside. Joyfully she flung the door open wide. Dughall stopped in midbark.

"Sheep!" the Auld Laird exclaimed as he stopped abruptly in the doorway.

"Father, I'm home!" Arms outspread, Seamus MacKenzie cheerily returned his father's unusual greeting. He was surrounded to midthigh by nearly a hundred crowding sheep.

"Sheep!" the old man repeated as he managed to overcome his shock long enough to make his way to the end of the front steps.

Katherine couldn't decide if the Auld Laird was upset or simply bewildered at the strange sight confronting them.

"I send ye to Londontown to seek your fortune—and ours—and what d'ye bring back? Sheep!" He waved his cane at the large fluffy flock in the drive, milling aimlessly about the tall young man. He shook his graying head. "I cannot believe my old eyes."

Stepping outside, Katherine couldn't believe her eyes

either. For six long months she had waited for Seamus's return. For half a year she had anticipated seeing again the twinkle in his emerald eyes and hearing the deep resonance of his voice when he laughed. She had yearned to hold Seamus tightly in her arms and cradle his head close to her breasts once again. Now, at last, he stood before her.

She took in all of him with her eyes, comparing everything to the image she had committed to memory to last her through their long separation. The light of the setting sun cast red-gold highlights in his brown hair, waving softly across his smooth brow and curling slightly about his ears. It was shorter than she remembered it—so short that she doubted she could entwine his locks about her fingers now. Still, she longed to try. The lights and shadows set into strong relief the familiar planes and angles of his cherished face.

"Seamus!" she cried, as breathless from running as with the long-awaited sight of him.

His eyes sought hers as if he had known all along that, at this very moment, she would appear. His eyes blazed green fire, setting her heart to pound.

"Kathie!"

His arms were outstretched. How she yearned to fall into his warm embrace and feel his strong body pressed gently against her. Yet even now she chafed in continued frustration. As she tried to move forward the sheep, bleating loudly and wandering as a tightly knit crowd, came between them.

"Why have ye brought back sheep, of all things?" the Auld Laird demanded. "Ye were supposed to be seein' about gettin' a banker's loan."

"They're *better* than any banker's loan, Father," Seamus maintained, reaching down to tousle the wool on one of the sheep's heads.

The Auld Laird grimaced skeptically. "A banker's loan wouldna be leavin' little piles upon my lawn. It wouldna smell half so bad either."

"But they'll improve the land," Seamus insisted. He made a futile attempt to step over one of the sheep. They shifted, nudging Seamus so that he almost toppled over. Righting himself, he continued, "They'll make our fortune."

"They make a mess," the Auld Laird replied. "And they'll probably ruin our shoes. Get rid o' the vile little beasties. Go on." He waved his cane in the direction of the outbuildings with their surrounding pens and the open fields beyond. "I always did worry that yer nanny tellin' ye that silly tale o' the boy wha traded his cow for beans would have some adverse effect on ye someday—causin' ye to bring home all manner o' useless things."

Seamus winked at his father. "And the useless things proved to be the most valuable of all, didn't they?" he pointed out with a chuckle.

"Oh, aye," the Auld Laird readily agreed. "We can always have a good mutton stew."

Seamus turned to the weathered, sun-browned man who had been standing unobtrusively behind him. The man whistled. A small, sleek, black, white, and tan collie circled about from behind the flock. Dughall set up a deep growl. The wiry collie slunk low, still circling. The two dogs eyed each other warily.

"Hush, Dughall," Katherine repeated. Instead of holding Seamus as she longed to do, she ended up picking up the fretful little dog in her arms.

"He won't hurt you, boy," Seamus called his reassurance. But Dughall wouldn't rest until Seamus had given orders to the shepherd to take the other animals away.

Now that the sheep no longer stood between them, Seamus rapidly took the front steps two at a time. The Auld Laird smothered him in a hearty embrace.

" 'Tis good to have ye home, son."

" 'Tis good to be home, Father," Seamus declared, returning his father's affection.

Dughall had wiggled out of Katherine's arms and now bounded up and down in front of his master. A loving scratch between the ears set him at ease.

"Oh, Seamus, I . . . we've all missed you so," Katherine said.

Seamus reached out toward her. She snuggled closer to him as he wrapped his arm about her. It felt so good just to touch him again, to feel the strength of his arms beneath the smooth fabric of his jacket.

She could smell the cool heather and musky horse scent clinging to his clothes after his long ride. Still, under it all, she could smell the clean scent that was, unmistakably to her, all his own. She could feel the rise and fall of his broad chest with each breath he took.

They had tried so hard to wait—until he returned, until he had enough money to restore the estate, until they could tell the Auld Laird of their love and their intention to be married. But the prospect of not seeing each other again for so long had been too overwhelming. All these months she had lived with the secret memory of that single, precious night before he left, when his bare body moved gently over hers while his manhood throbbed within her. Now that she was actually in his arms, she yearned to feel him, just like that, once again.

Would she look too bold if she placed her arm about his waist? She wanted so badly to feel the muscles of his back as they played beneath her hand. Nestled against him, still dreaming of his embraces, she murmured, "Ah, Seamus, how I've missed you."

"I could hardly wait to see you again either," he replied as he led them all inside. He leaned over and planted a light little kiss on her temple. "I couldn't wait to tell you all about the sheep!"

A wee peck! Katherine thought. And a brotherly hug. That's all! Her eyes grew wide with surprise and disappointment. Oh, not that she'd expected him to sweep her up in his arms and ravish her right there on the front steps with the Auld Laird and Dughall— not to mention a hundred silly sheep—looking on. But after six months of separation, she certainly would have thought his joy at seeing her again would amount to more than *that*!

Oh, men! She sighed with exasperation. At a time like this, why must they still be so preoccupied with business?

And what would it hurt, she wondered just a bit peevishly, if, as they walked along, he fondled her ear or stroked her

neck beneath her hair where no one else could see? She
waited, tense, for the sensation that never came.

Instead, here he was as they crossed the large, murky
laich, rattling on and on about his sheep! Even as they
ascended the narrow stairs that wound around the inside of
the wall of the tall tower house, he continued, "In London,
I met a Mr. Gilroy of Glasgow."

"Gilroy, ye say?" the Auld Laird asked with a frown that
only Katherine seemed to notice.

"Yes. Gilroy," Seamus answered, pushing open the door
to his father's solar at the top of the tower house. "Quite a
forceful personality—and an astute man of business."

The Auld Laird just gave a snort.

" 'Tis a wonderful agreement we've signed," Seamus
continued enthusiastically. "We'll supply him exclusively
with all the raw wool he needs for his mills. He'll pay us
the highest market prices."

Apparently the Auld Laird had heard enough. He shook
his head and sighed as he sank into his comfortable chair
by the fire. "Och, Seamus, how they've changed ye in
Londontown!"

"Changed? Me?" Seamus gave his father a puzzled smile.
He looked to Katherine, as if she could explain his father's
reaction.

"Aye. Changed," he insisted with a forceful rap of his
cane upon the floor. "Why, just look at ye! I sent a fine
Scot to Londontown—and what returns?" He pursed his lips
and made small, bobbing motions with his head. "Naught
but a fine, foppish gentleman instead," he replied in a high
squeak of a voice.

Seamus drew himself up as if affronted. Katherine tried
not to laugh.

The Auld Laird poked his cane in the direction of the
article of clothing encasing Seamus's legs and lower
body. "Now, just what would ye be callin' these . . .
these things?"

"Father." Seamus chuckled as if the man should know
better than to ask such a foolish question. "They are
trousers."

The Auld Laird grimaced as he continued to shake his head. " 'Twas bad enough when them wha rules us from Londontown took our kilt away," he grumbled. "Now a man goes there and cannot even wear a decent pair o' hose and knee breeches when he returns. 'Tis indeed a world turned upside down."

"While you may find them scandalous, Father," Seamus informed him proudly, "I assure you, among the *ton*—"

"The *who?*"

"All the fashionable people of London."

"Oh, *them*," the Auld Laird grumbled with scorn and disappointment.

"Trousers are all the crack."

"The crack? D'ye hear that, lass?" the old man demanded, turning to Katherine. "The crack, he says."

Katherine was too overwhelmed to acknowledge the Auld Laird's remark. She had been so filled with joy at the very presence of Seamus that she had not even bothered to notice his clothing. What did mere wool and linen matter when she had the man of flesh and blood before her?

Now that her attention had been drawn specifically to them, she was forced to admit that, for once, she disagreed completely with the Auld Laird. Trousers? Whatever they were called, she had to acknowledge that they certainly fit Seamus wonderfully. She could see every bulge and hollow of his leg, every curve and swell as the fabric stretched taut across his loins.

"Trousers are quite comfortable, actually," Seamus said, gesturing to his new clothes. He needn't have gone to any special effort to draw attention to them. Katherine could hardly miss them now. "Mark my words, before too long, all the gentlemen will be wearing them."

"Ye won't be catchin' *me* in such preposterous-lookin' things! Trousers. The *ton*. The crack. Och, there's naught to be done with the young," the Auld Laird continued to mutter to himself. Then he chuckled loudly and said, "Och, it dinna matter, lad. Ye're home at last is what matters to me."

"And I have brought these sheep—"

"Nay, I'll hear naught o' sheep tonight—nor o' the Englishmen's foppish fashions. Tell us o' yer trip to Londontown. Surely, in six months, somethin' more than meetin' sheep and Gilroy must have happened to ye there."

"Ah, indeed it did!"

After a while Katherine began to regret that the Auld Laird had not permitted Seamus to prattle on about his sheep. What cared she for his tales of extravagant wins or losses at games of chance by some unknown lord? What cared she for his descriptions of places she would never see? The very names—White's, Boodle's, Astley's Royal Amphitheatre, Vauxhall—meant nothing to her at all.

What cared she for his detailed accounts of the latest in ladies' fashions, supposedly given for her benefit? It did not benefit her in the least to be worrying how he would know so much about them, anyway.

The Auld Laird began to nod off in his chair. Dughall dozed comfortably by the fire. Seamus summoned his father's aging manservant to come up and assist his laird into bed.

He took up a lamp from the side table by the door and, followed by Katherine, left the solar. Immediately awake, Dughall sprang up from the hearthside and followed them down the corridor. They continued on to their individual bedchambers in the newer wing that had been added, not so many generations ago, at an angle to the ancient tower house. They passed the door to her room and moved on to his.

Katherine opened the door. A cheery fire was already burning, warming the long empty room. The servants had unpacked for him, and the housekeeper had set a bottle of whisky and a plate of her butteries on the table by the fireside.

Seamus entered and placed the lamp on the table by the bed. Dughall scampered in and bounded up onto the bed, but Katherine lingered by the door. Then Seamus turned to her.

She cocked her head to the side and peered into his eyes. If she ventured a smile, would he not take her seriously? Would he think she was merely flirting with him, as all the fine ladies of London undoubtedly had? And if she did not smile, could he tell from the light in her eyes, alone, how much she loved him and how she still longed for his touch? She swallowed hard with the anxiety of waiting and wondering.

"I have missed you so," he said.

She smiled, feeling her waiting passions welling up inside. "I have missed you, too."

He reached out his hand to her. Still fearing too much boldness would be unseemly, she moved slowly until she stood directly in front of him. If she took one more step, she could not help but press her body against his. She held her breath and dared not move.

"I have been waiting to talk to you," he said. Standing this close, he barely needed to raise his voice above a whisper.

"Not about sheep?" she asked with a wary grin. She began to back away just a step.

Before she could move away, he reached out to grasp her arms with both hands. "No. Not about sheep. Not even about you, Dughall," he added to the little dog who had jumped down from the bed and insinuated himself between them. His leaping enthusiasm threatened to topple them both. "Begone, fellow."

Dughall sulked his way toward the door. Seamus closed it tightly behind him.

"Now, where was I?" he asked, chuckling as he crossed the room to return to her. Then he ceased to laugh and gazed into her eyes. He reached out again and held her arms with both hands. Slowly he leaned forward. Katherine sighed deeply and closed her eyes to enable her to concentrate on the wonderful feeling to come. He placed a delicate kiss on her forehead.

Her eyes flew open in surprise, to be confronted by his green eyes twinkling with laughter.

"Well, you didn't expect me to sweep you up in my arms

and ravish you on the spot, did you?"

She giggled, embarrassed that his lurid thoughts should so exactly mirror her own.

Then suddenly, with no other warning, just one swift motion, he enveloped her in his embrace. His lips descended on hers. Softly at first, they gently touched hers, barely brushing them with butterfly-light sensations.

She entwined her arms about his neck in response.

"I have missed you, indeed," he murmured softly against her lips, kissing her again and again between each phrase. "The way you laugh, the way the sunlight brings out the fire in your hair." Each kiss grew more insistent. "The way you used to hide my breeches when you helped Morag with the wash."

"I *never* . . . !" she protested weakly.

He laughed and placed a playful kiss upon the end of her nose. Then the fire in his eyes rose again and he glided down to meet her lips once more.

Her heart beat more rapidly with the joy of having Seamus returned to her. Her smile curled against his lips as he continued to press kisses against her mouth and cheeks, earlobes and throat.

She heard his breath begin to come in ragged gasps. She knew he needed her as much as she needed him.

His hands roamed over her back, sending shivers of white-hot flame through her flesh where he touched her. Her breasts burned as they strained against the constricting bodice. His hands closed over the small of her back, pulling her hips closer to him.

She felt the heat of his tongue gently teasing her lips. She parted them willingly, allowing him to explore the promise of welcome within her.

His lips brushed past hers, across her cheek, feverishly pressing kisses into her skin where he passed. He nestled his face in the softness of her hair.

"Ah, Kathie, it has been a long, long time," he whispered hoarsely.

His hands slid up and down her back, coming to rest cupped about the softness of her bottom. Through the fabric of her skirt, she could feel the male hardness of him grinding into her, demanding entry.

She knew he would not stop. She didn't want him to. The same fires of passion consumed them both. She pressed her own body against his, responding with her silent consent.

His hands rose up her back again, searching for the top button of her gown. The tiny pearl slipped easily through the buttonhole. With maddening slowness, he unfastened each tiny bead, one by one. With great care, he eased his hands between her back and the fabric of the dress. His fingers traced shivers against her bare flesh. She hardly dared breathe as he pulled the sleeves from her shoulders. She drew in a great breath and held it as he moved the bodice away, revealing the soft swell of her creamy breasts.

"So lovely. You're so lovely," he murmured.

His hand glided softly over her shoulder, then downward until, with a single fingertip, he traced the blue veins pulsing through her translucent skin.

She shivered with delight, pressing forward, offering him her body to love.

"You'll never know how I've missed you—every precious part of you."

Opening his hand, he moved downward, to cup her entire breast in his palm. With his thumb, he teased the rosy tip until it grew taut with desire. She shuddered as tiny hints of pleasures yet to come coursed through her body.

He bent down slowly, kissing the softness under her jaw, then trailing his tongue down her neck and across the milky whiteness of her flesh. Her head arched back, and with the tip of his tongue, he caressed her nipple. A deep sigh of longing escaped her lips.

He lifted her in his arms easily and carried her to the large, curtained bed.

He stood at the side of the bed, with Katherine still in his arms. "How thoughtful of Morag to have turned the bed down already," he commented with a chuckle.

"I did it," she shyly admitted. "I kept your room ready—awaiting your return."

He nuzzled her ear. "Ah, Kathie, my Kathie. I've waited

so long to have you," he whispered, his voice breathless and husky. "I'll not wait another moment."

He lowered her feet gently for her to stand beside the bed. He slid his hands down her body until he bent on one knee to reach the hem of her gown. Slowly rising, he inched the hem higher and higher, exposing her ankles and knees, then more and more of her softly rounded thighs.

Katherine watched him as he studied the rising hem of her gown. He stopped. She waited, anxious. Had he changed his mind?

He looked into her eyes and smiled, then swept his gaze downward again. One stronger lift of the gown exposed her soft triangle of dark auburn curls. Shyly she pressed her thighs more closely together. Why should she feel so shy of him now, when she knew that soon, very soon, she would reveal to him, most willingly, every secret part of her? Or was it more to quell her own need, already pulsating for him there?

She stood, half-revealed to his burning gaze, and slowly lifted her arms. He continued to raise her gown until he had again exposed her breasts. She felt her nipples peak and her stomach tighten in anticipation.

He paused again. The soft folds of fabric imprisoned her head and arms. What was he doing? she wondered, until she felt again the pressure of his lips, gently pulling at first one nipple, then the other. He kissed the small hollow between her breasts, then trailed his tongue down the soft flesh of her stomach to circle her navel and rise again to kiss each jutting tip.

She could not stop the moan of pleasure rising in her throat. She didn't want to. She wanted him to know exactly how wonderful he made her feel.

Quickly he pulled the gown from her, flinging it into a corner. His jacket was shed just as rapidly and flung to join the abandoned gown.

He lifted her and placed her on the bed. Standing before her, he bent and removed her slippers, tossing them both away.

The soft feather mattress shifted as he joined her on the

bed. Kneeling above her, he tugged off his cravat and slowly began to remove his shirt.

As his head disappeared into the folds of fine lawn, Katherine stretched out her hand to trace the trail of dark hairs twining across the taut muscles of his stomach and rising to cover his chest. With her fingertip, she circled each flat brown nipple, then trailed her palm down the flatness of his stomach again, to come to rest against the searing bulge of his manhood.

He gave a low moan. Then the shirt was gone. His strong hand seized hers and raised it to his lips. Peering intently at her over the back of her hand, he tilted it upward to kiss her palm.

"Ah, woman, you're a rare delight," he whispered hoarsely.

Releasing her hand, he allowed her to recline upon the pillows. Slowly he crept toward her on his hands and knees until he straddled her hips. Reaching up, he began to unbutton the front of his trousers.

"A cunning vixen—knowing how to make a man's blood flow like lava in his veins."

He had reached the last button. Slowly he began to lower his trousers. Katherine could see where the patch of hair trailing down his abdomen grew denser. If he moved the fabric just a fraction of an inch, she could see where pleasure began.

Suddenly the wild howling outside rent the fierce silence of the room. Startled, they stared at each other, then toward the window.

"The sheep!" Seamus cried. As he sprang up his feet entangled in the covers. He almost fell as he leaped from the bed.

"Sheep don't sound like—"

"Something is wrong," he explained in quick, clipped syllables. He rushed about, gathering up his clothes. He pushed his arm through a sleeve, not much caring whether it was the right or the left. "With the sheep or the dog."

"But won't the shepherd protect them?"

"They're *my* responsibility," he insisted, pulling up his

trousers. He sat on the edge of the bed, tugging on his boots. Before Katherine could reach out to place a calming hand on his shoulder, he was up and heading toward the door.

"Oh, Seamus," she wailed, staring longingly after him. "Don't leave me now." As he continued toward the door she let out a little huff. "You care more for those blasted sheep than you do for me!" she accused.

His hand still resting on the doorknob, he stopped. "Kathie, the sheep are our only hope for a return to prosperity."

"But—"

"So you and I can be together."

"But—"

The howling resounded again.

He wrenched the door open. "Oh, I don't have time to explain!"

Before she could say another word, Seamus was out the door.

By the time she had scrambled about the room, retrieved her discarded clothing, and dressed, she could hear the Auld Laird and all the servants already assembled in the laich. Holding her breath, she slowly opened the door to Seamus's bedchamber and peeked out.

The two footmen carried glowing lanterns that sent shadows dancing up and down the stone walls with each pendulum swing. Dughall was already scratching at the door, begging to be let out.

She waited. Suddenly the howling echoed on the wind outside. All eyes turned toward the front door. Quickly she left Seamus's bedchamber and hurried into the laich. Hopefully everyone would assume she had come from her *own* bedchamber!

"Where's Seamus?" Katherine asked, looking nervously about.

The taller footman nodded grimly toward the closed door.

"He went outside," the Auld Laird answered, pacing anxiously. "Could he not hear that awful howlin'?"

"That's why he went. There's something wrong with his

blasted sheep." She could not hide the rueful twist of her lips.

"Did he take the musket?"

"I . . . I don't know." How could she tell the Auld Laird that Seamus was lucky he had made it out the door with all his clothes on, much less with a weapon? She was just glad he hadn't thought to ask her how she knew, this late at night, that Seamus thought there was something wrong with the sheep.

"I don't care how much he's invested in the wretched little beasties. They're not worth his life. I'd go, but . . ." He tapped his lame leg.

"You shouldn't have to," she told him. Turning to the footmen, she demanded, "Aren't you going out to help?"

"Won't catch me goin' out there," the taller footman replied, vigorously shaking his head.

"Not with whatever 'tis out there a-howlin' like that," the other added.

"You're cowards, the pair of you," Katherine declared. "You should be ashamed of yourselves!" Seizing a lantern from one of the footmen, she pulled open the heavy door. Barking furiously, Dughall scampered outside.

"Don't go, lass," old Morag warned.

Without making a reply, Katherine drew in a deep breath and ventured out into the night. The door slammed shut behind her, leaving her and Dughall alone in the dark.

"Maybe they're not so stupid after all," she remarked to Dughall. Slowly descending the front steps, she asked, "What on earth am I doing out here? What good could I possibly do?"

The howl echoed again through the blackness, sending a shiver through her spine. But Katherine truly jumped when Dughall unexpectedly answered with a howl of his own.

" 'Tis for Seamus," she told herself to bolster her failing courage.

Holding the lantern out to illuminate her way, she slowly descended the steps. "Seamus?" she called timidly into the wind, that answered her only with its own soft sigh. She felt a flood of immense relief when the horrendous howling suddenly stopped. "Seamus?" she repeated more loudly as she made her way around the side of the tower house.

The sound of bleating drifted again across the wind. It didn't come from the direction of the pens. From the sound of it, there'd be worse than hell to pay. If the sheep were where she suspected they were, there'd be Morag to face on the morrow!

Yapping, Dughall disappeared around the rear of the house. Quickening her pace, Katherine followed.

"Seamus!" she exclaimed when she spotted him in the moonlight. She stood there dumbfounded, watching the entire flock of sheep overrun the housekeeper's treasured herb garden.

The collie was running desperately back and forth, growling and nipping, trying to drive the sheep back toward their pens. Dughall was running back and forth, too, gleefully heading off every attempt to pen the sheep and scattering the groups the collie had managed to herd together.

"Dughall, stop that!" Seamus ordered. Dughall obeyed about as well as the sheep.

Seamus had one offender by the wool at the scruff of her neck. He was trying, without much success, to pull her from the patch of greenery.

"Seamus!" Katherine called in order to be heard above the barking and bleating.

"Ah, at last! Some help." Apparently he was so glad to see her that he eased his hold on the ewe. Quickly she slipped from his grasp and scampered after greener herbs on the other side of the garden.

"Seamus, what happened? What was all that howling?"

"The dog—letting us know they got loose."

"Sheep—staging a mutiny?"

"After nothing but scrub to eat on the way here, the sheep got a sniff of these herbs and just couldn't resist, I suppose," he answered with a shrug. He tried to give the nearest sheep another nudge back toward the pens.

"A revolution for a banquet of their own?" she asked.

"Who's to fathom these silly beasts?"

"But the howling? The Auld Laird, the footmen—we all thought it was a wolf."

"The collie tried to keep them in—he's really a good dog, but—"

"Where is the shepherd?" Katherine demanded.

"I don't know, but considering the inordinate amount of attention he was paying the village inn, I'd say he bolted like the sheep for something refreshing."

Katherine laughed.

"Well, don't just stand there," Seamus ordered. "Help me round up these silly beasties!"

Certain now that Seamus was in no mortal danger, she hung back. "Oh, I don't know," she answered slowly, swinging the lantern carelessly from side to side. "You look like you have everything pretty well under control to me."

Dughall suddenly sped by, nipping at the heels of several sheep. In their attempt to flee Dughall, they bumped into Seamus, almost toppling him to the ground.

"Stop your teasing, woman, and help me with these sheep," he commanded.

"They're *your* precious sheep," she pointed out. "Not mine."

"They may be my sheep, but it'll be all our heads rolling when Morag finds out about this." He nodded toward the decimated garden.

Raising the lantern high to expose all the desecration, she nodded. "You're absolutely right."

Setting the lantern on a stone bench, she spread her arms wide and began chasing after the sheep. Jumping over low bushes, bumping into each other, one by one the sheep shied away from their flailing arms and the collie's yaps and nips and headed back toward the pens.

One stubborn old ewe adamantly refused to be moved from her patch of lovage. Seamus stood behind her and gave her a gentle shove. Bleating her protest, she only circled her rear around and never once raised her head to stop eating.

"Help me with this one," Seamus called to her.

Katherine wasn't quite sure how to go about this. All the

other sheep had fled so readily. She wasn't even certain she wanted to touch the smelly creature.

"Come help," Seamus repeated, grunting with the effort of trying to move the stubborn sheep.

Katherine swallowed her dislike and sank her fingers into the thick wool. It was softer than she'd imagined, and warm and oily. She'd never admit it to Seamus, but it almost felt pleasant to her night-chilled hands.

"Come on, old girl," Seamus coaxed the ewe. He and Katherine gave a concerted push.

The ewe sidestepped, flipped her tail, and bolted across the garden. Seamus and Katherine landed facefirst in what had, only this morning, been Morag's well-tended herb garden and was now reduced to a puddle of mud. Katherine looked up to see the ewe placidly obeying the collie as she joined the rest of the flock in their pen.

Beside her, Seamus rolled over in the mud. "Ah, my Kathie, I couldn't have done it without you."

She wiped a clump of mud from her cheek. "I wish you had." Roughly she tried to brush away a sprig of lovage from her hair.

"Oh, don't be cross, Kathie," he said, reaching up to pluck the sprig. "You *do* care about the sheep."

"Do not bet any large sums of money on it."

Seamus flicked away the lovage, but his hand remained at her face. He moved to gently cup her chin in his hand.

"You are the most beautiful woman I have ever seen," he whispered, lying beside her in the darkness. "And dirt or no, I believe we have unfinished business to attend to." Slowly he moved his face closer to kiss her.

"Don't worry, Master! We'll save ye!" The two footmen hooped and halooed as they ran up to them.

Dughall propped his front legs on Seamus's hip and grinned.

Quickly Seamus released her. "'Tis about time!" he exclaimed. He rose, brushing his mud-caked hands on his trousers. Dughall continued to bounce about.

"We figured since the howlin' stopped, it'd be safe to come out," the taller footman said.

Seamus extended his hand to help Katherine rise.

Exhausted, she made her way to her room. She spared only enough effort to strip off her muddy clothes—and only enough thought to wish that Seamus could be there with her as she did so. After a quick sponging at her washstand, she collapsed onto her own bed only a few hours before dawn.

The rapid tattoo at her bedchamber door announced Morag's entrance. "Haste, lass. Haste," the housekeeper ordered as she stuck her head inside the doorway. "Are ye not up and dressed yet—and us with so much to do today!"

A feeling of immediate doom suddenly overwhelmed Katherine. Morag knew already! No, impossible. If Morag already knew of her decimated garden, there would be fire shooting out of her ears, the smell of roasting mutton in the air, and she'd be carrying Seamus's head on the end of a pike. Katherine sighed with relief—at least for the moment.

"Have you been outside yet this morning?" she dared ask.

Morag shot her a glum look. "All I can say is, the young Master's lucky 'tis his cousin Fenton who stands to inherit if he dies without issue—and he's *blessed* lucky I can't abide Fenton."

"So . . . so all is forgiven?" she ventured.

"For the nonce," Morag agreed. "Although I feel myself developin' a powerful hunger for mutton—and the thought o' havin' to eat it without my fresh mint or sage makes me even hungrier."

"Then 'tis something else that has you in such a blither this morning?"

"Mind now. I wouldn't be doin' this with so little notice from anyone but the young Master," Morag complained. "He tells me late last night we've guests a-comin'."

"Guests? Who?" she asked, trying her best not to sound overly concerned. Seamus had never mentioned guests to her or his father. Oh, they were probably just some fellows he had met at one of those places in London he had mentioned last night. Surely there was no cause for alarm.

Still, 'twas very strange for Seamus to overlook something as important as hospitality. 'Twas even stranger that he would not want others to know of his guests until they arrived. Why would he begin keeping secrets now when he never had before? she wondered. And from whom was he keeping them? His father or her?

Morag shook her head. "I dinna ken wha they are. But 'tis not so bad. There's naught but twa a-comin'."

" 'Twill not take us long, then, to make up the rooms," Katherine said.

"Their sleepin' is not what concerns me. They must eat, too."

"I'm certain a canny Scot like you can stretch the larder for a mere two extra people," Katherine said as she left her room with Morag following close upon her heels. "After all, the gentlemen should not expect to find luxurious accommodations in an old, dilapidated Scottish tower house, should they?" She gave an uncertain little laugh, then proceeded to the kitchen.

"Aye. That they should not," the housekeeper answered acidly, following behind.

"You . . . you said he told you last night?" Katherine asked cautiously, trying to keep an insouciant lilt to her voice.

"Aye."

"Late last night?"

"Oh, aye. Very late, almost as if he'd forgot—or dinna want anyone else to ken but me."

Why had he waited so long?

"Oh, I've no doubt . . . no doubt 'twas an oversight due to his being so . . . so tired," Katherine responded, trying to sound confident in her rationality.

"Well, he could not have been so very tired, as he's up and gone already," Morag replied.

"Gone?" Katherine asked, frowning. And without her. "Where did he go?"

Morag shrugged her thin shoulders. "Since when has the

Master been accountable to me for his whereabouts?"

"Indeed, Morag," she replied, already surprised by this new—and not altogether welcome—aspect to Seamus. "Since when has the Master of Dunkennet been accountable to any of us?"

It was nearly noon by the time she finished helping Morag.

"Now, dinna ye be gone too long with takin' the food to the clachan," Morag fretted, shaking her gray head and wringing her gnarled hands before her withered bosom. "I dinna ken when these strange guests will arrive."

"I'll not be gone long," Katherine assured her as she easily lifted the large basket from the kitchen table.

"Ye dinna want a footman to go with ye?"

She pressed her lips together. Each week the basket grew lighter. "I can manage alone."

"Och, 'tis a sorry state we're in. I can remember when ye first started takin' food and cast-off clothin' to the folks at the clachan," the housekeeper said. "Ye needed a footman to carry it then, 'twas so heavy."

Katherine shrugged her shoulders and readjusted her shawl. "What can we do when the crops have failed again this year?"

"They weren't all that bountiful to begin with," Morag reminded her morosely.

"Still, the Auld Laird is a generous man," Katherine continued. "He'd never stop helping them."

"Even if he can barely pay for it himself," Morag added tartly. "I wish the Master had waited until those silly sheep had done some good before he went and invited strangers here."

Katherine gave her chin a rebellious lift. "Morag, if one of Seamus's guests dares to make any comment—even just *one*—about the scant portions at dinner, I'll . . . why, I'll run him through with a claymore myself, and mount his head above the great fireplace in the laich!"

"Aye, ye're just the lass to do it, too!"

Morag's laughter followed Katherine as she made her

way out of the kitchen. The trill of the birds and the hum of the insects lulled her as she made her way down the path.

She heard the cheery calls of the women and children, already bringing their long-haired red cattle, with their wide-spreading horns and shaggy forelocks, down for the winter from their shielings in the high country. She smiled and waved to them as they passed.

As she drew closer to the clachan she stepped carefully through the muir. It only took one misstep in a cow pasture to ruin a perfectly good pair of shoes.

She picked her way over the outfield as well. The farmers rarely manured these fields. Still, she didn't want to twist her ankle in one of the ruts left since the oats and barley had yielded their meager harvest.

At the other side of the infield, she could see the black houses of the clachan rising from the worn-out earth. She managed to make her way over the rough rigs raised in S-shaped ridges between shallow, unplowed drainage trenches.

Against one of the black houses leaned the plow—the prize possession of all the people of the clachan. Katherine could remember many times watching four strong horses pulling it through the infield while three men guided it. Beside it leaned a *cas-crom,* with its crooked handle and iron-tipped wooden blade, which the people needed to farm the rocky land the plow could not reach.

It could hardly be called a street, this stretch of dirt that made its way through the small cluster of black, fieldstone houses. Ragged children peeked shyly out of each doorway she passed. She knew each child by name, but they were always too shy to respond to her greeting with anything beyond gap-toothed grins and giggles behind grimy hands.

She stepped over a rope of plaited straw held down by a large stone. The rope stretched across the thatched roof, keeping it in place. Ducking under the low doorway, she entered the black house.

To one side was the stable, with a scrawny cow snuffling in her stall. Katherine turned toward the family's living quarters. There was a small hole in the thatch overhead to release the smoke of the glowing peat fire and a small window in the side of the wall for light.

"Oh, Mistress Kathie, 'tis so good to see ye again," the woman greeted her. She was even thinner than the children who huddled bashfully behind her. From a small pallet at the far side of the room, a man coughed and wheezed.

"Good afternoon, Sorcha." Katherine nodded to the man on the pallet. "How fare you today, Mr. Nish?"

"Better, I'm thinkin'," the man answered, and wiped his dripping nose on his sleeve. "Lor' bless ye for yer concern, mistress."

Katherine set the basket on the grimy table. "Here's a crock of Morag's good chicken broth to help your cold," she said, removing it from the basket.

"Oh, with this the mister'll be doin' better soon," Sorcha exclaimed.

"I'm sure he will," Katherine said encouragingly.

"Thank ye," Mr. Nish replied, wiping his nose on his other sleeve.

"There's a thick stew for you and the little ones. There's meal for bread . . . a pot of jam . . ."

The children squealed excitedly over each disclosure. Katherine, for her part, felt abysmally wretched offering such meager charity.

Suddenly angry shouts outside broke the stillness. The children bolted for the door.

"Nay, nay! Ye bairns'll be stayin' inside," Sorcha ordered, loudly enough to be heard above the din. The children stopped in midstride and hung about the doorway. " 'Tis probably Mr. White, with too much o' the drink in him again and feelin' kind o' feisty." She turned to Katherine and explained. "Last time he knocked out Mr. MacLeish's front tooth. Served MacLeish right for interferin', it did."

The excited children, watching eagerly for any sign of a tussle in the street, remained huddled against each other in the doorway. Katherine, on the other hand, felt no such compunction against disobeying Sorcha. Making her way past the children, she marched outside.

The noise came from the Camerons' house at the far

end of the clachan. Hurrying around scrawny dogs and over shallow puddles, she made her way to the source of it. Drawing closer, she could hear the argument more clearly.

"I'll not leave!" Niall Cameron's angry voice bellowed. "I dinna care what ye say. Ye cannot make me leave!" ·

Then, much to her shock, Katherine heard Seamus's voice, clear and calm, reply, "You have no choice in the matter. You *must* leave."

Horrified by what she had just heard, she peeked into the doorway. Seamus stood with his back to her, facing the young couple.

"I'll not leave," Niall insisted. "This is our home!"

" 'Tis land that produces nothing. Once these fields and houses are demolished, 'twill be valuable pastureland for grazing sheep—and sheep produce wool, and wool earns money."

"Aye, and I'd earn money, too, if I could live off grass and grow wool on my back! Ye cannot make me leave!" Niall exclaimed, slamming his fist down on the table. "Ye have no right."

Seamus calmly placed his own hand on the table, leaned forward, and peered into Niall's eyes. "There you are mistaken, Mr. Cameron," he replied calmly. Katherine shivered with the iciness of his voice. Never had she thought to hear her fun-loving Seamus speak so coldly. "I do have that legal right."

"Ye cannot use it," Niall continued his protest. "I'll see ye dead and in hell first!"

The thin young woman's soft voice cut through the din. "Master MacKenzie's right, Niall. We cannot stay here. Why will ye not see his reasons?"

"Hush, Isabelle."

"We'll go to the Isles, like my cousin Tearlach did in aught nine," Isabelle Cameron suggested hopefully. "I ken he bides there still, burnin' kelp to make the barilla. He could find work for ye."

"There is no work there," Seamus answered bluntly.

"No . . . no work?" she stammered, her eyes wide with

surprise. "But . . . but what o' my cousin?"

"The war with Spain is over," Seamus answered. "England will lift the tax and get her precious barilla from them now. Do you honestly think Englishmen will bother with a Scots kelp burner when they can do business cheaper elsewhere?"

Niall glared at Seamus while his wife silently studied the bare dirt floor. There was no way to contradict the Master of Dunkennet.

"Of course, you must realize by now that you have no alternative but to leave," Seamus told them at last. "To make room for the sheep."

Katherine pressed her back against the outside wall of the black-house. Sick with shock, she held her hand to her throat. What was Seamus doing? She had heard of other lords cruelly evicting their tenants to replace them with flocks of sheep. Never would she have believed Seamus capable of removing his own people!

In her confusion, she began to run. In spite of her tears, she did not stop until, breathless, she was completely away from the clachan. Slowly, sides aching, she trudged back to Castle Dunkennet, taking far longer to return than she had spent going there. She needed some time to be alone with all her troubled thoughts.

"Come now, Niall. Let's not argue," Seamus said coaxingly. He tried to keep his voice as low and calm as possible to avoid agitating the already excitable young man. "Why must you be so stubborn?"

Why must they *all* be so blasted stubborn? Seamus wondered to himself. No one he had approached this morning had seemed the least bit interested in leaving the clachan—or, if they chose to stay, in helping to tend the sheep.

"Surely you can understand why you cannot remain."

"We'll go to Glasgow, then," Niall maintained. "There's plenty o' work there."

"You've never been away from the clachan in your life, Niall. You haven't seen what I have of the cities."

How could he make the young man understand that with the war over and England's industries steadily growing, these conditions could only get worse?

"Do you truly want your wife to live in the smoke and soot of a crowded city? Do you want your children growing up there—among strangers?"

"Of course not, Niall," Isabelle answered before her husband could respond.

"Don't you want to raise your family where there are trees and fields and cows?" Seamus continued.

"And no sheep?"

"You can raise whatever you want, Niall," Seamus told him. " 'Twill be your farm."

Niall pressed his lips together tightly and frowned. "Ye paint a glowin' picture, Master MacKenzie," he grudgingly conceded. "But can ye tell me where there's such a place for us to live?"

"There's land in Canada," Seamus stated.

"Aye. For those with the means to get there," Niall grumbled.

"I shall supply your means," Seamus told him. He hadn't suffered through bargaining with that shrewd old cheat just to use the Gilroy fortune for his benefit alone. He intended to see that everyone at Dunkennet benefited from the deal, whether they stayed at Dunkennet or not.

"I'll not take charity."

"Niall Cameron, ye're a stubborn man!" Isabelle exclaimed.

"Hush, woman."

"Then think of it as a loan," Seamus told him. " 'Twill be easy enough to repay with the cows and fields of corn."

"But *we're* still the ones who'll have to leave our homes." Niall shook his head forcefully. "I'll be thinkin' on it, Master MacKenzie. Just thinkin', mind ye."

"That's all you need do, Niall—for now."

Her long walk had eased the lines of worry in Katherine's face. She even managed to smile as Castle Dunkennet loomed larger as she approached. It was hardly a true castle. The earliest lairds had built a tall round tower for defense. Later lairds had added a series of large square rooms atop to form a tower house, with a wing to the side and gardens to the rear—and had had the audacity to call it Castle Dunkennet. But it was her home. She loved it as dearly as if it truly belonged to her.

Suddenly she frowned, in puzzlement rather than with worry. She lifted her head, trying to see better into the distance. Was that a carriage in the drive? And a very elegant one at that, she noted.

"Oh, blast!" she exclaimed as realization dawned on her. " 'Tis those fancy guests of Seamus's, arrived already, and me not there to help. Morag will have my head!"

Katherine lifted her skirts and broke into a run. The mud splashed over her shoes and up around her ankles as she heedlessly landed in puddles, then ran on.

Perhaps I can enter through the kitchen, she thought as she continued to run.

Her hairpins came undone. Her hair flowed out behind her, becoming more tangled in the billowing breeze.

Closer now to the tower house, she ducked behind the hedge growing along the drive. This way she could reach the side entrance easily, without being seen.

Apparently the carriage had just arrived, Katherine decided, watching curiously as she continued to move along. The ostler had just taken the horses' heads. A footman was just lowering the steps while two others waited for the baggage to be thrown down. Seamus was hurrying out of the wide front door to welcome his guests.

She had indeed taken too long returning if Seamus had reached home before her. Ah well, if she was this late, she reasoned, being just a wee bit later shouldn't land her in any more trouble with Morag. She paused to watch.

The liveried footman opened the door and lowered the steps. A fat, florid-faced man descended. She could not hear him at this distance, but Katherine was certain the man did not accomplish this maneuver without a great many grunts and groans and creaking of joints and seams.

She could hardly miss the man's gaudy yellow jacket,

with trousers much like Seamus's—although they never fit nearly so well.

Seamus bowed politely in greeting. The big man threw his heavy arms about him and clasped him to his barrel chest. He pounded on his back so vigorously that Katherine thought she could hear Seamus gasping for breath and his bones cracking, even from where she stood.

Then Katherine was the one to gasp for breath. From out of the fancy carriage descended a lady. A lady! Not two *gentlemen* from London. Seamus had invited a *lady*!

Katherine squinted harder to see if she could discern the lady's features, to get some hint of her appearance or age. As she drew closer, inching along the hedge, she could discern that she was young—and, much to Katherine's dismay, *very* pretty.

The lady descended from the carriage so gracefully that Katherine could easily have believed her dainty feet never touched the steps. Her traveling gown was a soft dove gray and cut so fashionably that Katherine had no doubt whose clothing Seamus had been describing to her yester evening.

Does his knowledge extend to her delicate silk-and-lace underthings, too? she asked herself as she ground her teeth together.

Dinna fret, lass, the little voice at the back of her mind consoled her. Perhaps she is the fat man's young wife.

Katherine wanted to believe this. But as she watched the way the fat man constantly maneuvered so that Seamus and the lady were continually at each other's side, she realized there was one reason, and one reason alone, for Seamus to invite a pretty young lady here.

She wanted to scream!

Dinna scream, lass, the little voice warned. 'Twill only give away yer hidin' place. Then won't ye be lookin' like the fool o' the world?

Katherine ground her teeth together until her jaws ached— and she screamed inside.

The group ascended the few short steps to the door. While Katherine admitted that she wasn't ordinarily a spiteful person, she thought it was a pity that the fancy lady, in her elegant little gray silk slippers, couldn't have found even just one of the piles that the sheep had left on the front lawn yesterday.

She watched them all enter the tower house. The cold lump in her stomach threatened to rise and escape as she realized she would have time—plenty of time—too much time—to see, up close, precisely what the elegant lady looked like.

Katherine quickly moved along to the servants' entrance into the kitchen. No one was there, not Morag or even the lazy young girl from the clachan who came to help in the scullery.

"Most likely they're all standing about gawking at the fine lady," she grumbled to herself as she trudged along. She admitted she felt more than a wee bit jealous. Even when she was dressed up in all her finest things for the celebrations at Hogmanay, no one had ever gawked at *her*.

She pattered through the kitchen. No matter how hard she had tried to scrape them before she entered, her ruined shoes left muddy wet marks on the flagstone floor.

"Won't Morag have a fit when she sees these?" she muttered, and continued on, hoping to reach her bedchamber before the housekeeper caught her and scolded her as she had done when she had misbehaved as a child.

She opened the kitchen door just a crack and cautiously peeked out. No one was in the laich. With any luck, she could make her way to her bedchamber without being seen.

Carefully she closed the door behind her. She drew in a deep breath and made a dash for the turn in the corridor.

"Your bedchambers are here—"

She collided headlong with Seamus, sending him reeling backward. Reaching out to catch himself, he bumped against the elegant lady, knocking her reticule from her hand and trampling her tiny feet.

The florid-faced man's beefy hands seized Katherine's arms and, fortunately, prevented her from falling. But he also prevented her from escaping. "Here, lass! Gently now, gently," he exclaimed. His tone was very kind, but his voice was so loud!

Seamus turned and glared at her darkly. "What are you doing *here*? And looking like *that,* for heaven's sake!"

"I was . . ."

How could she let Seamus know she had been to the clachan at the same time he had? What could she say to him about witnessing his horrendous behavior—at least now, in the presence of their guests? But, oh, she was so eager to talk to him alone!

"I was . . . out . . . taking a walk."

"You look like you walked through a peat bog," he growled. He cast a scornful look up and down her body.

Katherine shook herself out of the fat man's grasp and stared back at Seamus in surprise. He had never growled at her before! He'd been spending far too much time with those animals.

And he had certainly never looked at her body with *scorn*! As a matter of fact, only last night he had thought she looked rather appealing all caked with mud and plastered with leaves. Katherine had a sinking premonition that the arrival of this lady was going to cause even more harm than the blasted sheep.

Before she could recover her wits enough to respond, he turned his back upon her completely. He never even waited for her reply.

"I do beg your pardon. Are you quite all right?" he asked of the lady.

Not of herself—who could have suffered equal or greater injury—but of the lady. Could it be that all her terrible premonitions were coming true? Seamus cared more for the sheep and now, apparently, he cared more for this stranger than he did for her!

"I am fine, James. Truly I am," the lady answered in a voice Katherine thought only angels could possess, soft and low and elegantly civilized. Not like herself with her rough little burr, she thought morosely. But . . . James? She paused as memory overrode her shock. How could the

lady know him so well that she should call him James?
Obviously more had been going on in London than Seamus
had divulged during last night's conversation.

Her head was spinning from the collision and from her
confusion. Before Katherine could ponder any of this further,
Seamus suddenly spun around to her. Frowning, he issued his
command as if she were a naughty child who had forgotten
her manners. "Apologize to the lady."

"I . . . I . . ." She tried. Truly she tried to say something
polite and sincerely apologetic, but the events of the
past few hours had been too overwhelming. And all
things considered, she really was not sorry—not one
bit.

After what seemed an eternity of muttering and mumbling,
"Please excuse me" was all she could manage.

She wanted to flee to the security of her bedchamber, but
Seamus and the florid-faced man blocked the way. Turning
about, she fled back to the safety of Morag's kitchen, but
not before she heard the unknown lady, in her beautiful
voice, say, "It does not signify, James. Let the girl go.
Good servants are *so* difficult to find."

Servant! The lady thought she was a servant! Katherine
fumed as she tramped back toward the kitchen. The worst
part was, no matter how she had strained to listen, she never
heard Seamus contradict the lady's erroneous supposition.

Katherine looked at the mud still messing up the kitchen
floor. She looked down at her ruined shoes, the source of
the problem. The hem of her gown, brushing the tops of
her dirty shoes, was almost as muddy, and somehow, in
her dash home, a bit of the hem had been torn.

She glanced at her reflection in the polished copper
bottom of a saucepan. Her auburn hair hung down in her
face and flew out in several other directions as well. How
had she got a piece of hedge stuck in there? She hadn't got
that close to it.

Small wonder the lady had thought her a servant. She was
surprised now that she had not been mistaken for one of the
scraggly red Highland cattle!

"I never seen the likes of it in all my born days!" Morag

muttered as she trudged into the kitchen, shaking her head at the floor.

Why should Morag be so upset about mere mud?

"I hope I never live long enough to see the likes of it again!"

Morag was truly angry.

"I'll clean it up," Katherine said, wheeling about with a guilty look upon her face. "I promise I will."

Morag looked up, obviously surprised to see her. "Clean it up? What? Why, Miss Kathie, what are ye doin' in here?"

"The floor—"

"Och, that. I'll be takin' care o' that." The housekeeper dismissed it with a wave of her hand. Frowning, she glanced up and down Katherine's disheveled figure. "Lor', what on earth happened to ye, lass?"

" 'Tis only some mud I ran into on the way home," she said, holding out her ruined skirt.

"Looks more to me as if ye ran headfirst into the hedge," the housekeeper commented, pulling another small twig from the back of Katherine's hair.

"If 'tis not the dirt, Morag, then what has you so upset?"

The housekeeper placed both hands on her scrawny hips and glared at Katherine as if to display for her the full extent of her displeasure. "To think we'd be entertainin' the likes o' *him*! I vow, if I'd have known it would be him a-comin', I'd never have set up the second-best bedchamber. The barn's good enough for him!"

"You know that man?" Katherine demanded, incredulous. Even more unbelievable was the housekeeper's evident scorn for the fellow. And if she felt that way about him, what was her opinion of the lady who accompanied him?

Morag grabbed the besom from the hearth and began sweeping furiously at the drying mud on the floor. " 'Deed I do," she said with a snort. "That fat fellow is Iain Gilroy."

Katherine quickly suppressed a deep intake of breath. The man could be none other than Seamus's new business partner. She settled herself uneasily before the fireplace and tried to look unconcerned as she removed her shoes, leaving them to dry upon the stone hearth.

"Twenty-five years ago Iain Gilroy left the Highlands without so much as a pot to put his oats in. And everyone was glad to see him go, I can tell you." Morag vigorously swept the last of the dirt out the door, as if she could rid herself of Iain Gilroy as easily. "Went to Glasgow, worked as a common laborer in the new mills there, so I heard."

"I've not much experience of the world, Morag," Katherine commented as she pulled off her sodden hose, "but I don't think he looks much like a common laborer now."

"Och, nay. Not *now,* all dressed up like a Christmas tart," the housekeeper said, replacing the broom.

"I suppose he worked hard to get where he is today," Katherine ventured. She didn't care two figs for Iain Gilroy, his money, or how he got it. 'Twas the lady who had accompanied him that worried her.

"Just hard enough to make it into the good graces of the owner of the mill," Morag replied. "He managed to marry his English boss's daughter."

"Is that the lady . . . ?"

"Gilroy owns the factory now—weavin' woolens, I understand," Morag continued, oblivious to Katherine's question. "The overbearin' lout most probably comes to visit the Auld Laird just to be showin' off all the money he has and we don't. And brings his fine and fancy daughter with him."

"His daughter," she tried to say without her voice cracking.

"Glasgow-born, but raised in London by her mother's sister, I heard, after her mother died when the girl was still small. Brought enough baggage for three fine ladies, she has," Morag grumbled. "And a lady's maid who thinks she's the Queen o' Sheba!"

Suddenly Katherine's heart felt as heavy as the andirons standing in the fireplace. Of course Seamus would naturally be kind to any lady. But the fact that Miss Gilroy was the daughter of his business partner left all sorts of possibilities open to Katherine that she did not even want to consider. Still, her contrary mind refused to release her from its speculations. What *was* the lovely, pampered Miss Gilroy doing at Castle Dunkennet, so far from her elegant London home?

What, indeed! the small voice prompted her to face the harsh truth. Once they have money, there's naught else they seek but a title to adorn it.

Katherine harshly shook her head, scattering all her troublesome thoughts.

"Here, ye'd best be cleanin' yerself up for dinner, lass. Ye've just enough time for a wee bath. Then go to yer room and don a new gown," Morag advised. "And tie that wild hair back with a nice ribbon. We'll show those fancy Lowlanders we Highlanders can produce as fine as they ever could."

Katherine turned to heat the water.

Lifting her silver head, Morag commanded her, "Wear somethin' pretty so the Auld Laird'll be proud o' ye."

But would Seamus be proud of her? Katherine wondered as she quickly bathed away the grime. Especially after the way he had just treated her. With the fine and fancy Miss Gilroy here, would he even notice *her*?

She sighed as she quickly examined her own meager wardrobe. Morag had told her to look nice for the Auld Laird's sake, but she feared nothing she owned would be anywhere near as fine as what Miss Gilroy must possess.

At last she decided on a deep green velvet gown. It was hardly new, and a bit heavy even for this time of year. But it was the best she had, and at least their guests had never seen it. If she was lucky, she thought, they would not be around long enough, nor ever return, to see her wear it once more.

She ventured another quick glance in the looking glass. Ah well, she decided, she had done the best she could with what she had.

She hurried down the corridor and across the deserted laich, hoping that she might catch Seamus alone. She wished now that she had not been such a coward. If only she had confronted him when she first heard his argument with Niall Cameron, then she would not be suffering all these uncertainties now.

Katherine stopped abruptly at the doorway. It had been bad enough that she had made a fool of herself in front of their guests in the corridor. Now she stood in the doorway, looking out upon the small garden with its charming little arbor, queasy with terror and petrified with anxiety. They all were already assembled about the table, sheltered by the fluttering leaves. She would have no opportunity to speak to Seamus alone now.

"Come, lass," the Auld Laird called, beckoning eagerly to her. "We've been waitin' for ye."

All she had to do was walk the short path across the garden and up three small steps to the arbor. If only she could make her way to her chair without tripping and falling over her own icy feet. She swallowed hard and began to move, step by step, on her quaking legs.

All her fears were multiplied as every eye turned to her. The Auld Laird's eyes twinkled with their usual merriment. Miss Gilroy's smile was benignly pleasant. Mr. Gilroy had seemed such a fat, jolly sort in the corridor. Why was he now watching her as if she were a slug making her way up the garden path and he would love to squash her with the heel of his boot?

Seamus was watching her, too. Thank heavens, he no longer looked angry with her! On the other hand, he was not exactly gazing at her with longing either. As a matter of fact, his emerald eyes looked rather bored with the entire affair. How strange! Seamus had never looked bored before. Was there something else she had done wrong? Oh, she knew she shouldn't have chosen this gown!

If only she could manage to sit in her chair without falling off. The way the past two days had been going, with her luck, she would probably keep right on walking and fall off a cliff.

Cautiously Katherine took her place at the table. She breathed a deep sigh of temporary relief. She hadn't fallen after all. Now if she could just make it through tea without choking on a buttery.

"Miss MacKerlich," Miss Gilroy said, capturing her attention even before Katherine had time to settle into her seat. "Are you feeling quite the thing? I fear you took a dreadful bump earlier."

"I . . . I'm fine now," Katherine replied calmly. She tried her best to hide her surprise that Miss Gilroy's first thought should be for her welfare—and her disappointment that Seamus's should not.

"Och, so ye've already met," the Auld Laird said.

"Oh, aye," Mr. Gilroy said, still eyeing Katherine venomously. "Mistook the lass for a servant in the corridor."

"Imagine!" Miss Gilroy said with a little giggle and an elegant gesture to cover her mouth with her hand.

"Imagine," Katherine replied. She hated women who giggled like that! Not that she'd met that many, but she was now prepared to dislike Miss Gilroy just on general principles.

And although she and Morag had done their best, Katherine needed no looking glass to remind her how shabby even her finest gown still appeared in comparison with the elegant Miss Gilroy.

"I am so dreadfully chagrined by my terrible ignorance," Miss Gilroy continued her soft apology.

" 'Twas not ignorance, m'dear!" Mr. Gilroy protested in his loud voice. "At the time, how were we to be knowin' who the frumpy little baggage truly was." He cast Katherine another scornful look.

" 'Twas a logical mistake, considering Katherine's wretched appearance," Seamus grumbled.

If Katherine had been sitting closer, she would have jabbed him with the nearest fork.

"Och, well, she cleaned up real nice, didn't she?" The Auld Laird sprang to her defense before she herself could make any reply to Seamus. He gave her an approving nod.

"I was so surprised," Miss Gilroy exclaimed. "I never would have guessed you were the ward of his father's that James spoke of in London."

Katherine sat up straighter with silent indignation. His father's ward? Was that *all* he had explained of their relationship?

"Oh, did Seamus mention me?" Katherine asked. She found it wasn't difficult for her to sound surprised. While he was away she had spent every waking minute thinking of him. Even up to the time of the Gilroys' arrival, she had foolishly believed he had done the same. Now she could easily believe that, while in London with such a lovely lady, he had not bothered to spare her even a moment's consideration.

"James most certainly did mention you," Miss Gilroy assured her.

"Although, we never would have guessed that *she* was 'Little Kathie,' " Mr. Gilroy grumbled.

"Little Kathie?" she could not help repeating aloud. It was one thing to be labeled merely a "ward." It was an entirely different matter to be "little"! And it was altogether distasteful to be continually spoken *about* by Mr. Gilroy but never once spoken *to*.

"Quite naturally I assumed you were *much* younger," Miss Gilroy said.

"As did we all," Mr. Gilroy grumbled some more.

"As you can see, Seamus greatly underestimated me." Katherine turned her head to glare at Seamus while Miss Gilroy cast him a gently puzzled look that nevertheless demanded an answer.

Seamus shrugged. "Everyone changes with time," he offered as his excuse.

"Indeed," Katherine agreed.

Miss Gilroy gave a sigh and a shake of her head that set her golden curls to bouncing about her rosy cheeks, and Katherine's stomach to churning from sheer green-eyed envy. It took every bit of self-control Katherine could muster not to gnash her teeth and snarl. Must the lady have such a beaming smile? Must her blue eyes twinkle so merrily and her long blond tresses shine so golden? And must they all beam and twinkle and shine in Seamus's direction?

"Well, that just goes to prove what I have ever maintained," Miss Gilroy continued. "Men can be *so* un-observant!"

"I am just beginning to realize—" Katherine began to reply.

"Not *all* men, m'dear," Mr. Gilroy interjected. "Surely not *Mr. MacKenzie*." He shot his daughter a warning glance that she apparently chose to ignore.

"Miss MacKerlich. Kathie, if I may," Miss Gilroy said. "I do hope you will be able to forgive me my mistake and that we shall become friends."

"Och, let's not be doin' it up *too* brown now, Caroline," Mr. Gilroy fairly shouted.

Certainly Katherine could forgive her for mistaking her identity. But *friends*? Why would she ever want to become friends with a lady she hoped never to see again—no matter how nice she might seem. Still, for courtesy's sake, Katherine managed to respond, "That would be nice." She tactfully refrained from staring at Miss Gilroy in sheer disbelief.

Much to Katherine's relief, Morag at last approached the alcove, followed by the two footmen, each carrying a large tray. She bustled about the table, commanding the footmen, as proudly as if she were arranging all her finest fare, instead of the best gleanings from their rapidly diminishing larder.

The Auld Laird reached for the bottle that Morag had set before him.

"Seamus! In celebration of yer homecomin'—and in honor of our guests—let us have just a wee dram."

He poured himself, Mr. Gilroy, and Seamus a draught of whisky. Before Seamus and Mr. Gilroy could even reach for their glasses, the old man had shot back the amber liquid.

Seamus slowly swallowed his sip of whisky. He raised his eyebrows and blinked away the moisture that the fiery liquid brought to his eyes.

Katherine watched the Auld Laird's lips tighten as he tried to suppress a laugh.

"B'gads!" Seamus exclaimed when he was again able to speak. "I had forgotten."

"How can ye have forgotten the *uisge beatha*?" the Auld Laird demanded with a look of feigned surprise on his face.

"How indeed?" Seamus slowly replaced the glass on the table and turned to regard his father with his best attempt at maintaining a placid demeanor. "However, in London, I learned I rather favor wine, and port for after dinner."

"Och, they're not drinks for a *real* Scot." The Auld Laird poured yet another dram for himself and downed it just as quickly.

"Or perhaps even champagne," Seamus continued in spite of his father's good-natured ridicule. "For special occasions."

The worrisome thought flickered across Katherine's mind that these special occasions had included a special lady— and she had the most terrible suspicion who *that* might be.

She looked across the table at Seamus's handsome features, etched in the light of the lowering sun. No woman possessing the wits God gave her could deny that the man was as handsome as Lucifer himself. The thought that Miss Gilroy had not proved immune to his charms—and that he, in turn, had enjoyed the attentions of Miss Gilroy in London—gnawed at her confidence.

No! Seamus loved *her*. Had he not told her so himself so many times? Had he not shown her the depth of his love on the night before he left? Had he not tried to show her only last night that his passion for her was still as fierce as ever?

He'd not betray her love with another—and an Englishwoman at that! Katherine thought. Under lowered lids, she cast a dark glance at Miss Gilroy. Would he? She cast another worried look in Seamus's direction.

Indeed, anyone could see, Seamus *had* changed while he was away in London. His clothing, his speech, even subtle changes in his actions. Had she not just witnessed this afternoon how his outlook toward his own people had changed—and not for the better? Could his feelings for her have changed as well?

Oh, how she longed for the opportunity to speak to him alone!

*   *   *

" 'Tis a large mill," Mr. Gilroy was saying to the Auld
Laird and Seamus as they joined Katherine and Miss Gilroy
in the drawing room after dinner the next evening. "Powered
by water now, but 'tis steam I'm plannin' on usin' soon.
That's what the future holds, mark my words. Steam to
power the mills."

Katherine had still not found an opportunity to talk to
Seamus. Anxiety and impatience made her fidgety and cross
inside. But for the Auld Laird's sake, she held her tongue
in front of the guests, and listened and watched.

As much as she truly disliked Mr. Gilroy, she was forced
to admit, she was very interested in what he had to say about
his mill.

"Why, ye should just see that big loom, turnin' out
cloth much wider than a mere thirty inches," Mr. Gilroy
continued. "Well, ye've seen it, m'dear."

"Once," Miss Gilroy replied, and continued to toy with the
delicate lace on her sleeve. Clearly she had been unimpressed
by the thing from the start.

"Why don't ye be tellin' James all about it, then?" Mr.
Gilroy pointedly suggested.

"But, Papa, he already saw it—"

"Well, not everyone has," Mr. Gilroy interrupted quickly.

"Yes, I should love to hear—" Katherine broke off in
midsentence. No one but the Auld Laird was paying any
attention to her, anyway.

"Well, 'tis large . . . and dusty . . . and extraordinarily
noisy."

"Come, come, Miss Gilroy. 'Tis a shame to make you
discuss business matters," Seamus said.

"What would you have us discuss, Seamus?" the Auld
Laird asked with a sarcastic grin. "More descriptions of the
Englishmen's foppish fashions?"

"In London, we would never discuss business matters
when we had such a lovely lady in our company." He gave
Miss Gilroy a charming smile.

Was *she* not a lovely lady, too? Katherine's fingernails
made deep imprints into the palms of her hands before she

could calm herself enough to speak. "But, Seamus," she protested, "you know *I* have *always* been interested. . . ."

"Now, now, Kathie." He rose, but instead of pacing about the room, he made his way to the fireplace. Languidly he draped his arm on the mantelpiece and studied his fingernails.

How odd! Seamus had never paid an inordinate amount of attention to his fingernails before. He'd never draped himself on the mantelpiece, or worn strange apparel like trousers, or spoken odd words like *ton* and "crack" before either. Of course, they had never had a young, rather pretty, and very wealthy lady from London visit them either.

"You need to understand, Kathie. In London, a gentleman would consider it his duty to find more pleasant ways to entertain a lady."

"How would I be knowing that? I have never been to London," she reminded him tartly.

"Miss Gilroy is certainly more accustomed to lighthearted, frivolous things that make her laugh, not boring discussions of profits and wages, debits and credits. You would not want our guest to find us tedious companions, would you?"

Katherine fairly bristled at his unexpected—and altogether unnecessary—instructions on hospitality. She didn't give a tinker's damn how Miss Gilroy found them. In fact, she'd prefer the lady had never found them at all.

"*I* never considered our business tedious," she reminded him.

"Neither does my daughter," Mr. Gilroy interjected. "Do ye, m'dear?" When Miss Gilroy merely smiled and shook her head, he sternly prompted, "Especially not when James explains it."

"Oh, no," she answered quickly, her eyes wide—and rather guilty looking. "Not at all."

"Now," Mr. Gilroy continued, all the while prodding his daughter out of her chair and toward Seamus, "why don't ye be listenin' to all the fine plans James has for . . . for his future. Ye are interested in the future, aren't ye, m'dear?"

"Oh, indeed, Papa."

"And His Lairdship and I will be havin' a fine game o' cards." He turned to the Auld Laird. "Ye do play at cards, now?"

"I have been known to, from time to time."

"Och." Mr. Gilroy threw up his hands in what Katherine considered a fairly poor impression of dismay. "We'll be needin' another player." He turned and, for the first time since their visit, actually spoke directly to her. "Miss Mac—och, whatever yer name is. Ye'll be sittin' in a hand or two with us, won't ye?"

"I . . . I . . ." Katherine did not want to look so obviously worried, but she couldn't help but turn her gaze from the Auld Laird to Seamus. Much to her surprise, and reassurance, Seamus was watching her, a warm glow in his eyes. He *did* care more about her than he did Miss Gilroy, didn't he?

"His Lairdship won't be able to play if ye're not with us," Mr. Gilroy coaxed.

"Well, I . . ." What could she say?

"Of course ye'll be playin' with us!" Mr. Gilroy insisted, and before she could demur again, he began to deal her a hand as well.

What could she do but take her seat and take up her cards? And watch wistfully as Seamus and Miss Gilroy strolled about the small drawing room, stopping here and there to remark upon a few interesting objects.

Oh, every now and then Seamus would glance in her direction and smile, but that did nothing to free her from the tedious game.

Eventually Seamus and Miss Gilroy made their way out onto the terrace, alone, in the light of the waning moon— and much to her dismay, out from under her watchful eyes.

Katherine pulled her shawl about her shoulders. Reluctantly she followed the Auld Laird and Mr. Gilroy, Seamus and Miss Gilroy out of the laich. Dughall scampered merrily alongside.

For the past several days, in the evenings, Mr. Gilroy had conscripted her into games of cards with the Auld

Laird while Seamus was left free to entertain Miss Gilroy. Katherine could not have said how many hands she lost for lack of concentration upon the proper suit when all she could think of was hearts. During the daylight hours, they all toured the tower house itself, the new wing, and the surrounding gardens—not that the sheep had left all that much there to see anymore.

This day, they were to venture farther afield, into the wild countryside. Ordinarily Katherine would be the first to enjoy such an excursion. Now, as she trudged along, she thought she would even rather be stirring lumpy, rancid oatmeal over a smoky, sooty peat fire in one of the dismal little black-houses.

The Auld Laird, leaning on his cane, strolled beside Mr. Gilroy, who kept his hands in his pockets the entire time. Seamus assisted Miss Gilroy over each tiny hillock and minute rut. Katherine, on the other hand, walked behind the Auld Laird, with Dughall as her only companion, and fended for herself. Of course, she was quite accustomed to the rough terrain, but that didn't mean Seamus couldn't show some sort of concern for her well-being, too, she thought glumly.

They stopped at the top of yet another steep crag. Miss Gilroy extended her slender arm and pointed gracefully out over the view.

"I should never have believed Scotland could be so unutterably charming!" she exclaimed breathlessly.

"I've never seen any other country," the Auld Laird replied. "Never cared to."

Katherine agreed with him. She had always believed no other place could be as beautiful as the Highlands anyway. Yet even she had never felt the alarming ardor for its beauty that Miss Gilroy now displayed.

"Haven't seen the likes of it in nigh onto twenty-five years," Mr. Gilroy replied with what Katherine thought was a marked lack of enthusiasm. "Still," he agreed grudgingly, " 'tis a far cry from the smokestacks o' Glasgow and the chimney pots o' London."

Miss Gilroy's joy was not to be dampened by her father's

faint praise. At the edge of the crag, she turned excitedly this way and that, trying to view from every angle the panorama spread before her. She teetered precariously close to the edge.

"If you don't have a care, you will fall," Seamus warned, extending his hand to assist her.

'Twas not that he placed his hand upon her arm and attempted to draw her back from the edge. If the lady had been in imminent danger of falling, Katherine thought she herself might have done the same. 'Twas the way in which Seamus continued to hold Miss Gilroy's arm that filled Katherine with the horrifyingly uncharitable urge to lead her to the edge and there to give the lady just the *tiniest* push.

"Nonsense! I shan't fall."

Miss Gilroy laughed and brushed his proffered hand aside with a delicate gesture. She continued to draw closer to the edge.

" 'Tis so lovely! So exquisite!" she cried repeatedly, until Katherine thought she should scream. Then Miss Gilroy gave an unexpected sigh of deep melancholy and said wistfully, "Yet it all appears so . . . so unutterably lonely."

" 'Twas not so lonely—once," Katherine said, seizing the opportunity. Until now she had refrained from making any comments during their walks unless directly addressed, which was very seldom. But now she must speak. "Once, not so long ago, there were many more people living here—on small farms, in tiny villages—"

"Ah, and no doubt each was more picturesque than the next!" Miss Gilroy exclaimed. Her melancholy suddenly vanished, she spun excitedly to return to her view. Just then the dirt beneath her feet crumbled and she began to slip. She screamed.

Katherine gasped. She hadn't meant it—truly, she hadn't wished the lady *that* much ill luck!

Seamus caught Miss Gilroy's hand, then grabbed her about the waist. "Come," he said, pulling her away from the edge with a force not to be denied. "No matter how lovely you may think the country is from this vantage, I would venture to say you would not think it so charming if you were a mangled heap looking up from the bottom of the glen."

He led Miss Gilroy through the heather and gorse, along the narrow path that generations of feet had worn across the moor. Katherine followed silently behind.

Suddenly Miss Gilroy stopped. "What is that?" she asked, pointing to the low, jagged black outcropping in the distance rising just above the brown grass.

"The clachan," Seamus muttered. He attempted to draw her in the opposite direction. "Come this way, if you please. There is an exceedingly interesting—"

"Whatever is a clachan?" Miss Gilroy asked, turning her head so as not to lose sight of the strange-looking collection of houses.

"Ye dinna want to know," Mr. Gilroy answered gruffly.

She stopped and refused to budge. "Indeed I do, Papa," she protested. But Mr. Gilroy kept his lips pressed tightly together. She turned to Seamus. "*You* will tell me, won't you, James?"

" 'Tis nothing to concern yourself with now," he answered vaguely. "Come along."

" 'Tis where the rest of the people live," Katherine explained, taking a perverse delight in supplying the information that Mr. Gilroy and Seamus seemed so intent upon keeping from Miss Gilroy. Apparently the Auld Laird was delighted, too, if she could judge from his low chuckle. She patently ignored a dark glare from Seamus and continued to explain. "Farmers, laborers. You know. *Poor* people."

"Poor people? Why, I had no idea such a place existed here," Miss Gilroy exclaimed, her blue eyes growing wide with surprise. "I thought that . . . well, that in the Highlands, everyone lived in . . . in castles."

"Aye, and everyone has a fairy godmother, too." Katherine sniffed with derision. "I believe you would find the one-room black-houses vastly different from a castle—and far more numerous."

"Only *one* room?"

"Well, actually two."

"There!" Miss Gilroy cried exultantly. "I knew you were just teasing me."

"Their cattle are penned in the other room."

"Astounding!" Miss Gilroy exclaimed. Apparently she was not the least bit perturbed by this bit of news. "I truly would like to see such an unusual place."

"No, ye wouldn't, m'dear." Mr. Gilroy shook his head insistently. "I'll not take ye there."

"But, Papa . . ."

" 'Tis no place for a lady, lass."

"No," Seamus quickly agreed. " 'Tis no place for a lady like you at all."

"Oh, I don't know about that," the Auld Laird said hesitantly. Seamus and Mr. Gilroy shot him warning glares, but the old man just chuckled.

"Miss MacKerlich has been there—and lived to tell the tale," Miss Gilroy added with a coy little giggle. "Else how would she know what the place is like? If the clachan is safe for *her* . . ."

"Oh, perfectly safe," the Auld Laird assured her.

"Then surely it is safe for *me*."

"I'll not have ye goin' there, m'dear," Mr. Gilroy insisted in his booming voice.

Why did Miss Gilroy now turn a pleading glance to her? Katherine wondered. What influence could the lady possibly believe Katherine could have on these two obstinate men?

"But *Katherine* goes there," Miss Gilroy said with a stubborn pout on her pretty lips, and just the smallest hint of a sharp whine in her gentle voice.

"Kathie . . . well, Kathie . . ." Seamus began, but mumbled and coughed and could not—or would not—continue.

Apparently his hesitation gave Miss Gilroy some hope that she had gained an advantage, for she pressed her point. "I shan't go alone," she wheedled.

"Caroline, I *forbid* ye to go at all!" Mr. Gilroy commanded. "Do I make myself clear?" He waited for a reply that never came. "I'll not speak o' this again."

"Oh, pooh!" Defeated, Miss Gilroy kicked at a clump of grass and sighed her submission.

Katherine sighed with disappointment. What a pity Miss Gilroy had surrendered so easily. 'Twould have done the lady a world of good to see *all* that awaited her in the Highlands.

Seamus had been looking for Katherine everywhere. Miss Gilroy had pleaded weariness and gone off for a nap this afternoon, so he knew she could not be with her. She was not with his father and Mr. Gilroy, engaged in another game of cards. Disappointed, Seamus wandered into the small library. At least he could take this rare opportunity finally to be alone with his thoughts.

Mr. Gilroy was shrewd, Seamus thought as he thumbed mindlessly through a large volume. An admirable business associate, even if he was loud and overbearing. If Seamus managed to survive this partnership without going deaf, 'twould be a miracle.

If only Mr. Gilroy had not insisted upon coming *here*, Seamus thought ruefully. If only he had not brought his daughter! Ah well, if he had to play the gracious host to these people, the fact that Miss Gilroy was not a complete horror like most of the others he had met in London made his task just a little easier. But she was not his Kathie— and never would be.

He was so proud of his beautiful Kathie. If only she hadn't appeared the perfect hoyden when she first met such important guests! Oh, he probably shouldn't have snapped at her the way he did—but he had so wanted her to look her best, and there she was, looking more like one of the scraggly red Highland cattle!

"That's probably the first time anyone has touched that book since it was put there," Katherine commented.

Seamus looked up at the sound of her voice and smiled. "Aye, and 'twill be the last time, too," he answered, quickly closing the book and replacing it on the dusty shelf. He was so glad she had found him here alone.

Her hair was burnished gold in the light of the sunset

streaming through the library windows. Her fair skin glowed like translucent ivory against the dark blue fabric of her gown. Blast! Did she have to wear a gown that revealed so much of the smooth whiteness of her breasts? He had enough to worry about. He need not be constantly reminded of how much he longed to hold her close, to feel her soft lips upon his own. 'Twas the first time he had been alone with her in so long. Every ounce of will was concentrated on not making love to her on the spot.

" 'Tis an extraordinarily tedious tome," he said, and hoped that his voice did not shake too badly with his pent-up longing for her.

"Obviously it has nothing to do with sheep," she said with a wry twist of her lips.

Seamus wanted to laugh, but the strange uneasiness written upon her face prevented him. She'd been acting so unusual of late. What was troubling her? No doubt Mr. Gilroy was trying her patience as well.

"You care a great deal for the sheep."

Seamus blinked with surprise. So it wasn't Gilroy, but the sheep, who troubled her. "I would have thought, after our evening of chasing them around Morag's garden, that you had grown rather fond of the little beasties, too."

"But *I* still care more for people," she stated.

Seamus did laugh this time as he stepped closer to her. He reached out to slowly caress the length of her arm. He smoothed his hand from her shoulder down to her wrist. Taking her hand, he lifted it to his lips and winked at her.

"I am *not* like Arnie MacFee," he said with a lift of one dark brow. Leaning over her hand, he kissed it. "And I thought"—he kissed her wrist—"that I had pretty well convinced you that I much preferred human females." He kissed the crook of her elbow. His voice was deep and husky as he whispered, "One more especially than any other in the world."

He moved closer to kiss her shoulder, but she drew back quickly, as if his touch were no longer a blaze that ignited her heart to passion, but a fire that scorched her emotions beyond pain.

"Oh, Seamus, how can you be so cruel?" she cried, tearing her hand away from his grasp.

"I did not think what I was doing was cruel," he said. For the life of him, he could not fathom where she had gotten that silly notion!

"Have you no heart?" she demanded. "Or did you lose that in some fancy London drawing room, too?"

So the problem was not the sheep or Mr. Gilroy after all, but *Miss* Gilroy. Katherine was jealous, Seamus thought, with a surge of pleasure. That explained a great deal. He did his best to suppress a grin of eager anticipation. That problem was remedied very easily—and quite pleasantly, too, for both of them.

He took a step closer to Katherine, arms outstretched to embrace her, but she turned away from him completely. Clearly he had misinterpreted the situation. Oh, how could he ever understand women?

Well, whatever was bothering her, he'd better apologize for it, and quickly. "I am sorry if you think I have been—"

"*I* think! *You* don't believe you're being cruel, do you? You think you're doing these people good, forcing them away from the land they've called home for so many generations!"

He had heard—indeed, more than he ever wanted to— of the atrocities committed by some landholders in clearing the Highlands. Even now there were those who violently evicted their tenants with no warning, leaving them without resources, or recourse for relief. But, surely, that had nothing to do with *him*! With *them*!

"The people are starving on these farms they call home," he tried to explain.

"But I bring them broth and meal. . . ."

"No matter how many times you bring them food, there are always some who will be living near starvation, even in the best of times—which these most assuredly are not. Something else must be done." When she made no reply, he continued, "The land is poor, Kathie. 'Tis my responsibility."

"Your responsibility is to your people."

"My responsibility means nothing if I cannot make a profit from the land."

She stared at him, eyes wide with disbelief. "If money is all that means anything to you, why do you not find a way to profit from the people?" she demanded. "Instead of sending them away, why do you not use your money to make their farms better?"

"Because there is no money, Kathie," he stated bluntly. "I thought you knew that. I got a small advance from Mr. Gilroy, but unless I confirm this contract with him . . ."

"Does the contract include sending your people away?"

"Would you rather I left them here to starve?" he countered.

"Starve!" Mr. Gilroy exclaimed, bursting into the library without even bothering to knock. "That's just what I've been thinkin' myself. I'll die o' starvation before tea."

Seamus silently viewed Mr. Gilroy's rotund figure and decided that if they all were to die of starvation, he would be the one left to bury them—unless he ate them first. He turned to speak to Katherine, but she was already moving toward the door.

Troubled and puzzled, he watched her go. Whatever had given her the notion that he was *forcing* his people to leave? He tightened his jaw. If he was not able to explain his plans to Katherine—soon—he might as well be dead anyway.

Starvation, Katherine pondered as she poked at the small portion of potatoes on her plate and viewed the large mounds of food on Mr. Gilroy's. How the Nishes would appreciate such a feast.

From under lowered lids she watched Seamus and Miss Gilroy and found she could not eat even what little she had taken. At the moment starvation didn't sound like such a bad idea. At least that way she wouldn't have to sit through yet another interminably boring evening of cards with the Auld Laird and the obnoxious Mr. Gilroy while Seamus enjoyed himself in the company of pert and pretty Miss Gilroy. At least that way she would be out of her misery.

"Mrs. Armbruster's musicale was *quite* splendid," Miss

Gilroy said, punctuating her approval with another giggle behind her hand. "Did you not think so, James?"

"I beg your pardon," Seamus replied, as if slightly distracted. Could it be that he was not giving Miss Gilroy his undivided attention? Katherine could only hope. "Oh, it was passable."

Strange, Katherine thought. She recalled the name as one he had mentioned the first night of his return. Frowning as if that would improve her memory, she recalled that he had spoken quite favorably of his evening there, listening to several rather talented amateur performers. Was it more fashionable among the *ton,* Katherine pondered ruefully, for a man to be bored?

"What a pity," she remarked acidly, "that Mrs. Armbruster went to such lengths and you were not better entertained."

"You should be extremely flattered that Mrs. Armbruster wanted you as a guest," Miss Gilroy agreed. "Invitations to her musicales are quite coveted, James."

The Auld Laird coughed loudly, drawing attention to himself. "Now, just a minute. Just a minute. This has been goin' on and I've been meanin' to ask, so now I shall. What nonsense is this, Seamus? What is this 'James' nonsense they've been spoutin'?"

That was exactly what Katherine had been wanting to know for quite some time now.

"At first, I thought my old ears were deceivin' me, but it seems they were not."

" 'Tis not nonsense, Father," Seamus protested.

"Can the English not say a good name like Seamus?"

"Of course they can," he replied. Obviously uncomfortable with his father's continually probing questions, he rose and began to pace about the room. " 'Tis simply that in London society, I . . . I found it more . . ."

"D'ye find an English name *better*?" the old man prodded.

Katherine watched the merry twinkle in his eyes as the corners of his mouth turned up in a grin. She wanted to laugh herself. But Seamus looked so *serious*! Ever since the

Gilroys had arrived, he always looked serious. She greatly
feared he had also lost his sense of humor in London.

"Not better, Father," Seamus corrected. "Just more—
how shall I say, more expedient to be called James." His
face assumed an appearance of what Katherine could only
describe as haughtiness. How completely bizarre! In all his
life, Seamus had *never* been haughty! "After all, was James
not a name good enough for English *and* Scottish kings?"

"No more," the Auld Laird said, shaking his head sadly.
"Not Englishman nor Scot now sits the throne."

"Nay, nay," Mr. Gilroy loudly protested. " 'Tis still a
good name—James—signifyin' the happy union o' the two
crowns."

Happy for whom? Katherine wondered. From all she had
heard, and from what she could still see, the Highlands had
not fared half so well as the English from that union.

"England and Scotland," Mr. Gilroy exclaimed. He
reached out one beefy hand to pat his daughter's and
extended the other to indicate Seamus. With each phrase,
he continued to alternate between the two. "Mills and sheep.
Money and land. Industry and nobility. Oh, a grand union,
indeed!"

Union! The meaning of his words and gestures began to
dawn on her. A union. Impossible! Seamus could no more
be contemplating a union with the daughter of his business
partner any more than . . . than . . .

Than Mr. Gilroy could have contemplated a union with
the daughter of his English boss? the little voice in the back
of her head rudely reminded her.

Katherine felt as if she had just been plunged into the
icy depths of Loch Ness. A sudden coldness closed over
her, choking her as surely as if she were on her way to the
boggy bottom, drowning in the murky water of the loch.

"There's hardly anythin' this time," Morag commented.
She placed her hands on her scrawny hips. "If that Gilroy
fellow don't stop eatin', there'll soon be nothin' left to take
to the clachan at all." Peering into the basket on the kitchen
table, she shook her head in despair. "Sometimes I wonder

if we're doin' any good anyway. Perhaps the Master has
the right of it at that—makin' the people go elsewhere."

"Morag!" Katherine cried in anger and shock. Never
would she have believed the loyal housekeeper would turn
traitor on her! "*Never* say that again! *Ever!* What would
the Auld Laird, what would Dunkennet, what would *we* be
without our people? Someday Seamus will realize this, too.
I only hope he comes to his senses before 'tis too late."

Before Morag could respond, Katherine grabbed the
basket and fled out the door. By the time she reached
the clachan, her anger had subsided.

"Good afternoon, Sorcha, Mr. Nish," Katherine said
cheerfully as she entered the little hovel.

The smoky smell of the peat-fire, as well as something
else, invaded her nostrils. She sniffed. It was something
she had not smelled in a long time—not even at the tower
house. Where in the world could the Nishes have gotten
a roast of good, Black Angus beef? Surely her mind was
playing tricks on her!

Looking about, she spotted the remnants of the roast on a
chipped plate on a corner shelf, half-covered with a tattered
and stained, but nevertheless still-clean, linen cloth.

She pointed rudely in her shock and surprise. "Sorcha,
where did you get *that*?"

"Och, the pretty young miss from London . . ."

Katherine barely bothered to listen to the rest of Sorcha's
enthusiastic answer. She did not want to hear that Miss
Gilroy had been right here, in *her* very own clachan! She
did not like to think Miss Gilroy had been playing Lady
Bountiful—quite successfully too, from all appearances—
where Katherine had just been managing to scrape together
her puny offerings.

She pressed her lips together. It would seem terribly
unChristian to remark to Sorcha that she would be equally
charitable—if she had Miss Gilroy's father's fortune.

She was forced to admit a certain reluctant admiration
that the lady had managed to come to the clachan in spite
of her father's and Seamus's opposition.

Miss Gilroy had been kind to her. She had shown she

could be kind to the people. Katherine consoled herself with the thought that perhaps Miss Gilroy's generous spirit might be just the counterbalance needed to stop Seamus from his horrendous plan to evict all the people.

Perhaps she'll not be such a dreadful Mistress of Dunkennet after all, Katherine was forced to admit.

"Brought us beef and potatoes." Sorcha continued singing Miss Gilroy's praises, obviously oblivious to whether Katherine was willing to listen or not. "Brought us oranges, too—of all things! The bairns ate 'em that quick." She emphasized this with a snap of her gnarled fingers. "Och, I know the mister'll surely be mendin' quickly now, with all them good victuals in him."

"I'm sure he will, Sorcha," Katherine responded. "And look. Morag has sent some more chicken broth." She opened the basket and removed each item, although now, in the face of Miss Gilroy's generosity, she felt even more ashamed of its meager contents.

Come now, she silently chided herself. Does it truly matter who provides the meals as long as no one goes hungry?

Katherine found it did matter—it mattered to her a great deal. They were *her* people, as much as they were the Auld Laird's and Seamus's, and certainly more than they were an outsider's such as Miss Gilroy. Quite selfishly Katherine admitted that *she* wanted to be the one who helped them— not some Lowland stranger. Ashamed of the truth, she poked her head deeper into the basket to hide her blush.

"Did she come alone?" Katherine asked from the depths of the basket.

"No."

Katherine held her breath inside the basket. Oh, please let it be that Mr. Gilroy changed his mind and brought her—or that the Auld Laird had managed to sneak her out. Oh, please let it *not* be Seamus that had brought this foreigner to her clachan!

"Brought her servant, she did—a shriveled old biddy what talks finer than the lady herself." Sorcha gave a derisive laugh.

Katherine breathed just the tiniest sigh of relief.

She hurried back to the tower house. She knew she would be neglected throughout dinner, and only spoken to when Mr. Gilroy needed her for his game of cards in the evening. But some perverse stubbornness made her determined not to allow Seamus and Miss Gilroy any more time alone together than she possibly could. The Highlanders of old had fought to the death to protect what was rightfully theirs. Could she do any less and still be worthy of the name?

Her face was set with determination as she made her way from the kitchen, across the laich, down the corridor, and toward her bedchamber door.

She approached the bedchamber occupied by Miss Gilroy. The door stood half-open, and Katherine could hear the lady's wailing voice all the way out in the corridor.

"Oh, Huggins, how shall I bear another day?"

"Hush, now, or they will hear you," the high-pitched voice of Miss Gilroy's lady's maid quickly scolded.

Katherine stopped, poised in midstep. She had almost crossed in front of the open door. Surely they would have seen her then. Holding her breath, she flattened herself against the wall beside the door.

She dared move only her eyes, lest any other action should make a sound and give her presence away. She quickly searched the corridor right and left. She released a slow breath of relief. The corridor was empty. Thank goodness, she could now do some quite reprehensible eavesdropping without fear of being caught!

No doubt Seamus would haughtily point out to her that no one in London society stooped to eavesdropping. She didn't care. No one in London had sheep and Miss Gilroy to do battle with, either.

"Oh, pooh, Huggins." Miss Gilroy's elegant slipper gave a little thump as she stamped her foot. "Who is to hear us? The few incompetent servants are off lazing about somewhere."

Katherine frowned. Morag worked her arthritic old fingers to the bone for these ungrateful visitors.

"Poor Katherine is probably doing the work the servants *should* be doing. . . ."

Well, at least Miss Gilroy appreciated *her* efforts, Katherine thought, with a sharp little nod of satisfaction.

"I daresay she appears to be quite suited to it," Huggins replied.

Katherine clenched her jaw in an effort to remain silent.

"Papa and the Old Lord are in the drawing room playing cards yet again." Miss Gilroy heaved a heavy sigh of boredom. "And James has probably gone off to that wretched clachan of his."

Katherine blinked. How could anyone in full possession of their senses believe the clachan to be Seamus's? Had he not made it abundantly clear he had disassociated himself from his people?

"And left me all alone." Miss Gilroy pouted.

Huggins sniffed indignantly. "Just as well, too, if you ask me. You cannot think to be going there with him. *I* cannot imagine what possessed you to go there yesterday."

"I thought a visit to a clachan would be such a great adventure. That was the only reason I wanted to go," Miss Gilroy answered peevishly. Then she exclaimed, "How thankful I am you came with me!"

"Well, of course, I should go with you everywhere, my dear," Huggins replied gently. Then her voice sharpened as she added, "No matter how ill-advised. I cannot believe the Old Lord would condone a young lady directly disobeying her father."

The Auld Laird? Katherine thought with shock. Why ever should he be helping Miss Gilroy—unless he approved of the match! Katherine's toes turned to ice.

"Oh, Huggins, he was only trying to please me."

"Well, *someone* had to inject some sense into your madcap excursion."

"Indeed," she agreed. "I see now how wrong I was! You do realize I shall have to throw away the shoes I wore."

Huggins clucked her tongue in sympathy.

"I believe I shall throw away the gown as well, as I should never be able to feel at ease wearing it again for fear of continued contagion attached to it. No matter how often I bathe or douse myself with perfume, I cannot rid my nostrils of the wretched smell of that place."

Then Katherine began to grin. That clever old devil! Perhaps the Auld Laird was not so disloyal after all.

"The clachan is no place for the likes of you," Huggins insisted. "Your aunt and I taught you to be a lady—rising *above* your father's unfortunately humble origins."

"And I *am* ever so grateful."

"And you must surely see by now, my dear. Your papa is quite correct. That terrible place must be destroyed to make way for the sheep that provide wool for his mills that make the money to provide *you* with all sorts of lovely things."

" 'Tis not so much that I want to see the place destroyed," Miss Gilroy said. "In fact, it felt rather good to help those poor, miserable people. 'Tis simply that I found the place so . . . so exceedingly *melancholy*!"

"There, there, my dear." Huggins patted Miss Gilroy's shoulder in consolation.

Katherine grimaced. Miss Gilroy should be glad she didn't have to live there all the time.

"The next time do you think I could just *send* them money, instead of actually having to *go* there and *see* all those wretched people?" Miss Gilroy pleaded.

"You need not do it again, *ever*," Huggins promised. "All those horrible people will be sent away—very soon."

Katherine almost gasped in horror. Soon? *Very* soon?

"But where will they all go?" Miss Gilroy asked.

"Now, now. Do not worry your pretty little head about it, my dear," Huggins assured her sweetly. " 'Tis all arranged. By the end of the week, those dirty, nasty people will be gone, and lovely, fluffy white little sheepies will be grazing peacefully there instead. Now, won't that be simply splendid?"

"I . . . I suppose so," Miss Gilroy agreed hesitantly.

"Of course 'twill be. Your papa *is* right in this matter."

"I suppose so."

"I know he is—and *I* am *always* right."

Miss Gilroy sighed. "If you say so, Huggins."

Katherine's thoughts revolted. Miss Gilroy's charitable impulses were well intentioned, but extraordinarily ineffectual. She would prove no softening influence in getting Seamus to stop the planned eviction. She was merely the pawn of her avaricious father, urged on by her hard-hearted lady's maid. Katherine suddenly felt very sorry for Miss Gilroy.

Dughall sat perched on the backward-facing seat of the carriage between the Auld Laird and Katherine. His pink tongue lolled from his grinning black muzzle.

Almost as if he already has mischief on his mind, Katherine thought.

"I fail to see why you had to bring Dughall," Seamus complained to his father as they all rode along. "You know how he disrupts the sheep."

"Silly beasties, wha cannot abide a simple house pet," the Auld Laird grumbled. He scratched the little black head between the upright ears. "He's a good dog. He deserves a nice ride."

"But not today, of all days," Seamus protested. "I'm hoping once the people see how easily a shepherd and one good dog can handle an entire flock, they will be much more receptive to the idea of raising sheep."

For once Mr. Gilroy merely grunted.

"Oh, look!" Miss Gilroy exclaimed, gesturing ahead of them across the field. The people of the clachan had assembled at the edge of the outfield. The sheep milled aimlessly about. "They're here already, waiting for us."

"Apparently the people *are* interested in the sheep," Seamus remarked hopefully.

"People?" Miss Gilroy repeated. "No, the sheep are here waiting for us. My, aren't they clever?"

Only Miss Gilroy, in her unbridled enthusiasm, could ever consider sheep to be clever, Katherine thought with a weary shake of her head. "The shepherd has brought them here," she pointed out. "The only thing those sheep could find by themselves is Morag's garden."

Seamus leaped eagerly from the carriage as soon as it

had pulled to a halt. Katherine smiled with surprise when he turned to assist her down.

"We'll be stayin' in the carriage," Mr. Gilroy said. "We're close enough right here to be seein' all we need to."

" 'Tis a bit far for my old eyes, but if that's what ye want . . ." the Auld Laird remarked.

"I'll not have my daughter gettin' too close to the wretched place."

Katherine watched Miss Gilroy blush quite guiltily.

The Auld Laird handed Dughall to Katherine. "Hold on to him tightly now, lass," he advised, then settled himself comfortably into the cushions to watch the demonstration.

"But how can the shepherd earn his pay when he does nothing?" Miss Gilroy complained.

"Just watch," Seamus told her.

Miss Gilroy was right, Katherine thought. The shepherd merely stood on the sidelines, leaning on his crook and puffing on his pipe. From time to time he removed his pipe from his mouth just long enough to emit several sharp whistles, each series of pitches somewhat different from the previous ones. With each whistle, the sleek collie scurried or slunk or ran about the flock, directing them first this way, then that. He ran into the flock, singled out one ewe, and cut her from the rest, then chased her back.

"Oh, I see what he is doing!" Miss Gilroy exclaimed at last. "Why, what a clever man. What a clever little doggie!"

Dughall barked.

"Hush, Dughall," Seamus scolded.

"I don't blame you, boy," Katherine whispered into his shaggy ear. She stroked him soothingly. "I would be jealous, too." She shot a glance at Miss Gilroy, still seated in the carriage. The wind blew tiny tendrils of fair hair about her flushed cheeks. As a matter of fact, Katherine decided, she *was* jealous—very much so.

Dughall barked again and squirmed in Katherine's arms so wildly that she could no longer hold him. He jumped down and bounded across the field, straight toward the sheep.

"Oh, Dughall! Stop!" Katherine exclaimed.

Seamus shot her a sharp glare.

"I didn't let him go on purpose, Seamus. Oh, I vow I did not!"

Seamus took off at a run after Dughall. The shepherd dropped his crook and began to run, too. The collie tried to chase him away as well.

For his part, Dughall led them all a merry chase around the flock. Some of the sheep remained in a tightly knit clump, bumping into each other as they tried to stay in their circle. Other sheep darted off in different directions. Just when it appeared as if the shepherd or the collie had them in control, Dughall would cut through the very center of the flock, scattering them once again.

Instead of being duly impressed with the collie's efforts and remaining silent with dutiful awe and wonder, the people of the clachan roared with laughter at Dughall's sabotage.

At last Seamus managed to scoop Dughall up on the run. "Ah, Dughall, bad dog! Bad dog!" he scolded. "You've ruined the whole exhibition!"

A silent Dughall did not appear one whit contrite. In fact, he appeared to be grinning more now than ever.

Then suddenly he began to bark again. But this time it was not the joyous bark of a mischievous pet. Each deep bark was accompanied by a menacing growl.

With a fierce snarl, Dughall propelled himself out of Seamus's grasp. His bandy legs propelled him at breakneck speed across the field again.

"Dughall, come back!" Seamus commanded.

"Oh, Dughall, not again," Katherine called. "Once was quite enough to make your point."

"Has he gone mad?" the Auld Laird demanded. "I've never heard him growl so. Must we destroy him?"

Katherine could not bear to think this could be true. But this time Dughall completely ignored the sheep. He made a direct line for the clachan with Seamus following close behind. She lifted her skirts and began to run after them both, all the while keeping an eye on the little black dog.

It was only when she looked up that she noticed the lines of thick black smoke rising to the bright blue sky. The wind had been blowing away from them. Were it not for Dughall's barking, they never would have noticed the fires.

She entered a scene of horror. One of the black-houses had already collapsed into a heap of smoldering ashes. The house beside it had just flared into a full blaze. In the thick dark haze enveloping the village, she lost sight of Seamus and Dughall. All she could see were the hulking forms of several strangers, bearing lighted brands, running from house to house, igniting the village as they went.

A burly stranger roughly shoved her out of his way as he passed. He drew back his arm, prepared to release the torch into the doorway.

"Why are you doing this?" she screamed above the noise of the growing inferno. "Why?"

The man paused, as if the question had never occurred to him. At last he shrugged. "Well, them's our orders."

"Surely there must be another way to convince the people to leave," she protested.

"All that matters is that ye Highlanders are gone." He sneered. "The fewer there are of ye, the more room for sheep."

"Seamus MacKenzie would never allow *this*," she protested. "I demand you stop until Seamus MacKenzie can——"

The man laughed and shoved her aside again. "Seamus MacKenzie? Who's he? What's he got to do with this?"

Katherine paused, puzzled. "He hired you to——"

"Iain Gilroy hired me, ye ignorant tart. Gilroy pays me wages. Shows how much ye know about it." He gave a grunt of disdain. "Now out o' me way. I got a job to do." He gave Katherine another push, harder this time, so that she fell backward into the mud.

He drew his hand back again, prepared to throw his torch without interference this time.

Seamus's hand checked his swing. "You weren't hired for this!" Wrenching the torch from the man's hand, he quickly doused it in a puddle. "Leave now, while you can."

"Who are ye and what business is it o' yers?"

"I'm Seamus MacKenzie."

"Ha! D'ye think to stop me?" he demanded. "D'ye think to rob me o' me pay?"

By now the other ruffians had gathered around. Some still bore torches. The smoke of the burning houses and the red glare of the fires transformed their contorted features into the faces of demons.

Katherine pulled herself up from the dirt, slowly inching herself out of the way. If there was to be a fight, Seamus would need room to maneuver without having to worry about stepping over her. And she needed to be on her feet to do what she could to help.

"Leave this clachan walking," Seamus warned. "Or I'll see you carried out feetfirst."

The man sneered. Katherine swallowed the lump of raw nerves clumped in her throat as she watched the other rough-looking men each take a step toward Seamus.

"Ye're such a fine and fancy gentleman," the first man said. "D'ye think ye're man enough . . . ?"

He swung his arm in a side blow to Seamus's head. Seamus quickly sidestepped, without even allowing the dirty ruffian to touch him. The man's own momentum propelled him stumbling forward, headfirst, into the same puddle Katherine had just vacated.

Katherine wanted to smile with pride and satisfaction for Seamus. But the burly man rose, only momentarily stunned that his target had eluded him so easily. And now he appeared even angrier. It wasn't over with yet. Seeing their leader on his feet once more, the other men slowly began to advance.

The lump of fear began to swell once more within her throat.

"Ye think ye're so quick, eh?" the ruffian demanded, wiping the mud from his face. Suddenly he swung again.

Again Seamus sidestepped and, with a single blow to the jaw, knocked the man to the ground. The other men gasped in union as they watched their leader crumple.

In the distance, Katherine heard Dughall barking. She heard the shouts of the people of the clachan drawing nearer.

"Enough!" Seamus cried loudly in order to be heard by all. "There'll be no more of this."

The men and women, and even the children, began to pelt the strangers with mud and rocks, and even dung, driving them from their village.

Suddenly Mr. Gilroy's angry voice cut through the clachan. "What's the meanin' o' this, MacKenzie?"

Not until the ruffians were far away, running for their own safety, did Seamus at last turn to Mr. Gilroy. The man's face was more florid than ever, his eyes popping and his mouth gaping like a salmon on a hook. Miss Gilroy sat in the back, wide-eyed with surprise.

"I was just going to ask you the same question, Gilroy," Seamus replied. "*This* was *never* part of our agreement."

"Well, I got tired o' waitin' for ye to deal with these people yer way."

"That's the only way you will deal with *my* people, Gilroy. *My* way." Seamus stood his ground and glared up at the man in the carriage.

"But my way—"

"You're a despicable, unprincipled snake, Gilroy," Seamus told him, his lip drawn back in distaste. "You're lower than a snake—you're a worm! I will do *nothing* your way. I will *not* have these fields and clachan destroyed. And I will *not* force my people to do what they do not want to do. Some of my people have chosen to emigrate to Canada."

Chosen? Katherine's head shot up at the word. Seamus had given them all a choice? Not according to what she had overheard. But that was the trouble with eavesdropping. Sometimes you missed the truly good parts.

"Others have chosen to stay and tend the sheep," Seamus continued. "But it is *their* choice. I will not evict them. The loss of my people is not worth any price you might pay."

Mr. Gilroy fumed and flustered. "But . . . but we agreed . . ."

"We never agreed to *this,*" Seamus said, gesturing toward the black-houses still smoldering behind him.

"Ye'll . . . *we'll* be losin' a lot o' money. . . ."

"You will not lose a penny, sir. You will receive every bit of the wool we shear—and I expect you to maintain your part of the contract by buying it," Seamus reminded him sharply.

Heedless of the mud, Katherine caught Dughall up in her arms. "You did good, boy," she whispered in his perky black ear as she handed him to the Auld Laird. The old man looked about, his blue eyes dark with sadness at the destruction, but gleaming with pride as he watched his son.

"I . . . I . . ." Mr. Gilroy sputtered. At last he seemed to recover. "We have a contract, MacKenzie, and I'll hold ye to yer end. I'll abide by my end of it, too, but I'll be damned if I'll let ye marry my daughter now."

The smile vanished from Katherine's face. What had Seamus promised? she wondered. Oh, she knew she should never have allowed them to go out alone on that terrace!

Miss Gilroy gasped.

Would she protest? Katherine wondered, and worried.

Then Miss Gilroy gave a sharp little laugh. "Papa, I have no intention whatsoever of marrying James MacKenzie!"

Katherine was extremely relieved by the great conviction with which the lady said that.

"Hush, lass," Mr. Gilroy declared. "Ye don't know yer own mind."

"Indeed I do, Papa," Miss Gilroy insisted. "And I'll not be treated with the same high-handedness to which you subject your poor mill workers."

Mr. Gilroy flustered and blubbered, then settled down. "But ye've been so nice to him! I thought that's what you wanted!"

"Well, of course I was nice to him, for your sake, and for the business," Miss Gilroy answered. "Did you truly think I had any desire whatsoever to spend the rest of my life *here*—in such a wild and lonely place? With all these wretched, smelly sheep? I have found the Highlands to be quite beautiful," she said, looking about her. "But at the same time extraordinarily cold and empty. I cannot *wait* to get back to London!"

Mr. Gilroy huffed and fumed and said precious little that made sense. Suddenly he grabbed up the reins, slapped them over the rear of the horse, and took off across the field toward the tower house at a trot. The Auld Laird's laughter echoed after them.

Seamus turned to Katherine. A few quick strides brought him directly to her side.

"In their rush to be gone, they have left us quite without transportation," he said with a grin. "It appears we must return on foot."

"A pity," she replied.

"Return with me, Kathie." He held out his hand to her. She offered him her own.

The mist hung low over the glens as they walked along.

"Did you truly give the people a choice?" she asked.

"Of course. The Nishes are staying. Seems the children are quite partial to the sheep."

Katherine chuckled. "With that brood, I'd wager they'll think them delicious!"

"The Camerons are going to Canada," he informed her.

"Oh, I shall be sorry to see them go," she said. "But . . . but, they haven't so much as a pot to put their oats in. How can they afford their passage?"

"I suppose that is something else I neglected to tell you, and I am sorry for the trouble and misunderstanding it has caused. I shall pay their way."

"Of course," she replied. How could she ever have thought otherwise of her Seamus? In a small voice, she managed to ask, "Did you . . . did you ever love Miss Gilroy? Did you want to marry her?"

Seamus stopped in midstride. Turning her to face him, he peered deeply into her eyes. "How can you believe . . . !"

She shook her head. "I don't. Not anymore."

He drew her closer to him and kissed her. "Does that convince you?" he asked.

"Never again will I believe you love another."

At last they entered the tower house. Much to Katherine's relief, the laich was empty—except for the Auld Laird, who sat on an ancient chair, laughing.

"Och, I never saw twa people pack their belongin's as fast as they," he managed to explain between chuckles. "Why the old biddy of a maid fairly spat as she left!"

"I could not sell our heritage," Seamus said. "Nor will I sell our good name—not for any price."

"That's as it should be, lad," the Auld Laird agreed, nodding. "As it should be."

"While I will not sell our family name," Seamus continued, "there is one I wish to give it to. Father, I am in love with Katherine and I wish to make her my wife." Turning to her, he lifted her hand to his lips and placed a kiss upon her fingertips. "Now is the time, my love. We've waited long enough. Will you marry me, Kathie?"

"Oh, Seamus, yes."

"Will ye declare yerselves man and wife here? Now?" the Auld Laird eagerly demanded. "I'll summon Morag for a witness!"

"No, Father," Seamus answered, abruptly cutting off the old man's plans. "A declaration will not suffice for my Kathie. We'll have no common marriage, but a proper kirk wedding." He turned to her again. "Won't we?"

Katherine nodded. "I can think of nothing I should like better."

"Och, a nice kirk wedding, with a nice wedding breakfast," the Auld Laird murmured, rising. "That's what we've been needin' around here for some time now."

As he made his way up the stairs to his solar, Seamus and Katherine could still hear his contented chuckles.

"Of course, we'll not wait too long for this wedding," Seamus informed her.

"I've waited to marry you all my life, Seamus. I suppose I can wait just a wee bit longer."

"Of course, there is one matter that will not wait until later." His smile was warm, yet his eyes blazed as he looked down upon her. "I must see to this—immediately."

He bent down and swept her up into his arms. With a little squeal, she wrapped her arms about his neck. He carried her quickly across the laich and down the corridor. Still holding her tightly to him, he pushed open the door to his bedchamber. Once inside, he nudged the door shut with his foot.

He released her by the side of the bed so she could lower her feet to stand. He looked at the neatly made bed and shook his head.

"I see you have no longer been eagerly anticipating my wishes," he said. When she stared at him, puzzled, he replied, "For once, you have failed to turn down the coverlet."

She chuckled. "I was *that* angry with you."

He raised his hand to cradle her chin in his palm. Leaning forward, he placed a soft kiss upon her lips.

"Henceforth I shall make certain you are never again so angry with me," he promised. He reached down and threw the coverlet back. "As a matter of fact, I shall begin this very night to please you as no woman ever has been or ever shall be."

His green eyes grew dark with unsatisfied longing. He seized her in his arms, crushing her to his chest. He kissed her again, not gently as he had before, but warmly with igniting passions, and hard with growing arousal.

Katherine's breasts rose and fell with her rapid gasps for breath. Seamus's own breath quickened as he pressed kisses upon her lips and cheeks. Holding her flushed face between his palms, he continued to cover her with kisses. His fingers entwined in her auburn hair as his lips trailed across her ear and down the soft hollow of her throat.

His cheek brushed against hers as he nestled his face against her fragrant skin and gently moved his lips along her ear. "I'll wed you tomorrow, my Kathie," he promised, his voice hoarse and deep. "I'll wed you whenever you say— but I must have you tonight."

His hands swept over her shoulders and down her arms. Slipping his hands around her back, he cupped his hands about her shoulders and pulled her body closer to him. The pit of her stomach ached with white-hot longing as she felt his manhood pressing against her. The fabric of his trousers strained so tightly she need not see him naked to be certain of his desire for her.

He had taken his time before, but now he attacked the buttons at the back of her dress as if they were a bastion against him, the tiny turrets of the fortress holding his love imprisoned, small barriers to be conquered one by one. In his haste, he popped one button off, sending it rolling away.

"Fie upon it," Katherine told him with a little laugh. "I'll see to it on the morrow."

He buried his face in her thick tresses and nuzzled at her ear. "You'll be too tired on the morrow to worry with any buttons."

Seizing the shoulders of her gown, he pulled them down to expose her breasts. Still gripping the fabric tightly, he pressed her arms to her sides, causing her breasts to jut forward.

He slipped his thumbs beneath her breasts, lifting the tips until he could pull first one nipple into his mouth, then gently release it and move on to the other.

A low moan escaped Katherine's throat. She could feel the shivers of pleasure coursing up her breasts and rising from the warmth between her legs.

He released the fabric holding her arms pinioned to her side. He slid the gown completely from her shoulders, freeing her arms, and let it fall until it rested against the gentle swell of her hips. With one more swift motion, he sent the dress to the floor.

Quickly he tore off his own clothing. First the cravat and then the shirt, lastly the trousers. She stood naked before him, no longer shy, throbbing with the same pulse of passion as he.

She had seen him before. She recalled the splendid length of him and breathlessly awaited the sight and feel of him once again. But when he at last slipped the trousers to the floor, Katherine could not keep a little gasp of pleasure from escaping.

"Oh, Seamus, it has been so long. . . ." she murmured, reaching out to touch his manhood and the soft matt of dark hair curling about it.

Before she could reach him, he suddenly bent down to scoop her up into his arms and lay her gently upon the bed. "Patience, woman," he scolded with a little chuckle. "If we've waited this long . . ."

She leaned back against the soft pillows, groaning with longing and frustration.

His hands seized her ankles. Slowly the palms of his hands smoothed up her legs, over her quivering thighs. As his body moved over her with agonizing slowness, she felt his hot manhood glide along her skin. One hand lifted from her thigh. With a single finger, he traced the small dark triangle, finishing at the downward tip. Gently he slid his finger deeper.

She moaned again. "Ah, Seamus, if I don't have you now, I'll die."

"Then you must have me, my love," he answered.

He moved his hands upward across her stomach to gently fondle each breast. As he leaned on his elbows the weight of him pressed upon her. She raised her arms to entwine them about his neck, drawing him closer, and raised one knee to cradle him.

He moved up to kiss her lips while his manhood found slow yet undeniable entry. He groaned softly against her mouth, then continued to kiss her lips, cheeks, and neck. His bare body, hot with passion, undulated upon her. His manhood, thrusting and retreating, throbbed within her.

Her pulse quickened and beat to the rhythm of his thrusts. She gasped for air. She gasped in pleasure. When she could bear no longer the exquisite sensations, she cried in release. Seamus's body shuddered above her. His hips sank into hers. Perspiring and spent, Seamus hung his head, cradled against her neck.

She wrapped her arms about him, unwilling to allow him to leave, even now, when she knew he was hers for a lifetime. Sighing, he drew in a great breath of air.

"Are you happy, my love?" she murmured.

"I am the happiest man on earth," he answered. "And I shall do everything within my power to make you the happiest woman."

"I am, Seamus," she replied. "I already am."